MADAME DANICA

MADAME DANICA

Queens & Knights Book 4

M Kay Noir

Madame Danica

CONTENTS

DEDICATION

For the lost causes who became Queens, the villains who learned to kneel, and anyone who ever found their home in shadows others feared to touch. May you never stop believing in the kind of love that rewrites all the rules.

PLAYLIST

Navigate via mkaynoir.com/madame

K.Flay, *Blood In The Cut*
Måneskin, *Zitti E Buoni*
Muse, *Won't Stand Down*
Ashnikko, *Daisy*
Las Aves, *N.E.M.*
MEG MYERS, *Desire*
Cross My Heart Hope to Die, *Wild Side*
Garbage, Nellee Hooper, *#1 Crush - Nellee Hooper Mix*
Kingsborough, *Hard on the Heart*
Cathedrals, *In the Dark*
Lord Huron, *Vide Noir*
The Slow Readers, *Lunatic*
Thom Yorke, *Hearing Damage*
Daughter, *Run*
The Moth & The Flame, *Young & Unafraid*
Milo Greene, *Move*

Kiev, *Be Gone Dull Cage*
Iyeoka, *Simply Falling*
The Civil Wars, *Dance Me to the End of Love*
Florence & The Machine, *Stand By Me*

A WORD OF CAUTION

This book is intended for a mature audience only. It contains often graphic scenes between consenting adults. (Consent first, always).

Refer to mkaynoir.com/madame for the full TW/CW list (on-page and off-page mentions).

If at any point this book makes you feel unsafe, please take a break and consider whether you want to continue.

Mental health matters.

CHAPTER ONE

WEDDING

(DANICA)

W hen I imagined walking down the aisle one day, I never pictured myself marching toward a dangerous man with a nefarious empire—not willingly, at least.

Yet, I want nothing more than to become Mrs. Danica Fera today.

I could've done without it being such a lavish affair, though. Our backyard looks preferable *without* the rows and rows of strangers cranking their necks awkwardly to catch a glimpse of me as I journey toward the rose-laced arch where my Don awaits.

But Dante asked nicely, so here we are.

Taking a deep breath, I straighten my posture, smoothing out my dress for the umpteenth time.

The garment is heavier than I thought it would be; I'm wrapped in layers of silk, tulle, and other materials I never learned the names of. All I know is that it's a lot of white—*so*

1

much white on white. I look like one of those shower scrunchies.

It's a beautiful dress, nonetheless.

Initially, Dante wanted me to wear his mother's wedding dress today, but it wasn't my style—not at all.

Sadly (or perhaps fortuitously), moths had gotten to the antique garment before we did, destroying it beyond repair.

As much as that sucked, at least it meant I got to have this modern princess dress specially made for our grand wedding bonanza, as I like to call it.

If it were up to me, we would've had an intimate gathering somewhere in the forest or on a beach instead.

But it wasn't up to me.

It turns out the crime families have some sort of code, and it's custom to invite *everyone* to weddings. An entire garden filled with the most dangerous criminals in this city, all here to watch my short ass walk down the aisle.

I bet they don't even want me to marry Dante. I've heard the gossip. These mafia wives are vicious. I don't see myself ever joining their pompous tea parties (if I even get invited in the first place). These are not my people.

But hey, cake and champagne sounds fun.

I just need to get through this next bit, and then it will be all over; I will be Missus Fera.

That's if I don't freeze to death first.

The autumn breeze is nippy, sending shivers down my exposed back. I suppose having a February wedding outside was risky, but luckily, the rain spared us today.

We had to make it cute and get married on Valentine's Day—the one-year anniversary of our engagement.

I can't believe it's been a year since then.

Dante didn't object to my choice of date. He had no opinion on most wedding-related matters, only the guest list.

The last time I counted, that list was more than 300 people strong. But once you exclude the "business contacts" and people on our payroll, only Alessio and Adira are truly here for *me*.

It's not like I didn't invite my family.

They should have been here.

My brother's cruel words still ring in my ears, but I quickly push them out of my mind to focus on putting one step in front of the other.

Remember to smile, Danica.

The thought barely forms before piano notes fill the air—System of a Down's *Chop Suey!* transformed into something almost unrecognizable. Almost. My little act of rebellion, hidden in plain sight. A touch of chaos wrapped in wedding-appropriate packaging.

It's my cue.

Emilio's arm is solid under my grip, anchoring me as we commence our voyage down the makeshift aisle.

3

The grass crunches softly beneath my heels, already scattered with dried rose petals that two children I've never met are enthusiastically adding to.

I strain to see over the sea of unfamiliar faces, all these people who claim to be "family" but whom I wouldn't recognize in a lineup.

Designer suits and couture dresses, diamonds glinting like warnings in the afternoon sun. You'd think they're here to show off outfits rather than celebrate my union with Dante. Likely.

As we walk, I recognize Don Greco and a few other familiar faces that I must have met at some charity event. (*Always with the charity events.*)

Then suddenly, through a gap in the crowd—Dante.

The world shifts. Realigns.

Everything else falls away—the strangers, the politics, the weight of tradition.

There's just him, standing tall at the altar, looking at me like I'm something miraculous.

Besides my groom, Alessio radiates joy in his role as my person of honor. My boyfriend standing up for us at our wedding—another tradition bent to fit our strange, beautiful reality.

Let them whisper.

Let them judge.

Some loves don't fit into conventional boxes.

At least nobody can say shit about how cute Biscotti looks with his freshly washed white-and-brown coat and the little bow tie that matches his daddy's.

Yes, I called our Vegas rescue dog *Biscotti*, much to my future husband's dismay. At least it's Italian. Dante says that makes it worse. But see if I care.

Biscotti is so cute. The little shit tried to eat my flower arrangement earlier. But who can stay mad at our increasingly spoiled only child? His begging is much more effective than my groom's.

As the song reaches its crescendo, my steps find purpose now, though Emilio maintains our dignified pace.

The white dress flows around me like water, a costume for a role I never thought I'd play. Hours of professional styling have transformed me into someone who looks like they belong in this world of power and privilege.

The subtle makeup, the intricate braids crowned around my head like something from a period drama...I look straight out of Downton Abbey!

The closer we get to the arch in front, the more of Dante comes into view. His dark grey suit is tailor-made for the occasion, complete with a waistcoat that fits his broad frame like a glove.

He looks dashing!

I smile at my boys, and Alessio sends me a playful wink. He looks quite dapper himself in the elegant navy suit. Though, he always looks fancy as shit. Such style.

My vision closes in on Dante. I am walking to him, to be his—now and forever, *his* by law.

After all the effort it took to put this event together, I am happy the big day has finally arrived.

People always say that weddings are a lot of work, but that's an understatement. Even a year wasn't long enough to plan all this.

I quickly realized this event-organizing business wasn't my idea of fun, and Dante dropped some cash on a wedding planner. It's money well spent, for sure.

Other things? Maybe not so well spent. But who gives a fuck?

Did I need an eight-tier cake for my wedding? A cake that's taller than my 5'3" frame? Absolutely.

What about the candle-lit forest scenes as table centerpieces for the reception? Yup.

My motto was simple: If money was no object, why not go all out? I liked spending Dante's money, and he seemed to enjoy watching me do it. Win-win.

I just want the formalities done so I can wake up Mrs. Dante Fera, *La Donna* Fera, as my groom likes to call me.

Queen of the Fera empire at age 27 doesn't seem like such a bad life achievement. Sure, I finished my degree in the end and achieved some other minor milestones, but this is by far my most outstanding achievement—taming the untamable King.

After what feels like eons but what is, in fact, the length of a single song, we reach the front of the grass aisle, and Emilio takes his rehearsed best man's position next to his Don.

Alessio reaches out to me before Dante can, kissing my cheek lightly. "*Così bella, cara mia.*" (So beautiful, my darling.) Finally, after almost four years with Dante, my Italian is decent enough to understand, as long as they don't speak too fast or use too much slang.

The Vegas Joker steps aside and lets my husband-to-be, the fearless Don Fera—who, in fact, has many fears—take my hand.

"*Tesoro,*" is all Dante says, his eyes glistening at the corners with barely contained tears.

He brings my hand to his lips, and my heart swells. Could this moment be any more perfect?

The final notes of *Chop Suey!* drift from the piano, and everyone takes their seats.

Next, I have to get through the boring part where some old guy reads some holy text and makes me promise a bunch of old-fashioned things.

But anything to be Dante's. To have and to hold, to protect—which is very important in this line of business.

Focus, Danica.

The priest in the white dress starts to speak, greeting everyone formally. I still think it's weird that someone else gets to wear white to my wedding, but Dante said it wasn't that weird; it was pretty standard priest attire.

I wonder—

"Get down!"

The first shot shatters the world like breaking glass, cutting off the priest (and my thoughts) mid-sentence.

For a split second, my brain refuses to process it.

Tries to catalog it as something else.

A car backfiring.

A champagne cork.

Anything but what it is.

Then Alessio's hands are on me, yanking me down with such force my knees hit the grass through layers of white silk.

The bouquet explodes on impact, rose petals scattering like drops of blood.

Around me, all I hear is screams and more gunshots—so many gunshots.

This isn't happening. This can't be happening.

Alessio's weight half-covers me. I can smell his cologne, sharp and familiar, mixed with gunpowder.

Time stretches like taffy. Through the chaos, I see them—dark figures flooding in from the garden entrance, weapons raised. Twenty of them? More?

Their faces are masked, but their intent is clear. My wedding dress suddenly feels like a target, bright white against the green lawn.

Where's Dante? The thought repeats through my mind, urgent, relentless. I try to twist around to find him, but Alessio holds me down. "Stay here, *cara*," he hisses in my ear as he surveys the perimeter.

More shots.

Someone screams—high-pitched, terrified.

Biscotti's frantic barking cuts through the noise, incessant, urgent. But the sound is far away. I hope that means he's safe.

What the fuck is going on?

The perfect wedding transforms into a war zone in heartbeats.

Guests diving under chairs, men in expensive suits pulling weapons from hidden holsters, screaming women clutching designer bags like shields.

My hands press against damp grass, fingers digging into the earth. The elaborate braids pull at my scalp. Everything feels too sharp, too real—the weight of the dress, the smell of dirt and gunpowder, the sounds of mayhem.

And somewhere in this chaos is Dante. My almost-husband. Fighting or wounded or—

No. I can't think like that. I can't—

A body falls nearby with a dull thud.

I don't look.

Can't look.

But I know that sound will haunt my dreams.

This was supposed to be our perfect day.

Our fairy tale ending.

Instead, it's become a nightmare in white lace, our happily ever after hijacked at the last minute.

Where the fuck is Dante?

CHAPTER TWO

AMBUSH

(DANTE)

M y eyes are glued to my bride as Emilio slowly escorts Danica to me.

Every other sight and sound fade away, including the intrusive stares from our guests.

Dio mio, she looks incredible!

Alessio briefly squeezes my hand, and we share a knowing look before I return my full attention to the vision-in-white approaching us.

The wedding dress looks phenomenal on her! This is my first viewing, and my jaw is damn-near on the floor. The dress hugs all of Danica's curves in the right places, supporting her hefty cleavage with a modest neckline that fans out into yards and yards of fabric that trails behind her as she walks.

With every step my Queen takes, her beauty magnifies, captivating me. I've never seen her hair styled like this—classy, elegant, and utterly mesmerizing.

My heart swells with pride and love, knowing that in just a few minutes, this incredible woman will be my wife.

I never thought I'd ever get married again.

Not after last time...

But it's different now.

I'll protect her.

Nothing bad will happen—I'll make sure of that.

Mrs. Danica Fera.

I can't believe she's willing to take my name. I always thought she'd fight me on that, but Danica was eager to part with Matthews. Not sure why.

Perhaps it has something to do with why her family isn't here today. She's been quite tightlipped about that, and I didn't want to push. We had enough on our plate already.

Not that any of my blood relatives could be found among the rows of well-dressed friends, foes, and allies lining the seats before me either.

I couldn't let Luca come.

Even if he's my brother, his sins are unforgivable.

He's been banished from the city.

If it were up to me, he'd be weighted down at the bottom of the ocean, but Danica wouldn't let me get my justice. *Not like that*, she said.

The sunlight catches her earrings as she moves down the aisle, and suddenly, I can barely breathe.

My partner, my light, walking toward me like she isn't afraid of the darkness that clings to my soul. Like the blood on my hands doesn't matter.

If she knew half the things I've done...but she *does* know.

She's seen the monster and still chooses to love the man. Still looks at me like I'm something worth saving, worth keeping. *For life*, Danica always reminds me.

The concept seems impossible—good things don't happen to men like me.

I blink back tears, cursing my weakness.

Don Fera doesn't cry.

Can't cry.

Not here, not in front of these men who circle like sharks, waiting for any sign of vulnerability. Their respect is built on fear, their loyalty on the understanding that I'm more monster than man.

One bullet would be all it takes—nothing personal, just business. The price of power.

But watching my bride walk toward me, radiant in white...for the first time in decades, I want something more than power.

Something pure.

Something *real*.

Even if I don't deserve it.

Danica smiles at me, and my heart fills with happiness.

What an incredible woman!

How my life has changed since fate crossed our paths. She's grown up so much since then—my stunning Goddess, kinky and sometimes cruel but always kind.

She already owns my pleasure, but after today, she'll own all of me. What's mine will be hers, and I can't wait. I want her to have everything.

Nobody but Alessio knows that underneath this crisp shirt and tie, my leather collar tightly hugs my throat, reminding me who I belong to. Danica made sure I wore it for the ceremony, fastening it herself this morning after our shower together.

I am overly aware of it, just as I am of the pain in my ass from last night's play session. The future Mrs. Fera had me strung up on the cross, whipping me until my skin cracked and my knees grew weak, until all the stress around our big day evaporated, and my mind was clear, at peace.

Just the thought of last night makes my dick jump, and I quickly push the memory down. The last thing I want is to get a boner in front of all these people.

What Danica and I do behind closed doors is our secret. To everyone else, today just seems like another old Don (well, 46 feels old) marrying some young piece of ass with great tits.

And that she is, but she's also so much more.

Alessio leans in closer, whispering in my ear. "You lucky bastard."

"She's amazing, isn't she?" I don't take my eyes off my approaching bride for a second. She chose to forgo the veil,

14

and I'm not mad, not when I can see that stunning face as it approaches me in virtual slow motion.

I am so grateful Alessio could be here today. It wouldn't be the same without him. Our lives have been so different this past year, largely thanks to him as well. He's been a great inspiration for just letting go and having some fun sometimes.

We've run off to Vegas whenever we could. Danica was hooked on the city of sin and seduction. I couldn't blame her.

And me? I was hooked on having them both...The Queen and the Joker.

My mind runs through a million thoughts a second as Danica and Emilio draw closer, those little kids leading the way with their uneven scatterings of dried flower petals.

But when my bride reaches the front, all the thoughts disappear, replaced by a single one—*mine*.

Emilio takes his spot beside me as Alessio kisses Danica's cheek.

I hardly hear what the priest says; I'm drowning in my bride's gaze.

If only the formalities were all over already. Then I could just throw her over my shoulder and take her away, somewhere private, somewhere I can have her all to myself.

But not yet...

Time passes like a dream, slowly, sparkly around the edges...until Alessio's urgent "Get down!" shatters the illusion.

Was that a gunshot?

I know the answer without having to turn my head. The crack of gunfire is a sound I know in my bones, in my nightmares.

More shots follow, a deadly percussion accompanied by a symphony of screams in Italian, English, and...*Russian*?

They come in like a black tide—tactical gear, face masks, professional hardware.

Not street thugs.

Not amateurs.

My blood runs cold even as fury ignites in my chest.

How dare they? How fucking dare they turn this day into a battleground?

My body moves on instinct as Danica and Alessio drop.

Training kicks in, separating emotion from action.

Threat assessment.

Exit routes.

Variables.

Around us, our perfect wedding dissolves into chaos—chairs overturn, flowers scatter, white decorations stained red.

Emilio and Carlo already have weapons drawn, their movements fluid, practiced. We've danced this dance before, just never at my own fucking wedding.

My other guards materialize like menacing phantoms, dressed in their all-black suits, moving into formation.

The air fills with cordite and copper, the familiar taste of violence coating my tongue.

"Take the left!" I bark at Carlo, already moving right, creating a perimeter.

Through the mayhem, I catch sight of Danica—my almost-wife, my Queen—tangled in white silk, now spattered with mud, while Alessio shields her with his body. The sight hits harder than any bullet could.

"Stay with Danica," I tell Emilio, knowing he'll die before letting anyone touch her.

Questions race through my mind even as I return fire.

Who would be this bold?

This stupid?

Even the most ruthless families respect wedding neutrality. It's one of our oldest codes. To break it means...

A bullet whines past my ear, too close. I drop and roll behind an overturned chair, my suit collecting grass stains.

Bodies litter the garden—guests, guards, attackers. Later, I'll count the cost. Now, I just need to keep my people alive.

"Dante! Behind you!"

Alessio's warning comes a fraction too late. Pain explodes at the base of my skull as something heavy makes contact with my skin, stars bursting behind my eyes.

I didn't even see the guy coming.

Didn't see the steel pipe.

I'm losing my touch.

Fuck.

As I hit the ground, one thought burns through the pain: *This is not how I die.* Not today. Not at my own fucking wedding.

The grass is cool against my face, wet with dew and something darker.

I can hear Danica screaming my name.

Alessio barking orders.

The continuing pandemonium of gunfire and multi-lingual curses.

My vision blurs...

Cazzo!

LOSS

(DANICA)

"Enough, Emilio. Let me help!" I demand, shouting at my protector.

This inconvenient dress is a poor excuse to be sidelined.

I can't just cower on the floor.

Not while my boys are out there getting shot at.

It's not right.

Alessio happily handed me off to Emilio, drawing his weapon to join the fight. Like I'm some child that needs to be shuffled from one babysitter to the next. *Fuck that.*

"Miss Matthews—" Emilio starts, but I don't let him finish. I hate the sound of that surname. It grates my nerves. So close; I was almost rid of it.

Around us, guests flee in waves, abandoning us to our fate. *Cowards.* If they stayed, if they helped...

Ignoring Emilio's protests, I push myself up, straining to get a better view as I scan the mayhem for my groom.

21

I find him, but not in time.

Fuck!

The world slows to individual heartbeats when I see the pipe connect with Dante's skull.

The sound—god, that sound—cuts through the pandemonium like a knife.

No!

I'm moving before thought can catch up, ignoring Emilio's desperate grab for my arm. But I'm too quick; he misses.

My wedding dress tangles around my legs like a beautiful prison. Kicking off my stilettos, I hike yards of white fabric up to my knees, not caring what tears or stains.

None of it matters.

Nothing except getting to Dante.

He's sprawled on the grass to my right, the immaculate suit we spent hours fitting now stained with dirt.

The pipe—thick and shiny—hovers near his head, its owner gearing up to take another swing.

Please, god, let me get there in time.

The distance between us stretches like forever, each step as laborious as running through water.

Too slow. I'm too slow.

But luckily, I'm not the only one on this mission. Alessio reaches our fallen lover first, his shouting drawing the attacker's attention.

The Vegas Joker moves like a dancer, like a predator, buying precious seconds.

As I close the distance between us, my eyes suddenly catch on something glimmering in the grass—a knife, dropped in the chaos.

I grab it on instinct, tightening my knuckles around its handle.

By the time I reach the fight, knife in hand, Alessio is grappling with two attackers while Dante struggles to rise. The pipe hit must have been bad—his movements seem sluggish, unfocused.

Something primal rises in my chest, a fury that's been lying dormant.

Nobody gets to hurt *my* Dante. Not without consent.

What happens next feels like watching someone else move through my body.

The knife finds the first attacker's shoulder blade like it belongs there.

His scream sounds distant, underwater.

Alessio seizes his advantage, and I'm already moving again—knee up, blade out, just like training.

But this isn't practice.

This is blood and bone and the taste of metal in the air.

When the knife finds flesh again, the bleeding man's shout is guttural, foreign. *Russian?*

I've never heard anyone speak Russian in real life, only in those age-restricted action thrillers I sneakily watched with my older brothers as a child.

In hindsight, I'm rather glad the twins were above coming to my wedding, else I would've had to worry about saving their asses too right now.

Suburbia didn't do much to teach any of us to survive in the shadows. But I haven't been that girl from suburbia for a long time now.

Fuck being the damsel in distress.

"Don't you fucking dare lay a finger on her!" Dante's voice cuts through my battle haze. He's up now, fury giving him strength as he drives his fist into the guy's face.

"Who are you?" my groom demands, pulling the guy's mask off to reveal a thirty-something buzzcut-sporting thug with a gold tooth and creepy snarl. "Who sent you?" he tries again.

The apprehended man just laughs, making it clear he has no intention of squealing.

I watch Dante—my beautiful, dangerous Don—lose patience.

The gunshot that takes the gold-toothed thug's manhood is almost anticlimactic.

Just another sound in a garden of violence.

But the man's anguished screams pierce through. For him, it wasn't just another sound, another shot. It was someone shooting at his dick.

Asshole.

"Don't fuck with me," Dante growls, raising his gun again, and in that moment I see it all: the rage, the protectiveness, the pure love that makes him capable of such violence.

"Leave him, Dante," Alessio calls, another attacker pinned beneath his shoe.

Dante hesitates for a second, the gun still aimed at the bleeding guy's head.

I'm sure he's going to shoot the fucker, put him out of his misery, but he doesn't.

He just leaves him there, bleeding in agony.

"Go home, Danica. We'll take care of this," Dante tells me curtly, opening the gun's magazine to count the remaining bullets. Gone is the handsome hero who regarded my journey down the aisle with such adoration. The warrior is in charge now.

Instantly, the rage starts rising in my throat. He should know better than to dismiss me like that.

I cross my arms over my chest, resisting the urge to stomp my bare feet. "Fuck that, I'm not leaving." I know I should listen. That this is his world. But my mind isn't thinking straight. Up feels down and down feels like fuck knows what, but I won't let him push me aside, not now.

"Danica—" Alessio starts, but I shoot him a loaded look, and he instantly shuts up, returning his focus to the perp at his feet.

"No, Dante. I'm not some child you need to protect."

Dante meets my eyes, and I hold his gaze firmly, refusing to budge.

"Just let me help," I add, softer, "please."

Finally, Dante nods reluctantly, retrieving the knife from the bleeding assailant and handing it back to me, handle first.

25

"Thank you," I say softly, wiping the blade on my dress. "First things first..." Hacking through the material in uneven tears, I cut a slit into the side of my dress, ripping it from the hem to my hips.

"*Tesoro*..." Dante sighs, watching as I destroy my dress.

But now isn't the time for sentiment.

Like I'm the latest cast member on *Survivor*, trapped on a deserted island, I tie the material around my waist, cutting off some of the layers to make moving easier.

"Let's go!" I command once I'm free from the dirty offcuts, relieved to finally have the full range of my legs again, unobstructed by the heavy material of the wedding dress.

There was no chance in hell I would just sit at home and wait for this all to be over. I'm not the same weakling I used to be. It's been almost a year now since Emilio got me that bad-ass personal trainer.

Dante told me to learn something useful like Krav Maga or Muay Thai, but I wanted to do Taekwondo like Chung Li in the *Streetfighter* game.

Dante said it was dumb, but I was determined, so he tasked Emilio with finding me the best trainer money could buy.

I still have some ways to go before getting a basic black belt—at least another two years. But I am undeniably way faster and stronger than I used to be.

Before meeting Dante, my idea of working out was sometimes strolling through the park or maybe taking out the trash.

But now, I feel strong. Prepared. The anxiety is still there, the fear, but it doesn't freeze me—it propels me.

"Yes, Ma'am," Dante answers as he and Alessio follow me into the garden.

Things start to move quickly after this point.

With the help of Dante's well-trained guards, we quickly get the situation under control.

Nobody speaks.

Nobody answers any questions.

The invaders put up one hell of a fight.

But we have no intention of conceding.

Like some hodge-podge Charlie's Angels team, we help the remaining stragglers out.

It's too late, though; the damage is done.

Around us, chairs lie scattered, many broken, almost all upturned.

Even the arch that was supposed to cover us as I recited the vows I'd been working on for weeks, is lying uprooted on its side.

And then there is the human carnage...

Oh god.

A loud, piercing wail suddenly slices through the chaos, and I spin around, heart pounding.

It's Carlo.

To the right by the sound booth.

He's sprawled on the grass, clutching his chest, a blood stain growing over his once-white shirt.

I sprint towards him, dropping to my knees beside the hulk of a guard. Despite our past differences, I've grown fond of Dante's men. Carlo, especially, with his soft heart and collection of cat memes on his phone that he'd show me whenever Dante wasn't looking.

"Carlo?" I whisper, carefully lifting his hand from his chest to inspect the gnarly wound. The moment I do, blood gushes out at an alarming rate, and my stomach churns.

It's worse than I feared.

A bullet is lodged deep in his chest; he's fading fast.

The dark-haired man with the crooked smile tries to speak, but all that comes out is a gurgled mumble. His body trembles violently.

"Shh, Carlo. You'll be okay...*Dante*!" I scream, my voice quivering with panic.

I clutch Carlo tightly, trying to comfort him, even though he's too big to hold properly. But I do my best, wrapping my arms around him as far as I can reach.

"Miss..." he begins, but the word dies on his lips.

I watch in horror as his chest rises one last time under my blood-soaked hands, then falls still.

"Jesus, Carlo, please. Stay with me," I plead, shaking him, my hands slick with his blood. "Stay with me, please, please."

But he's already gone, the life drained from his eyes.

By the time Dante and Alessio reach me, Carlo is lifeless, stiff, in my grip.

"No! No! No!" I keep repeating as I beat his body with my fists, trying to elicit some reaction, *any* reaction, where there will never be any reaction again.

But there's nothing but silence.

The world comes crashing down as I lower my head, wiping my teary eyes with bloody hands.

Please, Carlo, please...

Dante crouches behind me, wrapping his strong arms around my shaking frame to lift me off the ground in one smooth motion. Like I weigh no more than a child.

I don't resist, my strength now gone.

Defeated, I wipe my bloody hands on the ruined wedding dress that will never be white again.

"Fucking assholes!" I shout in between my tears, unable to tear my eyes from the unmoving body on the floor.

Surely Carlo isn't really dead, right?

Right?

But he is.

I cry into Dante's chest, shaking in his arms, unable to keep it together any longer.

This is not how my wedding day was supposed to go.

"Come on, *Tesoro*." Dante's voice is soft as he picks me up like a baby and carries me home like he has no injuries.

"I hope you get what you deserve," my brother said in response to my well-meaning wedding invitation a few months back.

I guess this was it, what I deserved.

"People like you don't get to be happy, Danica."

Sniffing loudly, I close my eyes to focus on Dante's arms around me, the smell of his musky cologne now mixed with sweat and gunpowder, as he carries me over the threshold as his fiancé, not his wife as he was supposed to.

It was all for nothing.

CHAPTER FOUR

AFTERMATH

(DANTE)

The throbbing at the base of my skull intensifies with each movement.

Not now, I command my body. *She needs you.*

That asshole really did a number on me with that lead pipe.

As the adrenaline wears off, the pain slowly takes its place, radiating through my body.

But I refuse to let them get me down.

I've survived much worse than a blow to my neck.

It's not about me right now.

My heart breaks for the hundredth time today as I slowly wash the dirt off Danica's body while she sits in the bath, unmoving, staring ahead wordlessly. Usually, she's the one washing me, but there is nothing *usual* about today.

Next to the tub, her once-beautiful (now completely fucked) wedding dress lies discarded on the white tiles, angry streaks of blood staining the ripped fabric for life. Carlo's blood. *Fuck.*

33

Those cunts!

It still doesn't feel real.

Everything happened so fast.

They've fucked with the wrong wedding.

I will not rest until every last one of them has been wiped from this earth, I silently vow.

Later.

But for now, my Queen is my primary focus.

Gently, I kiss the side of Danica's head, trailing the sponge over her back in what I hope is a soothing pattern. "You okay, *Tesoro*?" I must have asked her that question 17 times since carrying her upstairs.

"Fine," Danica mumbles, her thoughts still keeping her far away, distant.

She would've been my wife by now if those assholes didn't ruin everything with their disrespectful ambush.

It is just a formality, though—in my mind, Danica is already mine, all mine, forever and always, until the end of our days. I don't need a piece of paper to prove it.

But she deserves a wedding. She deserves only the best. And the best doesn't include this much blood.

"I'll get those guys, don't worry," I try to reassure her, saying something just to say something. But the words hold little comfort for either of us.

Danica doesn't blink, just stares at the wall. "Yeah..."

"You really kicked some ass today," I try again, "I am so proud of you, darling."

Nothing, just a distracted, "Hmm."

"Look at me, *Tesoro*." I tilt her face toward me, finger under her chin, locking her gaze in mine.

It feels weird to see Danica so submissive; this isn't how our dynamic works. But I know it's a give-and-take; she doesn't always have to be the strong one. I will spend my life protecting her—my Queen.

"We'll make this right, I promise."

Danica simply nods, and I gently kiss her forehead, stroking a messy strand of once-perfect hair from her face.

Every time I raise my arms, the pain pulses harder.

But I force it down.

I focus on her face, using her presence to anchor me against the growing darkness threatening to pull me under.

Danica suddenly jerks her head up, her eyes wide, "Biscotti?" she asks in a panicked voice.

"He's fine. Alessio's given him some treats and taken him to his kennel; don't worry," I reassure her. His "kennel" being his own room right next to ours—a spoiled pup indeed.

"Okay." She sinks into the bath again, her concentration drifting away.

"Let's get you cleaned up."

Slowly, I move the sponge over her chest, covering her breasts in soapy bubbles. That finally gets some reaction out of her.

Danica gasps, her lips popping into an "O" as I roll one of her nipples between my fingers, teasing it into a little peak.

I smile. "Okay, time to get you dry. You've sat in this dirty soup long enough." The comment manages to elicit a weak smile from her, but it's something—I'll take it.

Kneeling before my bride, I slowly dry her from the bottom up with the fluffiest fluffy white towel I can find, ensuring I cover every inch.

"Let me take care of you," I manage to say, even as the room spins and my own voice sounds far away. Everything hurts now, but I won't let her see. She's seen enough pain today. I don't want her to worry.

Danica purrs softly when I part her thighs to dry between them, knees buckling ever so slightly when I flick my tongue over her clit, just for good measure.

"You're supposed to make stuff dryer, not wetter," Danica comments, frowning at me. *There she is, come on. Come back to me...*

"I made no such promise," I reply with a grin as I place a kiss firmly on her pussy lips.

She doesn't stop me as I move higher up with the towel, only to linger around those gorgeous breasts again.

When Danica's finally dry, on the outside at least, I wrap her in a soft bathrobe and pick her up again, cradling her in my arms.

My vision blurs as I lift her weight, lightning shooting down my spine. I clench my jaw, willing my arms not to betray how they want to shake.

"I can walk, you know," she tells me but hooks her arm around my neck anyway, resting her head on my shoulder.

"I know you can," I say, not bothering to find an excuse I don't need to find.

Today has been so messy.

Sure, I'm used to all the death and destruction, but I've been trying to shelter Danica from this world as much as I could. She's seen her fair share of violence since we met, but having Carlo die on her lap is not something I wanted to be engraved into her memory.

Fucking assholes. You'll pay.

When we enter our room, it looks different from how we left it. Alessio welcomes me with a big grin as I gently place Danica on the bed.

"And this?" I ask him, eyeing the giant slab of cake and champagne glasses on the dresser. It is the top tier of our wedding cake, the little figurines still planted in the icing—the bride with the groom chucked over her shoulder. It is cute, I have to admit. Danica had it specially made. *What a waste.*

"Well, I figured we might as well enjoy a bit of the wedding. No reason it should be a total write-off." My Vegas love grins, wrapping his strong arms around me for a solid hug. It feels good to be held, especially after this day. Maybe if he squeezes hard enough, he can put the pieces back together, make the spinning stop.

When we finally part, Alessio sits down beside Danica on the bed. "What do you say, *cara mia*?"

"I'm so, so tired," she says softly as she sighs.

He strokes her hair sweetly, weaving his long, elegant fingers through her locks to undo the plait. There is no way I would know how that thing works; I'm glad he's got it covered.

"You should have a little nap. It's been a long day," I suggest.

Danica nods slowly, pulling the covers higher up over her chest protectively. She doesn't even protest, how very unlike Danica.

It's so hard to see her like this—so defeated.

It takes so much effort not to punch a hole through the wall. I clench my fists tightly instead, the knuckles turning white.

"Sleep sweetly," I tell her, leaning down to kiss her, my hand on Alessio's shoulder. But she's already fast asleep, snoring lightly.

"Your turn," Alessio says, and I shoot him a puzzled look.

"I don't know if you've seen yourself recently, Don Fera, but you sure as hell could use a clean up too."

I look down. He has a point. My tux is messed up and dirty, the pants torn at the side...and the shirt covered in Carlo's blood. I hadn't even noticed the state of me. My main focus was not giving in to the nausea, to the pain taking over.

"You're right." I sigh, kicking off my muddy shoes. "You've looked better yourself, by the way."

"True, very true." Alessio gives Danica one more forehead kiss before taking my hand in his. "Come then."

I look back at Danica, but she's far away in Dreamland.

"She's fine. Come on," he encourages me, dragging me to the en suite where I had bathed Danica moments before.

With a heavy sigh that weighs my shoulders down into my chest, I sit down on the edge of the bathtub while Alessio turns on the shower.

It's a massive walk-in shower with all the fanciest of fittings. Since Danica officially moved in, the place has had quite an upgrade. I never cared much for decoration or modern furniture, but bit by bit, she's transformed our castle from my father's ancient fortress into a beautiful, tasteful home. The shower bench was her idea.

Alessio drags his shirt over his head and comes to me for a hug. I rest my head against his abs, exhaling slowly as I try to gather my racing thoughts.

"I'm glad you're here," I tell him, and Alessio kisses the top of my grass-filled hair.

"So am I. How's your neck?" he asks, lightly touching the warm spot above my shoulder.

I flinch, hissing between my teeth.

"That bad?" Alessio asks.

"I'm fine," I grumble. Physical pain is something I long ago learned to push down, to ignore. Endure.

"Man up, pussy," my dad used to shout as he hit me with his belt, again and again, until blood ran down my back. *"You need to be stronger,"* he'd tell me, voice thick with disappointment as he left my broken 10-year-old body outside in the backyard, in the cold, and walked off.

It was always Emilio who'd come to fetch me, who'd treat the cuts that now form little scars all over my back, weaving in between the tattooed lines.

Alessio runs his fingers over my cheek, releasing me from the fucked-up memory I haven't thought about in a long time.

"You don't have to be strong for me, Dante. I'm a big boy. Where do you keep your painkillers?" he asks, his stern tone making it clear that he's not here to argue.

I point at the cabinet under the sink, and the tanned god in the grass-stained pants brings me two pills, watching as I swallow them down.

"Happy now, *Mom*?" I ask sarcastically, and Alessio just rolls his eyes at me, ignoring the comment.

"Come, let's get clean. We can't get into the bed this dirty." Alessio unbuttons my shirt, undressing me layer by layer as the shower's steam mists up the space around us.

I let him, no fight left in my body.

I've been strong enough for one day.

Usually, Danica is the one who takes off my collar, but today isn't a usual day, and I know she won't mind that Alessio's taking it off, placing it neatly on the sink to keep it dry. It always feels momentarily strange not to have it around my neck anymore, to miss its familiar grip.

When we're both naked, he opens his arms, and I get up for a proper hug, both of us just holding each other, skin against skin.

A familiar comfort sinks into me, but also a tingle of lust. My cock perks up uninvited.

If you told me two years ago that I'd be living happily ever after with my Mistress-Queen and Don Santoro as our shared lover, I would've laughed at the ridiculous notion.

Heck, two years ago, I thought I'd never see Alessio Santoro again, never mind being allowed to freely fuck and be fucked by him.

But so much has changed—especially me. And Danica has been there for every step of the journey, holding my hand, supporting me, driving me wild with frantic lust.

It was all so perfect.

...And now it's ruined.

"We'll get them, don't you worry," Alessio says, pressing his forehead against mine like he can hear my thoughts.

I close my eyes. "I know. I just wish it went differently. Danica doesn't deserve this."

"Neither do you, *amore mio*. We'll make it right. But there is nothing you can do about it right now, so let's make the best of this situation."

"I know, I know." I put both my hands on his face, pulling him into a kiss. "At least you're finally here. Took you long enough to come visit us."

"Vegas waits for no one; I have stuff to do," Alessio replies with a grin, kissing me back fervently.

"You have stuff to do here, too."

"Are you making a pun?"

"Never. Come, we're wasting water." I pull myself from his embrace and step into the too-hot stream, letting it scorch my skin. It feels good on my neck muscles, easing some of the tension that's been threatening to pull me down.

Alessio follows me in, flinching as the water splashes off his body. He turns the hot water down slightly—probably for the best.

"The entire day doesn't have to be a waste." Alessio reaches for my cock, and it instantly comes alive.

Of course, I'm already hard.

He always seems to have that effect on my body.

A glance down confirms that I'm not the only one who is excited.

What a beautiful cock.

"Hmm," I groan louder as Alessio palms my dick to full hardness.

With my arms locked around his back, I pull him closer to me, kissing him desperately as he jerks me off.

It's a welcome distraction from the day we've just had.

His own erection grinds against my stomach, desperate for friction.

I love making him hard.

"Are you going to help me out here or what?" Alessio bites my ear seductively, and I smile, smacking his ass playfully.

"You could've just asked." I take his length in my hand, squeezing his tip as I kiss the moan from his lips.

"I just did," Alessio gasps.

With hungry kisses between rapid breaths, we stroke each other to completion, until we're just panting under the hot rain of the shower, holding each other close as our cum seeps down the drain.

Oh, sweet release.

He doesn't make me beg for permission, and I don't ask for any—only Danica gets to own my pleasure. With Alessio, we are equals, matched in every way, Don vs Don.

"Thank you," I whisper, my heart pumping too fast as we just hold each other for a while longer.

Perhaps all isn't lost...

CHAPTER FIVE

IMPALED

(DANICA)

I open my eyes with a start.

"What the actual fuck?" I ask, trying to decipher my surroundings.

Planted on either side of me, my Dons are covering my skin in what looks like...cake?

Have they gone insane?

Naked and streaked in chocolate, the boys are quite a sight to behold.

My sleepy mind does not know how to process this one.

Is this a dream?

Was the whole wedding a dream?

The aching in my exhausted body reminds me that nothing is, or was, a dream. The biggest failure of a wedding did, in fact, happen.

It's too much to process; it's too soon.

With a sigh, I shut down the image, compartmentalizing it into a back room of my brain. *Not now.*

Instead, I force my mind to the ridiculous chaos around me. So much for my restful sleep.

It's impossible to be mad at these two, though, not when the smiling faces are such a welcome change from the earlier gloom.

"Hey, you." Dante pampering me with sticky kisses like this, is something I could get used to waking up to. He tastes like champagne and chocolate.

My robe lies open around me, covered in cake and crumbs, just like my skin is. Some good that bath did.

"You were missing all the fun, *cara mia*. I'm only here for one night..." Alessio explains as he smears more cake icing on my stomach.

It's cold, unexpectedly so.

But I don't get to ponder the feeling for too long.

I gasp loudly as Dante suddenly licks the cake from my breast, trapping my nipple between his teeth.

Instantly, lust flares up between my thighs, shaking the last of my sleepiness from my limbs.

"We can't waste a good cake," Alessio explains like it's the most normal thing in the world to have an impromptu cake fight in bed after a day of death and destruction.

"Sure looks like you're wasting it," I retort, eyeing the massacred cake on the bedside, more than half of the tier reduced to crumbs. The happy couple figurine is nowhere to be seen.

Alessio doesn't reply. Just digs his long fingers into the chocolate to claw off another piece.

With a devious grin on his face, he parts my legs, dragging the cake through my pussy, smearing my skin in a move that ripples shivers from my center to my extremities.

My breath hitches in my throat as the Joker leans down to lick the cake crumbs from my cunt, pushing my thighs further apart like a hungry animal.

Oh god! Arousal grates my bones, stirring a fluttering of lust in my belly. The things that man can do with his tongue!

Alessio keeps going long after the last morsel of chocolate is gone, teasing my clit with his tongue until I'm humming in lust, my hips bucking toward him like they're being controlled by an invisible puppet master.

Dante does his part to arouse my nipples, teasing them until the little pebbles protrude from my skin, painfully hard. Like a good boy, he sucks and bites and licks until moans spill from my lips, a fountain overflowing.

I am no longer sleepy at all—just horny, oh-so horny.

The desire overshadows everything else, momentarily reducing my angst to a mere nagging feeling at the back of my head.

Alessio shoves one of his fingers inside my pussy, then two, and I come undone as the pleasure builds, forgetting any reality but the one that exists between these walls.

My moans speed up as Alessio's fingers quicken their rhythm inside me, focusing my attention on the electric sensations sparking through my body.

Like a well-synced team, my Dons work me to orgasm, drawing the climax from my body in violent shakes and screams until I'm a panting mess, clutching desperately at the sticky sheets simply to hold onto something.

My chest heaves up and down as I try to ride the wave of pleasure surging through my veins like an electric fire.

Letting go, I sink into the wave, letting it rupture my reality into bliss. I needed this more than I realized.

"Fucking hell," I gasp when the rush of my orgasm finally subsides enough for me to open my eyes again.

The boys are sitting beside me with their cake-streaked naked bodies, watching me intently.

"It was Alessio's idea." Dante shrugs, passing the blame.

"A bit of stress relief is always a good idea, no?" Alessio grins as I pull him towards me.

"I was sleeping," I say in mock protest as I kiss him messily, enjoying the cum, the cake, the desire dripping from his lips.

"There will be plenty of time to sleep later, *cara*. Tonight, we celebrate." He plants a kiss on my forehead affectionately and I stare into those intense amber pools I have lost myself in so many times.

I sigh. "What is there to celebrate? Everything is a mess." The heaviness sinks down on my shoulders again, threatening to ruin the mood.

"For now," Dante says, kissing the side of my head. "But we can plan another—"

I interrupt him. "No, I don't want to think about that now. Please."

"Of course. Champagne?" Dante thankfully changes the subject, saving the moment.

"It's time!" Alessio is far more excited about champagne than I would ever be, but I enjoy watching the naked god of a man open the bottle with an effortless grace.

The cork flies into the ceiling with a bang, and Alessio quickly wraps his lips around the bottle to prevent any gushing liquid from spilling.

When he hands me the bottle, I take a big swig, almost choking when the bubbles tickle my nose. A drop makes it down my chin, and Dante licks it off my neck like a thirsty predator.

Champagne in hand, I slip off my dirty bathrobe, joining the men in their nakedness.

With every sip, I feel myself get lighter.

We have the first bottle in bed and the second one dancing naked around the room to a playlist Alessio insists is *perfect* for the occasion.

The guys are so much taller than me; I'm dwarfed between their chests as they sandwich me between them—an act that gives me great joy. Especially feeling their respective erections digging into my abs, so hard, so ready.

Alessio on my left and Dante on my right, I take one cock per palm, rubbing them against my skin, against each other, as I first kiss my darling groom and then our lover, sipping on their moans until they're both mad with lust.

And me? I know I'm wet, so fucking wet. Who wouldn't want to be with two Italian gods ready to serve your every need?

Reaching an arm around Dante's neck, I pull myself up to whisper in his ear. "I want you inside me, boy." In my hand, his cock shivers at the mere suggestion.

Dante gasps, his voice barely audible, "Any day."

I look to Alessio, who just grins at me as I add, "Both of you."

"I hope you have enough lube," the Vegas Joker says confidently, looking down at his dick in my hand.

He's right; we'll need more lube—he's pretty big. Not as big as Dante, but still big—especially for my back entrance.

But it isn't the first time, and Alessio knows how to get me to relax around him, to take all of him.

The first time he entered me from behind was so uncomfortable, and I still prefer him at the other entrance, but there is something so incredible about having them both inside at the same time. It makes me feel like a powerful Goddess!

I push Dante down on the bed, and he offers no resistance, going where I move him. Keeping my eyes locked on his, I kneel before him in the same way he usually kneels before me. But it's not the same at all, because the power is still mine.

Seductively, I close my lips around his sensitive tip, slowly teasing his cock to full hardness as I suck him off.

Dante groans, quivering under my tongue as I lick the pre-cum from his skin.

When I am satisfied that he's hard enough, I climb onto the bed, stealing a messy kiss as I hover over my fiancé who should've been my husband by now.

I kiss his eyelids. "Hey, you."

"*Tesoro.*" Dante smiles, both hands over my tits like magnets drawn to metal.

Narrowing my eyes, I tell him exactly what to expect, "I'm going to fuck you into oblivion, you ready?"

Dante's breath hitches; it's beautifully obvious. "I'm yours," he pants in a whisper. "With or without the ceremony."

"And you're mine," I confirm as I affectionately brush a stray curl from his forehead. "Now, hold still, Don Fera. No coming without permission, yeah?"

Dante nods, and I reposition my body so his cock rests against my entrance, so close.

Just to tease him, I drag his tip through my wetness a few times before guiding him inside me, impaling myself on his length.

Oh god, he feels so good.

Familiar.

Home.

The perfect shape and fit.

Made for me.

Any and all of the above.

Biting down on my bottom lip, I allow the moans of pleasure to flow freely. Not for a second do I consider muffling my cries.

I don't care who hears me. All I care about right now is how good Dante feels inside me as I slowly push myself up and down with my knees digging into the bed, one on either side of his waist.

His hands never leave my breasts as he holds me up, massages my skin.

With a wicked grin on my face, I stop my thrusting as suddenly as I start, driving Dante to loud protests as he tries in vain to push deeper into me. But we both know he's not the one in charge. The Don beneath me sighs, relieved, as I start moving again.

Beside us, Alessio is stroking his cock leisurely as he enjoys the view of my thick ass bouncing up and down his boyfriend's cock.

Knowing that he's there watching fans my lust to a frenzy.

But I'm not through torturing my darling groom.

I slow my movements to a halt again, waiting to see what Dante will do.

"Please, Danica..." Dante whines, his cock just resting inside me, warm and needy. "Have a heart," he pleads.

I grin mischievously, leaning down to kiss him. "A heart won't help you right now."

"Is this my cue?" Alessio asks when I finally withdraw my lips from Dante's, leaving us both panting.

"My ass is yours," I tell the Joker, leaning back to accept a messy kiss.

"I like the sound of that." He playfully smacks my bum before getting into position.

I gasp loudly as Alessio's finger finds my backside, rubbing cold lube around my back hole before dipping inside.

Involuntarily, I clench tightly around his digit.

He caresses my ass, trying to get me to relax. "Breathe, *cara*," Alessio instructs, and I focus on Dante's eyes, counting to ten and starting over until the tension leaves. His eyes always center me again, those intense pools of emerald that look at me with such adoration—he is my calm, my rock.

"You ready for another?" Alessio asks, and I nod in confirmation.

His second finger stretches me even wider until I'm almost uncomfortably full. *Almost.*

The initial soreness wears off quickly as I breathe my way into relaxation while Alessio fingers my ass.

Beneath me, Dante is still rock-hard but diligently still as he watches my face intently.

Alessio kisses the back of my neck, moving my hair away to create a path for his lips, making my short neck hairs rise and my skin dimple.

Without warning, the Joker pulls his fingers out, and I bite my bottom lip to distract me from how empty I feel.

I know it's only temporary, though.

Weaving my fingers through Dante's chest hair for support, I try to brace myself for the next part.

Alessio adds more lube, as promised, before pressing his hardness where his fingers played moments before.

He's ready.

So am I.

We stopped using condoms with him a while back already—only with him. My birth control is still doing its job, and Alessio regularly gets tested. Well, that and he promised always to use protection with his other partners.

I hold my breath, focusing on the feeling of Alessio's cock pressed against me.

He definitely seems too big to fit.

But I know he isn't.

"Fill me, please," I moan, pushing my ass out towards him.

"Such a needy little kitty." Alessio laughs, smacking my bum playfully. "Your wish is my command. Relax, *cara*."

I take a deep breath and close my eyes, focusing on my ass. On taking Alessio. Stretching around him.

With his hands on my hips, he finally pushes inside, filling me to the brim and then some.

Oh god, it hurts.

I clench my fists around Dante's chest hair, tugging, my eyes still shut firmly. His gentle caresses are soothing as he grounds me in the moment.

And then it's all over, the pain, the initial discomfort. It all gives way to the most glorious pleasure. Oh god, to be penetrated from both sides.

Alessio kisses my neck, whispering dirty words of encouragement in my ear as I relax into the sensation. "There you go, all in. You take me so well," he says, his lips brushing my shoulder blade to pamper my skin with his kisses.

For a moment, the three of us just remain like that—interlocked but unmoving—Dante and I on the bed with Alessio's feet planted firmly on the floor behind me.

Not gonna lie, I had to Google this position to figure out the logistics the first time we tried it, but now it was no longer that complicated getting impaled from both sides.

"Can one of you just move already?" Dante complains beneath us, and I open my eyes with a smile.

"Almost ready," Alessio responds, sneaking a hand around to my clit, the other still firmly on my hip.

But I don't get to focus on the sensation. Because Alessio finally starts moving, fucking my ass in deep, slow movements that make the room spin and my insides twist with need.

I gasp as his fingers circle my sensitive bud, rubbing my clit in tandem with his thrusts while another orgasm starts to build between my thighs—far quicker than I ever thought possible.

"Fuck," I rasp as the tingling spreads.

My skin is instantly on fire!

Stimulated from all sides, there is no way I can last long like this.

But I don't want to last.

No, I want to fall apart entirely, fucked into oblivion, until nothing remains of this bloody day but cake crumbs and cum.

Make me forget, please.

CHAPTER SIX

SPENT

(DANTE)

E ven as pleasure builds at my core, part of my mind races with questions.

Who ordered the attack?

Why now?

The throbbing at the base of my skull matches my pulse—pain and pleasure tangling together until I can't tell which is which.

But here, between my Queen and my Vegas Joker, I can almost forget.

Almost.

My body moves on instinct while my thoughts drift to security protocols, to the guards I'll need to replace, to the weakness in our defenses that let this happen.

"Dante, darling..." Danica's kiss pulls me back to now, to this moment. To being just Dante. Just theirs.

I come undone as Danica pushes herself up on her knees, my painfully hard cock sliding out just an inch. *Fuck, she's so wet.*

After remaining still inside her for so long, so close to coming, so desperate, the little bit of friction is enough to drive me wild!

Even more so when Alessio pushes her back down, spearing her on my cock as we all moan in unison.

What a beautiful sight—Danica and Alessio hovering over me. I love looking at their faces, especially when they are so exquisitely etched with desire, with lust, with *need*.

I reach for Danica's breasts, holding them up as she bounces on top of me, propelled by Alessio's punishing pace. My circuits are ablaze with sensation.

There is nothing left in my mind but the aching need to come.

But that's not up to me.

I'm at their mercy, my body pinned to the bed.

No leverage.

There is nothing for me to do but submit. Let go.

I gladly sink into the freedom.

It takes a few beats before we all find our rhythm, but when everyone's movements sync up, the room fills with a symphony of grunts and moans in three different registers.

My Vegas love grins down at me, his long hair falling over his shoulders, and I blow him a kiss, much to Danica's delight.

She tugs at my chest hair, making me hum for her, and I shift my gaze to hers.

I don't know how she can concentrate on anything with us both filling her, but Danica slowly fans her fingers over my nipples before grabbing on, twisting with all her might as she continues to bounce on top of my cock.

The result is the most incredible pain-pleasure combo that almost sends me over the edge right there and then.

It takes every ounce of concentration to keep myself from coming inside her.

I can't, not now, not without permission.

Dio mio!

I try to focus on something else. Something other than *my* body.

Danica. I focus on Danica. She looks magnificent from this view, from any view. My lighthouse in the storm. My anchor.

Starting from her right ear, I slowly scan down, tracing the familiar contours of her skin as my own body turns to mush, boneless.

Her figure has changed so much from all the training and combat sports. Her natural curves are still there, the thick ass, the huge tits that I love so much, but her stomach is flatter, her arms gaining definition.

My favorite part is her thighs—they are still as thick as ever, but now they are more muscular. Sometimes, I imagine them around my neck, squeezing until I can't breathe anymore. It's an incredibly erotic thought, one that never fails to get me hard.

I would appreciate my Queen in any shape or form, but I love seeing how much fulfillment her newfound strength brings her. Her growing confidence is electrifying.

"Faster. Fuck me faster, boy," Danica tells Alessio, daring him. Not that he needs much encouragement.

He answers without missing a beat, "Gladly, *cara*."

My bride lets out a loud howl he complies, the most beautiful sound that drives me damn near feral.

And then she does something that *does* drive me wild—she wraps her hands around my throat like a collar, holding on for dear life, squeezing the sides with, as Alessio fucks us both into another existential plane.

When the Joker speeds up his fingers over her clit, Danica's face turns as desperate as mine.

I love how she bites her bottom lip, how her skin dots in goosebumps...

Time passes in songs playing softly in the background and increasingly desperate moans of bodies on the brink of climax.

When the third song starts, I know I'm in trouble. My cock is throbbing, ready—I'm moments from exploding.

"Please!" The word is but an urgent whisper, but Danica can see the plea in my eyes, the familiar desperation on my face.

"Do you want to come, my love?" she asks like she doesn't know the answer, her face twisting into a grin.

"I can't hold it," I tell her, trying to convey my desperation with my trembling voice.

"That makes two of us," Alessio adds between gasping breaths, slowing the rhythm of his thrusts.

Danica smiles. "Three if you keep going like that."

"Where do you want this cum?" Alessio asks, and a mischievous look befalls my bride's face.

"On my tits, both of you," she answers without missing a beat.

Alessio shoots me a look, and I nod. "On three," he announces before starting his countdown.

When the final number rings out, he pulls out quickly, and Danica topples onto me, gasping like someone's dumped an ice bucket onto her.

Alessio stretches out leisurely before wrapping his arms around Danica from behind, effortlessly lifting her off my dripping cock.

I instantly miss the warmth of her. Of them both.

Standing up feels strange, and I take a moment to get my bearings.

I'm slightly lightheaded, and my neck is achy despite the painkillers, but nothing trumps the need to come. The urge consumes me. Wholly.

When the world stops spinning and I look up, I notice that Alessio's as hard as I am, pre-cum leaking from his tip. No surprise there.

Holding her palms face up, Danica demands our cocks, and we gladly oblige, placing them in her hands. It's a ritual that never fails to bring a massive grin to that beautiful face.

Sitting on the edge of the bed, she pulls us closer by the dicks, pressing our hardnesses into her chest, rubbing sensitive skin on sensitive skin.

Alessio moans loudly and I'm not far behind.

We're in this together with Danica in charge, driving us delirious with desire as she rubs our cocks against her nipples, over her breasts, somehow keeping a steady rhythm in both hands.

"Are you boys ready to come for me?" our Queen whispers seductively, darting her gaze between Alessio and me. "You have permission," she adds, and I shudder in anticipation. Those magical words I've been waiting to hear. Permission. *Oh, Dio.*

Not that Alessio needs permission, but he politely waits for it whenever Danica demands it.

We both nod eagerly, primal groans filling the room as she milks the orgasms from our cake-crusted, tired bodies. It doesn't take long. Less than one song.

I topple over the edge first, my body jerking like a reed in the wind as ropes of cum shoot over Danica's beautiful tits.

Alessio follows close on my heels, adding to the spunk artwork on our Queen's skin.

"Good," Danica encourages, not stopping for a second as we wither in her grip, gasping, desperate, spent, "Give me everything you have." Mercifully, she lets us go before the overstimulation becomes unbearable.

Keeping her gaze locked on us, she smears the cum over her whole chest, her abs, mixing it all in a sticky mess that glistens on her milky skin.

Fuck, it's so hot!

Panting heavily, I reach over to kiss her, and she pulls me down onto the bed, her stickiness rubbing off on me.

Alessio joins us in the cuddle pile as Danica reaches for the bedside drawer to pull out her trusty wand.

"Don't move," she tells us, lying back down between Alessio and me, cradled in both our arms like a hammock made of flesh, our sticky bodies pressed against her.

As Alessio and I watch with rapid breaths, Danica reaches the wand between her thighs to finish the job quicker than any of us ever could.

She throws her head back, and a magnificent whimper dances into the room.

Pulling her into me, I kiss her deeply, swallowing her moans, my other hand massaging her breast in slow patterns.

Alessio lends a hand, or rather a mouth, closing his lips around a cum-stained nipple, biting down just enough to make Danica groan into our kiss.

Less than two songs later, Danica reaches her own crescendo as the music does, contributing a chorus of gasps and whimpers to the background tune as she orgasms.

We hold her close as she shivers and shakes, screaming in ecstasy as the wand achieves its mission of release.

When she finally comes down from her high, we just hold each other—all three of us—a sticky, spent mess of cake, sweat, and cum.

Soon after, reality crashes back as we lie tangled in sheets and each other. With the painkillers wearing off, my skull increasingly throbs—as much from my injury as from the dark thoughts I can no longer push away. Someone wanted us dead. Someone got close enough to try.

The Russians shouldn't have been able to get that far into our territory, let alone into our wedding. We had security. We had protocols. We had...

I pull Danica closer, breathing in her scent while watching shadows play across the ceiling. She could have died today. They could have killed her, my Queen, my home, all because I made her part of this world. Part of my war.

Alessio's hand finds my chest in the darkness, steady and warm, but even his touch can't quiet my racing mind. If they knew about the wedding, what else do they know?

You could emphasize the intrusive nature of the memory:

I close my eyes, but immediately, the image of Carlo's lifeless body appears unbidden, as if etched behind my eyelids—blood soaking into the grass, into the once-white dress.

Cazzo!

How many more will die before this ends? How many more lives will I risk trying to protect what's mine?

There are no answers. Just more questions. More threats.

It's Alessio who speaks first, saving me from the spiral. "So much for that shower earlier." He pushes a strand of hair from Danica's sweaty forehead before seeking her lips with his own.

"A second shower seems in order," she replies, dragging her finger over her abs before licking the cum mix from her digit like it's a delectable dessert.

It could be mine, it could be Alessio's, or both of ours.

What an arousing thought.

My dick perks up like it hasn't had enough attention yet.

"But first, I need to pee," Danica announces, as she usually does at this point. Something about avoiding infections...

As she wiggles out between us, I scoot closer to Alessio to rest my head in the nook of his armpit, enjoying his warmth, his proximity, as our heart rates slowly fall back into a regular beat.

Affectionately, he strokes my hair, planting a kiss firmly on my lips.

"Perhaps we should have some more champagne and see where the night leads us," the Joker suggests like our day has but begun, as he playfully tugs at my resting cock.

I wish I knew where his seemingly boundless energy came from because I am ready to sleep for days.

But it isn't time for sleeping yet...

CHAPTER SEVEN

REMATCH

(DANICA)

Consciousness creeps in slowly, accompanied by a hangover that feels like it's been crafted by Satan himself. *When did I start getting hangovers?*

Before I even open my eyes, I catch the rich scent of coffee mingling with the morning sun and hushed masculine voices.

They're by the window—my boys. The sight of them stops my breath for a moment.

Dante's robe hangs open at the chest, while Alessio has somehow squeezed himself into my silk robe, the fabric struggling valiantly to cover what it was never designed to hold.

They're whispering over steaming mugs, heads bent close, intimacy radiating from every line of their bodies.

Something warm unfurls in my chest at the sight. This could be my future—waking up to both of them, sharing quiet mornings and coffee-flavored kisses. *Imagine?*

Then reality crashes back like a tidal wave.

I should be waking up as Donna Fera today.

The thought brings everything else flooding back—gunshots scattering the crowd, roses stained with blood, Carlo's body growing cold in my lap. My throat closes up.

All those months of planning and for what? Just to have some disrespectful Russian dickheads destroy it all. It's not right.

Poor Carlo.

I'm overcome by heavy sadness as the memory of his lifeless body on my lap torments me, digging its painful claws deeper into my flesh.

Sure, I gave Carlo hell, especially when I first arrived at the Fera household, but we've been through so much together since then.

Last year, for my birthday, he even gave me a wooden bookmark shaped like a stallion that he'd carved himself. It was the most special gift...

They won't get away with it, I vow, wiping a stray tear.

This is not how our story is supposed to go.

"Ah, the Queen awakens." Alessio's voice is warm honey, but I hear the concern underneath. I try to school my features, to submerge down the grief, but I'm too slow.

The bed dips as Dante moves to me like the tide drawn to the shore. His arms envelop me, lips pressing gentle kisses across my face. "You're sad," he murmurs, those emerald eyes seeing straight through my defenses.

A sigh escapes as I burrow into his chest, seeking the steady thrum of his heartbeat. "Yesterday was a royal fuck-up, wasn't it?"

"I'm sorry, *Tesoro*." His voice rumbles against my ear. "We'll find those assholes. You'll get your big day."

The words should comfort me, but they land like stones in my stomach.

Before I can respond, Alessio joins us on the bed, his borrowed robe giving up any pretense of modesty. Despite everything, a smile tugs at my lips—trust Don Santoro to make even tragedy look somehow elegant.

"The next one will be even better. I'm sure we can pull something together in a few weeks, I—" Dante starts, but the mere thought of doing it all again makes my chest tight.

"No." The word comes out sharper than intended. "I don't want that. Not again. *Please*." I don't want another perfect day to be ruined. Another white dress to be stained with blood. Another chance for someone else to die protecting us.

"I thought you might say that." Dante's voice is soft with understanding. "I'm sorry, my love. I know you wanted your big day to be special."

I smile weakly, kissing his hand and placing it over my chest. "It's not that. I just really want to be your wife." My head is pounding, but I don't want to get up and do something about it. I'm too comfortable sandwiched between my Dons.

"You are already my wife. The wedding is just a formality."

My fingers trace the lines of Dante's palm, seeking patterns in the calluses and scars.

"You know..." Alessio's voice breaks the silence, gentle as morning light. "You could always just come to Vegas and do what people do in Vegas?" A pause, careful. "It's quick, it's easy, and completely drama-free..."

Dante doesn't speak, but I feel the shift in his energy. His brow furrows, thoughts turning inward like clouds gathering before rain.

"But the guests..." The words taste stale in my mouth. "The expectations, the traditions?" Even as I say them, I hear how hollow they sound. How many of yesterday's guests came for *us*, really? How many came for power, for show, for obligation?

"I'm sure you could be forgiven, considering the circumstances." Alessio's hand finds mine, his thumb brushing over my knuckles. His borrowed robe slips further, but none of us notice anymore. "Besides, *cara*, this is about you, not what everyone else wants." His eyes, warm and knowing, hold mine. "What do *you* want?"

The question hangs in the air like smoke. What *do* I want?

"That does sound like less hassle." I turn to Dante, searching his face. "Can we get away with that?"

"I'm not sure..." Doubt clouds those emerald eyes I love so much.

"Please." My voice cracks slightly. "I just want the next part of our lives to begin."

Something softens in Dante's expression. He brings my hand to his lips, pressing a kiss to my palm like a seal on a promise. "Okay. Fuck it. We tried doing it the right way."

"Every way is the right way," Alessio declares as he wraps us in his arms, pulling us closer together.

"I don't even know where to start planning..." The thought looms like a mountain.

"Don't you worry about that." Alessio's eyes sparkle with that look that usually means beautiful trouble. "Leave it all to me. You two just show up. I'll make sure it's special."

"I can't ask that of you, I—"

"My gift, *cara mia*. I will hear no objections."

I nod in quiet acceptance.

But the quiet doesn't last, not when my mind immediately starts working on a to-do list again.

"I would need a new dress..." The ruined white gown flashes through my mind.

"Whatever you want. Take the card," Dante offers immediately.

Hope flutters in my chest. "Does it have to be white again?"

Dante shakes his head. "It doesn't have to be. Whatever your heart desires."

"I like the sound of that."

"You can invite your family if you want?" Alessio's offer is gentle, careful.

"No, thank you." The words come quick, firm. "If you and Emilio are there, that's the only family I need."

Alessio shoots Dante a look I can't decipher, but Dante just shrugs. My family is a touchy subject, just like his.

Neither push me further on the matter. Thank fuck. I don't have the strength to have that conversation right now. I'm sure at some point I'll have to tell Dante why they refused to come to our wedding, why I was glad they weren't there. But not today.

"Then it's settled," Alessio declares, his smile bright enough to chase away shadows. "Give me a few weeks."

I lean over, pressing my lips to his. He tastes of coffee and possibility. "Thank you."

"Only a pleasure, dear. Speaking of pleasure, I have to leave in an hour. Do you think we can fit in a quickie?" He winks, and my stomach instantly flutters in lust. My libido is always so high in the mornings.

I reach my hand into Alessio's robe in answer, wrapping my fingers around his semi-erect cock.

"That sounds like the second-best idea you've had this morning." Anything is better than replaying yesterday's fiasco in my mind over and over again.

"Do you have to leave?" Dante asks, disappointment clear in his voice, and Alessio nods slowly in response. "You know it's hard for me to get away from my responsibilities."

"That's not the only thing that's hard." I bend down to close my lips around Alessio's tip, swallowing him whole as he grows to full hardness inside my mouth, until I can't contain the size of him, and I gag, spitting him out again.

In a fumbling of body parts and kisses from all sides and all variations, we draw the orgasms from each other's bodies until we're lying there panting, sticky, satisfied.

There isn't much time left for cuddling, but we make some anyway. I rest my head on Alessio's chest while Dante big-spoons me, pressing my naked body tightly against both of theirs.

"I wish you could stay." I sigh, kissing Alessio's neck as I lazily trace patterns over his beautiful skin, mapping his tattoos.

"You'll see me soon enough, don't worry." He strokes my hair, and I close my eyes for a moment, trying to hold onto the feeling that I know is impossible to hold onto.

"Sure," I mumble, unsatisfied.

"Okay, shower time," Alessio announces after a few minutes, breaking up the perfect morning after.

"I can help you?" Dante offers as Alessio untangles himself from our bodies.

"Don't tempt me. I would never leave. No, not this time, darling." He leans down to kiss us both and then disappears into the bathroom.

Dante pulls me closer to him, almost on top of him, locking his arms around my back and nearly squeezing all the breath from my lungs.

"It's not too late to change your mind, *Tesoro*. You don't have to marry me. Your life will be filled with endless chaos and death if you do." His fingers find my hair, strokes in soothing patterns.

I shake my head vehemently. "You're worth it. I don't care about all that."

Dante touches my cheek affectionately. "I don't want you to get hurt."

"You've never hurt me before."

"But there are a lot of other people who have. And so many more who will want to when you become Mrs. Fera."

"I'm a grown-up; I can make my own decisions. You are my person. Fuck those people. For better or for worse, or however those vows go."

"I'll sort out this mess, don't worry."

"*We'll* sort it out," I correct him.

"It's dangerous, Danica. You know I don't like involving you in the business."

"I *want* to be more involved. I'm going to be your wife. You can't keep me wrapped in cotton wool."

"But I need to protect you." If I had a dollar for every time Dante uttered those words since he barged into my life four years ago...

"Fuck that patriarchal bullshit. I'm not a child anymore. This is a partnership." I look at him sternly.

"Yes, Ma'am." Dante sighs, knowing there is no way to win this one.

"That's better, now...can I please have some coffee and an Aspirin? I'm dying over here."

"Coming right up. Will bring you some water too."

"Thanks, baby." I kiss him deeply, and then he's off, tying his robe firmly around his waist.

The room is so quiet without the boys, but it's also nice to have a second to catch my breath. Everything has been happening so quickly. It all still feels a bit like a movie rather than reality.

I trace the edge of the sheets where Dante lay moments ago, still warm from his body. Twenty-four hours ago, I was supposed to be saying, "I do." Now, all I have of yesterday is a torn, bloody dress and empty champagne bottles.

With a sigh, I force myself to get up, catching my reflection in the mirror.

My tired and hungover eyes see only imperfections, magnified and ugly. The scars I usually manage to ignore seem to glow like neon signs advertising my damage.

What am I doing here? Playing dress-up in a world I don't belong in, pretending I can be some mafia Queen when I can barely tell my salad fork from my dinner fork?

The mirror has no answers, only more questions, so I look away, forcing my gaze out the window instead, over the grounds. Everything has been put back into place, righted like it has never been wronged. But my mind still remembers...

Alessio finishes before Dante does, strolling back into the room with his crisp white shirt yet to be buttoned.

"So, see you at your next wedding?" He grins, wrapping me in a hug as he kisses my shoulder, pulling me closer to him.

I roll my eyes at him. "Too soon."

"Don't worry, *cara mia*. You'll be *La Donna* Fera soon enough. Nothing will stop that man from marrying you."

I want to believe him but the words bring little of the intended comfort. "I don't know if that's even a good thing." I lower my head. "He deserves more, someone with a better pedigree; someone who knows how wine pairings work."

My insecurities are waging a war inside my fragile mind.

But Alessio is having none of that.

"Nonsense. You can learn those dumb things if you want to, but they don't matter. You're more powerful than you think, Danica. Don't let the past define you. You're not that person anymore."

I nod, despite my mind still running a million miles an hour in the opposite direction. "Sure."

Alessio tips my chin towards him and stares me down with those intense amber eyes that always see so much. "Listen to me, *cara*; there is no one in the world more suitable to stand by Dante's side than you."

I sigh, shifting my gaze.

"It will work out. Just give it some time," Alessio tells me as he wraps his arms around me and holds me close, smothering me in his fresh aftershave. "See you in Vegas, okay?"

"Yeah, sure..."

For the first time, I'm not that excited to return to our shiny playground in the desert.

We need to take care of the threat first.

CHAPTER EIGHT

DEBRIEF

(DANTE)

A familiar knock draws my attention to the door—three short taps.

I call Emilio inside my office, not bothering with formalities. "What do you have for me?"

The old man was supposed to have the day off today, but that was *before* my wedding turned into a war zone.

Our whole routine was out of whack. Even poor Biscotti had to—begrudgingly—put up with getting his breakfast served more than an hour late. I make a mental note to ask Dario to take over that responsibility.

Closing the door behind him, Emilio hesitates, looking at Danica and then at me. She's not usually in our debriefing meetings.

Dressed in tights and a tank top like she's about to go work out, no shoes, my bride sits on my desk like I don't have at least four other chairs to choose from. I've long since stopped nagging her to conform to conventional seating suggestions.

"It's okay. Danica wants to be here for this," I reassure him. "Do you have an update?" I ask, my voice thick, assertive.

Emilio nods, continuing.

"*Sì, Don mio*. We had the crew in to clean everything up outside. The gardeners have fixed most the damage to the landscape," the old man starts. He looks tired, stressed. Usually, his crisp white shirts are impeccably ironed, but today, two creases tarnish the perfection—details too small for anyone to notice, but I've known Emilio for over three decades.

"You can sit down if you want, Emilio," Danica offers, but the old guard shakes his head, declining.

"No, thank you, Miss Matthews. I'm okay."

Danica visibly stiffens at the sound of her surname but doesn't say anything.

I return my attention to my second-in-command, who's been first-in-command more and more these days. Perhaps I've been relying too much on Emilio lately..."And casualties? What's the damage?" I continue my questioning.

"We lost Carlo, as you know, and someone from the Greco family. Four more heavily injured and a couple of minor cuts and bruises." Emilio lowers his head.

"*Cazzo*," I swear under my breath as I clench my fists, my knuckles cracking loudly.

That whole ambush was so unnecessary. *For fuck's sake.*

The responsibility weighs heavy on my shoulders. Part of me feels like I want to throw up, but that might just be the hangover. My body isn't as resilient as it used to be. Danica swallowed down an Aspirin earlier and seems back to normal now. I'm not so lucky.

My neck is killing me, but I don't tell Danica.

I don't want her to worry.

It's not the only thing in pain after yesterday's ambush of what was supposed to be our dream wedding.

I'm clearly not as fit as I used to be.

I used to take blows way worse than that without so much as a bruise.

But I am 46 now; I need to be more careful with my body. Especially since I've been skimping on my workouts and can no longer rely on my muscles to work the way they used to.

How will I protect Danica if my body can't be trusted?

The thought scares me more than a gun to the head.

"And on their side?" Danica asks, pulling my focus back to the debrief.

"Two dead and one captured," Emilio reports. "The rest escaped."

"Any luck getting the guy to talk?" I ask, despite knowing the answer.

"No, sir. We're keeping him in the basement. He's already a few fingers poorer, but we've got nothing."

"Thanks, Emilio. Keep trying." It's hard to keep my voice steady, but I force it. "Do we have any idea who these guys are?"

"*Sì*. It's the Volkov family. Russians. The Morettis had run-ins with them a while ago too."

"I thought I heard some Russian yesterday," Danica adds.

"The Russians?" I ask, trying to make sense of the information. That doesn't sound good. Not at all. "Didn't we deal with that problem decades ago already?"

"*Sì, Don mio*. It seems a new generation has taken power, and they don't feel as strongly about boundaries as their predecessors. Don Moretti's words were 'young and reckless with no regard for any tradition or established turfs.'"

I sigh. This is the last thing I need. "That explains the stupidity of attacking such a high-profile wedding in broad daylight with so many of the families present."

Emilio seems as restless as I am. "We've had them on our radar for a while, but I didn't expect them to be so bold."

"Why is this the first I hear of it?" my voice trembles with barely contained anger.

"Apologies, *Don mio*. You've been quite busy with the wedding, and I didn't want to bother you." Emilio lowers his head.

"I see."

I know what he's not saying.

It's not Emilio's fault.

We both know I've been neglecting my responsibilities lately, pawning it off to him.

I should have been on top of this.

"What do they want with us?" Danica's journalistic skills are working overtime, as usual.

"The attack appears to be a challenge to the families," Emilio explains. "The Volkovs are ready to expand their turf."

"Drugs?" Danica asks.

"Yes, Miss M—," he stops himself from saying her surname, "And human trafficking too."

"How?" We had such a good handle on all the routes. Trafficking was something the families never got involved in; we had an understanding. Such a nasty business. Even my heartless father didn't want any part of that. Those were people's daughters and sisters being shipped off as whores. It wasn't right.

"We believe they have infiltrated the ports—if our sources are to be believed." Emilio treads carefully, aware of the sensitivity around the issue.

"The ports? *Fanculo*!" I slam my fist on the desk, and Danica jumps—startled. Not the ports. *Jesus.*

It took so many years to negotiate a truce with the other families over the ports.

No one family could own it; it would give them too much power. So, we all agreed to leave it be, to keep people on the inside so we can move whatever we need quietly, discreetly.

With the ports compromised, all the families' businesses are at risk, ours included.

I can't do this all again.

Too many people died in that port war. My mother—

No, not now!

"I'm sorry, *Don mio*. I should have told you earlier. My sources weren't sure, and I thought this could wait until after the wedding."

"It's not your fault, Emilio. I should have been more available." I twist my rings, staring out the window. My head is still pounding, making it harder to think.

"We need to get these assholes. Strike while the iron is hot!" Danica jumps off the desk, fired up.

"No," I reply immediately, shooting her a loaded look.

She arches an eyebrow in question. "No?"

"We should wait," I say with certainty.

"What for? Those assholes killed Carlo. They ruined our wedding. You can't just let them get away with it." Danica crosses her arms over her chest, staring at me defiantly. Still my little firecracker, even after all this time.

"They won't get away with it, don't you worry about that. But we would be stupid to move in immediately. Not without more intel. We don't know what they're planning. We'd be walking right into a trap. That's what they expect us to do." My mind is racing, trying to put all the puzzle pieces in the right place for this all to make sense, but I don't have enough of the pieces yet. Something still doesn't fit right.

"The other families have expressed their willingness to work together for the collective benefit of all," Emilio reports in his usual monotone.

"We can't just do nothing. Who knows what they will do next?" Danica starts pacing around the room.

"Exactly. We don't know what they want. I say we take a step back and let them make the next move, play their hand, and then we can make a more informed decision. If we storm in blind, the casualties will be too high. There is no need to take that much collateral damage."

Danica doesn't reply. She may be in charge of my body and my mind behind closed doors, but when it comes to the business, this is *my* world. I've been running this family for longer than she's been alive. It is important not to make any rash decisions when playing with so many lives.

The loaded silence stretches on momentarily before Emilio clears his throat.

"What is it?" I ask, too short.

"Respectfully, sir. I don't think we have the time. The other families wanted to meet immediately, but I managed to bargain for tomorrow evening instead."

"*Cazzo.*" Damnit, Emilio. Always burying the lead.

"Apologies." Emilio straightens out his shoulders. "I tried to put them at ease, but the Dons are offended and want this handled."

I should have known the Dons would not take kindly to being crossed.

Fuck.

"Find out whatever you can before that meeting tomorrow, Emilio. Don't we have informants at the ports?"

"I'm doing my best to get hold of them, *Don mio*."

"Go." I wave him off with the flick of my wrist.

What a royal mess.

"You're being mean to Emilio," Danica says as soon as the door is closed.

"I'm not," I snap back, too loudly, rubbing my temples. "I'm just...frustrated."

"We all are. You don't have to yell." Danica sits down on the couch, crossing her arms, a sullen look clouding her face. Instantly, I regret my tone.

"I'm sorry, *Tesoro*." My expression softens as I take a seat beside her and pull her onto my lap. "Let me make it up to you."

Slowly, I run my palm over Danica's top. She isn't wearing a bra, and her perky nipples press freely (and noticeably) against the tight fabric.

"And how are you going to do that?" she asks, uncrossing her arms. Finally, a full smile.

"When was the last time I ate you out on my desk?" I suggest with a wink. Some distraction would be welcome right now—for both of us.

"Like literally last week." Danica laughs, shifting her ass on my lap. I know she can feel my burning erection beneath her, painfully hard for her as always, despite my injuries, despite the headache, the hangover.

"May I? Please?" My hunger for her is insatiable. Even after all these years. I could happily spend my days worshiping my

Queen and doing nothing else. Instead, I have to deal with asshole Russians and dead wedding guests.

"You can't just distract me with sex," my bride insists, her resolve quickly fading.

"Can't I?" I pinch a hard nipple through her shirt, and she gasps.

"Fair. Come here." Danica pulls me closer by the hair, trapping my lips between hers as she hungrily kisses me until I'm gasping for breath.

Without asking for permission, I stick my hands under her shirt, caressing her breasts and pinching her nipples between my fingers, just how she likes it.

My bride doesn't reprimand me, she just moans softly, purring into my neck like a cat who has gotten cream.

With my hands firmly under her ass, I get up and carry her to the desk, ignoring the protests of my body.

"My strong and sexy Don," Danica rasps as she clings to me, her legs wrapping around my waist.

"Yes, Ma'am," I reply, wildly scattering the contents of my desk onto the floor with one arm, clearing space on the large wooden surface to set her down gently.

Grinning mischievously, Danica pushes me away with her bare foot against my chest. "Kneel...*boy*."

Her wish is my command, and despite every ache and pain burning through my body, I fall to my knees without so much as a second thought.

Please call me good...

CHAPTER NINE

INTERLUDE

(DANICA)

The bedroom door closes behind us with a soft click that echoes through my bones. For the first time since we woke up on our wedding day yesterday, Dante and I are truly alone.

Like a good boy, he devoured my cunt in his office after our depressing debrief with Emilio. The release was glorious, necessary, and exactly what I needed to distract myself from our reality.

It's like I can only think of it in little bursts at a time, before it gets too much, too heavy, and I have to find something else to do with my thoughts.

Carlo keeps coming back to me, though...

As soon as my heart rate returned to its post-orgasm norm, I dragged Dante out of the office and back to the bedroom. It was a Sunday, after all, and there would be plenty of time for *work* soon enough.

Our room looks as fresh as an unlived-in hotel room.

The staff has cleared away the evidence of our celebration—no more cake crumbs in the sheets, no sticky champagne flutes on the nightstand. But they can't erase the invisible weight that hangs so heavy in the air.

Dante walks to the window, shoulders rigid, one hand absently rubbing the base of his neck where that Russian thug hit him. He's trying to hide the wince, but I see it anyway. My fierce, stubborn Don, always pretending to be indestructible.

"Come here," I say softly, patting the bed beside me. "Let me look at that."

"It's nothing, *Tesoro*. Just stiff." But his voice lacks its usual conviction.

The click of Biscotti's nails against hardwood announces his arrival before he pushes through the door. He's been extra clingy since yesterday, on high alert.

He beelines straight for Dante, nosing at his hand until my darling boy finally cracks a smile.

"See? Even Biscotti knows you're hurt." I raise an eyebrow. "And he's smarter than both of us."

Dante sighs but allows himself to be coaxed to the bed.

His attempt to hide another wince as he sits doesn't go unnoticed.

I position myself behind him, fingers gentle as they explore the angry bruising at his nape.

"Christ, darling, this needs ice." The swelling is worse than yesterday. "Why didn't you say something before?"

"More important things to worry about." His words end in a hiss as I find a particularly tender spot. "The other Dons will be here soon. We need to be ready."

"And you need to be able to turn your head." I press a kiss to his shoulder. "Stay put."

The kitchen is eerily quiet as I gather ice and a clean towel. Everything feels suspended, like the whole house is holding its breath. Waiting for the next explosion, the next attack.

I push the thought away.

Not yet.

Not today.

When I return, Dante has stretched out on his stomach on the bed, Biscotti curled against his side. Our dog's head rests on Dante's lower back, those soulful eyes tracking my movement. Keeping guard, as always.

"This will be cold," I warn, settling beside them. The makeshift ice pack draws a sharp breath from Dante, but he doesn't pull away.

We stay like that for a while, the only sounds being Biscotti's contented sighs and the occasional drip of melting ice.

My free hand cards through Dante's hair, noting the silver starting to thread through the black at his temples. When did that happen?

"What are you thinking?" he murmurs into the pillow.

"That we should order pizza." The words surprise even me, but suddenly, it's all I want—something normal, something that has nothing to do with failed weddings or Russian threats or family obligations.

Dante turns his head just enough to look at me, amusement flickering in those green eyes. "Pizza?"

"With extra cheese. And those stuffed crust things you pretend to hate but always steal from my plate."

"I do not—" he starts to protest, but Biscotti's tail thumping against the bed makes us both laugh.

"Even the dog knows you're lying, Don Fera."

His hand finds mine, squeezing gently. "Pizza it is. But please, for the love of god, please don't order a pineapple topping again. It's an insult to my people. My mother would turn around in her grave."

"You can pick it off," I tease.

"It's disgusting," Dante insists, but he orders me the bacon-pineapple combo I love so much anyway. As if he would deny me, ha!

The rest of the day passes in a haze of deliberate normalcy we haven't had for weeks as the wedding planning frenzy swept the house.

We eat in bed, the fresh sheets already collecting casualties of our impromptu feast. Strings of molten cheese stretch between slices, defying gravity until they snap.

Dante tries to maintain some dignity, dabbing at his mouth with a napkin, but there's something wonderfully human about watching Don Fera battle with stubborn mozzarella. He keeps telling me that pizza should not have that much cheese on it, but he doesn't stop me from ordering it either.

"You've got sauce..." I gesture to the corner of his mouth. When he misses it completely, I lean in to kiss it away, tasting tomatoes and herbs and him.

Biscotti's head appears between us, right on cue, those pleading eyes working overtime. "No," Dante says firmly, then immediately contradicts himself by offering a crust. "Just this once," he adds like he doesn't say that every time.

"You're getting soft, Don Fera," I tease, watching our dog delicately accept the offering with saliva dripping down his chin.

"Slander." But Dante's smile is gentle, even as he tries to suppress a yawn. The pain meds are hitting hard now—I can see it in the slight glaze of his eyes, the way his shoulders finally release their tension.

I put on an action movie on the TV for us. All explosions and car chases. The kind where the heroes always win and the violence is cartoonish enough to feel fake. Nothing like the real thing. Nothing like yesterday.

Dante fights sleep for a while, making occasional comments about the impossible physics of the stunts. His words get slower, softer, until they trail off entirely. His head droops against my shoulder, breath evening out into the rhythm I know better than my own heartbeat.

Biscotti settles at our feet, pizza crust victory achieved, ever-watchful even in this peaceful moment.

On-screen, the hero delivers another corny one-liner before diving away from an explosion. I turn the volume down, letting the flickering light cast shadows across Dante's sleeping face.

In his slumber, he looks younger. The constant mask of Don Fera slips away, leaving just my Dante—the man who feeds our dog under the table, and steals the covers, and loves me with a fierceness that still takes my breath away.

The bruising on his neck has spread like spilled ink, a violent reminder that tomorrow isn't promised. Not in this new life I've chosen.

I brush a strand of hair from his forehead, careful not to wake him.

Tomorrow, we'll have to be strong again.

But for now, in this quiet space between chaos and retribution, we're just us.

Biscotti shifts closer, resting his head on my lap as the sun begins to set outside, casting our room in shades of gold and purple.

Dante's breathing is deep and even, his hand still tangled with mine even in sleep.

I should be plotting revenge. Should be burning with rage about our ruined wedding, about Carlo, about all of it. Instead, I find myself memorizing this moment—the warmth of our dog against my legs, the weight of Dante's hand in mine, the soft evening light making everything feel soft and safe.

Because tomorrow, I know, the real war begins.

Tomorrow, the other Dons will arrive with their agendas and their armies, and my husband will have to put on his armor again.

Tomorrow, we'll plan revenge in wood-paneled rooms that smell of cigars and power, and I'll stand beside him as his Queen, not just his partner.

I trace the lines of Dante's sleeping face with my eyes, committing every detail to memory. The way his tattoos look in the fading light, the slight crease between his brows that never fully smooths away, the tiny scar above his lip from some long-ago fight.

I could have fallen for someone safe.

Could have found a nice accountant or teacher or literally anyone whose daily concerns didn't include territory disputes and rival families.

Someone who didn't need bodyguards.

But I fell in love with a Don.

With this man who carries the weight of an empire on his shoulders but still sneaks our dog extra treats when he thinks I'm not looking. Who can order destruction with one breath and quote Italian song lyrics with the next. Who looks at me like I'm something precious, even when I'm holding a weapon.

He's *my* Don, though.

My warrior, my protector, my beautiful contradiction.

And I would burn down kingdoms for him.

Would wade through blood and bullets and whatever else this life throws at us.

Because that's what we do—we survive, we fight, we protect what's ours.

Biscotti shifts in his sleep, letting out a tiny whimper. Dante's fingers tighten around mine reflexively, protective even in dreams.

Outside our windows, night creeps in like a tide, and somewhere in the darkness, our enemies are plotting.

Let them come, I think, as the last of my sadness turns to rage.

They don't know what it means to threaten something a Queen loves.

CHAPTER TEN

PLANS

(DANTE)

I wish we had more time, more information, more options, but all we have is a visiting party of unhappy Dons with revenge in their eyes and murder in their fists.

My throat tightens like someone is cutting off my airway, but in a non-consensual, unpleasant way. *Fuck!*

Emilio patiently waits for my response.

But Danica isn't known for her patience. "Those assholes!" she exclaims before I can say anything.

According to Emilio's early morning update, the Russians had been busy while we slept. Last night, they attacked one of our car dealerships and burned half of it to the ground before anyone could stop the flames.

The other families suffered similar fates.

If I was uncertain whether moving quickly was the right choice, now it's clear we have no alternative.

I know this cannot wait; I will not risk losing any more men.

This ends now!

They don't know who they're messing with. I once kept a man alive for four days while I slowly, strategically cut off pieces of his body with my hunting knife, stacking them in rows on the floor before him until, finally, I carved my signature on his unbeating heart.

The way he broke, piece by piece...those sounds were music to my ears.

There was artistry to my methods then. I'd take my time, orchestrate every moment of terror. Other Dons sent their soldiers to do their dirty work, but I believed in the intimacy of fear. In wearing three-piece suits spattered with red. In letting them see the monster behind the manners.

The sound a man makes when he realizes Don Fera himself is the one holding the blade...delegated violence could never feel that powerful.

The Russians think they know brutality? They should ask about the Marino family's former consigliere. Should ask what happened during those long hours when I personally extracted every secret, every betrayal. Should ask about the night I painted my office walls with the consequences of disloyalty. They never did get those stains out of the hardwood...

But that was before Danica.

Before I learned there were better ways to sleep than remembering the exact pressure needed to keep a man conscious while you peel away his reasons for silence.

I take a deep breath, twisting my rings in an attempt to tame the brewing storm inside. *Steady, Dante.*

This is no time to dwell on the past.

"Is everyone here?" I ask Emilio curtly, not responding to his account of the damage, the extent of the attacks. What was there to say? It was time for *action*.

"*Sì, Don mio.* The families are in the dining room."

"Thanks, Emilio."

The old guard hesitates. There is something on his mind. I know his body language too well.

"What is it?"

Emilio takes a deep breath. "I don't know if we can trust our contact, sir. Something doesn't feel right." He knows he can speak freely.

"Do we have any other leads, any other way in?"

He shakes his head—no.

"Let's see what the others think." I pick up my cup of cold coffee from the desk and swallow it down in one go. "This shouldn't take long. I'll meet you upstairs," I tell Danica, pulling her toward me for a goodbye kiss.

But she pushes me away, a scowl on her brow. "If you think you're sending me away, you have another thing coming." Arms crossed over her chest, her gaze meets mine in cold defiance and I know this isn't going to be as easy as I had hoped.

I sigh. "Danica..."

"No. We've spoken about this. I want to be more involved. This is my life too." I want to argue, but I know there is no point. Sure, I can have one of the guards take her to her room by force, but I'll have to spend a week groveling if I resort to such measures.

"Fine, but please stay quiet," I reluctantly concede. She did make a good argument.

Danica nods and follows me downstairs, where the five Dons and their various bodyguards are gathered around the large wooden table, making forced conversation.

The tension is thick, thicker than the air. Not everyone came, but the original families were all represented. All except the Riccis. I refuse to have those assholes on my property.

The men get up when we enter the room, looking at Danica questionably. But I ignore their scornful glances and start my round of greetings, respectfully starting with the eldest, Don Vinci, the one with the walking cane shaped like a scythe.

Don Greco covers my hands with his, holding me a moment longer. "I'm sorry about your wedding, Dante. Danica is a fine woman; you did well. Not as fine as our dear Elena, of course..." Hearing the name of the wife I couldn't save, couldn't protect, cuts me deep with guilt as it always does. But I can't think of Elena now. It's too late for her.

I am relieved Danica is on the other side of the room. She doesn't see me flinch, see me stumble as I try to regain my composure.

"Thank you, Don Greco," I say simply, patting my former father-in-law on the shoulder with what I hope comes across as an empathetic gesture.

Elena would never have joined me in the "war room"—she was far too delicate for that. Sure, she knew the business inside out, she grew up in this world after all, but she trusted my leadership, my protection...my dominance.

And then I failed her.

But I won't fail Danica.

Fuck these Russian assholes.

Everyone settles down, and the staff makes sure their drinks are filled, from the tea drinkers to the whiskey connoisseurs.

Taking the floor, I silence the men to recount the details Emilio shared during the debriefings. The Volkovs are nasty fuckers—drugs, human trafficking, manipulating the awarding of construction contracts, just to name a few. They came out of seemingly nowhere and brought the entire city to a standstill, playing by their own rules (or no rules at all) as they plundered their way through our territories.

Like thieves in the night, they came in and took the ports, undoing decades of peace negotiations.

"The ports are off limits!" Don Vinci interrupts me, hammering his shaky hand on the table with an assertive bang. The old man is well over 80 now, barely hanging on to life, but his rage burns no less bright.

"*Sì*, Don Vinci. That's why the families agreed to keep this as neutral ground all those years ago."

The men in the room nod while Danica sits quietly by my side, observing, playing the part of the perfect, obedient wife. *If they only knew...*

Losing control of the ports is the biggest threat to our businesses. If we can't get anything in or out of the city, things quickly become very complicated.

There used to be endless turf wars about the ports until the Feras negotiated peace nearly two decades ago. My father would never have settled for a white flag, but I am not my father. If he conceded earlier, maybe my mother would still be alive.

"The trafficking is nasty business," Don Greco adds, and everyone but Don Vinci nods. We all know that he's secretly got a side trade in a similar line, but the families have an unspoken rule not to interfere.

The men start mumbling to each other in hushed Italian, going off on separate tracks.

"*Silencio!*" I command in my deep voice, forcing them to settle down.

Standing up, I tower over all of them as I speak.

The Dons quieten down.

"What's your plan, Don Fera?" It's Don Marino who asks what on everyone's mind.

"We wait for the right opportunity."

Don Vinci jumps up. "We've waited long enough—"

"Sit down, *per pavore*." My voice is thick. I don't care how old he is, my house, my rules.

He sits down.

"According to our contact, on Wednesday, they're loading a new shipment of women. There is a lot of commotion on those days, a lot of people in and out, and that's our best chance to get inside."

The Fera family has many contacts and informants. This particular one owes a huge debt to my family. Many years ago, I paid his son's tuition to help him become a doctor.

For a long time, I took my job as Don seriously—everyone who sat down in my office, pleading for the assistance of the Fera family, was heard.

After Elena's death, work was my everything. I couldn't sleep, I couldn't keep the guilt from drowning me during every waking hour. So I threw open the doors and let them all in. Crying old ladies begging for mercy for their sons who got into gangs, young women with abusive husbands and nowhere to turn, outright thugs who got themselves mixed with the wrong crowd—I heard them all and did what I could for our people, our community.

It never took the pain away, the gnawing guilt, the feeling that it was all my fault that she was dead, my fault that our unborn son would never have a life.

But then Danica came along and gave me another reason to get up in the morning. Another way to repent for my sins.

"You can have as many of my men as you need," Don Greco offers, pulling me back to the present conversation.

"From the Antonios too."

The families all pledge their armies, eager to get rid of the Russian pestilence fucking up our delicate equilibrium.

They have no reason to trust me but even less reason for distrust. I have always been a man of my word, a man who has helped any family who came to him.

The rest of the meeting deals with the formalities, discussing the alleged security detail at the ports, the number of men we would need

The reality is that we only have two days to prepare.

It's not a lot.

Never mind the logistics, I'm not sure two days will be enough to get my body ready. I'm achy and nauseous, tired beyond belief.

But I don't mention any of my ailments, of course not.

I just shake the Dons' hands firmly as they leave, kissing their cheeks as I promise everyone the situation will be dealt with swiftly.

How foolish of me.

Once the last hand has been shaken and ushered out, I head upstairs to my office as Danica disappears to the kitchen in search of a snack. I need time to think.

My head throbs with the weight of today's negotiations, the tension of forced smiles and veiled threats still heavy on my shoulders.

I loosen my shirt's top button as I sink into my office chair.

The other families might show respect to my face, but their eyes tell a different story.

They think I'm getting soft.

And that's dangerous.

The familiar click of nails against hardwood announces Biscotti's arrival before his head appears around the door frame. In his mouth, that ridiculous purple dinosaur toy Danica bought him.

"Not now, *piccolo*," I mutter, but he ignores my protest, padding over to drop the toy directly in my lap. When I don't immediately respond, he nudges my hand with his wet nose.

"You're as stubborn as your mama, you know that?" The words come out gruffer than intended, but Biscotti just wags his tail, unperturbed by my tone. That's the thing about dogs—they don't care about the politics, the power plays, the masks we wear.

Despite myself, I pick up the dinosaur. One squeeze, and its ridiculous squeak echoes through my office. Biscotti's entire body wags with excitement.

Five minutes, I tell myself. Five minutes to play with my dog before returning to being Don Fera.

The toy goes flying across the room, and Biscotti tears after it, his nails scrabbling on the wooden floor. He brings it back, dropping it in my lap with such pride you'd think he'd just solved all my problems.

"At least someone around here is happy," I tell him, scratching behind his ears. "Though between you and me, *cane*, this ambush we're planning? It stinks worse than your breath."

Biscotti tilts his head, those loyal eyes fixed on mine like he understands every word.

"Yeah, I know. Your mama would say I'm being paranoid." I throw the toy again, watching him bound after it. "But something's not right. I can feel it in my bones."

The dinosaur returns to my lap, slightly soggier than before. This time, I just hold it, lost in thought, as Biscotti rests his head on my knee.

At least someone in this family still believes I know what I'm doing.

That makes one of us.

DISTRACTION

(DANICA)

My fingernails dig crescents into my palms as I force myself to remain silent. The ornate conference room that usually serves as our dining room feels too small for all the egos it contains—six Dons and their various guards, the air thick with cigar smoke and centuries of tradition.

At some point, Don Vinci's wrinkled face twists with barely concealed disdain as he addresses Dante. "Perhaps if you spent less time playing house..." The insult hangs in the air like poison. My jaw aches from clenching my teeth, the urge to defend my husband-to-be burning in my throat.

But Dante doesn't need my protection.

He rises slowly from his chair, and the temperature in the room drops ten degrees.

This isn't my Dante—the man who melts under my touch, who whispers Italian love letters against my skin, who submits so beautifully to my will.

This is Don Fera, and watching him slip into this role is like watching a sword being unsheathed.

"Careful, old friend." His voice carries the soft menace of a weapon wrapped in silk. "Your age earns you certain courtesies, but not unlimited ones."

It's somewhat jarring to see Dante be this person. At times, I almost forget who he is. Who he was.

My darling Don has never been too forthcoming about his past sins, but the internet is awash with supposed crimes—all those rumors, those whispered stories about the bodies Don Fera left in his wake before I knew him. Looking at him now, it's not hard to imagine. I've experienced the wildfire of his rage, the violence that lives in his bones.

But he's so much more than that.

These men see only the Don, the killer, the legend. They don't know about the man who kneels at my feet, who gives me his power willingly, who found redemption in submission.

Both versions are real—the Don and the submissive, the killer and the lover, the monster and the man.

But it's not the lover who's in charge now.

Don Vinci sinks back in his chair, properly chastised. Dante's eyes meet mine briefly across the table, a flash of warmth in the winter of Don Fera's mask.

The meeting drones on with plans and counter-plans, alliances and threats. Watching Dante navigate this deadly dance of power, I understand why he needs our dynamic at home. Without a release, this job would consume anyone's soul—perhaps it already has. But in our bedroom, on his knees, he finds his way back to himself.

I just pray the price of power doesn't break him before then.

This job is too damn stressful; it brings out the worst in my darling groom. I wish there was a way for him to get out, to start fresh, to live the life he's always wanted but never had the luxury of living.

But I don't have solutions, only concerns.

As the meeting carries on, Don Marino, the one with the wispy goatee and scary face tattoo, keeps looking at me strangely, but I pay him no mind. I bet he's one of those dickheads who believes a woman's place is in the kitchen. Well, I have news for him—I'm absolutely shit in the kitchen.

But I have other skills.

As Dante tells them the improvised plan of attack, I watch closely to gauge everyone's reaction. Even though I was initially all for immediate action, I still can't shake the thought that this is a bad idea; Emilio's words keep replaying in my head.

Then again, *all* of it is a bad idea.

But what choice do we have?

What else must the Volkovs ruin before they get what they have coming?

Besides, with so many families and so many armies, surely we'd be fine, right?

Surely...

The proceedings drag on for a bit, for almost three hours, until the grumpy old Italian men finally take their leave, their oppressive cologne lingering in the space long after their exit.

Dante closes the door behind the last guest, sighing loudly in either relief or frustration, but my guess is both.

He looks worried beyond belief, absentmindedly twisting the rings on his fingers as he heads to his office under the pretense of catching up on work.

I give him a moment, making up some excuse about needing snacks. When Dante gets like that, he either needs space to figure it out or something to distract him altogether. I've learned it's best to give him a few moments to figure out which one it is.

When I walk into his office 15 minutes later, munching on an apple, Dante seems even more restless than when I left him.

Biscotti demands an ear scratch before trotting off, the purple dinosaur in his mouth. He clearly senses things are about to get intense.

"You can't come," Dante says without any context, fidgeting with his pinky ring, his mom's.

"Not this again. Come on, Dante. Aren't you tired of having this conversation? I am."

He looks away from me, refusing my gaze. "I don't want you to get hurt."

My face softens. "Baby, the chances of you getting hurt are way higher. I'm in peak physical form. Maybe *you* should stay home."

Dante's quiet for a long time, mulling over my words before finally conceding. "Fine," he grunts, slumping his shoulders as he exhales.

But something's off. I've spent four years learning to read every flicker of emotion that crosses that face. Right now, his eyes are darting around the room, unfocused, pupils slightly dilated. His right hand has started that familiar twitching as he toys with the rings—the tell he gets when his mind is spinning too fast. The air is thick with the words he's not speaking.

"It's going to be okay, my love," I try to reassure him, taking his hand in mine. His skin is clammy, pulse racing beneath my fingers. This isn't just stress—it's the beginning of one of his spirals.

"I don't know. This is different. We need to prepare immediately." His voice has that hollow quality, the one that appears when he's disconnecting from himself. The muscle in his jaw jumps as he grinds his teeth, a habit that always precedes his darkest moments.

Dante tries to leave but I hold onto his hand, keeping him in place. I've seen this before—when he gets like this, he'll work himself to exhaustion, make reckless decisions, put himself in danger. As his Domme, as the person who promised to take care of all of him, I can't let that happen.

"I don't think that's a good idea, baby." I raise my voice slightly, injecting some assertiveness. The soft approach isn't working—he needs his anchor right now, not a supportive spectator. "I think you should get some rest first. Else, you'll be no use to anyone."

But it's like he doesn't hear me at all.

"I can't. This is all my fault. I've been slacking on my duties—" His breathing has quickened, words tumbling out faster than he can control them. The dark circles under his eyes make him look haunted, almost feverish. His hands are shaking now.

I recognize this pattern. If I don't intervene, he'll disappear into his head entirely, lost in a spiral of guilt and responsibility that will leave him raw and broken. As his Queen, I need to pull him back before he falls too far.

"Stop!" Before he can even finish his sentence, I slap his cheek, hard. Not in anger, not to hurt—but to shock his system, to break the circuit of thoughts threatening to drown him. Like hitting the reset button on a machine that's overheating.

Dante growls at me angrily, the sound primal, instinctive—but his eyes focus for the first time since we started talking. He lowers his head, and I watch the shift happen: his breathing slows, his shoulders drop from around his ears, the frantic energy draining from his body. His knuckles go white as he grips the desk, breathing slowly, deeply. "I'm sorry, Tesoro."

Relief floods through me. The slap did exactly what I needed it to do—jarred him out of his downward spiral and back into his body, back to me. It's not something I do lightly, but in our dynamic, it's sometimes exactly what he needs. The physical sensation cutting through the mental chaos.

"Your mind is a mess, baby. Perhaps I can help you clear it?" I gently touch his cheek, caressing the warm skin my fingers bruised moments before. The redness will fade, but the grounding touch—the reminder that he's here, with me, not lost in his guilt—that will stay.

"I don't think I can sleep now, Danica." His shoulders slump even further as he finally meets my imploring gaze. But there's clarity there now, awareness rather than blind panic. He's back with me.

"I'm not talking about sleeping...*boy*."

The *boy* instantly triggers his submission, his entire posture changing. "Ah." Dante finally grasps what's on offer.

Playfully, I smack his ass, and my tired Don jumps. "Maybe a quick session..." He looks at the open door nervously, but we're alone, alone enough for me to grab his crotch, caressing his hardness that's noticeably pressing against the non-stretch pants.

"Someone seems ready," I tease, spinning the web of seduction around him. My darling boy's cock instantly responds to my touch despite the various fabrics separating our skin.

"I don't want to think anymore." His voice is small, almost pleading. The big Alpha-hole mask is gone, and it's just Dante, the little lost boy, *my* little lost boy.

Without another word, I take his hand and lead him upstairs, straight to the playroom.

With a single snap of my fingers, the well-trained Dante strips out of his clothes until he stands before me in only his socks. It's a ritual that instantly brings out his submissive side, undressing under my watchful gaze.

Like I've done hundreds of times before, I put my hand out, and he brings me his cock, placing it in my palm, surrendering his body to me.

"So pretty when you're being obedient," I praise my big boy, leading him to the large St. Andrews Cross in the corner, pulling him along dick-first.

When every limb is secured to the cross, custom-built for Dante's extra tall physique, I slowly drag my nails down his bare back. He's facing forward.

"You have your safe word, right?" I check in like I always do, even after all this time.

"Yes, Miss."

"The flogger?" I ask, aiming soft, but Dante shakes his head.

"The whip, please, Miss," he asks, needing more.

I fetch the implement in question, trailing the leather over Dante's exposed flesh when I return, watching him shiver.

"Ten lashes, okay?" I tell him as I take a step back. I used to be wary of the whip, of doing too much damage. But I've been practicing, just as Adira taught me, whipping glass bottles off high walls with expert precision.

Dante nods as he whispers, "Please."

As I swing the elegant black whip through the air like I'm commanding a serpent, my darling husband-to-be counts like he's been trained, sputtering numbers from hurried breaths until he can't anymore.

We get to number eight, and then, for the first time in over a year, Dante utters his safe word, barely audible in a broken voice.

I stop immediately, dropping the whip to the floor.

"There you go, baby; it's okay," I coo in a soothing voice as I kneel to unclasp his ankles. "Let's get you cleaned up and ready for bed."

The big man doesn't say anything, just whimpers softly as I free his limbs, helping him to the bathroom.

Careful not to hurt him, I treat his fresh cuts properly, covering his body in ointment as he flinches, gritting his teeth.

In this moment, the fearless Don of the meeting earlier now looks so vulnerable, and I know it will take more than just a whipping to calm his mind.

"It's going to be okay," I try to reassure my broken sub as I lead his hunched-over figure to our bed, tucking him without bothering to clothe him. Dante doesn't speak, just balls the duvet up in his fists and pulls it over himself tightly.

Stripping out of my clothes, I slide in next to him on the bed, pulling his face to my bosom.

Slowly, I stroke his hair, barely touching him, holding him close to my body, his face nestled between my naked breasts.

With a heavy exhale, Dante presses his body against mine fully, wrapping himself in my skin, holding on like he's afraid he'll float away if he doesn't.

Not a word leaves his lips, but I know his mind is anything but quiet. There is nothing else I can do for him, though. As much as I want to fix this, I know I can't. All I can do is be here, hold him, try again tomorrow.

I don't let go until my husband-to-be's breathing turns slow, his chest falling into a sleep rhythm against mine. Only then do I allow the nagging sleep to overcome me, to take me to dreamland as well.

It will be okay, right?

It has to be...

Chapter Twelve

MORTALITY

(Dante)

As beautiful as the garden looks in its early morning hues, I have to stop mid-run. My body simply refuses to carry on. *Fuck!*

Bent over, hands on my knees, I try to will away the aching in my neck that's quickly spreading to my back, to my legs.

My running partner slows to a halt beside me.

"Everything okay, sir?" Dario's face is expressionless, as always. In the six years he's worked for me, I don't think I've ever seen any other look except that deadpan seriousness. He is a great guard though, no nonsense.

When it came to training—or anything for that matter—he was no Emilio. But my second-in-command wasn't getting any younger, and keeping up was slowly becoming an issue. I had to find a new running partner.

And now I'm the one who can't keep up.

"I'm fine. You go ahead, I'll catch up," I grind out, still bent over.

My body is on fire, and not in a good way.

I clench my teeth, trying to hide the discomfort from my face.

How will I be ready for tomorrow if I can't even get through a run?

The muscular man with the thick beard and the solid-black tattoo sleeves hesitates. His job is literally to protect me.

But we're still on the compound, in the back where the forest trail is—nobody can come in or out without using the front gate. The entire property is surrounded by thick 20-foot walls topped with electric fencing, and guards with dogs are always patrolling. We've beefed up security since the wedding.

"*Signore...*" Dario stops, unsure how to word his thoughts without sounding disrespectful.

I know what he's thinking: the boss is getting weak.

He might be right.

It feels like my body is literally falling apart.

But even more reason for it to do so in private.

It's been three days since the wedding ambush on Saturday; how can I *still* be sore?

I stand up straight, giving him a look that has made weaker men shit their pants before. "Dario." My voice is stern, assertive, piercing through the pain.

The guard nods, remembering his place. "*Sì, Signore.*" He lowers his head.

"And Dario..."

"Sir?"

"Not a word."

"Of course." He jogs off like he can carry on for miles without even breaking a sweat, and he probably can. At that age, early 30s, so could I.

When did I get so creaky? Jesus.

I'm not even that old!

Though, I'm older than my father was when he died—two years older already.

My mortality falls on my shoulders like a boulder dislodged from a mountain—heavy, unstoppable, crushing.

This is not the time to fail, I tell my body stubbornly.

With clenched fists and gritted teeth, I force my feet to start moving again, grateful to be out under the watchful eyes of my guard.

My struggle is between me and whoever is manning the property surveillance now. It's probably Nikko, but he'll never say a word.

Despite my determination, I don't get far as the aching in my legs quickly turns to cramping a few steps later.

Swearing under my breath, I drag myself to a nearby bench, one of the many wooden ones my mother had specially made for the grounds.

The garden was always her sanctuary. She liked to sit outside and read or go for long walks, especially in the rain. My father used to think she was mad, shouting at her from his office upstairs to come back in, that she would get sick, but she never listened, not about the rain walking at least.

All these years later, and I still miss her. Still wish that the bullet could've found its intended target that day instead of robbing us of our mother, too young.

How different things would have been...

There is no rain today.

And the bench looks much more worn than in my memory.

I make a mental note to ask the new house manager to have it taken care of. Missus Nell. She came highly recommended, and we haven't had any issues yet. Sure, she isn't as efficient as Alicia was, but she seems less likely to fall in bed with my brother and betray me.

Though you never know. Luca always liked them older.

Luca...

As soon as the name enters my mind, I force the thought of my degenerate younger brother away, or at least I try.

Danica doesn't know this, but Luca messaged me on our wedding day.

He congratulated us, apologizing for the umpteenth time for selling me out to the Riccis to pay his gambling debt.

I didn't bother replying. There was nothing left to say. He's as good as dead to me.

Before, Luca was all I had. But now I have Danica. I don't need his chaos in my life anymore. I'm done bailing him out—literally and figuratively.

The many (many) *"I'm sorry"* messages from Luca will continue to go unanswered.

I am tired of looking after him, of cleaning up his messes. Sure, he had a shit deal too, but at least Luca didn't have to live with the unbearable weight of becoming the head of the family before even hitting his 20s. A job I didn't want. One that took everything from me—all my dreams, my aspirations...How foolish of me to ever believe that my destiny held anything but death and destruction.

While Luca played video games in his room, I was out on the streets, ripping people's eyeballs out with my bare hands, doing what needed to be done to keep the family safe, to keep it thriving.

But Luca never appreciated any of it. So naive.

When I was learning how tax worked and how to avoid it, he was seducing the kitchen staff, sneaking bodies of all genders into his room at ridiculous hours.

Sure, it wasn't all bad. We had good times too, despite being so different. Luca used to be such a kind soul, so soft, so sweet.

I'll never forget how vulnerable he used to be. My little brother didn't stop crying for weeks when our mother died. He was only seven.

I thought him lucky; he didn't remember her as much as I did.

But perhaps we were both unlucky, being stuck with a father so cruel.

Forcing my mind back to my present challenge on the weather-worn bench, I massage my leg, trying to get the cramping to stop.

It's not just my leg that hurts—it's my lead-pipe accosted neck, the fresh whip bruises on my ass, the various healed-over stab wounds scattered over my skin like tattoos I never consented to, decorating me in the painful memories I can never escape.

At some point, I probably have to accept that my past is catching up to me, to my body at least.

But not today.

With a heavy sigh, I force myself back on my feet. If I stay away too long, Danica might get worried.

She was still asleep when I snuck out to catch a run, hoping it would clear my mind, maybe make me feel calmer about tomorrow's attack on the ports.

But it had the opposite effect, adding more worries to my already stressed mind.

Even after all these years, it never gets easier—this business. I expected it to, but it didn't. So many tough decisions, so many impossible situations.

But what choice do I have?

Nobody gets out alive...

I take a shortcut to the back door by the kitchen, forcing myself to straighten up and walk normally. To wipe the pained look from my face and greet the kitchen staff with a simple nod.

"Sir?" It's Missus Nell, scurrying around nervously as she eyes me through those thick, square glasses that always slip down her nose, forcing her to push them up again mid-sentence.

The kitchen isn't usually a place I frequent often, so I understand why she is nervous.

"Not to worry, Missus Nell. As you were."

She nods, returning to what appears to be the stocktaking of the pantry.

"Would you please send up some coffee to the master bedroom in 20 minutes?"

"No problem, sir." She nods, wringing her small hands like she's washing them under an invisible stream.

"And something sweet for Danica. Maybe one of those Danish pastries she likes, if we have any." I force a smile, grabbing a bottle of water from the fridge.

"I'll see what I can arrange." A faint smile curves her thin lips for less than an instant, and then she looks down again.

I want to tell her she doesn't have to bow her head for me, but instead, I just thank her and drag my tired body up the stairs, one painful step at a time.

Danica is still fast asleep when I sneak back in. My snoozy Queen.

She looks stunning as ever, even with her hair all messy and standing up in weird places. But it's not her hair that's got my attention; it's the gorgeous left breast peeking out from under the slipped covers, inviting me to caress her skin.

Danica opens one eye, a soft smile on her face. "You staring at me?"

"Maybe a little." I smile. "Good morning, my love."

The mattress dents in as I climb into bed with her, not even bothering to shower first. Building up a proper sweat would require managing a proper run, not just a few yards. But nobody else needs to know that.

"Hey, baby. Come here." Danica opens her arms, and I sink into the comfort of her embrace. She kisses me deeply, enveloping me in her familiar early morning scent that could be bottled and sold as an aphrodisiac.

I am instantly hard.

My hand finds its way to her breast like a moth to moonlight, drawn to those little hard nipples instantly.

"Hmm," she hums softly, pressing her breast into my hand, her back arched.

"May I?" I pinch the nipple between my fingers, drawing a quick moan from her lips, and she nods, closing her eyes and lying back, allowing me the honor of pressing my lips to her skin, to suckle like a hungry infant in need of nurturing.

It's my turn to moan when Danica's palm unexpectedly closes around my cock, pulling it from the running shorts.

All my pains and aches are forgotten as my bride pumps my erection while I suck on her nipples, biting them ever so gently from time to time, just to hear her moan.

No liquid comes forth from her breasts, only from my cock, and it lands on both of us, a sticky glue that bonds us together momentarily.

Danica kisses me deeply, swallowing the heavy pants from my lips, holding me close until my climax subsides.

"Thank you, *Tesoro*," I tell her, enjoying the surprised gasp she lets out when I stick my fingers between her folds, teasing her clit. "How are you feeling down there?" I rub the sensitive bud slowly.

"You know I wake up horny as fuck...and my nipples are so sensitive, especially now."

"Well, let me return the service." I start moving lower down but Danica stops me suddenly, grabbing my arm.

"Not today." She looks alarmed.

"You know I don't mind you unwashed. I prefer you dirty." I grin, continuing my path downward, kissing her belly, lower...

Danica shakes her head. "It's not that."

I look at her, my brow knitted in confusion. "Should I be worried?"

"No, it's just a bloody mess down there." She laughs, shrugging. "That time of the month and all."

I don't answer, just pull the sheet from her body and continue my trail of kisses.

"Dante..." she gasps as I take her clit between my teeth.

I don't respond; just follow the path until the familiar coppery taste fills my mouth.

Like a bit of blood has ever put me off...

CHAPTER THIRTEEN

ATTACK

(DANICA)

The glowing digits on my watch flick to 4:52 AM, their faint green light barely visible in the pre-dawn darkness.

My breath fogs in the cold air as we move like ghosts through the shadows, a lethal procession of nearly thirty armed men—and me.

The weight of my weapons feels foreign against my body, a constant reminder that I'm not the same woman I was before I met Dante.

Emilio's whispered "*Good luck*" still rings in my ears as he settled into the getaway car earlier, his face dark, focused. Like all of us, he knows what's at stake.

My muscles ache with exhaustion, protesting with every careful step. The Kevlar vest beneath my black tactical gear seems to grow heavier by the minute. But I force my breathing to remain steady, my movements precise. I won't be the weak link. Not today.

There's a bitter irony in how familiar this feels—the black boots, the face mask, the anticipation of violence humming in the air. But last time, I was desperate to save Dante, to free my kidnapped love. Now, we hunt together, equals in the darkness.

When he'd seen me gear up earlier tonight, his eyes had met mine with quiet understanding. No arguments, no protests—just a nod that carried the weight of trust.

The 2 AM wake-up call feels like a lifetime ago. The briefing blurs in my memory, lost in a haze of caffeine and adrenaline that makes my heart race and my hands tremble slightly.

I flex my bare fingers, trying to work warmth back into joints stiff from the spring chill. The cold bites through my tactical gear, but gloves would only slow my trigger response.

Dante moves ahead of me like a shadow given form, his movements fluid with years of experience. I'd know his silhouette anywhere—the set of his shoulders, the precise way he places each foot. He glances back occasionally, his eyes finding mine in the darkness. There's no tenderness there now, no trace of my husband-to-be. This is Don Fera, and we're at war.

Part of me worries about him. He looked so exhausted yesterday, his body so tender. I couldn't help but notice that flash of pain clouding his face whenever he thought I wasn't looking.

But I didn't say anything, just held him closer as we pressed our naked bodies together.

We fucked up those sheets for good. Missus Nell might have to burn the blood-stained linen, but it sure didn't stop Dante from entering me with zealousness, his spent cock dark red and sticky afterward—just like the sheets.

Oh god, what a way to wake up. I forgot how much more sensitive I became on my period. How intense sex felt when my hormones were all over the place. I was damn near feral!

For so long, I avoided Dante on those days. But not anymore...

Focus, Danica! I force the distraction from my mind.

This is no time for lustful thoughts.

This is life or death. (And not the little death, *la petite mort.*)

The port gates loom ahead, harsh security lights creating pools of artificial day against the dark grey sky.

My arsenal feels simultaneously reassuring and insufficient—two holstered guns, one in my hand, a knife strapped to my calf.

Yet something gnaws at the edges of my consciousness, a creeping unease I can't shake.

We press ourselves against the cold brick of a warehouse just outside the gates. The concrete scrapes against my back through the tactical gear as I try to steady my breathing.

4:57 AM.

Our contact should be cutting the power soon.

My fingers tighten around my gun as doubt whispers through my mind. Disabling an entire port's electrical system isn't like flipping a switch—there are redundancies, backup generators. So many things that could go wrong.

But we're out of options. Every day we wait, the Volkovs chip away at everything we've built.

Yesterday, when lying in bed, as Dante explained the history of this conflict, our plan seemed more straightforward, simple almost. Clinical.

Now, with dawn approaching and so many lives hanging in the balance, nothing feels simple at all.

I catch Dante's eye in the darkness. For just a moment, I see my darling boy there—the man who held me through my orgasm, who promised to love me until the end of time.

Then he nods once, sharp and professional, and Don Fera returns.

I straighten my spine, squaring my shoulders.

I might be a suburban girl playing at war, but I'm also the future *La Donn*a Fera. And today, we're going to make the Russians regret ever thinking they could touch what's ours.

What is taking so long?

5:12 AM.

Four delivery trucks lumber toward the harbor, their diesel engines cutting through the pre-dawn silence.

My legs tremble from maintaining the crouch position, muscles screaming in protest, but I force myself to remain still. Waiting. Watching.

The restlessness is unmistakable in my bones. We should've been inside by now, but the glaring lights still angrily illuminate the space around us, trapping us in the shadows.

The third truck is still being inspected when darkness crashes over us at 5:28.

One moment, harsh security lights bleach the world white, the next, we're plunged into night.

Finally!

We move like a dark tide across the concrete, dozens of shadows flowing as one.

My heartbeat drowns out everything except the scrape of boots and the controlled breathing of the men around me.

The first Russian guards go down silently, efficiently. Our silencers make wet clicking sounds—nothing like movies, more like muffled coughs.

The smell hits me first: copper and cordite, that distinct mixture that means death. A body crumples near my feet, and I force my eyes forward. Don't look at faces. Don't count the fallen. Just move.

This morning's briefing runs through my head on a loop—Dante's voice steady and sure as his finger traced our path on the blueprints. The boss's office was circled in red marker, our target clear.

But now, in the grey space between night and dawn, nothing makes sense.

The buildings are wrong, the distances distorted. It's like trying to match a child's drawing to the Mona Lisa.

The first hint something's wrong is a soft *pop* to my left.

Then, the world goes white.

Smoke billows up from out of nowhere, thick and chemical. It claws down my throat, burns my eyes until tears stream down my face. Through the chaos, I hear Dante's voice: "*Via! Via! Via!*" But the thick smoke turns sound strange. Makes it impossible to tell direction.

Panic rises like bile as I stumble forward blindly. My training screams at me to stay still, but instinct drives me toward where I think the main building should be. Every step feels wrong.

The blueprint in my head shatters like glass as the realization hits: We've been played. It was a setup.

My foot catches on something soft. I know what it is before I look down. One of ours, face-down on the asphalt. Dark hair, broad shoulders—for one horrifying moment, I think it's Dante. The relief when I realize it's not makes me hate myself a little.

The concrete tears at my palms and knees as I crawl forward. The smoke is starting to thin, but what it reveals makes my blood freeze.

Dark figures emerge from the shadows, too many to count. Their weapons gleam dully in the pre-dawn light. Russians. We're surrounded.

The building ahead promises at least some cover. I get up and sprint the last few yards, lungs burning, fingers grasping for the door handle.

Pull.

Nothing happens.

Again.

Still locked.

"Danica!"

Dante's voice carries a note I've never heard before—pure primal fear. I start to turn—too slow, too late.

The Russian asshole's fingers bite into my shirt, lifting me like I weigh nothing.

He's massive—one of those men built like a brick wall, all muscle and menace. A scar runs from his left eye to his jaw, twisting his features into a permanent sneer.

Vodka and cigarettes are thick on his breath as he pulls me close, his pale eyes as icy as a Siberian winter.

Something cold and sharp presses against my ribs, and time fragments into crystal-clear moments stretched out in slow motion. It's a blade and it's somehow found its way to the soft flesh unprotected by my vest.

Dante appears through the thinning smoke, running toward us. But he's too far—might as well be miles away.

My trainer's voice fills my head, clear as if he were beside me: *"Use their size against them, piccola. Bigger they are, harder they fall."*

Months of training, of being thrown around the gym mat, of learning to turn disadvantage into opportunity—it all comes down to this moment.

I stop fighting the grip on his trunk-like arm. Instead, I go loose, letting my weight drop suddenly. The unexpected shift pulls him forward slightly.

My knee drives up, finding its target with brutal precision.

His grip loosens—just a fraction, just enough.

A string of Russian curses spills from his chapped lips as he tries to regain control.

He's quick, despite his size. The blade catches me as I twist away, tearing through fabric and flesh along my stomach

White-hot pain blooms across my side. Blood immediately begins soaking my shirt, but there's no time to check how bad it is.

Dante reaches us like an avenging angel. His movements are pure predator—no hesitation, no mercy. The knife in his hand disappears into the Russian perp's thick throat. Arterial spray arcs through the air, dyeing the grey morning crimson.

The giant makes a wet sound as he falls, those ice-blue eyes widening in surprise before going blank.

"Retreat! Retreat!" Dante's voice carries over the chaos, the command cutting through the gunfire and shouts.

His hand finds mine, pulling me close. I can feel his heart hammering against my back as he shields me with his body. He doesn't ask me if I'm okay; the answer won't change the fact that we need to get out of here and soon.

Around us, our plan dissolves into chaos. We're surrounded, outnumbered, betrayed. The exit seems miles away, every step between here and safety promising more blood.

We need to move. *Now.*

My side burns with each breath, blood warm against my skin, but survival comes first. Pain can wait.

Step one is getting out of this trap alive.

"Run, Danica!" Don Fera urges, and I beeline toward the exit with everything I have.

The weight of unseen eyes bears down on us, the threat of bullets in our backs very real. But we don't slow down, don't look back.

Emilio's van idles by the truck-blocked gate, our exit-strategy in matte-black steel.

We dive in as shots pepper the air around us. I stumble, almost lose my footing, but Dante grabs me in time, pulls me inside.

The van peels away before the doors even close, carrying us from the trap we walked right into. *Fucking hell.*

Wordlessly, I reach for Dante, pressing my ear to his heaving chest as our bodies try to find a regular rhythm of breathing again. I'm so glad he's here. Beside me. *Alive.* But we're far from safe.

Behind us, more black vans are filling up with defeated, bleeding men in black as we retreat.

We won't know the extent of the loss until later.

As the sun rises higher in the sky, the adrenaline begins to fade, replaced by the bitter taste of failure and betrayal.

My gut feeling had been right—I should have listened.

But there's no time for regret now.

Somewhere in the growing light, our enemies are celebrating their victory.

They won't be celebrating for long.

Mark my words.

Fuckers.

CHAPTER FOURTEEN

COMEDOWN

(DANTE)

I watch Danica's movements carefully as she paints the gold, shiny polish over my toenails in precise streaks.

It's the first time I've ever had my toes painted, and I'm not sure how I feel about it, but I have bigger concerns right now than the color of my toenails.

"Whatcha think?" Danica smiles, catching my gaze. She's lying belly down on the carpet in our bedroom, naked, just like I am.

We both pretend we don't see the massive erection between my legs as I sit with my back to the cold wall, leaning against it, knees pointed to the ceiling to let her do her thing.

Everything hurts, but I force a smile. "Good."

Danica sighs and gets back to work, leaving me to my brooding thoughts.

By now, she knows that trying to get more elaborate answers from me is probably a futile exercise.

Yesterday's failed ambush occupies too much space in my mind.

I can't think of anything else.

So many foolish mistakes.

We should never have gone in at all, not like that. I put everyone's lives in danger; the carnage was unnecessary—seven men, including Matteo. *Fuck!*

My body aches in places I didn't know it could ache, and I silently curse my fate. I'm not as fast as I used to be. I couldn't even save Danica yesterday. That's the thought that plagues me the most—my slowness almost cost my Queen her life.

Before witnesses, I will soon have to vow to protect her, but I can't make that promise.

The thought of her almost coming to serious harm yesterday is still too much to bear. The second time in less than a week...I torture myself with the fear but can't bring myself to voice it.

Danica would just tell me that she can protect herself, that she doesn't need me for that. But it doesn't ease the unease gnawing at my insides.

Even after all these years, I can't get rid of the guilt. I used to drink myself into a stupor every night to try and shut it out. Still, it always resurfaced during the inevitable hangovers that got messier and messier after Elena's death.

Who knows what would've happened to me if it wasn't for Emilio's intervention that fateful June afternoon when I almost drove my car off a cliff in a drunken fit of rage.

I wouldn't be here today, not with Danica.

That man has always been more of a father to me than my own flesh and blood. *Oh, Emilio.*

Neither of us is getting any younger...

My body used to take so much punishment, and I would still wake up fine the next day, have my coffee like nothing is amiss.

So much fighting. So much killing. So many cruel things that still haunt my dreams—I don't want to be that person anymore. My body can't handle it. Nor can my mind.

I suspect my mind never could.

I'm becoming a liability on the battleground, and the thought is too much to bear.

Who am I if not the great, fearless Don Fera?

I clench my fists by my side, cracking my knuckles.

Danica looks up at me but doesn't say anything, just wedges her tongue back into the corner of her mouth and resumes concentration. Something about *clean edges*, she said earlier—whatever that means.

I didn't protest when she suggested sprucing up my toes after our bath, nor when she pushed me down onto the floor, reaching for her favorite shade of gold.

Like she doesn't have a care in the world, Danica blows warm air over my toes, tickling the little hairs, before sitting up, eyes narrowing as she regards my distant expression.

"One more coat and then you'll be pretty as a princess," she says with extra enthusiasm that I know she's faking for my sake. My eyes keep wandering to the thin red line over her stomach where the asshole's knife had cut her yesterday. Luckily, it was just a surface wound.

So close. Too close.

I just sigh, nodding.

"We'll get them, baby. It's not your fault," Danica says for the millionth time, taking my hand in hers and bringing it to her lips for a soft kiss.

It sure does feel like my fault though. "I've made a mess," I tell her, looking away again.

"You're doing the best you can, my love." She holds my hand, pressing it against her cheek.

"As always, it's not good enough." I grit my teeth, painful memories of my father's endless disappointments stabbing at my mind.

Nothing was ever good enough for him, especially not me. He'd probably be so embarrassed about how I've run this family. I was never the man he wanted me to be.

"We'll make a new plan," Danica says with conviction, leaning over to kiss my cheek before dropping down to her stomach again.

It is soothing to watch her paint, the up and down strokes of the small brush—so precise, so careful. I don't know if it's cheering me up as promised, but it's not harming me either.

I don't deserve her; I know I don't. So beautiful, so young, so caring. Danica shouldn't be with a thug like me, but here she is, naked on our bedroom floor, caring for me and trying to lighten my mood.

She even made me some toast earlier to have with my painkillers. Sure, it was burnt, and she should definitely leave the cooking to the staff, but it's the thought that counts. I don't remember the last time anyone who wasn't on my payroll offered me a meal at home.

"There it is, you're done." Danica looks pretty chuffed with herself as she sits back to view her handiwork.

I follow her gaze and can't help but smile.

My toes look ridiculous, big and hairy—and gold.

But the joy on her face makes it worth it. It's not like anyone ever sees my bare feet but her (and maybe Alessio).

"Thank you, my love." I try to get up, but Danica quickly stops me.

"Don't you dare! I'm not letting you undo all my hard work."

I look at my feet and then back to her, confused.

Danica grins, her expression shifting. I know that look—she is up to no good.

"You can't move those feet, baby," she tells me, stroking my inner thigh seductively.

I shudder at the intimate touch. My cock jumps.

"If so much as a single spec of my hard work is smudged before it dries, you will spend the rest of the week in chastity, do you hear me?" Her voice is playful but I have no doubt that her threat is serious.

Quickly, I nod. "Yes, Miss."

"Hands on your thighs, baby."

I do as I'm told, placing my hands on my legs, golden-toed feet flat on the floor.

For someone who doesn't want kids, Danica sure loves her games. But I'm not complaining. That's who she is, what makes her, her.

We discussed the possibility of children at length before; I was willing to give her whatever she wanted. But Danica didn't want my sperm, at least not for that. As headstrong as she is beautiful, she's always known parenthood was not the life for her. It was a relief for me. Having a feline child was enough.

"Don't move!" Danica reminds me before jumping up to fetch something.

Dio mio, I love watching those naked hips sway, the slight sag in her breasts as they rest heavily against her waist. Even in broad daylight, she looks stunning—every flaw, every imperfection, beautifully perfect because it's her.

As she walks away, I can't help but wonder about the scars on her back again, for the umpteenth time. I wish I knew what happened to her, where those marks came from, who hurt her. Even after all these years together, it's a secret she still keeps close to her chest. I try to probe every now and again. But I know better than to push. She'll tell me when she's ready.

Danica returns after a few minutes, her hands full.

I can't tell what she has in mind, not until she places the items before me on the carpet.

"Pain or pleasure, darling?" she asks, and I consider my options, looking at the items on offer.

"Both," I answer with conviction. My mind needs it.

"Good. Remember, I want those toes perfect!" Danica reminds me as she positions herself between my thighs, her skin brushing against my cock ever so slightly, enough to make it jump to full attention.

"Yes, Ma'am."

Danica kisses me deeply, holding my face between her hands. "It will be okay, baby. It's not your fault."

I still don't believe her, but I'm grateful for her attempt at comfort anyway.

Her kiss moves down my chin, down my neck, my collarbone...until she's kissing my nipples, licking them, coating them in a layer of saliva that comes in handy when she attaches the weighted clamps moments after, pinching the sensitive skin tightly.

It stings, but in a good way.

She could've chosen way more dangerous clamps, but she went light, and I know it's probably a good thing. Last time, the butterfly clips did some serious damage.

Once properly fastened, Danica kisses my sore nipples one more time before reaching for the second object—a single black feather.

She traces it over my nipples, gently nudging the dangling weights to make them swing more, pulling on my stretched skin.

"How does it feel?" she asks, slowly dragging the feather lower down, barely touching the skin, as she makes her way down between my thighs.

"So good. Thank you, Miss." I mean it. The distraction is almost soothing.

"Don't thank me yet." Danica's face is twisted in a devilish smirk that could only mean my torment has just begun, and I fall more in love with her every passing second.

I gasp loudly as the feather tickles my cock, floating down my shaft to my balls.

The touch is so light, barely there at all, but it's enough to drive me mad with lust.

Pre-cum glistens on my tip as my wife-to-be strokes my balls with the feather, teasing me into submission.

My nipples are on fire, but I only spare them occasional thought, the climax building between my thighs overwhelming most of my mental faculties.

"Do you want to come, Don Fera?" my naked tormentor asks as she circles the head of my cock with the feather.

"Please," I rasp. "So badly."

"Please, *who*?"

"Please, Miss. Please." I am whining, but it was impossible to hold anything in my head except the urgent need to explode all over that feather. I am dangerously close to blowing my load. It's been a few days since my last release, not since before the failed ambush, and I'm extra sensitive.

But Danica just grins, dropping the feather to the carpet like a discarded toy. "Hmm...no."

No?

Dio mio! I never even considered the possibility that she wouldn't let me finish. How foolish of me.

Instantly, I'm desperate, whimpering on the floor.

I start to move toward her, but Danica simply puts her foot on my chest and pushes me back against the wall, keeping my ass firmly on the floor.

"Don't you dare smudge those toes, baby boy..."

Please!

But silly me, I should know by now that her "no" is final.

Oh, fanculo.

Chapter Fifteen

MOONLIGHTING

(Danica)

The Sinful Moon club's staff locker room is bathed in harsh fluorescent light that leaves nowhere to hide. I hang my coat in the creaky locker and slam it shut with enough force to keep it closed.

My heart beats at a million beats per minute as I stare at the "uniform" laid out for me. It hardly comprises enough material to be called a uniform, but it suits the job, I guess.

The short leather skirt barely fits over my wide hips, and it sure doesn't cover my whole ass. The top half is a black sheer mesh crop top that's pretty much fully see-through, leaving my breasts on display for the world to see. I suspect they were the reason I got the job in the first place.

"No underwear," I was told during onboarding earlier. "And no speaking without being spoken to."

I glance at my phone as Dante's name flashes across the screen again, ringing silently for the seventh time in the past 10 minutes.

I send a quick text before dropping the phone in the locker too, locking it this time.

> I love you. Don't worry. See you later. D

Breathe, Danica. Just breathe.

I'm in the belly of the beast now. The crown jewel in the Russian mob's collection. The main poaching spot for their female exports—if rumors are to be believed.

It's been a depressing week at the Fera compound; not even Dante's golden toes could cheer me up. After days of nobody coming up with a viable plan, we were getting desperate to find a way to put the Volkovs in their place once and for all before a full-on war broke out between the families. Dante has been moodier than ever, and we're no closer to peace.

At least he no longer cuts me out of business meetings, debriefings, or strategy sessions, but it feels like we're going in circles. Every lead becomes a dead end, every ray of hope, another "it can't work."

Until the idea hit me two days ago. I woke up in the middle of the night with the perfect plan. Some problems can't be solved with violence. You need a more discreet solution—like someone on the inside. It all made sense.

Much to my surprise, it was easier to get a job at the Sinful Moon than I thought it would be. I just sent in my "audition tape" (just some video I recorded on my phone), wearing a wig and something revealing. They literally phoned me the next day, asking if I could cover a shift on Saturday—today. One of the other girls hadn't shown up to work.

I immediately agreed, despite the nervous feeling in my stomach that threatened to upheave my lunch.

Dante didn't know I applied until they called back. His response? Less than enthusiastic.

"It's too dangerous, I won't let you," he told me this morning as I fastened my coat around my waist, ready to head out. I tried to lay out my argument calmly, but my husband-to-be was anything but calm.

He actually threw me over his shoulder, despite it still being injured and achy, and locked me in the bedroom.

"I'll be fine!" I insisted as I hammered my fists on his back, but neither of us believed it.

Furious but determined, I snuck out while he was on a call with Luigi, the accountant. It wasn't that hard—our bedroom balcony has a low wall I could scale to reach the open window of the guest suite next door.

Dario saw me leave but didn't try to stop me; none of the guards did. They watched me get into the Uber and smartly chose to turn a blind eye. Their job descriptions were to keep people out, not in.

Even Dante knows he can't just rush in here and grab me from the club. We are on enemy turf. His main argument against me finding a way in from the inside was that they would simply capture me if they found out who I was.

Hopefully, the long blonde wig and blue eye contacts will help with disguising that, or at least the many layers of makeup I'm about to plaster on my face. Conveniently, the staff also wear masks when out on the floor, or at least that's what the chubby man with the greasy palms told me when he handed me my *workwear* earlier.

I take a deep breath and start to get changed.

I'm here now. No turning back.

The name tag on my useless shirt says *Jasmyne,* and I practice saying it out loud one more time before exchanging the locker room for the dressing room—you'd think they'd be the same room, but nope, not here. You leave your personal belongings in this sterile room and then enter into the dark wonderland of sin and desire through the side door.

"Those shoes will never do." A redhead in a green leotard regards me in the massive mirror wall as I enter. Save for the lights around the mirror, the lighting in here is much dimmer than in the locker room, and it takes a few moments for my eyes to adjust.

She gets up, her make-up half done, and pulls a pair of the highest stripper heels I've ever seen from a nearby drawer. "Try these. I'm Sasha, by the way." She smiles broadly, handing me the shoes that look more uncomfortable than the outfit I'm wearing—something I thought impossible.

"Hi, Da—" I start but catch myself in time. "Jasmyne. Nice to meet you."

"These should be your size, but if they're a bit big, just shove some toilet paper in the front. I take it you're the new recruit?"

"Yeah, they needed someone urgently." I sit down to change my shoes, looking around the room. Two other girls are busy getting ready amidst a scattering of make-up and accessories.

"They always do." Sasha takes a deep drag from her discreet black vape, blowing a soft cloud of vanilla smoke my way.

She seems about my age, probably a few years younger. However, it's hard to tell with all the makeup caked on her tired face. It would be days later before she told me that she was only 22 but had been working here for almost three years already to support her six-year-old.

I want to pry, but I know it's too soon. The aim of my undercover mission is seemingly simple: get to know the girls, find out what I can, and get to the big cheese Russian dude in charge here—without getting kidnapped or recognized, of course.

Foolish, I know, but so is sitting at home, watching Dante brood and worry about our safety.

I'm tired of looking around every corner, worrying about what's waiting for us. I just want to be free to live my life as Mrs. Fera already, and the fucking Russians are standing in my way.

"I'm not sure what I'm supposed to do," I admit, sitting down beside Sasha to do my make-up.

"Yeah, Nikki is usually better with the onboarding but things have been a bit crazy as of late. It's easy: just take people their drinks and get on stage when it's your turn. If anyone wants to book you privately, you can take them to the dungeon downstairs. Ivan works the door there; he'll let you in. And if there is any funny business with the client, he'll step in and make sure it's resolved."

"Does that happen a lot?" I ask cautiously. The idea of walking around the club in this skimpy outfit and having strangers lust over me is incredibly erotic for some reason that I don't even question. But the thought of having to go to a private room with an unknown man seems scary.

"Sadly, not all of our customers are as well-behaved as they should be. But don't worry, they don't usually let the new girls work the dungeon. At least not for the first week, not before you've done the rest of the induction course."

The dungeon is where all the money is, apparently.

You can make good tips down there.

But I'm not here for the money.

Sasha blows another vanilla smoke cloud my way, smiling sweetly. I find myself staring openly as she gets up, straightening out her skimpy outfit, the back a mere G-string that leaves her entire ass uncovered. What a beautiful ass—so full, thick, tanned. Like the rest of her, it's curvaceous, round, and incredibly enticing.

She winks at me in the mirror and shakes her ass, twerking until everything jiggles. *What a Goddess!*

"I'll see you out there. Mommy needs to go make some rent money." She blows me a kiss and disappears out the black door, a big red feather boa draped around her neck.

On paper, this is a burlesque club, but everyone (including the cops) knows it is so much more than that—according to Emilio's intel.

For the right price, everything goes in here. Ask no questions and hear no lies. Way shadier than the club where Adira works.

I take my time with my make-up, trying to ease the anxiety in my stomach.

Who knows how long before I cross paths with one of the Russian big bosses? They look pretty mean in the photos we have in the ever-growing intel folder that lives in Dante's desk drawer.

What if they recognize me first?

What if I get raped by some asshole before Ivan can break it up?

Too many questions. Zero answers.

You got this, Danica, I try to feign some confidence.

I flick the whore-red lipstick over my lips, smacking them together as I drink in my image in the mirror.

A complete stranger stares back at me, a stranger with long blonde hair that drops down over her shoulders and stormy blue eyes hiding behind pounds of thick black eye makeup layered onto her unrecognizable face.

One of the other girls smiles at my reflection, catching my gaze. "Don't worry, babe. With those knockers, you'll get dungeon privileges in no time." Her accent is British, thick.

I blush slightly, overly aware of how little modesty my outfit offers. "Thank you."

The final touch is the delicate black Venetian mask I fasten over the top half of my face, completing the uniform. It makes me feel more secure, more inconspicuous. But I know that, in reality, I'm no safer than I was a week ago when we stormed the ports in the hopes of overthrowing the Russians with pure force.

I jump as the door opens, and the chubby man peeks his head inside.

"Jasmyne? You're up!"

Oh god, what am I doing?

CHAPTER SIXTEEN

GOOD BOYS

(DANTE)

I can't eat.

I can't work.

I can't find a second of rest for my mind as I pace around my office.

Emilio stands by the door silently, keeping his distance but refusing to leave, making sure I don't harm myself or accidentally burn the house to the ground.

Around me, the contents of my entire bookshelf lie scattered on the floor; everything that was on my desk now lives on the carpet among the books. Two of the paintings are broken—I shouldn't have, but the anger tore through me uncontrolled, untamable.

Biscotti has long since made a run for it, hiding somewhere in the house. Probably for the best.

A cool breeze wanders in through the newly smashed window, my bloody knuckle evidence of the rage that drove me to destroy my office when I realized Danica had snuck away while I was on my call, despite me clearly forbidding it.

I wanted to run after her, guns blazing, tearing that club down to its foundations, but Emilio managed to talk me off that ledge.

The realization that I'd 100% risk Danica's life if I did that was the only thing that convinced me to get out of the car and stay at home.

But staying at home meant there was nothing to distract my mind from the thought of Danica in the enemy's lair, alone, unprotected, whoring her body for the world to see. That part didn't bother me—Danica could do with her body what she wanted. But if any harm were to befall her, I would never forgive myself.

After realizing she had gone, I tried to focus on the work that had been piling up while I was distracted by my wedding, but focus was a scarce commodity.

My calls went unanswered, and when she sent me that text, I lost it, smashing my fist through the window and sending Dario and Emilio running in.

The old man took one look at me sitting on the floor, my fist bleeding, and he sent Dario away, closing the door behind us.

I wish Danica would come back already.

Every time I hear the door, I look up hopefully, only to be disappointed.

Time goes slowly.

My imagination is playing every trick in the book on me; I'm going mad with the thoughts of what Danica could be doing now.

I demand a bottle of whiskey from Missus Nell, and she obliges despite the hesitation I see in both her and Emilio's eyes. But they would never dare question me.

I drink half the bottle, collapsing on the floor among the scattered books, papers, and glass. None of this would have happened if I was stronger, if I was better. I vowed to protect her but I can't. My dad was right: I was destined to be nothing but a failure.

At some point, I must have blacked out. I don't remember it.

When I finally come to, Danica is hunched beside me, picking glass shards from my arm, her face coated in concern.

"Danica!" I sit up, too quickly, and almost throw up on my fiancé.

"Shh, baby. I'm okay. What happened here?" She looks from Emilio to me. The old man wordlessly takes his cue and closes the door behind us, leaving Danica with the mess.

I grab her in both arms. "You're okay!" The relief of having her home, safe, makes all the anger dissipate instantly.

I hug her close.

"Totally fine. Though I can't say the same for you. Jesus, Dante." She helps me up onto the couch as I regard the mess I've made.

"Don't ever do that again. You could've died." I take her face between my hands, staring into her eyes intently, trying to force the message into her mind, imprint it in her cranium forever.

"I'm fine. I told you I have a plan." She smiles sweetly, but she smells anything but sweet; a mix of smoke and sweat and something else covers her like a veil.

"Not like this. You can't go back. I forbid it." I say sternly, getting up from the couch to resume my pacing.

My head is pounding like a motherfucker.

I need water.

Not now!

"My darling boy..." Danica laughs and climbs up onto the couch, shoes and all, standing a head taller than me. "If you think I'm going to let you forbid me anything, then you clearly don't know me at all."

I spin around, anger returning to my body, starting at my fingertips and seeping through my veins like hot lava. "This is serious, Danica."

She sighs and reaches her arm to me. "Come here."

I don't move.

"*Dante.*" Danica raises her eyebrow but not her voice, yet the way she says my name, in that tone, I know I have already lost.

When she uses that voice, I know the tables have turned—I am no longer in charge; my Queen has taken command.

Like a humbled Knight, I go to her.

Her eyes soften, a smile curling her lips as she reaches for me, stroking my cheek affectionately.

I melt. Instantly.

Without her touch, I go mad, my compass lost.

But she is home now. Danica is here.

And everything feels less like the end-of-days.

"Dante, you have to trust me, baby. I'm not stupid. If it's dangerous, I'll get the fuck out of there quicker than Eminem can rap a four-bar verse."

"I don't know what that means." I can't help but smile at my Millennial Goddess with her ridiculous metaphors and hypnotic eyes. She always knows how to disarm me so quickly, even if it makes no sense. When she looks at me like that, speaks to me in that way, nothing matters but this moment, right now.

She pulls me to her chest, and I let her, resting my head on her breasts.

"It means I'm a big girl, and I can look after myself."

"I just don't want to lose you. I can't bear the thought of it." It's hard to look her in the eyes as I confess my vulnerability, my dependence on her.

"This is the only way we'll ever be free to live our lives the way we want to." Danica kisses my forehead tenderly.

"We can never be free, *Tesoro*. Not with this life." My eyes sink to the floor, my shoulders with them.

"I have a plan, don't worry," she repeats.

"I wish you would let me help you. We could send anyone else in there but not you." I'm pleading.

"No, Dante. It has to be this way. We've come this far, I'm already in. When the time comes, of course, I'll let you help me.

I'm not gonna muscle that guy out of there myself. But it's not time yet." She strokes my hair from my brow. I wish she could stroke away the pounding headache too.

"I don't know how you can be so relaxed."

"I'm trying not to think about it." She's clearly lying about that part. I know her better than that. But I also know that no good can come from making her doubt herself. Her superpower is her confidence, among many other things.

I sigh, grumpy, unsatisfied with the answer. "You smell like a hooker, by the way."

"Thanks, you're not doing so hot yourself, Mister Half-a-Bottle-of-Whiskey-Like-My-Life-is-a-Spanish-Soap-Opera."

I don't need to be a Millennial to know what that one means. She's right, I reek.

"It's been a long night."

"Well, let's go get ready for bed then. I suggest a shower first. Care to join me, Don Fera?" Danica winks at me. "Then you can personally make sure that not a hair on my body was harmed."

"Sounds good." Ignoring my aching shoulder and the blinding white pain behind my eyes, I throw Danica over my shoulder and carry her to our room as she squeals with delight, playfully pounding her fists on my back.

Emilio smiles as we walk past.

He simply nods. It's a scene he's encountered many times before. Emilio has seen Danica's bratty behavior in play more times than anyone can count.

"Night, 'Milio!" Danica calls.

"Good night, Miss Matthews."

Barging through our bedroom door, I throw her on the bed. She bounces before sprawling out on the pure black sheets.

In the minute it takes me to close the door and take off my shoes, Danica has stripped off her pants and underwear.

She lies waiting for me, knees bent, thighs apart, her fingers fanned over her clit.

Instantly, I harden, my pants straining under the burden of my desire.

"I...I thought we were showering?" I slowly walk to the bed, my cock aching with every step, desperate for release—from the pants and so much more too.

"Oh, we are, but you know, we don't want to waste water. Need to make sure we're as dirty as can be..." Her argument is silly, but I'm not even paying attention to anything but the slow, rhythmic motion of her fingers.

The closer I get, the harder it gets to concentrate.

"Danica..." I'm virtually salivating, just standing there like a buffoon, entranced by her exposed pussy.

"What do you want, darling?" she asks coyly in between soft moans as she slips a finger inside, just one.

I groan, lamenting the fact that words are not my strong suit. So many things, I want so many things all at once. But none of them correspond to words, to sentences.

"Mommy…" My desperation turns me stupid, reduced to mere lust, as I watch her fuck herself, my own erection still trapped in my pants, unattended.

"I'm not your Mommy. Tell me what you want," Danica demands in a stern voice.

"I need a taste. Please." Desperate to get closer, I kneel down beside the bed, my eyes locked on her fingers. A second one dips inside, and I groan. I'm so close, I can smell her lust, and it's driving me wild!

"No, darling. Not tonight. Tonight you get to watch me finish while you sit there, hands on the bed, no touching." A cruel smile befalls her face.

"No…Please, I'll be good." I'll beg if I have to, we both know that. But begging won't help me today.

"Good boys don't try to tell their Queens what to do, do they?"

My heart sinks. My punishment has been served.

"No, Ma'am."

"Do you think they use words like '*forbid*'? Hmm?" Not for a second do her fingers leave her pussy, stroking, flicking, pinching, pumping…working herself to a climax that becomes inevitable the moment she pulls her magic wand from the bedside drawer and presses it to her clit.

"No, Goddess. I'm sorry." My balls ache, knowing they won't get any relief today, but there is no universe where I would defy her orders and touch myself. I can't, even if I want to. My pleasure is hers. It feels wrong any other way.

"Hush, boy. And watch," Danica hums, closing her eyes.
Look, but don't touch...

Chapter Seventeen

FEET

(Danica)

I t's been two weeks since I started at Sinful Moon, and things are starting to look desperate. I am no closer to the Volkovs than I was before I started flashing my tits at strangers.

On the upside, though, I love my new job.

I love the freedom. The power. The purpose.

Who knew I'd be a great stripper? Sorry, I meant *dancer*.

Well, technically, I'm rubbish with a pole. I may have a core of steel from all my combat training, but those pole skills need to be learned, practiced.

I found that out the hard way by almost falling on my ass the first night I confidently strode to the pole, imagining my life as a movie where I could just walk up to it and instantly swing around like a graceful creature.

It did not happen like that—not at all!

Still, the clientele didn't care whether I fumbled around or danced like some talented Bollywood movie heroine.

All they cared about were my tits.

Not that I can blame them, these have always been my best assets. I seriously considered a cam girl life when I was a student, but I couldn't bring myself to do it. Well, maybe I could have if I weren't living with my parents at the time...And before that, my asshole boyfriend, James, awho was as vanilla as they come.

The dressing room mirror flickers under the unforgiving lights as I trace bronzer along my cheekbones. Around me, other dancers chatter and laugh, the familiar pre-show energy electric in the air.

My altered reflection stares back at me—smoky eyes, red lips, confidence I never thought I'd wear so easily.

It wasn't always like this.

Nobody had to teach me to hate my body. The lessons came naturally, written in raised scar tissue and whispered in every reflected glance.

I learned at an early age that love was meant for others—for whole, unmarked people who didn't carry their childhood trauma etched into their skin.

I remember the heavy sweaters, even in summer. The way I'd pull them down over my hands, creating armor from wool and cotton. My thick glasses became a shield, letting me hide behind smudged lenses and unfashionable frames.

In high school, I had swimming class down to a science—always the last to change, first to leave, scars safely hidden beneath layers of chlorine-soaked fabric.

Only ballet brought me joy. In the studio's forgiving shadows, beneath leotards and wraps, I could pretend to be graceful. Beautiful, even. Until the recital lights threatened to expose me, and I'd retreat back into my fortress of baggy clothes.

Then came James. So many years later. At varsity. After I had already given up on finding someone who could accept me as I was.

He called it love, but love shouldn't need darkness to thrive. *"It's more romantic with the lights off,"* he'd say, but I heard the truth beneath the words. I thought I was lucky—who else would want damaged goods?

But now...

I adjust my leather corset, watching how it hugs my curves. In a few minutes, I'll dance under spotlights that hide nothing.

Dante changed it all. The way he looks at me like I'm the most beautiful woman in the world has worked a miracle on my confidence. I don't have to fake it anymore; it feels right.

Oh, Dante.

The stage manager calls out a five-minute warning, refocusing me on my mission.

I smile at my reflection, ready to own every inch of who I've become.

Knock 'em dead, gal.

I step onto the stage, beaming with confidence, ready to put on the show of my life.

But I never finish my act.

I am called upstairs, Nikki pulling me right off the stage mid-number, much to the disgruntlement of the audience, whose boos follow me all the way to the office upstairs where *The Boss* sits.

It's happening.

I've never met "The Boss." All I knew was that he was the guy I'd been trying to get to, one of the Volkov brothers—the youngest of three.

If we can't get them at the ports, we might as well hit them where they are weakest—the clubs.

According to dressing room gossip, Mister Boss-Man is quite the hedonist, with a soft spot for curvaceous divas and French wine.

It turns out Sasha was feeling ill, and The Man Upstairs needed a stand-in for whatever Sasha does for him.

My heart is pounding in my chest as we make our way up the narrow, dark stairs next to the dressing room entrance.

Two guards stand by the door at all times. They let Nikki and I pass with a simple nod. Nice guys, I've been chatting to them a lot over the past two weeks. Definitely seems like Mister Boss-Man treats them terribly—poor things.

This is my chance to find a way in. If he doesn't kill me first. But I'm hoping my fake hair and real breasts can distract him.

"Now, Jasmyne. You want to do exactly as Mister Volkov says, understood?" Nikki straightens out my dress like there is anything to straighten out.

Tonight's assigned outfit is a red micro-skirt that has half my ass hanging out with straps like dungarees running over my shoulders. No shirt, nope, just two little straps trying to hold my titties in place and failing with every step I take.

I look like a grade-A hooker, and I'm not even mad; it's a fun fantasy to play out. Though I'm not sure what's about to happen here will be a fantasy, it sounds more scary than fun.

Nikki knocks and then leaves, instantly disappearing down the stairs again.

Oh god. The urge to flee is overwhelming, but the moment the door slowly swings open, the urge quickly turns to a freezing response.

Another guard stands on the other side, ushering me in. A real thug-looking piece of work, the kind with face tattoos and metal-capped teeth. You could probably scare children with this dude. He sure scares me. But I force my mind to focus and my shoulders to straighten out. *Stomach in, chest out.*

The room is dark, lit only by a yellow glow from an antique lamp in the corner.

The figure behind the desk waves the guard out, making him lock the door behind us with an echoing click.

"Come here, *dear.*"

I shiver. The word dear has always just made me cringe—except when Alessio says it with that hint of an Italian accent that has long since been smoothed out by the Vegas life.

I walk towards the bulky figure in the chair, nonetheless. The closer I get to him, the clearer his features become. He's not bad-looking—for a fucking human trafficker.

The mere thought makes me want to throw up on him, but I keep it together.

His beard is thick, dark against his pasty skin, his neck covered in gold chains. Clean-shaven head, a fancy suit...he looks every bit how I had imagined a Russian mobster would look—full of his own shit. And not my type at all. He's much older now than in the blurry photos from our intel file.

Keeping my shoulders up high, I lean over onto his desk, letting him get a good view of my breasts.

The man smiles and reaches for my right nipple with his coarse fingers, pinching it.

I keep my poker face firmly in position, willing my body with every fiber of my being to not flinch outwardly.

"Not those," he says simply in that cliched thick Russian accent. "Feet," he demands.

This is it, Danica; your moment to shine.

Without missing a beat, I climb onto his table, steadying myself against the low ceiling beams running across the surprisingly non-luxurious room.

Volkov stares at me. I have his full attention.

Holding onto the ceiling beam, I slip my left foot out of my heel to run my toes over his gross, hairy chest that pokes out beneath a shirt that should be buttoned higher up but isn't.

The man purrs like a cat, grabbing my foot halfway down and stuffing it in his mouth.

I gasp, almost losing my footing, but I hold onto the ceiling beam for dear life to regain my balance.

Oh Christ, what am I even doing?

I push him away, pulling my foot free. It takes every ounce of self-control not to jump down and crush his balls.

Two more girls have disappeared since I started here, and I know this asshole is to blame.

But if I fail to be patient, I will ruin it all.

Quickly, before he can catch me, I jump off the table, kicking off my other shoe, too, before I trip. "Let me tie you up," I say simply, keeping my distance behind the table.

Big boy is already drooling, I can see his need. "Tie me." He laughs, crossing his wrists and offering them to me.

There is nothing sexy about the encounter, at least not for me, but I force my hips to sway seductively as I walk to the door where I left my toy bag. Sasha told me to always take it with me when I go upstairs, *in case*. Her texts also warned me never to get bratty or try to be in control.

Only 50% of that advice will be adhered to. Control is not something I give up willingly. Not anymore.

We have a playful struggle, but I manage to cuff the big man's hands together.

"Now this." I pulled the blindfold out of my bag, fastening it over his eyes before he could object.

"Ooh, very kinky, Miss Jasmyne." He growls in a way that probably seems sexy to him but seems off-putting as fuck to me.

"You have no idea how kinky I can be, Mister Volkov." I pull his wheeled chair away from the desk and notice his little hard cock, tenting in his pants.

With his eyes closed and his hands bound, it's somehow easier to stomach the encounter.

It's just a mission, I remind myself.

"Hmm, I like you. Feisty. Call me Tolya, please, dear Jasmyne."

"Yes, Mister Tolya." My voice is sickeningly sweet. It's a good thing he can't see the cruel streak in my eyes.

He laughs in that raspy voice of a smoker who should've stopped many years ago. "Touch me with your feet," he instructs despite being the one in the vulnerable position.

For today, I let him believe the reins of control rest solely with him.

"Yes, Mister Tolya," I say obediently, climbing onto the table again, this time to sit down. It's a relief not to have that creep stare at my body. I would've pegged him a tits man, maybe ass. Definitely not feet. But hey, you never knew what people were secretly into.

I reach for his zipper, but he knocks me away with his wrists. "No. Keep them on."

"Aww, does Mister Tolya want to make a mess in his pants?" I can't help it, it's my Mommy voice, patronizing, sweet, cunty.

He responds instantly to it, pressing his groin into my stockinged feet, desperate to rub himself on me.

"Please, Miss Jasmyne." I yearn to make him beg, but not tonight.

I'm glad he can't see the disgust on my face as I drag my feet over his erection, but not as glad as I am for the pants separating my skin from his.

Jesus, Danica. This is a new level of weird, even for you. This man is so revolting.

But I don't stop, no, I continue to rub my feet over his pathetic erection until he sweats and pants and cries out in a language I will never understand, a little wet patch forming to the right of the zipper.

Quickly, I jerk my foot away. I don't want to touch it, touch his cum. *Gross!*

When he's done panting and grunting, I free my boss's wrists first before removing his blindfold, stepping back quickly to busy myself with packing up.

"Well, Miss Jasmyne, I'll have to order you again," the creepy man says, rubbing his now-free hand over the wet patch on his pants.

I can feel the bile crawl up my throat, but I swallow it down.

"Yes, Mister Tolya."

Dickhead.

Chapter Eighteen

TAKE TWO

(Dante)

I'm thrilled about the insider info regarding Tolya Volkov. Less so about the part where Danica jerked him off with her feet.

It's not jealousy, more guilt—she shouldn't have to do this; it's not her mess to sort out.

But Danica is nothing if not determined.

At least we now have a plan for the next phase. We know how many guards there are, how many entrances. It's only a matter of time before he calls Danica again, and then we'll be ready.

She's been working on the Sasha girl from day one, gaining her trust, trying to get her to help. I'm still not sure whose side she's on and whether she'd be a hindrance more than an aid, but Danica seems to believe Sasha's got her back.

I make sure that I'm near the club at all times when Danica's at work. It's all I can do not to feel completely useless, to keep myself from going crazy, just sitting at home, imagining the worst.

Time passes slowly, but Danica recently introduced me to podcasts, and I quickly found distraction in true crime—it was amusing to me more than anything else, and I kept going back episode after episode.

Usually, it's incredibly frustrating when the murderer does something stupid and doesn't cover his tracks. I would never get caught like that.

My favorite part is lying in Danica's arms at night, telling her about the episodes of the day and how I would have done it differently.

She humors me, but I know her vibe is more those smutty sports romances. Fuck knows why, neither of us are big on sports.

We don't have to wait long for another chance.

Mere days later, on a Wednesday, that Russian creep upstairs sends for Danica again.

She sends me a quick text from the extra phone she's been hiding in her make-up bag, and I know we have to act quickly.

This is not a big operation. We have to be discreet. Get in and out with Volkov in tow. He's our way in, the weakest link in the chain.

"It's time," I tell Emilio, and he and Dario slip on their ski masks. I do the same.

We're by the staff door within minutes. Danica conveniently left it unlocked, a piece of tape wedged over the lock to keep it from slamming fully shut. It looks closed, but it gives up instantly when I touch it, and we push inside quickly before anyone sees us.

As planned, Sasha greets us, leading us through to the dressing room. She must have said something to the others before because nobody screams or runs away, the girls simply carry on with their make-up.

I hide behind the giant wardrobe on the left, Emilio by my side, as Dario takes the heat, putting our plan into action.

Nodding at Sasha, she checks in with the other girls—everyone is ready. On my signal, she starts wailing loudly, causing a massive commotion.

The other girls join in, screaming and shouting at Dario as the two guards come rushing in, guns drawn.

Before they can grab Dario, we jump from behind the wardrobe, overpowering them before they even have a chance to react.

Dario slaps some cable ties around their wrists and ankles, securing the guards in the fetal position on the floor. Their lips get taped to ensure their silence.

Emilio carefully ties up the girls, too, to make it look believable, absolving them from any blame. Danica made me promise, repeatedly, that the girls would come to no harm.

I have many flaws, but I am a man of my word.

There is no time to waste, though. The third guard, the one with the face tattoos, is already on his way down the stairs.

I tackle him into the metal steps, jamming my knife into his stomach.

He growls, struggles, but can't find enough leverage to throw me off him. Blood gushes from his stab wound, staining my shirt.

I wish I could shoot him, but I don't want to alarm anyone else in the club. Not while Danica is in that creep's office, alone, unprotected.

Kicking him in the face for good measure, I leave the bleeding guard to Dario to clean up and restrain. I need to find my Queen—ASAP.

Oh god, I hope she's okay; that we're not too late. That cunt must have heard the commotion by now...

Taking a deep breath, I barge into the room upstairs, preparing myself for the worst. Danica had left the door unlocked, as planned.

But my fears are in vain.

The big, scary Mister Volkov is whimpering in his chair, a knife to his balls.

Danica is standing over him, a smug look on her face. She blows me a kiss. "Hey, baby. About time."

My heart leaps, relieved.

"What's going on here?" Volkov asks, voice cracking. Despite the blindfold over his eyes, he looks around wildly, trying to figure out what's happening.

"I don't think you're in any position to make demands, Mister Tolya," Danica says.

"Do you know who you're fucking with? You're making a huge mistake." His tone changes to a threat, but his voice is no less uncertain. I can't blame the man; even I'd count my words if someone had a knife to my nuts.

The club owner is tied up in his chair, no doubt part of Danica's kinky play set-up. I'm sure he let her willingly, enjoying the idea of being tied by her.

Silly man, look at you now.

"Oh, we know exactly who you are. That's why we're here." Danica increases the pressure of the knife, and the slimy man gasps for breath.

"Please, Jasmyne..."

"Jasmyne?" I raise an eyebrow, and Danica laughs.

"Yeah, my stage name. Do you like it?"

"So slutty." I smile.

"Right?"

"Do you want money? I've got lots of money," the pathetic man tries again.

"Shut up. Nobody's talking to you." Danica smacks him across the face. It's such a turn-on to see her being this ruthless. "We don't want your filthy money."

"Anything. Take anything." He's begging now, desperate.

"Oh, we're not just taking anything. We're taking *everything*," Danica laughs.

The sound of approaching footsteps grows louder as Emilio and Dario join us.

Dario stops in the doorframe, mouth agape, his unbreakable expression breaking as he takes in Danica's blond figure, dressed like a complete slut, bent down over the poor man with the knife against his balls.

Emilio just smiles, unphased. He looks proud.

"Take him home. Put him in the basement. We'll deal with him later," I tell them, and Dario chucks the man over his shoulder like he's as light as a feather. Not before Emilio adds some tape to his mouth.

"We'll meet you there," Danica tells them.

"What?" That was not part of the plan. We need to get out of here, right now.

But Danica has other ideas.

She closes the door behind them, turning the key in its lock.

"*Tesoro*, we have to go..." I start, unable to take my eyes off her. She looks incredible, so seductive in blonde.

"Hush. Now, don't move." She pins me down on the desk and grabs my belt, undoing it quickly, efficiently.

"We don't have time," my mouth says, but my body responds only by getting more erect, my cock desperate for her touch.

"I said hush." Danica pulls my cock out and I gasp, loudly, ready to obey her every command.

"Yes, Ma'am." The adrenaline surges through my veins.

"This is *my* desk now," she says, despite the fact that neither of us will ever come back here again.

Danica pushes her hands under my shirt and drags her long nails over my chest, drawing blood as she cuts into my skin.

I hiss between my teeth, closing my eyes, as she rips open my shirt and licks the blood from my skin. *Oh god, it's the hottest thing in the world.*

I do not dare tell her that, or anything else for that matter.

In this moment, I'm reduced to a mere object, my dick's only function to bring her pleasure as she impales herself on me, fucking me on the Russian mobster's desk until we're both screaming profanities, climaxing together minutes later.

The power surging through Danica's body is unmistakable as she brings herself to orgasm, taking me with her, riding me with vigor without bothering to take off my pants.

"You're a fucking crazy woman," I pant between rapid breaths, kissing her sweaty face as our post-climax bodies heave up and down together on the large wooden desk.

"Thank you, I love you too." She kisses my nose and gets up, standing over me as my cum leaks out, dribbling down her leg.

Instantly, I sit up, shoving my face between her thighs to lick our spent orgasms from her skin.

"Hmm...Such a good boy," she coos, weaving her fingers through my hair, tugging just hard enough to make my scalp tingle as I clean her up.

This time, I get my reward.

Every last drop of it

When I'm done, I help her down, kissing her deeply when both feet are planted firmly on the floor. Her taste mingles with mine, and I can feel her smile against my lips.

"We finally have one of the Volkovs," I say when we finally break apart, tucking myself back into my pants, the taste of victory still sweet on my tongue. "And all thanks to you."

Danica's eyes flash with pride. "I told you I had a plan."

"Have I ever told you how fucking incredible you are?" My voice drops low, reverential.

"All the time," she says, tracing my jawline with her finger, "but you can tell me again."

When Danica looks up at me, her eyes gleam with that fierce intelligence that first drew me to her. The same brilliance that got her into the Sinful Moon, that identified Tolya as our target, that orchestrated this perfect trap. But her expression changes, grows serious suddenly. "No one will even notice he's missing for a while. Not with the girls at the club covering for us."

"Perfect," I smirk, zipping up but not bothering with my belt yet. The adrenaline is still coursing through me, making my movements jerky, impatient. "From what you've told me about him, he'll break easily."

Danica pulls her skirt down, but her movements are slow, thoughtful. "Oh, he will. That man is all hedonism and no backbone. And definitely not much brains." She smiles, something dangerous in it that makes my blood run hotter.

"And we'll use everything he gives us," I say, moving toward her and cupping her face between my palms. "Dismantle the Volkovs piece by piece, one Russian asshole at a time."

She leans into my touch, her eyes now alight with possibility. "They're all going down."

"The whole operation," I agree as I stroke my thumb across her cheekbone, wiping away a smudge of makeup that survived our encounter.

The office is quiet now, just the sound of our breathing and the distant thump of bass from the club below. The desk is still in disarray from our impromptu celebration, papers scattered across the floor like confetti.

"Nobody will see us coming."

"That's the point." I pull her closer, our foreheads touching. The scent of her—sweat and perfume and arousal—anchors me in this moment of possibility.

Her eyes search mine, understanding dawning. "So, what now?"

My heart hammers against my ribs, but my decision is already made. "Well, I'm calling Alessio as soon as we get home," I say with conviction. "I believe I promised you a wedding."

"We don't have to—" she starts, but I cut her off, drawing her fully into my arms.

"I want to, *Tesoro*. You deserve it," I murmur against her hair. "You deserve the world."

She melts against me for a moment, then pulls back. "But the Volkovs—"

"We'll get them," I reassure her as I tuck a strand of fake blonde hair behind her ear. "Besides, I need an excuse to go see Alessio, don't you?"

She smiles at the mention of his name, a private smile that makes me grateful, not for the first time, that we found someone who fits so perfectly with both of us. Someone who loves her as fiercely as I do.

"Let's do it," Danica says finally, taking my face between her hands, her eyes holding mine in that way that still makes my breath catch. She brushes her lips against mine, gentle now after our earlier frenzy. In that kiss, the entire world shifts, rights itself again.

I squeeze her tight, unwilling to let go.

Her smile grows wider, and I can feel her heartbeat quicken against my chest—a rhythm that has become as familiar to me as my own.

As Danica takes my hand and we leave this shitty club, the cool night air hits us like a blessing. My mind is already plotting our next moves...

Because I am done waiting, done denying Danica the new chapter we both so badly want, badly *need*. Done letting these Russian bastards dictate our lives.

This time, nobody will stop us.

Nobody.

CHAPTER NINETEEN

OPULENCE

(DANICA)

Today is the day I become Missus Fera.

Fucking finally.

Three months after the initial wedding that ended in carnage, I'm ready to try again. Three months of rebuilding, of fighting, of clawing our way back to this moment.

Outside the tinted windows, Vegas shimmers like a mirage. The autumn sun beats down mercilessly, creating ripples of heat that dance above the asphalt as we glide toward the hotel.

Even in May, Vegas doesn't believe in subtle weather. When our private jet touched down around 10 AM, the air already clung to my skin with oppressive intensity, promising a scorcher of a wedding day.

Alessio was waiting for us on the tarmac, his tall frame cutting an elegant silhouette against the desert backdrop. The moment he saw me, his face broke into that smile that still makes my stomach flutter. He held the limo door open with a flourish, then pulled me into a kiss that tasted of mint and promise. We both kissed Dante goodbye—him with passion, me with the tingling anticipation of separation before reunion—and left him and Emilio to get ready at another location. I wanted the look on his face to be genuine when he first sees my new dress.

The only shitty part is that we couldn't bring Biscotti with us. But Dario is looking after him, so I know he's in good hands. I've caught that mountain of a man sneaking the little mutt treats when he thinks no one is watching, seen how the statue of a guard breaks character to give soft head scratches that make Biscotti's tail thump against the marble floor. The two of them will be just fine—probably having more fun than they would admit.

I can't believe the day has finally arrived. After everything we've been through...

Involuntarily, my thoughts turn to Tolya Volkov currently enjoying our *hospitality* in the basement back home. Such a slimy guy; still makes my skin crawl just thinking of his little cock. The girls at the club have been keeping his cover story intact—telling everyone he went off-grid for a while, which apparently isn't unusual for him.

He was instrumental in helping us take down the rest of the Volkovs. All I had to do was threaten to staple his balls to the table with an industrial stapler, and he quickly sang to my tune. I was ready to do it too, stapler in hand, his pathetic shriveled-up balls on the splinter-rich wooden table in our basement.

Convenient for us, the asshole had high-level access that allowed us to dismantle the syndicate from the inside much quicker than anticipated, crumbling their businesses, their connections, before they had a chance to catch on.

The extended plan of taking down the Volkovs required minimum violence and maximum patience, not my idea of fun.

We moved quickly—the accountant first, then Dimitri. He didn't talk as easily as his slimy baby brother, but he sure spilled all his secrets once we threatened his secret lover—a tall, elegant red-headed pole dancer with a huge cock (if the hype was to be believed).

Piece for piece, we took them apart swiftly, effectively, until it was just that main dickhead, Boris, left—the eldest brother, the one calling the shots.

There was no reasoning with that cunt, so hardened, so cruel. Dante's patience finally wore thin, and he just shot the guy right there in the basement, putting a bullet between his eyes without so much as changing his expression.

I don't feel an ounce of remorse. Not after what they did at our first wedding. Not after everything they've done to countless innocent people.

We're keeping the other two brothers alive, tied up in our basement but alive. Insurance, Dante calls it. Something tells me we haven't seen the last of the Russians' network, regardless of what we've accomplished.

For now, though, we've earned this moment.

The sleek black limousine glides to a halt, bringing an end to my wandering thoughts.

For a moment, I'm frozen in disbelief at the view. My eyes widen as they trace the contours of the towering structure before us, its gleaming facade reflecting the crisp sunlight.

"We're...here?" I breathe, my voice barely above a whisper. Even I know the reputation of this hotel. Only the elite get to walk through those doors.

Alessio's warm chuckle fills the air as he opens the door, offering his hand. "Indeed we are, *cara*."

As I step out, the desert heat hits me like a physical wall.

"Alessio, this is..." I trail off, struggling to find words that adequately capture the grandeur before me.

My lover squeezes my hand gently, his touch grounding me. "Nothing is too much for *Donna* Fera," he murmurs, soothing my frayed nerves. "Time to get ready for your big day.

It seems crazy to get a hotel this fancy just to get ready. The reception later will be at a whole different venue.

But I have zero intentions of overthinking this; I'm going where Alessio takes me. Most of the plans are still a surprise to me. It's way less stressful than the first time around.

A rush of cool air envelops us as we step inside the building, the air conditioning working overtime. Taking off my sunglasses, I blink rapidly, adjusting to both the temperature and the dazzling interior.

The lobby is a feast for the senses—crystal chandeliers cast prismatic rainbows across marble floors while the gentle tinkling of a nearby fountain mingles with soft classical music.

I'm so entranced by the surroundings that I nearly collide with a pillar. Luckily, Alessio's quick reflexes save me from embarrassment, his strong arm wrapping around my waist to pull me aside.

"Careful, darling," he teases, his eyes twinkling with amusement. "We can't have the bride with a bruised forehead, can we?"

I shake my head, grateful for his presence—not just to keep me from injuring myself, but also to distract me from my intrusive thoughts.

As we make our way across the lobby, I can't help but feel out of place in my casual jeans and blouse combo. Around us, people glide by in designer dresses and impeccably tailored suits, their heels clicking rhythmically against the polished floor.

"How did you manage this?" I whisper, leaning close to Alessio. The subtle notes of his cologne—sandalwood and something uniquely *him*—fill my orbit. "Isn't this place fully booked for months?"

A knowing smile plays on Alessio's lips as we approach the reception desk. The woman behind the counter hands him a key without a word, her eyes lingering on him a moment too long. I've grown accustomed to the effect Alessio has on people, but it still stirs a complex mix of emotions within me—pride, amusement, and just a hint of possessiveness.

"*Cara mia*," Alessio begins as we step into the elevator, "in Vegas, everything has a price. And for the Santoros, that price is often quite negotiable."

I roll my eyes playfully, but there's no real annoyance behind the gesture.

As the elevator doors close, sealing us in our private bubble, I intertwine my fingers with his. "Thank you," I say softly, meeting his gaze. "For all of this. You didn't have to—"

Alessio silences me with a gentle kiss to my forehead, his lips warm and comforting against my skin. "I wanted to," he assures me. "Your wedding day will be unforgettable for all the right reasons this time."

The mere hint at our previous nuptial attempt sends a cold shiver down my spine. Unbidden, the image of Carlo's lifeless body flashes before my eyes, and I feel the phantom sensation of his blood on my hands. My breath catches in my throat.

Alessio, ever attuned to my emotions, pulls me closer. "It wasn't your fault, dear," he murmurs into my hair.

I know he's right, but the weight of guilt and grief still presses heavily on my chest.

I take a deep breath, inhaling Alessio's comforting scent, and try to focus on the present. On the man holding me. On the fact that I'll be marrying Dante in a matter of hours.

The doors ping open on cue, forcing me to untangle from Alessio and step into the spectacular space that is way too lavish to even dream about.

The elevator took us all the way to the top—oh, Alessio and his endless penthouses. This one is big enough to fit a whole football team, I swear!

Such good taste. So modern. Bold colors. Dark hues and aesthetics. Rich emerald couches and abstract artworks hung from too-big frames off textured walls. And the lights...*What is it with rich people and fucking chandeliers?*

There's even a grand piano in the corner of the massive space. Like, who comes to Vegas to sit around playing the piano in your bedroom? I've never met such a person.

The master bedroom has an extra-long king-sized bed and floor-to-ceiling windows that offer stunning views of the Las Vegas skyline. I put my handbag down on the bed.

Outside, on the expansive terrace, the view gets even better. Is that a firepit *and* a jacuzzi? *So extra.*

"It's too much, Alessio."

It's overwhelming. Even after all these years of spoils and luxury since entering the Fera household, I still couldn't get used to living this way. Growing up, my idea of luxury was getting to order a large pizza instead of a medium or buying name-brand cereal from the grocery store.

The Vegas Joker smiles as he watches me fan-girl over my surroundings, his empire, technically. "No such thing."

"Seriously, though. This is probably where Beyonce stays when she comes to Vegas."

"Perhaps. But we both know you're the real *Queen*." Alessio winks at me playfully.

"I'm not worthy." I try to curtsy, but the move carries little grace, and I nearly lose my balance. Alessio catches me before I can topple over, kissing the side of my head.

"Nonsense. Now, come, we're already late for our spa booking."

"But we just got here." The outside seating looks so inviting; I don't want to go anywhere. It's been such a busy day, such an early morning, just to get here.

"We're on a tight schedule, dear. So leave all your things, and let's go."

"I thought we were going to relax, have some drinks, ease into it..."

"We're having all of those, but just at the spa. Come. *Vamos*!"

"Spanish? You're just trying to confuse me now."

"Well caught." Alessio laughs heartily, and that's that. Without any further explanation, we're back in the elevator for a short three-floor ride down.

"Surely we can't just go relax in a spa...Isn't there stuff to do? Like arrangements that need to be made and shit?" It feels strange not having a million last-minute errands. The previous wedding was a ball-ache until the very end. But this time around, it feels like nothing is done yet.

Alessio just shakes his head, placing his hand on my arm in a reassuring gesture. "Everything is taken care of, dear. Relax. I want you to enjoy today."

"That all depends on who's on the guest list." I laugh like I'm joking, but I'm not.

"Don't worry, no family, just like you asked," he confirms as the elevator door opens to reveal another level of luxury—this one all white marble and gold accents with luscious bamboo trees lining the entrance like we've somehow ended up on a whole other continent.

I exhale, relieved. "Thank you."

"I take it your family doesn't see eye-to-eye with Dante?" Alessio tries to fish as the spa staff ushers us into fluffy white bathrobes, shoving a mimosa into my hand.

"Something like that," I mumble into my drink, letting the bubbles burn away old hurts.

Alessio doesn't press.

"Well, luckily, you have a new family now." His eyes are warm, kind, and I give him a grateful smile.

"A massive upgrade, for sure." I attempt lightness, but the smile feels brittle on my face.

We're led into a private suite before he can dig deeper.

Two massage tables wait like altars in the center of the room, draped in linens that probably cost more than both my wedding dresses combined. The air is heavy with jasmine, tranquil music falling like mist from hidden speakers.

But my mind drifts to the last time I saw my family, to the final door I had to close to begin this new chapter of my life.

I tried. God, I tried. At Dante's insistence, I extended one last olive branch—a wedding invitation delivered in person. One last chance at being the family we pretended to be in public.

Instead, it became another scene in our lifelong tragedy.

My mother's lips twisted around the words *"thug wedding"* like she was tasting poison. My father stared at his plate, silent as always—a habit learned from decades of choosing peace over protection. The twins...well, Marko spoke for both of them. He always did, Filip's spine long since surrendered to his brother's will.

I fled before the tears could fall, determined not to give them the satisfaction of breaking me again. But Marko followed—he always did love an audience for his cruelty.

"A slut like you deserves a man like him!" His voice chased me across the driveway, each word aimed with sniper precision. *"A scumbag."*

I stopped dead, fists clenched so tight my nails cut half-moons into my palms.

"You'll never be anyone," my brother continued, voice dripping with the familiar venom of childhood as he threw fresh matches at old wounds. *"Just little crying Danica with nobody to listen to her. He'll throw you away like they always do."*

A thousand responses burned on my tongue—about surviving their games, about finding love despite their best efforts to convince me I was unworthy, about becoming stronger than their cruelty. But I swallowed them all.

Instead, I straightened my spine. Lifted my chin. Walked away.

For good.

Some doors need to close forever so others can open. Some families need to be found rather than born into. Some names need to be changed to become who you really are. I'm done being a Matthews.

I sink into the massage table's embrace, letting warm hands soothe away old tensions. Soon, I'll become Danica Fera—not because I'm running from who I was, but because I'm finally becoming who I was meant to be.

Can it just be tomorrow already?

Chapter Twenty

VOWS

(Dante)

T welve years after the first time I said *I do*, I'm ready for it to be the final time I utter those words.

This time, I'm more restless, though.

My fingers twitch, longing for the familiar weight of a gun. Alessio's reassurances echo in my mind— *"We're fully protected, amore mio. My men won't let anyone pass."* But the memory of the first failed wedding refuses to fade. The sound of gunshots still rings in my ears, drowning out the soft music playing in the quaint hotel chapel with the golden pews and draped walls that looked more like a movie set than a place of worship.

Earlier today, I had high hopes that a quick workout would clear my head and settle the nervousness that twisted my stomach into knots. But now, as I stand in front of a room full of mostly strangers, waiting for my bride to approach (again), I feel anything but settled. Perhaps I should've joined the spa day outing instead.

The door creaks open, and my heart leaps into my throat. But it's just another of Alessio's friends—a tall woman with cascading purple hair and a suit that shimmers like starlight. She catches my eye and winks, her easy smile a stark contrast to the tension thrumming through my body.

"A weird and wonderful bunch of queers"—that's what Danica calls Alessio's crew affectionately, and it's a fitting description. Such beautiful people.

There is no one from any of the crime families here, no business contacts, no relatives. Not today. The only other familiar face outside the wedding party is Adira and her partner Rani.

Adira and Danica have remained friends after the former helped us establish our dynamic. The two of them often go to shows and random events together. It was good to see Danica finally make some friends.

The door opens again, and I grab Alessio's hand for support, safe in the knowledge that I don't have to worry about who clocks our familiar intimacies today.

And then I see her.

On cue, Danica appears in the doorway, a vision that steals the breath from my lungs.

I look from my bride to my boyfriend, and both are grinning as wide as their faces allow. So am I.

Dio mio, she looks out of this world!

Danica is dressed from head to toe in black. Leather and lace intertwine in an intricate dance, cascading to the floor in a

212

collage of textures. The dress clings to her curves before flowing out into a river of midnight that trails behind her. Sheer lace embraces her arms to the elbow, a delicate contrast to the leather harness straps hugging her bodice like a lover's embrace.

Emilio guides her down the short, carpeted aisle, this time a path lined with only five rows of seats.

Dark red roses and white tulips brighten up the space, their perfume mingling with the heady scent of anticipation that hangs in the air.

My wedding attire pales compared to my bride's—a simple black suit, unremarkable save for the deep red rose nestled in my breast pocket.

Alessio planned it all, pinning the rose to my jacket before we entered the chapel.

My shirt is buttoned up all the way, my collar hugging my neck securely, making me feel safe.

It feels different today.

No children this time, no violence either. Just my stunning wife-to-be with her dark make-up and pinned-up, curled hair walking towards me, looking like the gothic bride of the year.

As Danica draws closer, the world around me blurs and fades. The music becomes a distant hum, overpowered by the thundering of my own heart.

Her eyes, rimmed with smoky shadow, lock onto mine. A smile plays on her painted lips, and suddenly, my knees threaten to buckle. Alessio's hand in mine becomes my anchor, his touch a silent reassurance that this is real, that we're finally doing this despite everything.

The song—whatever it was—finishes, and Emilio's hand clasps mine, firm and warm, as he places Danica's hand in my own. The weight of her familiar touch sends a jolt through my spine, catching my breath in my throat.

Alessio leans in, his lips brushing Danica's cheek in a gossamer-light kiss, careful not to disturb her artfully applied makeup. As he takes his place beside her, I can't help but glance back at the chapel doors, half-expecting them to burst open at any moment.

Danica blows me a kiss, and I have to clench my fists to keep them from shaking. Part of me wants to grab her and kiss her immediately, fully, but I know I have to wait until the formalities allow such actions.

As we turn to face the officiant, I steal one more glance at my bride. In her black gown, she embodies everything she is—strong, unconventional, breathtakingly beautiful. A far cry from the traditional white dress from before, this is pure Danica. My dark Queen, my partner in crime (literally), my everything.

Our officiate is a slender figure with a radiant smile and long black hair cut into a mullet. They must be about Danica's age, dressed in a loose-fitting purple suit and shiny loafers.

I struggle to focus on any of their words as my eyes keep drifting to Danica—who is even more magnificent up close.

She is still so young, only 27, but my god, she's grown up a lot in the past few years. The older she gets, the more she settles into her features, becoming more breathtaking with each passing day.

Emilio pats my arm, and I smile like a fool.

Today, I want to remember every detail of our special day. More than anything, I just want to be married already. I want to be Danica's, forever—officially—*owned*.

Unlike my first wedding, the ceremony is short, concise. It's also not in Italian like when I married Elena.

Twelve years ago, the pews in the cathedral were packed with our family and friends, Luca by my side as my best man.

The thought of my delinquent brother makes me wince for a second, but I push the thought away. So much has changed since then; *I* have changed so much.

Twelve years is a long time when you're in the business of death and debt. I feel like I've aged three decades since my first wedding.

After Elena's death, I vowed I would never love again, never get married to anyone else. But for Danica, I would give it all, whatever she wanted. My Queen deserved to have all her wishes fulfilled.

And her wish was for us to write our own vows...

It's been giving me sleepless nights for months as I tried to perfect my awkward wording, the bin in my study littered with crumbled-up papers of earlier attempts.

Even with Alessio's help, I'm still not confident it's good enough. But there's nothing else I can add now.

The realization doesn't slow the rhythm of my racing heart, though.

I'm relieved not to be going first.

"Danica, are you ready?" the officiant asks.

She nods, reaching into her cleavage with a playful smile that makes my heart skip. The folded paper she withdraws bears creases from being read and refolded countless times.

As I hold her hand, Danica reads her vows like a letter, promising me more than I am worth...

Her voice shakes, but she pushes through, catching my eye between sentences to share a soft smile that melts me into a puddle of mushy feelings.

My beloved Dante,

I am filled with overwhelming love and gratitude as I stand before you today.

You, my darling Knight, have given me strength I never knew I had.

In your arms, I have found refuge from the chaos of life.

I can never thank you enough for believing in me, even when I didn't believe in myself.

With you by my side, I feel invincible because I know that, together, we can conquer anything.

I vow to cherish and honor you for all the days of my life.

To stand by your side through every trial and triumph that may come our way.

I will protect you with all that I am, shielding you from harm and keeping you safe.

With you, I have found my true partner, my soulmate, my everything.

I can't wait to spend the rest of my days as your wife.

My darling boy, I love you.

More and more each day.

You are mine.

To have and to hold.

Until the end of my time.

Forever and always.

As Danica's final words hang in the air, a profound silence settles over the chapel. My vision blurs, the world around me softening at the edges as tears well up unbidden.

I blink rapidly, trying to clear my sight, unwilling to miss a single moment of this. A droplet escapes, trailing down my cheek, but I make no move to wipe it away.

Danica's eyes meet mine, a universe of understanding passing between us in that single glance. Her smile, soft and knowing, breaks through my haze of emotion like a ray of sunlight.

Without conscious thought, both my hands reach for hers. Our fingers intertwine, the warmth of her skin grounding me in this moment of beautiful, terrifying openness.

Words crowd my throat, a jumble of gratitude and love and disbelief, but they tangle on my tongue.

How can I possibly articulate the magnitude of what her vows mean to me? The idea that someone—that

Danica—would choose to declare such devotion, not just to me but before all these witnesses? It's almost too much to comprehend.

She is about to crumble up the paper again when I take it from her and shove it into my pocket. I want to keep it, always.

A soft chuckle escapes Danica's lips. "Silly boy," she whispers, her voice carrying a fondness that washes over me like a warm breeze. The familiar endearment, so at odds with the formality of the occasion, breaks through the last of my emotional paralysis.

A smile tugs at my lips, mirroring hers, as a sense of lightness spreads through my chest.

And then it's my turn.

I take a deep breath, feeling the weight of Danica's hands in mine, the steady presence of Alessio and Emilio at our sides.

The words I've prepared suddenly seem inadequate in the face of Danica's heartfelt declaration.

But as I look into her eyes, patient and loving, I know that whatever I say will be enough.

With one final squeeze of Danica's hands, I steel myself.

It's time to bare my soul.

Please don't stutter!

CHAPTER TWENTY-ONE

I DO

(DANICA)

The woman I saw in the hotel mirror an hour ago still feels like a revelation—someone I've waited all my life to become. No white wedding gown this time—thank fuck—just pure, unapologetic me.

Alessio outdid himself with the spa day earlier, transforming hours of pampering into art.

"Bellissima!" the Vegas Joker had exclaimed in the hotel suite, spinning me around the dressing room like a dark fairy tale princess. His joy was infectious, pure, making me laugh in a way I hadn't since before the first wedding disaster.

In that moment, the weight of family expectations, brothers who tried to break me, and parents who never saw me—it all fell away like shed skin.

This time, we do it *our* way.

Now, standing at the chapel altar, I feel Dante's eyes on me. I haven't lost his attention since I walked in. He's drinking in every detail like a man dying of thirst.

There's something beautifully primal in his gaze—part reverence, part hunger, pure devotion.

I love it!

Despite expecting someone to barge in at any moment, our second attempt at a wedding is proceeding as planned, the only minor hitch being that I forgot to put in my contacts and have to struggle my way through the vows. But nobody notices.

Eyes glued to the paper, I push through the handwritten lines, avoiding Dante's gaze until the end in fear of losing my place.

I feel corny as shit, but he deserves it; he deserves everything.

My heart warms to see his teary eyes when he snatches the crumbled paper away from me.

Maybe it was worth all those nights editing and re-editing those damn lines, after all. Alessio offered to help, but I wanted to do it on my own.

I straighten out my posture, reminding myself to pull my shoulders back as the photographer flashes away, capturing the beautiful moments I want to cherish for life.

Now that the vows are over, my part at least, I let out a heavy sigh of relief.

This shit had me so nervous. Being sentimental wasn't my vibe, but Dante was worthy of sincere vows.

And I meant it. All of it. He *is* mine.

I'm nervous for him as Dante's turn arrives.

My heart squeezes as my dark Knight fumbles with his phone, adjusting the font size back and forth with trembling fingers. The feared Don Fera, brought to uncertainty by words of love.

Alessio's hand finds Dante's back, whispering something that relaxes my groom's shoulders slightly. That man always knows what to say.

Dante wipes his eyes with a crisp white handkerchief he fishes from a pocket discreetly—so perfectly him, so old-world formal. My father is the only person I know who still carries a handkerchief wherever he goes. He insists it's his favorite Christmas present to receive (well, that and socks). Though, he's not getting any more presents from me, ever.

Focus, Danica.

I brace myself for the moment, knowing how my darling Don struggles with emotional expression. The traditional vows would be enough—any words, really—coming from him.

Dante clears his throat, catching my eyes briefly before returning all his attention to whatever is typed on his phone.

I watch every move intently, every twitch of his eye, every crinkle on his forehead that glistens with little dots of sweat.

Nobody has ever declared their love for me publicly before...

"Dearest Danica," my dapper Knight begins, his voice rough with emotion, "My love, my Queen, my world..."

The words wash over me like warm rain as I shift from one foot to another.

"You have made me the man I am today, and I cannot wait to call you my wife," Dante's voice gains strength with each word.

"Before these witnesses, I vow to protect you with my life—now and forever. I promise to shield you from harm and end anyone who so much as harms a hair on your body." A shiver runs down my spine, knowing the truth behind this vow, the blood it promises.

"I will cherish and adore you until the end of time; worship you the way you deserve." His eyes meet mine on the word worship, and heat floods my cheeks at our shared understanding. We both know he doesn't use that word frivolously; it was intentional.

"In good times, and in bad. At all times, I am yours." The possessive note in his voice makes my knees weak. I know he truly means it.

"My love, you make me happier than I ever knew possible." Dante's voice cracks slightly, and I see Alessio wipe his own eyes discretely.

But my groom pushes on, clutching the phone with such might, I fear he might crush it in his large hand. Beside him, even Emilio's usually unbreakable face shows signs of feeling something.

"Thank you for accepting me and for loving me." The vulnerability in these words nearly breaks me as I stare at my almost-husband like a K-pop fan at her idol.

"Your strength is an inspiration, and I am proud to have you by my side," he continues, filling my heart to the brim. "Words cannot express how much I love you, my *Tesoro*." The familiar endearment rolls off his tongue like honey. I've never seen him be this soppy.

"I will spend the rest of my days proving it to you." His voice strengthens with determination as he concludes, "I am forever yours, Queen Danica."

As Dante's final promise fills the moment, I reach for the handkerchief peeking from his pocket, dabbing at my eyes while silently praying I haven't ruined my makeup. Alessio's thumbs-up reassures me all is still well.

I needn't have lowered my expectations—it was so perfect. I want to frame these words one day, maybe even pay someone to embroider them for me, maybe on a pillow, or wherever, something to remind me of this moment.

It's not time for our kiss yet but I kiss my groom anyway, squeezing my arms around his broad chest, bathing in the familiar musk scent of a man who doesn't bother with fancy scents.

"I love you so fucking much," I whisper in Dante's ear. His lips press against my forehead in response, a gesture so tender it makes fresh tears threaten.

A whoop echoes through the chapel, breaking the spell, and I laugh through my tears.

The officiant's warm smile guides us back to the ceremony, to the rings I'd almost forgotten about in the emotion of the moment.

Emilio pulls the rings from his pocket and hands us each our partner's one—a solid black band made from titanium for Dante (simple, sleek, durable); and a thin platinum band encrusted in diamonds for me (beautiful, elegant, strong).

The rings slide on easily, they were perfectly fitted after all, and with a simple "I do," I promise to be the best wife I can be to the worthiest Knight in the whole land.

Dante doesn't hesitate, his *I do* is instant, clear.

"I now pronounce you husband and wife," the officiant tells us, and this time, more than one person whoops.

Our rent-a-crowd jumps up, applauding enthusiastically as we execute the *"You may kiss your bride"* command with zealousness, Dante dipping me low in his arms like we're doing the tango before kissing me for the first time as Missus Dante Fera.

Oh god, I'm Missus Fera.

Finally!

Well, technically not yet, not until the officiant oversees us signing the wedding license and other necessary legal documents moments later.

But then it's done—final, over—without any interruptions or gunshots.

The moment Dante lets me come up for air, Alessio sweeps in like a force of nature. His hands find my waist, lifting me effortlessly as his lips claim mine in a kiss that tastes of spearmint gum and victory.

When he sets me down, he turns to Dante, cupping his face with those elegant hands before kissing him with equal passion.

"Congratulations, darlings." Alessio's eyes dance with mischief as he pulls back. "You're one step closer to being a kept man." His finger traces Dante's jaw playfully, and though my husband—*god, my husband*—shakes his head, his smile is pure contentment.

"Thank you," I manage, emotion making my voice thick. "For *everything*."

They envelop me between them, my safe harbor of broad chests and familiar scents.

"Only a pleasure." Alessio's voice rumbles through his chest against my back. "You two deserve a good wedding. That last one was a mess, to put it lightly."

"I appreciate it," Dante adds softly, reaching past me to touch Alessio's cheek with tenderness.

Alessio catches Dante's hand, pressing a kiss to his palm before announcing, "Okay, so now for the fun part. The reception."

The gleam in his eyes reminds me of our planning calls, of his increasingly outrageous suggestions that had me crying with laughter. Dante had just smiled and said, "*Whatever pleases you,*" content to let us plot our perfect celebration.

"You sure you don't want to do the gambling and cocaine party platter, Missus Fera?" The new name sends shivers down my spine, even as I laugh at Alessio's teasing.

"Hundred percent sure!"

"Danica, dear, you are an enigma." Alessio's fingers play with a loose strand of my hair, twirling it thoughtfully. "I don't know anyone who loves Vegas this much but doesn't give a single fuck about the actual gambling."

I shrug, still pressed between them both. "Why would I waste time and money with that when there is a giant playground to explore? I prefer my Sin City with extra sin, thank you."

"Such a strange yet incredible woman." His voice drops to that velvet tone that makes my knees weak.

"Then kiss me already!" I demand, straining upward on my toes, the black lace of my dress rustling between us.

Alessio's hand cups the back of my neck as he bends down, kissing me until stars dance behind my eyelids. When he finally releases me, I'm gasping, grateful for Dante's steady presence beside me.

"Come," Alessio purrs, taking Dante's right hand and my left in his. "Your guests await." His eyes promise wickedness to come as he leads us outside toward people who will soon become way more than strangers.

Looking up at my Dons—my husband and our lover, both so beautiful in their own way—I know I've found my perfect version of happily ever after.

CHAPTER TWENTY-TWO

AFTER PARTY

(DANICA)

They say Vegas weddings are supposed to be quick, messy affairs—drive-through chapels and Elvis impersonators. But nothing about loving Don Dante Fera has ever been conventional.

A surprised squeal escapes my lips as Dante sweeps me off my feet, the layers of my black dress rippling around us like a dark ocean.

His arms are steady, secure, but his face is pure joy—so different from the man who was fighting for his life at our first wedding attempt just months ago. Amazing how much can change between one almost "I do" and the next.

"What are you doing?" I laugh as we enter the mansion Alessio arranged for our reception. The space is clean and sparkling with money, a far cry from the blood-stained garden where our first ceremony ended in gunfire. I wanted something more private than the hotel.

231

"Practicing for home." Dante's eyes sparkle with mischief before he captures my lips with his. I melt into the kiss, my arm tightening around his neck.

Behind us, I hear the murmur of guests filing in, their footsteps and voices creating a soft symphony of celebration.

When we finally part, I open my eyes to find Dante gazing at me with an expression that makes my heart flutter. His usual sharp edges have softened, replaced by something almost boyish—a smile that reaches all the way to his eyes, crinkling the corners in a way that makes him look years younger.

"What is it?" I whisper, though I already know. I've never seen him this unguarded, this openly happy.

"Nothing. Just can't stop looking at you." His voice is rough with emotion. "How did I get so lucky?"

"You're being so mushy." I press a kiss to the tip of his nose, feeling him smile against my skin. "Put me down."

His arms lower me gently, but he keeps one hand on the small of my back as I find my footing. The marble floor is cool beneath my feet, even through my shoes.

We made it.

Despite Russian attacks, despite family disapproval, despite a lifetime of scars telling me I didn't deserve love—we're here.

"I can't help being mushy. It's your fault," he says with a shrug that does nothing to diminish his grin.

"Come, let's go find something to drink. I'm thirsty as fuck."

I take his hand as I lead him into our wedding reception.

It's been an insane few months, but tonight we celebrate. Tonight, we prove that sometimes the most beautiful love stories start with bloodshed rather than "once upon a time." That the most devoted hearts often beat in the chests of those society calls monsters. That in our world, happy endings aren't given—they're taken, with both hands, whatever the cost.

Twin staircases sweep upward like arms reaching for the sky, their dark wood railings gleaming under crystal chandeliers. The space is all marble and abstract art, wooden surfaces with black metal finishes, expensive shit.

I'm sure long-term rich people or those journalists who write 15-page features on houses for a living could describe it way better, but to me, it is *spacious* and *open* and *so classy*—that's all I need to know.

The rooms are huge, the ceilings high, and the furniture made of brown leather that feels (and smells) real. Through the back, the entire wall opens like an accordion, sliding away onto a massive patio that leads into a garden the size of a small public park.

The property, all eight rooms and 12 bathrooms of it, belongs to one of Alessio's friends, a mansion realtor with access to incredible places like this. It was far more intimate than hanging out at the hotel or any of the casinos or clubs; it was exactly what I wanted for my first night as a married woman.

Around us, waiters waltz around carrying trays of drinks and canapés, but I'm not hungry for anything available on a platter.

I snag two flutes of champagne from a passing tray, the bubbles racing to the surface like my pulse when Dante looks at me that way. Golden liquid catches the light as I raise my glass to his.

"To Missus Danica Fera," he says, his voice low and intimate despite the grand space around us. The title makes my whole body tingle—not because of the power it carries in our world, but because of the way he says it.

"That's *Madame* to you." I grin as I toast him.

Dante takes a sip. "Madame Danica Fera, hmm, that sounds good."

"Doesn't it?" It sounds right. "Speaking of, I don't think you need all those buttons anymore." I tug at Dante's shirt to open the top three buttons, revealing his beautiful collar.

Slowly, I trace the edges of the leather band before slipping my forefinger through the metal hoop and tugging, pulling his face down to my eye level.

"Are you going to be a good boy today?" I whisper seductively, and Dante groans in response, his whole body softening like it's melting.

He looks around quickly. "Please, don't...You'll make me hard in no time."

"Well, darling, that's kind of the point, isn't it?" I gesture around the room where our guests enjoy their drinks while lightly swaying to the music.

"We haven't even met half these people yet," Dante says with a hint of nervousness, looking at the two dozen bodies around us.

"Not yet. But they all know what kind of party this is." I wink at him, my stomach knotting in little butterflies at the mere thought of the excitement to come.

When Alessio asked about my preference for the reception, I told him all I wanted was a fuck-you to societal norms, something that was truer to us.

He suggested we go to one of the sex clubs, but I wanted something more exclusive.

A few days later, Alessio sent me a voice note with an alternative suggestion, one that sounded oh-so-perfect.

Describing it in detail, he told me about this massive house on the outskirts of the city, about his various friends and partners he would like to invite, about the type of parties they had at houses such as these, about the fully-equipped playroom that's included...

I was sold. Immediately. "*Yes!*" I squealed in an unnecessary voice note that definitely could've been a text.

Dante was nervously excited for our reception party—he had told me as much before—but I was just excited.

The consent forms were detailed. We all knew what was on the table, the rules of engagement. The game had been set; all that was left was to play it.

"Do we even know what we're getting into?" Dante asks, looking around suspiciously. "I think I need to go to the bathroom again."

"Go. I'll be by Alessio." I give him a quick kiss, smacking his bum as he walks away.

I find Alessio by the bar and he leads me to the couches outside on the patio to enjoy the incredible Vegas sunset as it tints the sky in pinks and oranges—for once, not from a penthouse balcony.

"Your glass is empty, *cara*, let's fix that." He takes a swig from my glass, finishing it himself, before grabbing another one from a floating tray that appears with the mere click of his fingers.

"Are you trying to get me drunk so you can take advantage of me?" I trace my fingers over his crotch, following the outline of his cock.

Alessio laughs, reaching over for a kiss. "We both know I don't need to get you drunk for that."

"That's true. Though you have to be careful, I'm Missus Dante Fera now...My husband might get jealous." *My husband.* I've never had a husband before. The thought is amusing. It all still feels so new.

The Joker smirks. "I still can't believe you took his surname. So much for feminism."

"Why be another Matthews when you can be Queen of the Fera empire?" I wink at him, my hand still resting on his crotch. "This is my destiny."

"Fair point, dearest Danica, fair point. Good catch, hey?"

"The best," I beam, looking at the new ring on my finger. "Are you jealous?"

"Oh no, I'm not about jealousy. I have the best deal; I still get to have you both."

"And you don't want someone of your own, just yours?" Strangely enough, we've never had this conversation before. Our time together is always so limited, so rushed, so feverish with need and lust.

"You know I'm a relationship anarchist; things like that don't appeal to me. I need my freedom. The mere thought of co-dependence is enough to give me grey hair." Alessio laughs.

"So you just fuck everyone all over?"

"Sometimes. But it doesn't take away anything from my other intimate relationships. Many of them are here today. The beautiful misfits. There is a lot to say for platonic love, you know. I never understood what was so wrong about fucking your friends."

"I would need friends before I could fuck them." I laugh despite the sting of the truth. Sometimes, I did miss having other people around. But not the friends I used to have; they were all two-faced vain bitches who chose my ex's side.

"Well, *cara*," Alessio's eyes sparkle with barely contained excitement, "there's no time like the present. My crew is dying to meet you properly." His fingers brush my arm, gentle and reassuring. "We may not pick our blood, but that doesn't mean we can't have family."

"I like that." I take a sip of champagne, letting the bubbles dance on my tongue. "People always did get that blood is thicker than water saying wrong."

"Well, they just left out the second part, completely giving it the opposite meaning." His smile is knowing, intimate.

"Found family, hmm." I fidget with the leather strap on my bodice. "I hope they like me..."

"Who wouldn't like you, dearest Danica? You are a Queen! I—"

A familiar voice cuts through the air, and I snap my head around. "There she is, the woman of the hour!"

My heart skips as I turn to see Adira gliding toward us, her presence commanding attention like gravity itself.

Her blue dress ripples like liquid gold in the fading light, the fabric clinging to every curve before flowing to the floor.

My breath catches at the sight of her generous cleavage, memories flooding back—the taste of her skin, the softness of her breasts against my lips.

"Adira!" The name bursts from my lips as I practically leap from my seat. She catches me in an embrace that smells of sun-ripened peaches and something darker, more primal—a scent that ignites a familiar heat low in my belly. Her lips find mine in a brief but electric kiss.

"Congratulations, honey." Her words brush against my skin like velvet.

"Thank you so much for coming."

"I wouldn't miss it for the world." She pulls back slightly, her eyes dancing. "Plus, I wanted you to meet my Rani." Adira gestures to her partner behind her.

The 30-something woman who steps forward is all sharp angles and quiet power. Her black suit jacket hangs open, revealing a leather bra that catches the light like obsidian. The severe cut of her fade haircut emphasizes her striking features—high cheekbones, angular jaw, dark eyes that seem to see right through you. Silver hoops climb her ears like a constellation.

"Nice to meet you." I pull her into a hug, feeling the cool press of her jacket buttons against my chest.

"Congratulations." Rani's voice is slow and deliberate. There's an energy about her that makes the air feel charged, like the moment before a storm breaks.

Through the windows, the last traces of purple surrender to the Vegas night, city lights beginning to sparkle like earthbound stars. The conversation flows around us like wine, easy and warm, until Adira's hand finds mine. Her touch sends electricity racing up my arm.

"You look incredible," she murmurs, and despite everything—despite being a newly crowned Queen of the underworld—I feel my cheeks flush.

"Thank you."

"May I kiss the bride?" Adira's eyes hold a promise that makes my pulse quicken.

"You didn't ask before..."

"That wasn't a kiss." She winks, and suddenly, the room narrows to just us, the sounds of the party fading to a distant hum.

I manage a nod, and then she's drawing me in. Her lips part mine with practiced skill, tasting of champagne and steamy memories. I surrender to the kiss, to the familiar perfume of peaches and desire, to the way the world seems to tilt on its axis when Adira kisses me like this.

For a suspended moment, I am weightless, caught between past and present, between what was and what will be. And somehow, impossibly, it all feels right.

Oh god, I'm wet already.

Chapter Twenty-Three

SUNDOWN

(Dante)

I don't know how it goes from a *normal* wedding reception to a sex party, but the change is sudden. As soon as darkness ascends outside, the music's volume goes up and the inhibitions down.

The lights have been dimmed, and the entire vibe is different now, increasingly relaxed by a free-for-all alcohol selection and platters of designer drugs floating around.

Oh god, I really need a release.

My dick has already been painfully hard so many times today. Danica always has that effect on me, Alessio too. But it wasn't just their proximity that sent my blood rushing to my groin. No, it was the mere thought of tonight's pleasure *menu*, the scene that's been unfolding since we arrived at this house with the sandy walls and out-of-place palm trees in the driveway.

Tonight will be an amalgamation of Danica and my fantasies, a hedonistic buffet brought to life by Alessio and a selection of willing (consenting) play partners.

At first, I wasn't sure how to voice my desires, but many (many) conversations later, we found the perfect way to celebrate our union.

It was Danica's idea to invite Adira and Rani. I didn't think they would accept. I know Rani could be quite uptight sometimes. We go way back, once even dueled over the same woman. Rani won, of course. I am no match for her.

Suddenly, the music cuts.

"Friends, lovers, and lovers-to-be, welcome." It is Alessio's voice, flowing from the overhead speakers like a Lord beckoning us to him in the lobby where he towers seven marble steps above us.

Like zombies drawn to fresh meat, we move toward him, Danica's warm hand wrapped in mine. I keep looking at her, at that insanely beautiful face, those playful eyes, and I can't believe she's mine, on paper too—Missus Fera.

"I call our newlyweds to the front; it's time to cut the cake," Alessio announces, and Danica drags me with her through the crowd of applauding strangers who are slowly becoming familiars...

It is a mix of people so unique that they look like they could only have met on the internet. Such beautiful people, so kind, so sexual. Alessio sure did collect a certain kind of magical creature. Only he could.

I completely forgot about the cake-cutting and all the attention is quite overwhelming as Danica takes the giant sword to the tiered cake. The image is absurd, and I can't help but laugh; it's perfect. Of course, my Queen would forego a basic knife and bring out an actual sword.

Danica messily cuts the cake, and I join the others in a cheer—despite the mouthful of rich chocolate cake my wife stuffs in my face with a triumphant laugh.

She kisses me deeply, stealing a bite of chocolate from my mouth before I can swallow it all down. And then she licks the icing from my chin in a way that makes every hair on my body stand to attention.

Fuck, I'm so horny.

"Well, before this goes any further..." Alessio picks up the mic again. "Because I'm sure I'm not the only one who's noticed the groom's raging erection," he teases, sending laughter through the room as my cheeks flush in humiliation. We both know I love it. Danica knows too. She pats my crotch like I'm just a silly puppy as everyone cheers. *Down, Sonja!*

"My darlings, I cannot tell you how happy I am to celebrate the union of these two incredible humans—finally." People laugh knowingly, us included, and Alessio pauses a perfect length of time before continuing.

"Dante, my love, after all those years. The fact that we finally found one another can only be serendipitous. And the fact that you found Danica, well, that was serendipitous *and* oh-so fortuitous. You better look after her."

Danica firms her hand in mine, resting her head against my shoulder as we listen to Alessio's speech on love and lust, on the beauty of bodies and consent, the nature of boundaries and communication. It's a poetic journey that warms my heart and raises my cock at the same time. Such a fucking charming man—always so smooth, so eloquent.

"A toast, my gorgeous friends. To Danica and Dante, our guests of honor," he concludes, "Let's show them a good time." Alessio raises his glass, and out of nowhere, flutes of champagne appear on floating trays. "Let's feast!"

He's definitely not talking about actual food.

Everyone knows that.

Why am I so nervous?

I bring Danica's fingers to my lips, kissing them gently as I watch the bodies around us move.

Even the staff have gotten the memo, it seems.

The waiters are no longer in uniform, no, they're wearing only thongs—regardless of what genitals they've been assigned or chosen, chests exposed in the cool evening breeze.

Grabbing two flutes from a tray, I fall into Danica's dark eyes as we bring our glasses together, chasing my drink with a sparkling kiss afterward.

Alessio snaps his fingers in a single command in the direction of the person in charge of the sound, the guy who's been watching like a hawk, waiting for that one signal.

The music comes back on. Louder than before. The beat more urgent. More sensual.

It's time!

Danica holds my forehead against hers with both hands as people around us start to make out and grind against each other in the pulsing beat raining down from above. I have my arm around her, and we slowly sway, my erection trapped between us, her voice warm on my skin.

"Are you ready for our banquet, my darling husband?" Danica whispers, and a chill runs through me like lightning. My cock jumps. *Fucking Sonja.*

"I'm ready." *I think.*

Danica kisses the corners of my eyes, my nose, before leaning into my ear: "Let's go make some friends, *Tesoro.*" She pronounces the Italian word flawlessly.

"Yes, Ma'am."

Danica holds me close as the song finishes, every friction of her moving body making my cock ache even more.

"May I have this dance?" Adira interrupts, and I hand over my bride with a kiss to them both.

Alessio doesn't let the opportunity pass him by, grabbing my hand as soon as my wife lets me go and forcing me to dance with him. The one time he knows I can't say no. Not at my own wedding. "Aha, now you're mine."

"You know I hate dancing," I say with fake grumpiness as I let myself be steered through the bodies in various stages of undress.

This feels like a wet dream and I still can't believe it's actually happening—only with a wife, a Domme, a Queen, like Danica.

But we didn't plan this alone, or out of the blue, oh no, Alessio has been tempting us with the pleasures of his companions for a long time now.

I was hesitant before. But now I'm ready.

"Well, if you don't want to dance, let's go mingle then." And just like that, Alessio drops out of tune with the music, leading me to the bar on the veranda instead.

I'm relieved to be excused from the dancefloor. The fresh air is a welcome change too.

"Two whiskeys," he orders.

"Make that four."

I turn around to two identical images of pure health.

"Ah, my babies." Alessio kisses each twin in turn, with open mouths and tongues, before turning to me. "Meet the man of the hour, Dante." No surname. No title. Just Dante. It feels good. Freeing.

"We've heard so much about you," the one says. I don't know which one; they look the same to me with their blonde fringes and beefy muscles poking out of identical neon green crop tops.

Scanning them, I can't help but run my eyes over their fit physique. Oh, to be that young again.

"This is Ciaran. This is Jo," Alessio adds without giving any indication of who is who, leaving the smiling boys almost interchangeable.

"Nice to meet you," I say almost formally. "Thank you for coming to my wedding?" We laugh awkwardly. It is quite a bizarre situation if you think about it—our rent-a-crowd cum rent-an-orgy. But they are so much more than that; they are Alessio's people, and I have every faith in this sensual Joker's taste in humans.

We take our whiskeys and toast to my big day, the space between the twins and us diminishing with every sip until Cieran-or-Jo looks at Alessio and me through hooded eyes and says: "If you'd follow us upstairs, we can give you your *gifts*."

I want to protest that we said no gifts, but one look at the grin on Alessio's face makes me realize that that wasn't the *gifts* these two boys had in mind, oh no.

And so it begins...

CHAPTER TWENTY-FOUR

ASK NICELY

(DANICA)

Adira holds me closer as we navigate the crowded dance floor, other bodies moving around us like waves around a rock. The air is thick with perfume and promise, with the kind of freedom that only comes when everyone present understands the beauty of unconventional love.

"Congratulations, Missus Fera," the Goddess in blue tells me as she steers me through a waltz despite the EDM pulsing from the speakers, the furthest thing from waltz music. "You deserve all the happiness."

"Thank you." I smile, content, as I rest my head on her shoulder. "And you. I hope Rani treats you well."

"Oh, the best. Two Dommes together create a beautiful chaos. But I wouldn't want it any other way." Her lips brush my temple as she smiles. "She's probably going to beat the shit out of your husband at some point tonight."

"Such a lucky boy. He'd be into it, I'm sure." Our laughter mingles with the music as we spin.

Movement catches my eye—Dante and Alessio ascending the grand staircase, followed by twin blonds who look like they stepped out of a candy rave fantasy. My heart swells seeing them together, seeing how far we've all come from rigid rules and hidden desires.

Halfway up, Dante turns back, his eyes finding mine unerringly across the space between us. From afar, I give him a simple thumbs up, encouraging whatever he is about to get into. I know he's in good hands with Alessio.

It has been so incredible to watch him make peace with his sexuality, his masculinity, his desires. The Don who once hid every softness now openly embracing all parts of himself.

Adira turns to follow my gaze, smiling at the foursome heading upstairs.

"Seems like he's found some entertainment. Do you want to join them?" she asks, her brown almond-shaped eyes peering deep into mine, a playful smile curving the corners of those full, plump lips painted in nude-colored lipstick.

"No, thank you. I'm sure they'll be fine. Alessio is good with taking the lead. Besides—" I stop myself from finishing the sentence, averting my gaze to hide the blush creeping up my cheeks.

The mere thought of the words I can't form out loud is enough to make the lust coil at my center.

Adira tilts my chin towards her with a single finger, forcing my gaze back on her. Her voice is commanding, authoritative, but in a quietly powerful way—soft but stern. I've forgotten what influence that voice has over me. "Tell me," she demands, and I know I will give her whatever she asks; we both know. "Besides..?" she starts my sentence again where I left off.

"Besides..." I hesitate, searching her smoldering eyes. "Besides, I don't want to leave here," I finish the sentence I never planned on finishing.

"Why?" Adira's gaze is piercing, amused. I know she knows what I'm trying to say, but just as I torture Dante, she is giving me a taste of my own medicine, forcing me to speak my words.

"Because you're here." My cheeks are burning, but I boldly keep her gaze.

"And?" She arches a single, perfectly-plucked eyebrow.

"And...I want you," I exhale in almost a whisper, barely audible. The mischievous smile on Adira's face makes it very clear that she heard.

"I see..." She pulls me closer to her until our bodies are pressed into one another like a mold, my curves yielding against hers. If I had a cock, I know she'd be able to feel my hardness trapped between our stomachs right now. But the only tell of my incredible arousal is how hard my nipples have become.

Adira's got a few inches on me, height wise, but my wedding heels narrow the gap, bringing me almost eye-level with the most enigmatic woman I've ever known.

I gasp, holding my breath as she seductively runs her fingers over my chest, stroking my breasts over the layers of material I wish weren't there.

My eyes are glued on her lips, the thin layer of sweat forming above them in that little hollow space. *Oh god, I want to kiss her so badly!*

Softly, I whimper as I come undone in her arms.

The student and the Master.

Adira is who I channel when I try to project my inner Goddess. She's the one who inspires my inner Domme. Even all these years after she trained me. Her effect on me is no weaker than it was the first time I watched her make a sub beg.

But before I can melt into a puddle of humiliation and need, Adira spins me in tune with the beat, catching me again—so fast that the world swirls.

My breath quickens as we just stand there, holding each other in the middle of the dancefloor, no longer dancing.

I know Adira is waiting for me to speak.

But I can't find the words I know I should say, want to say.

"We should get some fresh air. Care to join me?" I ask instead.

I know I don't need this charade but I keep it up, nonetheless. If I asked her to take me right here, in the middle of the crowd of sweaty, swaying bodies, she would. But I don't ask, not yet.

Adira nods and follows me beyond the veranda into the garden. Two rows of fairy lights line our path, making me feel like a Fae Queen.

The evening breeze is slight but a relief after the sweaty dancefloor. It's almost cool, but I feel nothing but anticipation.

At the bottom of the steps, there is a bench in the most perfect place. Surrounded by greenery, vines sneak up a metal arch to create a secret cove around the bench.

I have Adira alone finally, or perhaps she has me alone.

"Thank you." My voice is soft as I regard the Goddess in blue through hooded eyes.

"For?" She rolls the last R off her tongue slowly, seductively.

I'm trapping myself further in her web with every inch of distance I close between our faces until my lips are almost touching hers.

"For coming," I whisper, staring at her lips.

"Oh, this isn't about me coming—that's the bride's job." Adira gives me a wink and we both burst out laughing, cutting the tension.

"Wow, what a dad joke."

"No regrets," she says before putting a hand behind my head and closing the final distance, swallowing any reply I might have as she slides her tongue over mine—a breathless kiss filled with desire.

I gasp, and a soft whine escapes my lips.

Desperate, the kiss intensifies as I turn my body to hers, my hands roaming over her chest.

My wetness pools under my dress, and I clench my thighs. I wish I didn't have all this material between us.

Adira releases my lips to take her kisses elsewhere, exploring my face, my neck, my exposed collarbone.

She whispers filthy, sweet nothings into my ear as her tongue darts over the shell of my sensitive lobe.

Oh god, my ears have always been such an erogenous zone for me, almost as much as my sensitive breasts. Hard like candy, my nipples perk up fully, my breath hitching.

Adira's kisses trail down my neck, following the dress's neckline as she kisses my skin, leaving behind a pathway of goosebumps. I don't dare speak. Don't dare move.

Slowly, delicately, Adira pulls the neckline of my dress to the side, briefly flicking her tongue over my nipple before gripping it between her teeth, biting down ever so softly, just enough to make me whimper in her arms.

"Such a good little girl, aren't we?" Adira asks, and I know I want nothing more than to please this great Goddess, the one who knows all my buttons, who has seen my kinks written black on white because she was there when Dante and I negotiated them. She knows; she remembers.

"Whatever you want me to be," I hum the words softly. Every cell in my body is focused on Adira's lips on my nipple, her teeth, her tongue.

I can no longer form any proper sentences.

My body knows only lust in this moment. Lust for what I've wanted for so long. Since the moment I first saw Adira perform in that sex club three years ago. Before she was even my teacher, my guide—a muse so alluring, so magnificent.

I would throw myself to the floor to worship at her feet if I could so much as will a single muscle to move right now.

Instead, my body is dancing to the tune of Adira's dexterous fingers as she draws little sounds from my lips while bestowing a cocktail of pleasure and pain onto my needy flesh.

Too soon, she pulls away, and I instantly miss her lips on my skin.

"Sit back, honey," Adira instructs, and I obey like a Bene Gesserit has commanded it, leaning my body against hers on the broad bench, grateful for the support of the wooden slatted backrest.

Adira shifts slightly, putting her leg up on the bench. She pulls my knee up as well, parting my thighs where an ocean of black material pools between my legs.

Big-spooning me from behind, I fit into her perfectly as we reposition ourselves sideways on the bench.

I lean my head back, resting it on her shoulder.

A sigh of relief as the familiar fingers return to my chest, distributing the attention to the other breast as well.

"Pull your dress up for me, honey," Adira whispers in my neck, licking me in a single broad stroke.

The evening breeze feels extra cool against that spot, refreshed by her saliva.

I do as she says, needing both hands to part the layers.

Not far behind us, the house continues buzzing with beats and shadowy bodies dancing and swaying.

I hope Dante was also getting what he needs upstairs somewhere.

I can spare only a quick thought for my husband and his activities. As soon as Adira snaps the elastic of my panties against my stomach, I'm here. Fully present. All hers.

"Is someone wet down here?" She lightly taps my pussy over my underwear like she's petting it.

"So wet," I rasp, trying to move closer to her hand.

"Let's see..."

My breath stops doing the one thing it's supposed to do as Adira's fingers part my panties to slip underneath, snaking down to my clit. Two fingers. They part my lips in a V, snugly sliding down on either side of my sensitive bud.

I fall apart as Adira rubs my clit in little circles, never touching it directly, head-on, but always the pressure, the pressure building. *Oh god!*

Her fingers slide further down, and I gasp, perhaps in disappointment of missing her touch, perhaps in relief of having a moment of reprieve before I come completely undone.

She pushes her fingers down, lower, until they reach my entrance...and then up again. Her movements are graceful, perfectly delicate yet powerful at the same time—a fine art.

"Just as I thought. Dripping!" Adira shoves her fingers into my mouth, and I suck my lust off her digits.

"Hmm," I mumble over her fingers, trying to tell her how it's all her fault but not succeeding in anything other than making her fingers even wetter. Drool runs down my cheek, but I don't care.

"Don't speak. Don't think. Just listen to my voice. You're safe." I know every word is true.

Even if I wanted to speak, I couldn't, no, Adira reduces me to an unorchestrated symphony of moans and groans, small gasps that turn into big ones, until I'm panting like a rabid dog, delirious with need.

First one finger, then another, she plunges into me with ease, lubricated by my desire for her.

At any moment, someone could walk out and see us in the garden's shadows. The bride getting fingered on a bench, her thighs spread wide, head thrown back.

But I don't care.

The thought of being caught makes my little exhibitionist spirit happy, even hornier.

Without bothering to be quiet, I rock my hips, shoving myself onto Adira's fingers again and again, faster, even faster still as I moan for her.

I float away to another plane until my body starts to stiffen, my eyes mere moments from rolling back in my head with pleasure, the tingles of pre-orgasm already starting to build towards a spike.

"Do you have permission, girl?" Adira asks, her fingers slowing their pace.

Almost frantically, I move my hips, trying to compensate for the reduced pressure of her fingers. *Fuck!*

"Please. I'm close!" I moan, too needy to appreciate the fact that I am finally getting some of my own medicine.

I loved making Dante beg. But now I am the one begging, close to tears, teetering on the brink of the perfect orgasm.

"Ask nicely." Adira pulls away to hold me against her with both hands. Hands I wish she'd use to touch my needy parts instead.

"Please, Goddess Adira, please let me come." My voice is small, submissive. Only for Adira.

"Hmm...only because it's your wedding day," she says as she lowers a hand between my thighs again. "Come for me, Missus Fera. You have permission." With each word, she pushes deeper inside me, deeper and deeper, until I let out a loud howl, tumbling over the edge without so much as an ounce of shame.

"I'm coming!" I cry, my body shaking to its own accord as ripples of pleasure wash over me, crashing and crashing over my skin, my insides, everything.

The world blurs around me, my eyes closed. The only thing I can hold onto is Adira's arms around me, keeping me safe as I ride out the most spectacular orgasm bathed in her peach scent. Everything tingles. I swear I see actual sparks behind my closed eyelids. The warmth floods my body, consuming me.

When it's all over, Adira pulls me into a tender kiss while my heart pounds in my chest like it has zero intention of ever returning to its usual base rhythm.

"You did so well for me," she coos as she licks her sticky fingers clean like she's just had a delectable meal. "Such a good little dirty girl."

Oh god.

CHAPTER TWENTY-FIVE

DOUBLE DELIGHT

(DANTE)

*J*ust *act cool, Dante. You're fine.* I try to talk down my racing heart as my eyes dart around the room.

"Surely they're too young?" I whisper hurriedly at Alessio, my eyes locked on the pair of dancing brothers passing the nearly empty bottle of whiskey between them. Their matching crop tops lie discarded on the floor of the upstairs bedroom we found unlocked not too long ago.

Alessio regards the twins momentarily before returning his attention to me, shifting even closer on the mustard-colored velvet couch. "You need to work on your definition of *young*." He smirks and reaches for my chin, pulling me in for a kiss, gently biting my bottom lip when he pulls away.

"They're at least half our age, Alessio. You're not as young as you think you are," I retort as I playfully shove him away from

263

me. But he just pulls me closer, trapping me in his arms, his familiar scent putting me at ease.

"Darling, they're 32, way older than your wife. So hush now and enjoy your wedding gift," Alessio scolds in a mock tone.

The word *wife* rolls around in my mind like an unfamiliar wine on my tongue. Even now, hours after the ceremony, it feels surreal. I have a *wife* again.

Except this is nothing like the first time.

Standing here in this extravagant room, watching the city lights twinkle beyond the windows, I can hardly believe this is my life. That I'm here. About to do...I don't know what.

For so long, I'd convinced myself that men like me weren't destined for love—we had empires to build, enemies to watch, promises to keep.

After losing Alessio the first time, I buried myself in work, trying to figure out how to keep the family afloat after my father died. It consumed my every waking hour.

Then Elena came along—a brief flicker of light in the darkness. For a moment, I almost thought I could be happy.

When she died, when I couldn't save her or our unborn child, I built walls so high that I thought no one would ever scale them.

For more than a decade, that worked just fine.

But then Danica came along.

She didn't scale the walls—she walked right through them like they were made of smoke.

And now I'm here, on a couch with Alessio, contemplating the virility of the half-naked twins dancing sluttily before us.

"You lucky, lucky man," Alessio murmurs like he can read my mind, his voice carrying that familiar warmth that still makes my chest tight like it did when we were three decades younger.

His eyes drift to where the twins are swaying like very limber reeds, their movements fluid and graceful. "Most wives wouldn't trust their new grooms with me, let alone with my entire crew."

One of the twins—Cieran or Jo, I still can't tell them apart—blows a playful kiss in our direction. My stomach tightens with an uncomfortable mix of attraction and uncertainty.

"I suppose not. Danica was even more excited than I was, though." We share a knowing laugh.

"Come," Alessio says, "let's join them. I'm getting thirsty." He moves with that casual grace I've always envied, sliding between the pair to grab the bottle of whiskey. He takes a big swig before offering it to me.

I accept it dutifully, letting the liquor burn away some of my hesitation.

The music from downstairs thrums through the floorboards, a steady bass line that matches my pulse.

One of the twins gravitates toward Alessio, their bodies finding a natural rhythm together.

As Ciaran-or-Jo grinds up against Alessio, he locks his wrists around the much taller Joker's neck, pulling him in for a slow kiss that builds into something fervent.

Watching them, I stand frozen, the empty bottle dangling from my fingers. This is Alessio's world—all fluid boundaries and easy affection. Even after everything we've shared, I still feel like an outsider here, caught between who I was raised to be and who I might become.

Stop overthinking it, Dante!

The music downstairs changes, something slower now, more intimate. I sit down on the couch again, close my eyes for a moment, feeling the vibrations through my feet, trying to find my place in this strange new world.

When I open my eyes again, the remaining blond is staring at me, his smile gentle but suggestive. In his eyes, I see an irresistible invitation.

"Don't even think about it. I don't dance," I inform the pretty boy as he approaches, feeling incredibly awkward, shifting on the couch as I clench my fists to hide my restless hands.

"We don't have to dance," the young gym-bunny whispers, reaching for my hand to drag me off the couch. I let him. Don't push him away even as he closes the distance between us, looking up at me with those needy eyes, pouting lustfully.

Frozen, I hold my breath as I regard the shirtless figure before me, perfect, like he was sculpted by the gods.

I'm not sure what to say or even what to do.

This is not the kind of situation I've ever trained for.

Alessio is the only man I've ever done anything with.

What was this kid expecting of me?

Man, not kid, I correct myself.

He does look way younger than 32, though.

There is no denying he is fit—maintaining those muscles must take so much work.

Cieran-or-Jo takes my silence for consent and puts his hand on my chest, forging our bodies together.

His cock is hard, unmistakably so—it presses against my own, stirring the desire that's been bubbling under my skin.

The blond notices me noticing and grins. "Hmm...You're quite hard yourself."

It's a fact.

I feel like shrugging but manage to restrain myself. How am I supposed to be sexy right now? What does that even mean?

Luckily, Cieran (he only tells me later, when they leave) isn't one for awkwardness. The beautiful boy with the shining light blue eyes leads me back to the couch, pushing me down with the slightest guidance.

"Let me dance for you then." He doesn't wait for an answer before starting to sway his hips provocatively, touching himself all over as he performs for me.

The movements are elegant, trained; I can't take my eyes off him.

"Talented, aren't they?" Alessio plonks down next to me again, his shirt unbuttoned and flailing open. He doesn't seem to notice.

Jo joins his brother to put on a choreographed strip tease that looks like something Danica might show me on a social media video.

For a minute, I can tell the boys apart by their underwear—black for Jo, navy blue for Cieran.

I gasp.

But it's not the strip tease that instantly makes my pulse race to dangerous levels; no, it's Alessio sliding down my zipper and pulling out my cock, stroking it almost absentmindedly as he watches the performance.

My natural instinct is to panic. My cock is out in front of strangers!

But Alessio's dexterous, long fingers quickly command my full attention, massaging the nervousness from my hard flesh as I feel my body relax into the couch, my shoulders slumping.

Without having to look, I reach over and return the favor, feeling my way to that familiar thick dick I know every inch of.

Suddenly, it is no longer just the twins putting on the show; they are getting a performance of their own with the Dons on the couch, moaning and touching, gasping and whispering.

Mister Blue Underwear strips fully naked first, his brother allowing him the stage before dropping his black pair to the floor as well, kicking it out of sight.

The pair of nearly identical cocks are adequately sized and uncut—more detail than that, I don't know what to observe.

Those muscular asses, though, I am unable to take my eyes off them, fully mesmerized.

Not nearly as mesmerized as Cieran, who forgets all about dancing and returns to me with his eyes glued on my cock between Alessio's fingers.

"Oh god, you're so *big*," he whispers as he kneels before me.

"I'm sure you've seen way bigger," I try to dismiss him, but he has no intention of being dismissed.

The naked boy boldly pushes my thighs apart, leaning down to get a closer view.

Alessio winks at him. "It tastes great too."

The blond looks at me with feral desire in his dilated eyes, virtually drooling before me. "May I?"

I look at Alessio for help, but that's not what he's there for; it's my decision. He just winks at me and pulls his hand away.

"All yours," I reply only after a brief hesitation.

I am *desperate* for a release. Alessio's fault.

That, and I am curious to know how those whiskey lips would feel around my cock.

The mere thought sends a jolt down my spine. When he licks my shaft from end to tip, I gasp loudly, grabbing onto Alessio's hand for support to keep myself from toppling over the edge.

First just the tip, then all of me, Cieran swallows me whole, gagging, and then taking more. *Jesus!* How can anyone take that much?

Beside me, Alessio is receiving the same *gift*, as Jo kneels next to his brother on the luxurious charcoal carpet.

"Aren't they exquisite?" Alessio hums, stroking the kneeling Jo's hair as his blond head bobs up and down on the Joker's cock.

My only response is a mumbled grunt while I buck my hips toward the expert lips currently working me in a rhythm I've never experienced before.

Alessio pulls me in for a kiss, and I lose myself in his scent, his taste, devouring him in sloppy kisses as we swallow each other's moans, gasping through mixed breaths.

I hold his face to mine, close. There is no way I can last like this, but I don't have to. Danica has given me a free pass for tonight, permission to come as much as I want to, whenever I want to. She promised me that by the end of the night, I would beg for it to stop, but somehow, I couldn't imagine that situation. *Silly me.*

But the night is still young.

"I'm close." I pull away from Alessio's lips only long enough to warn the kneeling twin.

"Give me everything," Cieran whispers, much to my surprise, before going back down and sucking even harder, devouring my head like it was an ice cream moments from melting into the pavement on a hot summer's day.

"I can't hold it," I gasp, clutching at the couch for stability that doesn't come.

"Then don't," Alessio breathes in my ear, and I know I'm about to come undone. He takes my hand, holding it too tightly as we reach the pinnacle of our climaxes together, groans mixing with grunts as we let go and tumble off the edge.

Dio mio, it feels incredible!

The twins lap up every drop, drinking our cum until there's nothing left.

When they're done, the job completed satisfactorily, the pair join us on the couch. There's not enough space, but Jo happily takes a spot on Alessio's lap.

His brother forces my attention back to him, grabbing my chin to go in for a messy kiss before jumping up in search of more liquor.

I'm surprised to taste myself on Cieran's lips, though there is clearly no reason for surprise. It's just been so long since I tasted my orgasm from anyone except Danica or Alessio.

There is something about it that feels dirty, forbidden—even though I have full permission.

It makes my heart race and my spent cock perk up again.

I can't wait to tell Danica about the experience.

She would be proud of me...

As much fun as this is, I instantly miss her, the feeling of something being missing burning through me like an electrical fault.

I wonder what she's been up to.

Something vibrates next to me, and it takes my post-nut brain a few seconds to figure out it's my phone buzzing from where it had fallen into the side of the couch.

A single message pops up on the screen when I pick it up.

From Danica.

As if almost on cue.

Seems I'm not the only one having these thoughts.

[Meet me in the lobby bathroom, husband]

CHAPTER TWENTY-SIX

CHECKING IN

(DANICA)

T he click of the door makes my pulse jump.

Dante's relieved exhale echoes off marble walls as he finally finds the right bathroom—one of four in the oversized lobby.

"Moglie mia." (My wife.) His voice is rough velvet as he slides the lock home.

When he turns, his eyes find me perched on the counter between twin sinks, black lace spilling around me like a poisoned waterfall. The perfect updo Alessio's stylist crafted is decidedly less perfect now—Adira made sure of that—but my makeup has survived the night's adventures thus far.

I feel powerful.

Divine.

Fuck being a Goddess—I am a God.

Dante crosses to me in three long strides, and I reach for him, drawing him into the dark pool of my dress, my legs wrapping around his waist with practiced ease.

His mouth finds mine—tasting of whiskey and lust—and I kiss him like I'm trying to consume him.

When we finally part, I cup his face in both hands, forcing his eyes to meet mine. "Did you have fun, baby?"

Dante grins, those emerald pools sparkling in a way I've never seen before. "So much fun." He looks pleased. "And you, *Tesoro*? How's our good friend Adira?"

"She's highly *skilled* as always." I grin mischievously.

He licks his lips, need flashing in his eyes. "I wish I could have seen it."

"Is that so?" I raise an eyebrow.

"I'm hard just thinking about it. Feel."

I drop my hand to Dante's pants. The belt is already undone, his shirt untucked. With a single quick motion, I guide the zipper lower.

When I slip out his erect cock, I know he is telling the truth.

Dante hisses between his teeth as I wrap my fingers around his shaft, enjoying how it grows even harder in my hands.

"Very hard indeed. Tell me, little *Sonja*, did you have a good time too?" I laugh, squeezing the tip of his hardness.

"You crazy woman. You'll drive me mad." Dante gasps as I reach for his balls, rolling them gently in my palm, adding pressure in all the right places...pressing all the buttons to make my aroused sub even more desperate.

"I will spend the rest of my life driving you mad, dear Dante," I say against his neck. "That is a promise."

"Please," he moans and I swallow his pleas with my kisses, devouring his exclamations of need like they're rewards.

When I suddenly drop his cock, the great Don Fera complains bitterly, cursing under his breath in Italian. But I don't want him coming all over my hands, no , I want him inside me.

Burning for him, aching, I pull Dante's face to mine. "Fuck me, *Tesoro*," I whisper in his ear. "Fuck me as your *wife*." It feels like a lifetime has passed since I first dreamt of saying those words.

"Oh, *Dio mio*," is all Dante can muster as he hurriedly fights through my layers of dress to find my bare pussy, no underwear in sight. I enjoy the look of surprise on his face when he realizes my panties are gone.

"I'm ready, Don Fera. Give it to me quick and dirty," I shamelessly demand in hurried breaths as my pulse quickens.

Dante pulls me closer to the edge of the counter, his cock finding my entrance without much effort, like the opposite ends of two magnets hurling toward one another.

He hesitates for an instant, peering deep into my eyes.

"Do it!" I demand, holding onto his neck as my Dante obeys, plunging into me like he's about to split me apart.

"Oh, god!" It's my turn to come undone, for words to fail me.

How can it feel so good? *Fucking hell.*

Dante entering me is like coming home, so perfect, so complete.

Fighting my dress to get closer to him, I kiss his neck, his chin, every inch of his face I can find as he thrusts into me, his pants around his ankle, like I'm a runaway bride. Could it be any more perfect? Any more *us*?

Dante steadies me with one hand on my hip as the other finds my clit, dragging his thumb over my sensitive bud in a move that sends my knees jerking like I don't control them.

"Don't stop," I whisper in rapid breaths as Dante fucks me like he's trying to shatter my whole world.

Oh god, I am so wet. He drives even deeper, deeper still.

"Harder!" I command. I want it all.

I'm drowning in his kisses when Dante suddenly falters beneath me, breathlessly trying to warn me of his imminent release.

"Do it!"

Dante holds his rhythm over my clit as he continues to fuck me on the bathroom counter, keeping a punishing pace until I scream his name, digging my nails into his back. I see stars as the shock of the orgasm rips through my body, burning my skin with its release.

Seconds later, my husband comes inside me for the first time as my legally-wed spouse.

He thrusts a few more times before going still, but he doesn't pull out.

Despite my ragged breathing, I kiss him tenderly, holding him tight as our chests heave up and down together.

My *husband*. I can't believe it's finally real.

"I love you so much, *Donna* Fera," Dante whispers, trapping my gaze in his, showering me in sincerity, intensity.

"I love you so much, my darling." I kiss his forehead. "I want to be a good wife to you."

Dante smiles, momentarily putting his head on my chest, listening to my heart. "I couldn't have asked for better."

We hold each other for a few minutes until our breath slows and the goosebumps fade.

"Shall we get out of these clothes?" I finally break the silence.

"Is it time?" Dante looks up at me, his eyes peaceful, content, but fired up.

"Phase two. Are you ready, baby?" I stroke a stray lock of hair from his brow affectionately.

Dante bites his lip, but nods. "Nervous," he admits. "But I'm ready."

"Everyone has read the Ts & Cs, and you know you can stop at any time. Your safe word remains unchanged."

His cock is still inside me, but we talk like it isn't.

"I know. I want this. Thank you for being so open to it."

"My wedding present, from me to you. You know nothing makes me happier than bringing you pleasure. That look on your face..." I grin like a silly girl. It's true. I want to spend the rest of my life bringing that man pleasure. *My* man.

"I thank my lucky stars every day that I saved you that day at the restaurant." Dante smiles.

"You were the reason I needed saving, remember?"

Dante shakes his head. "I know, I know."

"Who would've thought we'd end up here, about to do something so...daring."

"*Dio mio*," Dante whines, but I don't give him time to overthink it.

"Let's get you out of these clothes. Strip!" I demand, my voice swelling with authority, an easy switch.

"Yes, Ma'am." Dante springs into action, holding my eyes as he slowly pulls out.

I gasp. The emptiness always takes some getting used to again.

Cum leaks onto the black fabrics of my wedding dress, staining it white.

It seems fitting. Perfect.

Under my watchful gaze, Dante cleans his dick over the sink and then drops his pants, finally stepping out of his underwear as well. The shirt goes next, until he's standing naked before me in only his socks and collar.

"Shoes back on."

He does as he is told, and it makes him look ridiculous. I love it!

"Now help me out of this, please." I ask nicely because why wouldn't I?

Dante helps me with the zip and finally, I'm free, the black, cum-stained garment dropping on the floor like a discarded pom-pom. Rather a cum-stained wedding dress than a blood-stained one.

"Thanks, darling." I hold out my arms to him, and Dante presses his tall body against me, crossing our hollows to touch as much skin as we can, desperate for one another.

There are no words to label the feeling of Dante holding me tightly in those muscular tattooed arms; it's somewhere between safe, home, and desire.

"Okay, I gotta pee," I break up the perfect moment, and we both laugh. "Get my bag, won't you?" I add as I sit down on one of the toilets without bothering to close the stall door.

My bag holds many wonders, including, but not limited to, a cock leash for Dante and a stunning black leather harness and lingerie combo for me.

Sheer to the point of see-through, only the tiniest triangle between my thighs is covered by the new outfit that slips on like it was made for my body, my nipples pink and hard behind the lacy black fabric.

Dante stares like he's never seen my bare skin before as I admire myself in the full mirror near the door.

"You look incredible," he rasps as I smile at our reflection.

Thank fuck rich people have mood lighting even in their bathrooms. I'm sure my ass would look lumpy under fluorescent lighting. But lighting is not on my list of concerns tonight—very few things are.

Even the ports have been pushed down to the back of my mind, the door locked for the night. *Later.*

If there's one thing I know how to do, it's how to compartmentalize. With a family like mine, it was the only way to survive.

Fuck that. I want to think about my family even less than I want to think about the ports.

Instead, I focus on the present, on my beautifully naked husband leaning against the wall.

"Thanks, darling." I grin. "You look ready to be used."

Grabbing the other goodies from the bag, I fasten the leash around Dante's balls, making sure it's on tight, before tugging him towards me. "Come here, Sonja."

Dante gasps, freezing beneath my grip.

Leaning in, I close my lips around his right nipple, enjoying how his body shivers, how his cock jumps when I take it in my hand. I don't stop. I suck until he's fully hard in my hand, until the outline of my lips is imprinted on his chest, a dark hickey marking his flesh.

"You are mine, Don Fera," I whisper, tugging on the leash and drawing a heavy moan from Dante's lips.

"Yes, Wife. Yours," Dante answers obediently as he turns to admire his new mark in the mirror.

"So handsome when you're being a good boy, aren't you?" I smack his hard cock with my backhand, and Dante bends over, a deep growl echoing off the bathroom walls even as fresh pre-cum glistens on his tip.

To have and to hold, in pain and pleasure.

It's time.

CHAPTER TWENTY-SEVEN

FREE

(DANTE)

My scantily clothed wife leads me to a private room down a hidden passage behind the kitchen, pulling me along firmly, dick first.

She knocks loudly before entering the unmarked door, tugging me along like a naughty puppy, dressed in nothing but my shoes.

It's more spacious inside than I expected. A fully kitted-out sex dungeon, stocked with even better equipped than our one at home. Hooks and whips and toys and cages—we are clearly in the right place.

The music from upstairs trickles down, softened but ever-present. It's not loud enough to drown out the sound of my pounding heartbeat, though.

Breathe, Dante.

Alessio is already there, shirtless on the couch, flute of champagne in hand. Beside him, Rani and Adira appear to be locked in an intense conversation, holding hands and whispering to each other.

All three look up as we enter, cheering and clapping as Danica parades me before them like I'm a show pony, my semi-hard cock on a leash.

It's a bit awkward, for me at least, but I give myself over to Danica's direction, letting her lead me.

There is nobody I trust more in the world.

Nobody I trust more to give me exactly what I need.

What I crave deep down.

So deep down that I've never dared voice it until recently.

The need to be Don Fera falls away with each step through that doorway.

Here, surrounded by the people I trust most in this world, I don't have to be strong.

Don't have to make decisions.

Don't have to protect anyone.

I can just...be.

Just Dante.

Just a body.

A body with needs.

"Now, isn't that a beautiful sight," Adira remarks, clapping her hands together enthusiastically as we draw closer. "May I?" she asks Danica, reaching for the leash as my wife nods.

When she gets up from the couch, my jaw nearly drops to the floor; Adira is dressed in a deep-red baby doll lingerie dress that barely covers her ass as it fans out over her curves in layers of sheer lace. Her voluptuous breasts spill over the top, barely contained by the flimsy fabric. *Oh god, I just want to touch her.*

Wordlessly, my bride hands me over like I'm a real pet, kissing Adira with such passion that you'd think they haven't seen each other in years instead of just minutes.

And I? I just stand there like a horny spectator. Mesmerized. I am unable to tear my eyes away from the way their bodies respond to each other. Like long-lost lovers finally found.

With a final "be good," Danica leaves me to my desires, dropping down beside Alessio on the couch to accept a glass of champagne. Instantly, Don Santoro's hands are all over my bride, tracing the thin fabric of her new lingerie, exploring the textures, pinching her scantily-covered nipples.

My semi-erection is no longer so *semi,* growing along with my humiliation as Adira tugs me, dick first, to where Rani has gotten up to run her fingers over the various devices of pain and pleasure mounted on the walls, taking stock.

Adira holds my leash taut, reaching up to kiss her partner. "Look what I've brought you, my love."

"Ah, a willing slave," Rani remarks as she takes a whip from the wall—a thick braided nylon bullwhip that uncoils like a long snake.

Dressed in a skintight PVC black body suit and tall-as-fuck heels, Rani looks like a Dominatrix fantasy in her second outfit for the night. It fits her so well. I can't stop thinking about how she got into that suit in the first place. It looks impossibly tight.

But I don't have much time for thoughts. Rani unrolls the whip, cracking it expertly, loudly, and I jump involuntarily. And so does my cock.

"See for yourself. He bruises so beautifully." Adira runs her long fingernails over my bare chest, teasing me, lingering over my new hickey. It's been a while since we played together, not since she spent all those days at the mansion, training Danica in the basics of Domme-life with me as the willing guinea pig. But my body still remembers her touch—soft yet firm at the same time.

Rani, however, we've never played together. But her reputation precedes her. She's considered one of the best in the city in all matters pain-related. A shiver runs up my spine at the mere thought.

"And his Mistress consents?" Rani looks over to Danica on the couch beside Alessio, their eyes firmly glued to me as they playfully grope each other. I can't help but notice his open zip, that thick cock wrapped in Danica's palm while they watch the two Dommes circle me like prey.

My wife nods, smiling mischievously as she gives the duo the okay.

"Please go ahead. I'm sure he's looking forward to it," Danica responds before turning to me. "You good, *Tesoro*?"

I nod enthusiastically. "Yes, Ma'am." Nervous as hell, but good.

"Well, in that case, won't you help me get him ready?" Rani asks Adira, and the Dommes make quick work of tying my wrists to a hook above my head.

"Be a good boy now. Tap out when it gets too much, okay?" It's Adira, being so sweet, kissing my lips softly before pulling the satin blindfold over my eyes. The world goes dark.

This is it.

My gift.

Oh, Dio mio, I'm nervous.

We've been discussing a free-use scene for a long time, but finding the right partners seemed like an impossible task.

But today, right now, it is time.

Everything has been planned.

I can't believe this is really happening.

Tied to the ceiling, I'm at the mercy of the four of them. Sure, I have my safe word, I always do, and they have full consent, but it doesn't make the anticipation any less nerve-wracking.

I feel so exposed, standing before them, tied up and cock out.

Yet it's exhilarating.

Anything could happen.

Well, *almost* anything.

Submission settles into my bones like a familiar companion. I clear my mind. Let go. "Yes, Miss."

"Mistress," Rani corrects me, voice stern, harsh.

"Yes, *Mistress*."

I shiver as the untangled whip is dangled over my shoulder, tickling my skin. The calm before the storm. But I'm ready.

"Take a deep breath," Rani instructs, her breath warm on my skin.

I do as I'm told, trying to brace for impact. But when you can't see what's coming, the anticipation reaches near-unbearable levels. My skin is tingling, and nobody has even touched me!

The sound reaches me a fraction of a second after the first lash lands on my ass with perfect precision.

I exhale all the air I've been holding, my lungs burning as much as my behind.

Fuck!

It stings like a motherfucker!

My skin is hot, almost burning, but still intact. Rani knows what she's doing.

"She can whip a fly off a glass without breaking the glass," Adira once bragged.

The second lash cracks through the air like thunder and lands across the back of my thighs, instantly setting my skin on fire.

Groaning like a caged beast, I pull on the restraints holding me, slumping against them as my knees weaken, threatening to fail me.

"Count with me," Rani demands, and I obediently croak out a "three" and a "four," each with diminishing strength.

My back feels warm, my ass aches...but my mind, my mind finally calms down as I sink into the familiar feeling of the pain, a singular thought that blacks out everything else, soothing the edges of my restlessness.

I exhale deeply, counting my way through ten out loud. Just as Danica trained me to do.

Lash 11 breaks the skin—I can feel it.

Oh god. The pain. It hurts so much. So much more than anything has hurt in a long time—physically, at least.

"Still no safe word?" Rani asks in a snarky tone. "You're a wild man."

My only response is an unintelligible grunt.

The whip moves but doesn't come down again.

"Shall we give him a bit of a pain break?" It's Danica. She sounds concerned, but she needn't be. I want to tell her, but I have no words. My brain is pure mush.

There are kissing sounds, but no more whip sounds. Danica's familiar hands feel so tender as her soft kisses pepper my burning skin, soothing the fire. Her scent makes me feel safe. Grounds me.

"You okay, baby?" she asks, kissing my neck.

"*Sì,*" I manage, forgetting the English word altogether.

I gasp as someone's lips close around the tip of my cock, licking me like a lollipop. It's Alessio. I would know that tongue anywhere.

A loud groan tears from my lips as he licks my shaft around the leash before carefully taking the leather harness off.

"We're going to ruin you, *amore mio,*" my first love promises before he swallows my entire dick in a move that makes my eyes roll back in my blindfolded skull.

"Careful, you know what that mouth does to him," Danica teases, flicking a finger at one of my nipples.

Much to my dismay, Alessio spits me out again, playfully slapping my ass before unhooking my wrists from the ceiling without untying them from each other. "You heard the Missus."

"Bring him here," Danica orders, and I'm led in the direction of what I assume is the bed. I only briefly saw it when we entered earlier—massive and on top of a cage. But we won't be using the cage tonight.

"Look how beautiful you are, so perfect, so good," Danica coos, bending me over the bed and spreading my whip-bruised ass cheeks apart before her. Before everyone.

The praise coats my skin in tingly feelings, and I sink deeper into the bed.

It feels nice to give my legs a break.

But I know it's no time for resting.

"I think it's time I fuck my husband, don't you?" my Queen asks, and a shudder of anticipation sneaks up my spine.

"*Per favore,*" a plea so soft, I'm sure she didn't hear, but Danica clearly did.

With familiar care, she slips a lubed finger into my hole, preparing me for the thick silicone strap-on I feel pressing against my thighs shortly after. She must have put it on during my whipping.

A second finger fills me, and then she pulls out quickly, smearing my entrance with even more lube.

My eyes are still blindfolded, heightening my other senses, especially touch. I feel every point of contact, every thrust inside me.

With difficulty, I focus on my breathing as my wife slowly pushes her cock inside me, fucking me for the first time since becoming legally hers.

Fucking me while the others watch.

Fucking me as I shamelessly come undone.

A loud moan echoes through the room, mine, as Danica stretches my ass around her.

So full, oh god. My hard cock presses uncomfortably into the bed under me, but I don't move—I'm not sure I even can.

"Such a pretty little slut, aren't we?" Danica whispers in my ear, fucking me into the bed, each thrust deeper, longer than the first.

I try my best not to clench, to think about the pleasure instead of the pain, but it's hard to focus on anything when every feeling seems to demand my attention simultaneously.

My mind is lost in sub-space somewhere when Danica suddenly pulls out, too quickly, leaving my head spinning and me empty.

Not for long.

"Your turn," she says to someone, tagging them in as she lies down beside me, stroking my cheek affectionately.

He doesn't have to speak for me to know it's Alessio taking over from Danica. I can smell his cologne, for one, but mostly, I know the shape of him, the feel of his cock inside me, thick and warm, perfect.

Alessio chuckles softly in my ear as he pushes himself inside me. "Congratulations on your marriage, Don Fera."

I'm still trying to get used to the discomfort when he pulls me off the bed, still inside me, holding me up with both arms as someone else slips a condom over my cock. I don't know who, not until Alessio pulls out and throws me onto the bed. *How is he this strong?*

Someone undoes the ties binding my wrists together, only to stretch my arms apart and secure me to the bed posts, spread to all four corners.

At first, I think it's Danica, but I quickly realize it must be Adira as someone else climbs onto the bed with me to massage my condom-covered cock.

Keeping me firmly in her grip, Adira guides me inside her.

Fuck! She feels amazing.

I can't move, can't do anything other than just lie there as Goddess Adira bounces up and down on my cock like she's riding a stallion through the mountains.

After this moment, it becomes hard to keep track of what happens when.

I lose myself time and time again.

In pleasure.

In pain.

In the pure bliss that comes from giving one's brain cells a rest.

The room is a mix of moans and groans and utterings of desire that have no name. I wish I could witness it. Wish I could see them all play together. But Danica will tell me every little detail later on.

Who knows how much time passes?

I hear Danica's cries of orgasm multiple times, but none by my doing.

My own cum lies smeared all over my body, over the sheets, the floor, as time and again they milk me dry to the point of agonizing overstimulation.

It's all a blur.

My senses are overwhelmed; it's impossible to tell where one climax begins and another one ends.

I know the nursing handjob is Adira, repositioning me and instructing me to suck on her full breasts while jerking me off with rapid movements.

I know Alessio came over my stomach at some point with a deep, throaty grunt.

That Danica spit on my hole before plunging into my ass again, my knees pressed up next to my ears...

Rani is nowhere to be found, though.

Not until someone undoes my wrists and drags me onto the floor by my ankles.

My legs don't remember how to do their job and I fall to the floor, bent over. Before I can move, my cock is trapped under the foot of a shoe.

A howl of pain rips through my body. *What the fuck?*

"Enough pleasure, I'd say." It's Rani. *Dio mio.*

"Finish him," Danica encourages, sounding far away.

Moments later, I feel the unmistakable sting of a cane on my bruised ass, and I cry out in agony. The cane always causes such destruction. Instantly.

Still bent over, I remain kneeling on the floor as Rani hits me again and again until I know I'm bleeding, the warm liquid running down to my thighs. I want her to simultaneously stop immediately and never stop at all.

It's everything I need. I feel free.

Sometime later, the cane-wielding Mistress grabs me by my collar, pulling me to my shaky knees.

I go where I'm guided, still blinded, in the dark.

"Well, well, well…" is all Rani says as she taps my hard cock with the cane.

I try to steady myself, but everything goes red and then black as soon as that cane touches my sensitive head.

The pain is excruciating!

Fuck!

Exhausted, circuits overflowing, I collapse on the floor in a puddle of blood and cum, content.

No more.

I can take no more.

The pain burns through my body without any sign of letting up, making me dizzy, woozy, as I trip out on endorphins.

Finally, I reach for my safe word, the only word I have left in my mind.

Danica stops the scene immediately, wrapping her arms around me as she lies down on the floor beside me. My ears tickle as she whispers proudly, "What a pretty mess you are."

The world shines in color behind my closed eyes. I have no words, just rapid, short breaths.

Bliss. Pure bliss.

CHAPTER TWENTY-EIGHT

AFTER CARE

(DANICA)

When his breathing finally returns to its usual rhythm, Alessio and I help Dante to his feet.

Despite the discarded blindfold, my darling sub's eyes are still firmly closed, shutting out the world.

"Will you manage?" the naked Joker asks as I shove my shoulder under my exhausted husband's arm to keep him from falling back down.

"Yeah, I'll be fine. You kids have fun. I think the big boy needs some cuddles." I smile, caressing Dante's cheek.

He just grunts, "I'm fine," without looking up, convincing nobody.

Alessio tsk-tsks, shaking his head at Dante before giving me the directions to our room. I'll have to drag the big man upstairs. But luckily, his legs are regaining some of their stability, it seems; he's holding his own weight now.

"I think I'll stay here for a bit..." Alessio casts an eye to Rani and Adira relaxing on the couch, body parts mingling like they're being woven together.

"Please. Stay, darling," Adira insists as Rani nods in agreement.

"We'll manage," I repeat, kissing Alessio deeply in parting. "Besides, it has been a long day of formalities and informalities, and all I want is to have my husband all to myself."

"Fair enough." Alessio reaches for Dante, kissing him sweetly. "*Fai il bravo, amore mio.*" It's a bit late in the night to tell Don Fera to "be good," if you ask me, but I think it's sweet, nonetheless.

After parting kisses to the Dommes on the couch, we're off, weaving through the party that has spread all over the house, guests fucking on all available surfaces, some against walls.

Part of me wishes we could've stayed, that I could've watched Alessio and the Dommes explore their needs. But honestly, my tank is running on empty too. It's been a crazy long day.

For now, it's aftercare time—for Dante's sake as much as my own.

The Don in question always thinks he can take more, but his bruised and broken body says otherwise.

After much huffing and puffing up the stairs, we finally find our room among the closed doors that emanate symphonies of pleasure as other guests find the pinnacles of their pleasure.

I hardly take in any details about the room, just head straight to the en suite bathroom before letting go of Dante. The aim is to set him down gently on the toilet, but he has other ideas.

Like a monolith toppling, my darling boy collapses on the floor, seeking relief from the cold tiles or perhaps the ground itself. The dirty floor beneath his fresh cuts can't be sanitary, but I'll clean him up soon enough.

The tub is big, footed, Victorian—expensive like everything else in the massive bathroom that comes complete with indoor plants and walk-in his-and-hers showers.

Opening the hot water tap all the way, I let the tub fill up as I ease out of my heels. The relief is instant.

I return my attention to the man with the bruised backside lying flat on the floor, smearing the cream-colored tiles crimson with his blood. "You okay, baby?"

Dante still hasn't said much anything other than the unconvincing "I'm fine" earlier. He hasn't even opened his eyes. Not for long, anyway.

There is so much I want to talk to him about, but I take a step back, giving him the space he needs, stroking his hair sweetly as the tub fills.

I know he'll come back to me. He always does.

After adding in some cold water as well, I test the temperature to make sure it's manageable before squatting beside the 6'5" beast that no longer has any of the threatening qualities that make him the feared Don Fera. In this moment, he is just a little boy.

My beautiful Knight.

Could I love him any more than I do right now?

It's not possible.

Bringing my face closer, I inspect the new bruises decorating his skin. Rani sure did a thorough job.

Dante's body is a beautiful tapestry of purples and future-yellows-that-are-still-blue, little red cuts running over his back, his ass—Rani's souvenirs.

Just thinking back to the scene instantly makes me aroused too. I still can't believe it all happened in one day. We've lived so many lifetimes in these past hours.

So many firsts...

Like watching Rani at work. She's so different from Adira, but no less attractive—that's for sure. There's something about the way she commanded that whip so elegantly that instantly made me want to throw my body before her, despite usually not being much into impact play.

A few smacks on my pussy with a riding crop, maybe, but that's about as far as my enjoyment of pain goes. I much prefer receiving *pleasure* to pain.

And pleasure, there was plenty to be had in that room.

The free-use scene may have been for Dante, but we all got what we needed—more.

At some point, Rani ate me out while Adira sucked Dante off. At another, Alessio fucked me so hard I came multiple times, especially the time when Adira joined, taking my sensitive nipples between her teeth as the Joker reduced me to a puddle of spent lust.

So many hands, so much touching, groping, clawing...in the dimly-lit room downstairs, everything was free-use, not just my husband.

The only difference was that, unlike Dante, the rest of us could see, could touch, could move.

Poor boy. I'm sure he'll be bleak to have missed the sight of me sandwiched between Adira and Rani, penetrated from both ends, filled to the brink. But he was busy getting fucked by Alessio, ever-exchanging partners rotating in a variety of formations, giving and taking power, sometimes sharing.

I thought things would be a bit more awkward, but Alessio had a way of making people feel at ease. His natural charm quickly disarmed the Dommes, even Rani, who rarely found a male specimen she enjoyed, according to Adira.

It all worked out so perfectly, the most amazing wedding gift.

Now it's time for damage control.

Despite Dante's strict health regime and regular workouts, the human body can only take so much—especially once you hit your mid-40s. And his body clearly needs a break.

But first, time to wash the various liquids from our skin. Not before I make sure his cuts are cleaned. I'll add salve to them after.

"Upsy-daisy." I lift from my legs as my trainer taught me, almost tumbling us both into the bath as I perch Dante on the edge of the tub. "Look at me, darling." I tilt his chin toward me, kissing his closed eyelids.

It's clear that it would probably be impossible, and quite dangerous, to get him into the water without his cooperation.

Dante grumbles something in syllables that don't form words, his eyes still firmly closed.

"You're going to have to open them peepers, Don Fera. Gotta get you into this bath." Still holding him firmly so he doesn't topple over into the steaming water, I gently kiss the side of Dante's neck, whispering recently-learned Italian sweet nothings into his ear.

Finally, after what was probably a few minutes but felt like ages to my aching arms holding up the giant sub, Dante sighs and flutters his eyes open.

He quickly closes them again with a groan. The bathroom lights must be very bright for eyes that have grown used to the darkness.

"Easy does it. Whenever you're ready," I encourage him, hoping *whenever* is soon, before my arms give in and I drop him.

Dante tries again, forcing his eyes to remain open for longer this time. They fall shut a few times, adjusting, until he can keep them ajar, looking around wildly as he tries to orientate himself in the foreign surroundings.

My husband smiles weakly, looking up at me like an awkward kid. "Hey..."

"Hey, you." I kiss his nose.

Dante blushes. "That was, um...fun..."

"Yeah? I'm glad. Only the best for my husband." I want to say that word over and over again. It feels so right.

He rubs the back of his neck. "Your very sore husband."

"Should we get that bum clean so we can get some rest?" I can't believe we woke up at home this morning, that this has all been one day—the flight, the hotel spa, the wedding, the after party, the scene...But my body knows it's all been one day; my limbs are aching, tired.

Dante nods, and I help him into the steaming water through winces and pressed lips, occasional grunts, and a little whimper at the end as his sore ass hits the porcelain below.

"Are you okay?" I repeat my earlier question, slowly guiding the washcloth over Dante's body, careful not to hurt him more. He's sensitive in some parts, so bruised—a beautiful tapestry of pleasure spent to remember tonight by.

"*Sì*. Just exhausted."

I kiss the side of his head, inhaling the new scents covering him. "You did such a good job; took it so well."

He smiles at the praise. "I wish I could have seen it."

"Next time, we'll film it."

"I hope there will be a next time." Dante looks up at me through messy curls, and I kiss him tenderly.

"Such a brave boy."

"Only with you by my side."

The words make me smile, filling me with warmth.

"Do you think there is space for me?" I ask, getting up to slip out of the little clothing I still had on my body.

Nodding, Dante scoots over, and I join him.

Sitting down between his legs, I lean back against his chest as he wraps both arms around me, holding me close. I can feel his heart beating against my back...and his cock pressed between us. This is what home feels like.

Leaning my neck back on his shoulder, I close my eyes, enjoying his skin against mine, familiar, warm, content.

With a heavy exhale, I weave my fingers through his, interlocking them over my heart. "I love you so much, you know that, right?"

"I do, Missus Fera. I love you too. Too much." He strokes my nipple, almost absentmindedly toying with the little bump that grows excited under his touch, perking up.

"Hmm...Missus Fera. I like the sound of that. Say it again."

"Missus Fera. My Queen." Dante pinches my nipple, and I giggle in response as his unmistakable erection grows against my back.

"You're hard."

"For you, always."

"Don't move."

Careful not to slip, I get up on my knees to reposition myself over Dante, slowly guiding his cock into me, reverse cowgirl style.

A deep moan echoes off the tiles as the familiar shape fills me, completes me.

For a moment, we just sit there, with him inside me, unmoving.

"*Dio mio,* you feel incredible," Dante whispers in my neck, his hand fanning over my stomach, holding me close.

"As do you, darling. Slowly now," I tell him like I'm not the one in control of the speed, of the movement of impaling myself on his large cock.

I move gradually, grinding myself down on that magnificent appendage again and again as the water splashes around us.

Dante's hands move down to my hips, holding on as I ride him like I'm trying to fuse our bodies together. When he moves a hand around, to my clit, I know neither of us will last long. Not with the pleasure building so quickly, despite my slow movements.

I pick up speed, not caring about the water spilling from the tub, or how tired my body is, or whether Dante has any cum left inside him after the night we had.

"You have permission, baby. Come for me," I instruct between rapid breaths and numb legs, grinding down on Dante's dick as he moans my name on repeat, louder and louder, until we both tumble off the climax cliff together. Until he comes inside me for the second time as my husband and I collapse against his chest, both of us breathing heavily.

Later, when we finally succumb to exhaustion, our naked limbs intertwined beneath silk sheets, I rest my ear against his heartbeat, counting each beat.

Time seems to stand still in our darkened room, the world narrowed to just this: skin against skin, Dante's arms locked around me like he'll never let go, that rhythmic beat that drowns out all the negative thoughts.

Even though our problems are far from solved, I know we'll be okay. Because we have each other. From now until forever.

My last conscious thought drifts through my mind like a satisfied sigh:

Missus Dante Fera.

Finally.

PROBLEMS

(DANTE)

I push my pasta around my plate, the same way I've been pushing problems around my mind all week. Even Missus Nell's mouth-watering carbonara can't tempt me tonight. My body craves sustenance, but my mind is too full of endless complications.

"You need to eat, my love," Danica says softly, reaching across the antique table to touch my hand. Her fingers are warm against my skin, which I know must feel cool to her touch—I've spent too many hours in that basement interrogation room again. I wonder if she can smell it on me.

We've only been back from Vegas for four days, but it's been beyond stressful. Dealing with missing shipments and frozen bank accounts and unhappy investors, and, and, and...It's just been one thing after the next.

It feels like we never left home. Like Vegas was but a drug-induced fever dream.

The weight of the world rests heavily on my shoulders, tainting everything with its darkness, its weight.

The world never pauses, no matter how hard you try. It certainly didn't while we were away.

Outside the window, I notice Marco adjusting his patrol route to keep us in sight. The new security protocols are second nature now, but they're a constant reminder: we're not out of danger yet.

It doesn't stop my mind from daydreaming about Vegas, though. About the most incredible wedding reception. My *gifts...*

Even now, I carry the bruises from Rani. Beautiful purples and yellows with healing red lines where she broke skin.

Every night, Danica makes me strip fully naked to inspect every single bruise, every cut, kissing them better before putting on salve.

She refuses to let me come though, much to my frustration. Something about needing to keep a clear head to solve our problems with the Russians. As much as I tell her that it's having the opposite effect, that I can't think when I'm so damn horny, my Queen has been impossible to sway.

I haven't had a release since we left Vegas.

Since we got back, Danica's been spending her days with the trainers, working on her fitness, her fighting skills, and even shooting practice. That and endless research, trying to find a way out of this mess.

I tried to get her just to relax, to enjoy the luxuries our status has to offer, but she wasn't having any of it. "*Stop wrapping me up in cotton wool*," she complained, and I dropped the subject.

It's not like I would take my own advice either.

Last night, I fell asleep at my desk again.

Our happily ever after isn't quite proceeding as planned.

Turns out dismantling the Russian mob isn't as straightforward as we thought. As soon as I found a charger for my mobile after our intensely beautiful wedding night, the barrage of missed messages and calls flooded in.

There were complications. Unexpected deaths. Uprisings.

And just like that, our peace was shattered. Our honeymoon put on hold. An early flight home organized.

Now, trying to force myself to eat a table and not my desk, I can see Danica trying to keep her mood light, trying to make things easier for me. I wish I could tell her how much I appreciate it, but I don't know how. Everything feels like it's too much. Like we can't ever catch a break.

Biscotti's head appears in my lap, drawn by the untouched food. For once, I don't even attempt to maintain discipline, just absently offer him a piece of pancetta. His warm weight against my leg is oddly comforting.

"Tolya talked again today," I say finally, my voice rough from too little sleep. "Gave us another shipment schedule. Another shell company. Another..." I trail off, rubbing my temples where a persistent headache has taken up residence.

"That's good, isn't it?" Danica's voice is hopeful.

"It's endless, *Tesoro*. Every answer leads to ten more questions. The ports are a maze of paperwork and shell companies and fuck knows what else. Even with that idiot singing like a canary in our basement, it'll take months to untangle." I hear the despair in my own voice, feel my fingers cracking my knuckles out of nervous habit.

"But we got them out," she reminds me. "The Volkovs are finished."

"Are they?" My laugh feels bitter in my throat. "We've got their operations, their territory, their headaches. Those opiate shipments? They're still coming in. We can't just stop them—legitimate businesses are waiting. But I won't deal in that poison."

Biscotti whines softly, sensing my distress. I find myself scratching behind his ears—a gesture as much for my comfort as the dog's.

"We'll figure it out, darling. You need to pace yourself. This is too much stress." Danica's concern is evident in her eyes.

"Ha! There are so many problems we never even considered. Now the dock workers are threatening to strike, Emilio tells me." I sigh, finally taking a small bite of pasta. "Can't blame them. The management changeover hasn't exactly been a smooth transition."

"I spoke to their union rep yesterday," Danica offers, and I feel my eyebrows rise slightly.

"You did?"

"What? You're not the only one who can handle business. I've been learning, darling, figuring it out."

"What did the rep say?" I'm genuinely curious now, feeling a small spark of hope.

"He's worried about job security more than anything. I assured him we're keeping all legitimate operations running." She takes a sip of wine. "Though that accident at Pier 7 yesterday—that wasn't an accident."

My fork freezes halfway to my mouth. "What do you mean?"

"The crane operator said the controls malfunctioned, but I had our tech team check. Someone tampered with them. Could have killed three workers if he hadn't noticed something off about the cable tension."

"*Cazzo*." I rub my face, feeling the stubble I haven't had time to shave. "And now this morning's threat..."

"The note about *'rivers of blood'* at the security gate? Bit dramatic if you ask me." She keeps her tone light, though we both know how serious it is. "I've already increased security at all access points, and I'm having cameras installed at the blind spots we found during the audit."

I stare at her for a long moment, struck by her competence. "When did you become so...capable?"

"I've always been capable. Now I just have better resources." She meets my gaze steadily. "Let me do more, Dante. You don't have to carry all of this alone."

"I don't want you—" I start, but she cuts me off.

"Get hurt? Yeah, I know. But keeping me locked up like Rapunzel won't keep me safe."

"I'm doing my best." My voice sounds defensive even to my own ears.

"I know you are, baby. But let me be by your side where I belong. I'm not the damsel in distress you saved at the restaurant all those years ago when we met."

"I know," I say softly, looking down at my barely-touched meal. She's right. We both know it.

"What are the other families up to?" she asks, pushing her finished plate aside. Unlike me, Danica has no issues with stress eating.

"Circling like sharks. Everyone remembers the port wars. Nobody wants another bloodbath, but nobody trusts anyone else to control them either." My voice catches slightly as unwanted memories surface—my mother's death, the bullet meant for my father that made me an unwilling part of port history.

"When was the last time you slept properly?" Her question draws me back to the present.

"It's been a while." I don't even try to lie. "Every time I close my eyes, I see paperwork. Shipping manifests. Bank accounts. And somewhere in all of it is the key to making this work, to keeping the peace, but I can't find it..."

She stands, moving around the table to massage my shoulders. Under her fingers, I can feel how tense I've become, muscles like solid granite.

"You're not alone, my love," she murmurs. "The other families helped us take down the Russians. They'll help us figure out the ports."

"Or they'll tear each other apart trying." I lean back into her touch, craving the comfort. "We need a solution that doesn't end in war. That doesn't end with more bodies, more grieving families..."

"We'll figure it out." She presses a kiss to my temple."

I know she's trying to comfort me, but the dread refuses to leave my body. It's a risky game.

"We better, because if we don't—" I stop myself from finishing the sentence. We both know that if we don't find a solution soon, it won't just be our honeymoon that is ruined...but our lives too.

Not too long ago, I vowed to protect my Queen for the rest of our lives. But right now, I have no idea how I will make good on that promise.

"You won't solve it all tonight," Danica says. "Tonight, you're going to eat, then sleep."

"Danica..." I start, even though I know she's right.

Biscotti chooses this moment to steal the pancetta directly from my plate, making us both laugh. The sound feels foreign after so many heavy discussions lately.

"Terrible guard dog," I mutter, but my hand is gentle when I push him away.

"Good timing, though." Danica returns to her seat. "Eat. Then bed. Doctor's orders."

"You're not that kind of doctor, *Tesoro*."

"No, but I am your Domme, and that's still an order."

I pick up my fork with a mock salute. "Yes, Ma'am." I'm too tired to argue.

We both know tomorrow will bring more complications, more decisions. The Volkovs might be handled, but their ghost lingers in ledgers and shipping lanes and nervous dock workers wondering if they'll keep their jobs.

But for now, in this moment, we have pasta and each other and a spoiled dog who thinks he's people.

One day at a time.

CHAPTER THIRTY

SECRETS

(DANICA)

I f Dante wasn't getting uncharacteristically impatient for my company, I could've slept at least another three hours. Two weeks since our Vegas wedding and we were no closer to solving our conundrum with the ports.

Begrudgingly, I open my eyes, squinting against the light streaming through the half-drawn curtains. He's been hovering this morning, checking on me every half hour like I might disappear if he doesn't. That's usually my first clue that something's on his mind.

"Good morning, moglie mia." Dante kisses me fully awake, and I grin, despite wishing I was still asleep. The clock on the bedside makes it clear that we're way beyond "morning" already, but Dante will always tell me good morning, no matter what time I wake up.

"What do you want?" I growl at him, pretending to be mad. But I know that look in his eyes—he's been building up to something. The careful way he's watching me, the slight tension in his shoulders that wasn't there last night.

"We have work to do," he says simply, planting a kiss on my nose. But his hands linger a moment too long, his touch more deliberate than usual. Almost like he's trying to memorize me.

I can't help but smile, taking his face in my hands. "Hey, baby."

"Hmm, I'll never get tired of you calling me that," Dante tells me as he covers me in caresses. There's a new tenderness in his touch this morning, something almost reverent about the way his fingers trace each curve. It's like he's fortifying himself for something.

When his fingers reach my lower back, I flinch, as always. It's an involuntary reaction, one I've never been able to control even after all these years together. His hand freezes, and the atmosphere in the room shifts. That's when I know.

Today is the day he's finally going to push.

He's touched my scars before, of course—accidentally at first, then carefully, cautiously, as our relationship grew. But he's always respected my silence, my subtle withdrawals when his fingers grazed those raised lines. Even in our most intimate moments, when his hands would map every inch of my body, he would skirt around those damaged territories with careful reverence.

Four years of looking away when I turned my back from him while changing. Four years of questions caught behind his teeth, curiosity swallowed down with silent understanding. Four years of watching my face tighten whenever anyone mentioned childhood or family.

He hesitates, seeking my gaze, before asking the question I've been avoiding for as long as we've known each other.

"These marks..." Dante's fingers trace the raised lines that map my back, his touch feather-light against the scarred tissue. The mattress dips as he shifts closer, his chest warm against my skin. "Tell me, Donna Fera, who did this to you? You're my wife now; I want to know who hurt you."

There's a quiet desperation in his voice that I've never heard before. Not just curiosity, but necessity—like he can't move forward without this piece of me. Like something inside him needs to know who to hate for marking his Queen.

The question pierces through my post-sleep haze like an ice shard. The silk sheets suddenly feel abrasive against my skin, the room too warm yet somehow freezing. My throat constricts as memories I've spent years burying claw their way to the surface.

I sigh.

Is this it? Is it time?

I don't want to keep living in fear of that question...

Not from my own husband.

"Promise you won't hurt them." The words come out barely above a whisper.

I'm not actually going to tell him, am I?

But I think I am...

What is the point of keeping secrets from Dante? He already knows everything else—my darkest desires, my greatest fears, my cruelest impulses. He's seen me at my worst and loved me anyway. This is the last wall between us, the final door I've kept locked.

Might as well get it all out.

I turn to meet Dante's gaze, searching those emerald eyes for mercy I already know I won't find. In the dim light of the bedroom, my husband's features are cast in shadow, but I can see the muscles working in his jaw.

"Tell me." His voice has shifted—no longer my tender submissive but Don Dante Fera, the man who makes grown men tremble. His body becomes rigid against mine, muscles coiling like a predator preparing to strike. The change in him is palpable, electric.

"Dante, please promise me." I hate how my voice wavers, how vulnerable I sound.

"I can't." Two simple words, delivered with the weight of a death sentence.

The silence between us feels thick enough to cut with a knife.

I close my eyes, drawing in a shaky breath. My heart pounds so hard I wonder if he can hear it. This moment feels a hundred times scarier than taking on the Russian mob...

"It was my brothers." The words I've held back for so long taste like ash in my mouth. "It was long ago," I quickly add like it would absolve them their sins.

Dante's fists clench beside me, knuckles bleaching white against tanned skin. The temperature in the room seems to drop ten degrees as fury radiates off him in waves. I can feel the tension vibrating through his body where it touches mine.

"Go on." The words come through gritted teeth.

I lean back against his chest, needing his warmth even as I dread his reaction. My fingers work to uncurl his, threading through until our hands are intertwined. His pulse races against my palm as I speak.

"I was nine. They were almost seventeen..."

The memory writhes up like a serpent. How many years has it been since I've spoken of this? The last time, they called me a liar. Said I was seeking attention. Blamed me for my own torture. Even now, decades later, their voices echo in my head, mocking and cruel.

"My parents were very strict..." My voice sounds distant, hollow. "Always working, never around. Raising kids is expensive, you know, especially when a third one shows up unplanned." A bitter laugh escapes me. "*Moi*. The mistake. The financial burden. The one who ruined everything."

Dante's free hand moves to my hair, stroking gently. The tenderness in his touch nearly breaks me.

A tear escapes, rolling down my cheek. I don't try to wipe it away.

"Before me, everything was perfect. At least, that's the story they all cling to. Two golden-haired twins, Marko and Filip." Their names feel like poison on my tongue, and I feel Dante tense at the mention of them. "They excelled at everything—academics, sports, life. Marko especially...God, he could sell ice to an Eskimo. So smart. So *conniving*. Always planning, always three steps ahead. And Filip..." My voice catches. "Filip just wanted to be like his brother. Always following, always trying to impress. Together they were...they were monsters wearing angel masks, pretending to be exemplary."

"Not so exemplary in reality?" Dante's question is soft, encouraging, but I can hear the lethal undertone, feel the barely contained rage in how his fingers tighten slightly in my hair.

"Angels in public. Devils at home." The words tumble out faster now, like a dam breaking. "They'd torment me when our parents were out. Make up games where I was always the victim. Cut my hair, break my toys, lock me in closets...And when I'd cry or fight back, they'd turn it around and gaslight me. Poor troubled Danica, they'd say. Can't control her emotions. Making up stories for attention."

Dante's breathing grows heavier, his chest rising and falling against my back in controlled fury. "Your parents never intervened?"

"They saw what they wanted to see. Two perfect sons and one problem daughter." My laugh comes out sharp, brittle. "Do you know how hard it is to keep up your grades when living in constant fear of your own family? When your brothers steal your homework or keep you up all night with their 'games'?"

"You were just a kid, Danica..."

"I don't remember a time when it was different. I was always their guinea pig, their slave, their prisoner—depending on what movie they watched that week. Our parents didn't allow us much TV; they were so strict. But the boys did what they wanted when our parents were at work. Watched what they wanted. And then they always had to reenact their favorite scenes with their poor little sister as the *star* of the show."

"Tell me how you got these scars, *Tesoro*." Dante's fingers trace the raised lines on my back, and suddenly, I'm nine years old again, small and scared and so very alone.

The words stick in my throat. Four years he's waited for this story. Four years of patience, of gentle questions met with silence. I've been too scared to tell him. To relive it. But his touch grounds me to now, to him, to safety.

"Hide and seek," I whisper. "That's what they called it. Just another game." A bitter laugh escapes me.

I feel Dante go still behind me, but he doesn't interrupt. Just waits, his heartbeat steady against my back.

"I was so small then. So trusting, even after everything they'd done before. They tied my hands—rough rope that bit into my skin. Kingsly followed me into the shed..." My voice catches. "He was my only friend, that dog. Golden retriever. Used to sleep outside my door to guard me from them."

The memory crashes over me like a tsunami wave. "The shed was their favorite place. Dark. Private. Far enough from the house that no one could hear...They left a candle. Said I needed light to play their game properly. Kingsly was nervous—he always knew when they were planning something cruel."

My fingers dig into Dante's arm as the panic rises, decades old but still sharp as glass. "It happened so fast. Kingsly bumped the candle. It wasn't his fault. They were banging on the walls; he got startled. The flame caught the old wood like it was waiting, hungry. I screamed...god, I screamed so loud. But they just laughed outside. '*Those are the rules,*' they kept saying. '*You have to stay inside.*'"

Tears fall freely now, but I can't stop. The story pours out like poison from an old wound. "The smoke came first. Thick. Black. Couldn't breathe. Kingsly was barking, panicking. I pulled at the ropes, but they were too tight. Then the heat..." My hand moves unconsciously to the scars. "The ropes started to melt. Into my skin. The smell...burning rope, burning flesh. My flesh."

Dante makes a sound like he's been wounded, but I barely hear him. I'm back in that shed, nine years old and dying.

"I kept waiting. For my parents. For anyone. Kept thinking someone would save me. But nobody came. Kingsly was howling. The fire was everywhere. On my back, in my lungs. I couldn't see. Couldn't breathe. Just felt the excruciating pain of my skin bubbling, melting..."

My breath comes in gasps now. "I remember thinking: this is it. This is how I die. Tied up in a shed while my brothers laugh outside. Nine years old, and this is all I get."

"*Tesoro...*" Dante's voice breaks on the word.

"I don't remember getting out. The ropes had melted enough...or maybe the wood was weak. Everything was fire and smoke and screaming. Next thing I knew, I was in the hospital. But Kingsly..." A sob tears free. "He didn't make it. My only friend, and they killed him."

"Tell me they paid," Dante's voice is deadly quiet. "Tell me someone made them suffer."

The laugh that tears from my throat is ugly, broken. "One weekend grounded. That's what they got for nearly killing their sister. Because what would people say if they knew? *'Think of their futures,'* my parents said. *'It was an accident,'* they said. *'Don't ruin this for them, Danica.'"*

"Your parents..." The rage in his voice is barely contained.

"Blamed me. For making a fuss. For ruining the perfect family image. The twins got to keep playing their games, just...differently after that. No more fire. But they made sure I never enjoyed another second of my childhood."

"You were nine..." Dante's arms tighten around me like he could shield me from the past.

"Poor Danica, making a fuss about a stupid dead dog," I mimic Marko's voice. "It never got easier. The scars healed, but the memories...they loved hiding my pain medication. Loved watching me suffer."

"And now?" His voice has gone deadly quiet.

"Now?" I wipe roughly at my tears. "Now Marko's an architect. Has a perfect wife, perfect kids. Filip's some hotshot engineer. And me? According to Marko, I deserve marrying a criminal because nobody else would want damaged goods."

I turn in Dante's arms, needing to see his face. "Now you know. Know why—"

The sob breaks free before I can stop it. This is it—the moment he sees how truly broken I am. How ugly. How worthless.

But instead of pushing me away, Dante wraps me tighter in his arms. His eyes burn with an intensity that steals my breath. "I am going to fucking end them," he hisses, the words vibrating with barely contained rage.

"No...please. This is why I didn't want to tell you." Part of why. The other part, the larger one, was the fear that he would see me differently, treat me like I'm fragile, treat me like a *victim*...

"They can't just get away with it, *Tesoro*." Dante's voice breaks on the endearment. "The thought of you going through that...I wish I could have protected you."

"It wasn't your job; I had parents for that." My voice sounds small, even to my own ears. "But I guess I wasn't worth the trouble."

"Look at me." His hands cup my face, thumbs brushing away my tears. Those emerald eyes bore into mine, fierce with love and fury and protection. "You are worth everything. You are a Queen. *My* Queen. And anyone who ever made you feel otherwise..."

He doesn't finish the threat, just presses his lips to my eyelids, kissing away the tears that won't stop flowing. I can feel him trembling with suppressed rage, even as his touch remains gentle on my skin.

The secret is finally out, hanging between us like smoke from a long-ago fire. But for the first time, the telling of it doesn't leave me feeling hollow. Instead, wrapped in Dante's arms, his heartbeat strong against my cheek, I feel something else entirely.

I feel free.

Raw, but free.

CHAPTER THIRTY-ONE

THE FURY

(DANTE)

I hold Danica until she cries herself back to sleep, my chest soaked with her tears, my mind aching with her trauma.

It's hard to marry the reality of little nine-year-old Danica stuck in the burning shed with the Queen wrapped in my arms.

The mere thought that someone could do this to her is enough to make my blood boil to the point of blind rage.

But I kept quiet—for her sake. As much as I wanted to punch a hole right through the solid wall, I clenched my fists and listened, letting her get it all off her chest.

Seeing her so broken, so vulnerable, felt like a dagger piercing through my heart.

How could they do this to her? She didn't deserve it. *What narcissistic cunts...*

I stroke her hair, inhaling her scent—familiar, home, mine. In this moment, Danica looks her age, even younger. She seems more like a child to protect than the fearless Goddess who boldly took on Tolya Volkov like he wasn't one of the cruelest, most dangerous men in the city.

I had no idea...

The signs were there, literally etched on her beautiful skin, but the thought never even crossed my mind. I suspected it was some sort of accident, maybe something she was embarrassed about...

But *accident* is not the word I would use to describe the torment Danica went through at the hands of her own brothers.

I should probably try to get some sleep too, but sleeping in the middle of the day has never come naturally to me. And with my mind overburdened like this, there's not a chance in hell I could switch off.

The anger burns through my body, getting stronger and stronger the more I think about the pain my Danica carries around with her.

Fuck-it. I'll go mad if I just lie here.

Careful not to disturb my sleeping beauty, I detangle myself from Danica. She murmurs softly but quickly resumes her slumber.

For a moment longer, I just watch her, watch how those magnificent breasts heave up and down with her breath.

And then I sneak out, tip-toeing on my bare feet.

It's afternoon. Our whole schedule has been upside down since our failed attempt at a wedding.

The house is quiet. The staff know not to disturb me when the door is closed.

I head downstairs to the gym.

Biscotti lifts his head as I pass his room but doesn't follow me. Sleepy, just like his mother.

The first punch feels good, the second not so much. Still, I pummel all my frustration into the poor punching bag, destroying it as my fists drive into it again and again, until my pesky shoulder forces me to a standstill, aching like my gunshot wound hasn't been healed for years. *Fucking, body!*

A loud roar echoes through the room as I let it all out. I'm shaking in frustration, in fury, in all the emotions other people have names for, but I can't recognize as anything but shades of anger and disgust.

"Everything okay, *Signore*?" It's Dario who responds to my outburst, hesitating by the door.

My heart rate is still sky-high from the punches, but I force my voice steady. "Fine. Please call Emilio," I reply, and Dario disappears with a nod.

My best man appears moments later, taking one look at my deranged state before closing the door behind him. He doesn't say anything, just patiently waits for me to gather my thoughts.

"Emilio."

He nods. "Boss."

"I need you to track down some people for me."

"Anything you need, *Don mio*."

"Filip and Marko Matthews. They shouldn't be too hard to find."

Emilio nods. I know he knows who they are, that they're Danica's brothers, but he doesn't say anything.

"Do you want us to make them disappear?" he asks.

"No, I thought about it. But Danica would never forgive me for it. She probably wouldn't forgive me for interfering one way or another, but I can't just do nothing while those cunts walk free, living a life without consequence."

Emilio doesn't answer, just waits for me to give the order.

"Don't hurt them, not physically, at least. But make sure they never work again, not in this country, not anywhere. I want their careers destroyed. Their lives. Just how they destroyed Danica's."

"*Sì, Don mio.*"

"And Emilio?"

"Yes, boss?"

"Please be discreet. I want none of this to be traced back to us."

"Of course."

"Everyone has skeletons in the closet and I bet these assholes have a few. Find it and exploit it. Are we clear?" I drop the boxing gloves on the floor and crack my knuckles, loudly.

"*Sì, Don mio.*"

"Don't hurt the children."

Emilio nods before taking his leave. I know he'll take care of it; he's never disappointed me.

Danica will find out soon enough, I can never lie to her. But not now. There is too much else going on; I'll tell her later.

I call after Emilio before he disappears. "Please ask Missus Nell to arrange something to eat and some flowers. Tulips. White and red ones, please. She can leave them in the dining room for me."

"*Sì.*"

"Thanks, Emilio." I try to be nicer to him, remembering Danica's earlier reprimand. "Close the door behind you."

As soon as he's gone, I collapse on the floor, flat on my back on the rubber mat that spans across the area of the box gym we've had since my father's days. It's not very big, just a square room with the necessary equipment. In my younger days, I'd spend hours in here every day, fighting my demons, trying to find peace.

But today, it gives me no calm, no shelter from the chaos. The khaki-colored walls seem depressing, the windows dirty. I make a mental note to remind Missus Nell to come clean down here but I know I will forget again, just like all the other times I've made the same mental note.

I don't know how long I lie there for, long enough to almost fall asleep. But I need to get back to Danica; I don't want her to wake up alone.

Taking a deep breath, I gather myself, washing my face in the small basin by the door. The mirror is mounted too low for my tall frame, forcing me to crouch down to see my blood-red eyes and messy hair staring back at me.

As best as I can, I smooth out my hair and try to force my breath to its normal rhythm. Danica doesn't need to worry about me as well, she's got enough on her mind already.

I just wish I could go back in time and cut this memory out of existence like it never happened at all. But I can't.

Missus Nell is efficient as always and the flowers and a covered tray stand ready on the dining room table when I finally gather myself enough to leave the gym.

I make a quick detour to my study first before collecting all the items to take upstairs. One of the guards offers to help me carry, but I dismiss him, trying my best not to project my emotions, my frustration, onto an innocent bystander.

Careful not to spill, I carry the tray upstairs, the bouquet of fresh-cut flowers from our garden tucked under my arm.

"Dante?" Danica's voice is soft with sleep as I maneuver through the door with my offerings.

"I'm here, *Tesoro*." The tray finds a home on the dresser before I slide back into bed, pressing a kiss to her forehead.

She curls into me immediately, then pulls back. "You're all sweaty. Where did you go?"

"Had to work some things out with the punching bag." I try to keep my voice light, but she reads the tension in my muscles, the barely contained fury still simmering beneath my skin.

"Oh, darling..." Her fingers trace the fresh splits in my knuckles.

"I also brought us something to eat. And flowers—thought the room could use some brightness." I force a smile.

338

I didn't even look at what was under the silver plate covers, but I knew Missus Nell would not disappoint. By now, she knew all about Danica's peckish eating habits and my endless need for protein.

"You're too good to me." Danica's attempt at a smile breaks my heart— still so wounded, still trying to be strong.

"I have something else for you." I retrieve the wrapped bundle from the dresser beside the food, holding it out to Danica with both hands. Even through the leather, I can feel the weight of history it carries.

"What is it?"

"My grandfather's combat knife." I unwrap it carefully, revealing the ancient weapon. The handle is dark wood, polished by decades of use, inlaid with intricate silver work that catches the light. The blade itself is a masterpiece—nearly 12 inches of Damascus steel, the distinctive rippled pattern speaking to its craftsmanship. "Forged in some ancient mountain city—I never paid attention to his war stories. But I remember him saying it was extremely rare, extremely lucky."

Danica sits up straighter, eyes widening as she takes the blade with reverent hands. She unsheathes it slowly from its leather scabbard, the steel catching light like it was forged yesterday instead of decades ago. The curve of the blade is elegant, deadly—a perfect marriage of beauty and lethal purpose. "Dante...this is incredible. Are you sure?"

"It's yours." *Like my heart.*

"It's stunning." Her fingers trace the intricate handle before placing it carefully on the bedside table.

"My grandfather said it was a knife for only the best warriors." I pull her close, breathing in her scent. "And you're the strongest warrior I know."

"Oh, Dante." She melts into me, and I rest my chin on her head, letting her warmth chase away some of the darkness.

Never again, I vow silently. *No one will ever hurt her again.* The knife is symbolic—she already has the most dangerous weapon in the city at her disposal: a Don who would burn the world to keep her safe.

And after hearing her story, burning the world suddenly seems like a reasonable response.

Biscotti shuffles in like he's been waiting for the right moment, his nails clicking on the floor, head tilted as if sensing the heavy emotion in the room. I don't stop him when he jumps on the bed, forcing his adorable face between us to join the hug. His tail thumps against the mattress as he settles, managing to take up more space than seems physically possible for his size.

Danica hugs us both closely, kissing first my forehead and then the dog's. "My boys," she murmurs, a real smile finally touching her lips. "My protectors."

Biscotti lets out a contented sigh as he drools on thousand-thread-count sheets, and some of the darkness recedes.

Just a little.

Just enough to breathe.

For now.

CHAPTER THIRTY-TWO

NEW EMPIRE

(DANICA)

The morning sun streaks through our bedroom windows, casting patterns across the rumpled sheets. My body aches—partly from crying, partly from Dante's gentle lovemaking after I shared my darkest truth.

After he gave me that knife, the most precious gift ever, I hugged him so tightly. Hugged his sweaty body until I felt his cock stir and my heart race. Until he slipped his erection inside me carefully, intentionally, fully, pressing our broken pieces together until we climaxed like one.

For years, I've carried those memories like poison in my veins. Hidden them. Buried them. Let them fester into doubt and self-loathing. I was so sure telling him would change everything—that he'd see me differently, damaged goods, a victim. That was what they wanted, after all. To break me. To make me feel worthless.

But Dante...

I watch him sleep, his face peaceful for the first time in days. The weight of the port crisis has been crushing him, but he set it all aside last night to hold me, to listen. My heart swells. He didn't push me away. Didn't see me as broken. No, he just loved me harder.

In the soft morning light, I can still feel the echo of his touches—reverent, claiming, healing. The way he whispered "mine" against my scars like they were battle wounds to be honored, not shame to be hidden. The fierce promise in his eyes when he swore my brothers would pay.

For the first time since that night, I feel...whole. Not despite my past, but because I've finally faced it. Claimed it. The weakness I feared admitting has somehow become a strength.

I trace my fingers over the marks on my skin, seeing them through new eyes. They're not badges of shame anymore. They're proof I survived. Proof I'm stronger than they ever imagined I could be. My brothers thought they were breaking me that day, but they were forging something else entirely—a woman who refuses to break.

The insecurities that have haunted me—the fear of being seen as weak, of not being enough, of losing Dante's respect—they feel distant now. Not gone completely, but quieter. Like they've lost their power over me.

I look at my sleeping husband again, love squeezing my heart. He knows everything now. Every dark secret. Every scar. And he's still here, planning revenge against those who hurt me, loving me not in spite of my past but with it, through it, because of it.

This morning feels different.

I feel different.

Lighter, yes, but also...harder somehow.

More certain.

The girl who trembled at the thought of her secrets being revealed is gone.

In her place is a woman who knows her worth, who's done playing small, done letting the past dictate her future.

In search of fresh air, I slip from bed, wrap myself in Dante's discarded shirt, and pad to the terrace.

The city sprawls below, morning fog rolling in from the harbor. From here, I can see the ports that are causing so much trouble—metal containers stacked like children's blocks, cranes reaching into the sky like mechanical giants.

There has to be a way...

My phone buzzes. Alessio.

"Your timing is perfect," I answer, not bothering with hello. "I need your business brain."

He chuckles. "And here I was calling to check on honeymoon plans. What's on your mind, *cara mia*?"

I outline the port situation—the families fighting for control, the endless bloodshed, the impossible task of untangling decades of corruption. I know Dante wouldn't mind; him and Alessio often discuss business. Most of it he already knows anyway.

"The way I see it," I say, leaning against the railing, "if Dante keeps going like this, he'll either burn out or get killed. And for what? Territory? Shipping routes? It's all so..."

"Primitive?" Alessio offers.

"Exactly." I watch a cargo ship glide into the harbor. "There has to be another way to control the ports without this endless cycle of violence."

Alessio is quiet for a moment. When he speaks, his voice has that razor-sharp edge I rarely hear—the voice that rules a Vegas empire. "You're looking at it backward, Danica. The most dangerous men I know aren't the ones who control the streets. They're the ones who control the boardrooms."

Something clicks in my mind. "Clean money."

"Now you're thinking." I can hear his smile. "What's more valuable—a street corner or a corporate headquarters? A protection racket or a majority stake?"

I watch the massive cranes loading and unloading millions in cargo. Legal cargo. "But the families would never—"

"Wouldn't they? Think about it. Most of them are already laundering their dirty money into legitimate businesses. What if you offered them a way to skip that step? To have power without the constant threat of prison or death?"

My heart races as the pieces snap together. "A legitimate company."

"With legitimate shareholders," Alessio adds. "And a legitimate Managing Director who happens to have no criminal record."

I grip the phone tighter. "Me?"

"You." His voice is soft with pride. "The suburban girl with a squeaky-clean history who just happens to be married to Dante Fera."

The fog is burning off now, the sun illuminating everything with stark clarity. I can almost see it—the future laid out before us like a new kingdom.

"Alessio," I breathe, "you're a fucking genius."

He laughs. "I've been called worse."

I hear Dante stirring inside. "I have to go, my love. Thank you, just thank you."

"For what? You figured it out yourself. I just asked the right questions. See you in Bali, *cara mia*." He hangs up before I can respond.

I turn to find Dante in the doorway, sleep-rumpled and beautiful, watching me with those midnight eyes.

"You okay, *Tesoro*?" His voice is rough with concern. "After last night..."

I cross to him, pressing my body against his. "I'm good. Guess what?"

Dante looks at me, confused. "What?"

"I think I just solved our problem."

"You'll have to be more specific than that."

I gesture at the ships in the distance.

His eyebrows lift. "The ports?"

"All of it." I take his hand, pulling him back inside. "What's the one thing every family wants?"

"Power." His answer is immediate.

"No." I shake my head. "Legitimacy. Clean money. The ability to walk in the daylight without looking over their shoulders."

His expression shifts, interest sparking where there was only exhaustion before. "Go on."

"We give them what they want—every last piece of the Fera empire. The protection rackets, the gambling, the drugs. All of it."

He stiffens. "My father's legacy—"

"Was built in blood," I say gently, taking his face in my hands. "And it's drowning you, Dante. But what if we could build something better? Something lasting?"

"The other families would never agree to—"

"They will if we offer them something better." I move to the open door, gesturing toward the harbor. "Look at those ships, Dante. Look at all that legitimate cargo. Billions in legal commerce. What if we created a corporation to run the ports? Clean. Professional. With shares for every family."

Understanding dawns in his eyes. "And who would run this corporation?"

I meet his gaze steadily. "Me."

"You." He says it like he's testing the idea, turning it over in his mind.

"I have no criminal record. Just a journalism degree and a rich husband." I step closer, heart pounding. "I can learn business.

Get an MBA. Build something that can't be taken away by a bullet or a raid."

Dante's eyes narrow, calculating. "They'll never accept an outsider."

"They will when they realize what they're getting. Safety. Legitimacy. Profit without risk." I press my hand to his chest, feeling his heartbeat. "And they respect you. You'd be there, behind the scenes. The power behind the throne."

He's quiet for a long moment, his mind working through the angles. Then, slowly, a smile spreads across his face—not his usual dangerous smirk, but something genuine. Something hopeful.

"You would do this?" His voice is soft with wonder. "Take on the families? The business world? All of it?"

I lift my chin. "I've faced worse demons than corporate lawyers and grumpy old Dons." The scars on my body seem to pulse with affirmation. "Besides, I handled Tolya Volkov, I can handle a boardroom."

His hands come up to frame my face, his eyes searching mine. "You're different this morning."

"Good different?"

"Powerful." His thumb traces my lips. "Like you've finally seen what I've always known was there."

The last piece clicks into place. This isn't just about saving the business or stopping a war. It's about claiming my place. My power. Not as Dante's wife but as my own force to be reckoned with.

"A legitimate empire," Dante murmurs, pulling me closer. "Built on our terms."

"With no more bodies in the harbor," I add, letting myself believe it's possible. "No more nights waiting to see if you'll come home."

His kiss is answer enough—deep and certain and full of promise. When he pulls away, the weight that's been crushing him these past weeks seems lighter.

"Where do we start?" he asks, and those four words tell me everything. He's with me. He believes in this. In me.

I smile, trailing my fingers along his jawline. "By packing our bags and going to Bali. We need to think this through properly before proposing it to the families." My mind races ahead, already strategizing. "Let them stew a little longer. Let them get even more desperate while we're away. They'll play right into our hands when we return."

His eyes light up with understanding—the tactician in him appreciating the move. "Beautiful and strong, *and* smart—how did I get this lucky?" Dante pulls me closer for a kiss that feels like a seal on our new future, a promise between equals.

When we break apart, I look back toward the harbor one last time. The sun is high in the sky now, the fog completely burned away. Below our terrace, the city is bustling as always, unaware that its underworld is about to be transformed by a woman who once thought her greatest achievement would be surviving her past.

Now I know better. Surviving was just the beginning.

This—this moment, this idea, this future we're about to build—this is what I was surviving for.

I'm done playing by their rules.

Time to write my own.

CHAPTER THIRTY-THREE

BETRAYAL

(DANTE)

The basement air hangs thick with the familiar scent of fear and blood. Dimitri Volkov whimpers pathetically in the corner, his once-defiant posture now permanently stooped from weeks of questioning. Ever since we captured him, he's been a reluctant fountain of information—names, routes, connections we never would have discovered otherwise. He had way more access than his little brother Tolya.

But one question continues to gnaw at me: Who betrayed us? There was no way those thugs would've gotten into our wedding without insider help. And who fucked us over during that first failed ambush?

While Danica's been upstairs revolutionizing our future, I've been down here hunting the ghosts of our past. Somewhere, I smell a rat. And I don't tolerate rats.

"Tell me again," I demand, circling the chair where Dimitri sits trembling. "The night before the ambush. Who did you speak with?"

"I told you everything!" His accent thickens with desperation. "My contact—he said you were coming. Said when, how many men."

"A name, Dimitri." My patience, worn thin by weeks of damage control and family politics, threatens to snap entirely. "I want a name."

Dimitri's watery eyes dart around the room, seeking escape where there is none. *"Bozhe moy*...he will kill me!"

"I'm not feeling particularly merciful either." I lean in close enough to smell his fear-sweat. "The difference is, I can make it last for days."

He mumbles something I can't quite catch.

"What was that?" I grab his chin, forcing his face up to mine.

"Vitale," he whispers, the name barely audible. "Leo Vitale."

The floor seems to shift beneath my feet. Not possible. Leo has been with the family for fifteen years. He's godfather to Emilio's youngest grandson, for fuck's sake.

"You're lying." My voice sounds distant, even to my own ears.

"Why would I lie now?" Dimitri's laugh holds the hysteria of a man with nothing left to lose. "He reached out months ago. Said he was tired of working for scraps while you lived like a king."

The pieces slot together with sickening clarity. Leo's recent purchases—the new car, the vacation home his salary couldn't possibly cover. His convenient absence the day we moved on the club. The way he always seemed to be away from his post when crucial information needed relaying.

I straighten, my decision already made. "Thank you for your cooperation, Dimitri."

"Does this mean I can go?" Hope flickers across his battered face—a hope I have no intention of fulfilling.

I don't bother answering. He knows the truth as well as I do. There is no walking away from this basement. His brothers are already rotting in the ground for their sins.

Upstairs, the house is alive with activity. Through the open door of the library, I glimpse Danica with Luigi, poring over financial structures and legal frameworks for her brilliant new plan. It's been three days since her revelation on the terrace, and I've never seen her so focused, so alive. While she builds our future, I need to clear the debris of our past.

This is old business—the kind of work I've been trying to leave behind. The kind she wants to transform into something legitimate. But before we can move forward, I need to cut out the cancer in our ranks.

Emilio answers on the first ring. "Boss?"

"Bring Leo in." I keep my voice steady, controlled. "Tell him it's about security for the new company venture. Be discreet.

A pause. Emilio knows me too well. "Understood, *Don mio*."

Four hours later, as evening shadows lengthen across the garden, Leo Vitale stands in my office, shoulders squared, face betraying nothing but professional interest.

"You wanted to see me, Don Fera?" He's clean-shaven, immaculate in his dark suit. The perfect soldier.

The perfect traitor.

"Sit down, Leo." I gesture to the chair across from my desk. "Drink?"

"No, thank you, sir." He sits, posture relaxed but alert. Fifteen years of service has taught him my routines, my tells. He's watching for signs of trouble, but I've had decades to perfect my mask.

I pour myself two fingers of whiskey, taking my time. "How do you feel about our progress with the ports?"

He blinks, clearly thrown by the question. "The ports? It's going well. We're winning."

"Seems that way." I nod, swirling the amber liquid. "New beginnings all around."

"Yes, sir." He shifts slightly. "It will be a significant change."

"Change is inevitable." I study his face. "We adapt or we die. Wouldn't you agree?"

"Of course, Don Fera."

I sip my whiskey, letting silence fill the space between us. Leo holds my gaze, but I notice the faint sheen of sweat at his temple.

"Funny thing about new beginnings," I continue finally. "They often require cleaning up old messes first."

His fingers tighten almost imperceptibly on the armrest. "Sir?"

"The port ambush, Leo." I set my glass down carefully. "Before we move forward, I need to understand what went wrong."

"We were double-crossed," he says smoothly. "The Russians were waiting."

"Yes, they were." I lean forward. "But how did they know? Who told them?"

Leo's expression remains neutral, professional. "We've been investigating—"

"No need." I cut him off. "Dimitri Volkov has been very...forthcoming."

The blood drains from his face so quickly it's almost comical. "Sir, I don't—"

"Don't insult me further by lying." My voice drops to a dangerous whisper. "*Traditore.*" Traitor.

Leo's hand twitches toward his weapon, but Emilio steps from the shadows behind him, pressing the cold barrel of a gun against the base of his skull.

"How long?" I ask, genuine curiosity mixing with fury. "How long have you been selling us out?"

Leo's shoulders slump, the charade abandoned. "Five months. Since the new territories opened up. I—"

"Five months." The words taste like ash as I cut him off. "Seven men died at those ports. Carlo died."

"I didn't know it would be so many," he whispers. "They promised just enough resistance to make it look real. Then things...escalated."

"And what did your honor cost these days, Leo? What was the price for our blood?"

His silence is answer enough.

I stand, moving around the desk to face him directly. "I trusted you. Brought you into my home. Let you near my wife."

"It was just business," he pleads. "Nothing personal."

A laugh escapes me—bitter, cold. "That's where you're wrong. Everything in this life is personal."

The next part is mechanical, practiced. The questions that need answers. The information that must be secured. Leo talks, of course. They always do. Names, dates, meeting places. The full extent of his betrayal mapped out in trembling confessions.

When it's done, when there's nothing left to learn, I nod to Emilio. My oldest friend, my most loyal soldier, understands without words.

"Your family won't suffer for your mistakes," I tell Leo as Emilio prepares to lead him away. "Your daughter will finish university. Your wife will be provided for."

Gratitude and shame war on his face. "Thank you, Don Fera."

"Don't thank me." My voice hardens. "This mercy isn't for you. It's for them. They deserve better than a traitor's legacy."

He nods, accepting his fate with what little dignity remains to him.

"One more thing, Leo."

He turns at the door, eyes already dead.

"Was it worth it?"

The question hangs between us.

"No," he whispers finally. "Nothing could be."

At least in this, he tells the truth.

Later, when Emilio returns alone, I don't ask for details. Some actions belong to the shadows, even between us. It couldn't have been easy for him.

"It's done," he says simply, accepting the glass I offer.

"Quietly?"

"*Sì, Don mio.*"

We sit in silence for a long moment, the weight of necessary violence heavy between us.

"Will you tell the *Donna*?" Emilio asks finally.

I consider the question, thinking of Danica in the library downstairs, excitement in her eyes as she builds something new, something legitimate. Of the future we're planning, the life we're trying to create.

"Yes," I decide. "No more secrets between us. She needs to know it's truly over."

Emilio nods, understanding. In our world, truth is often the only luxury we can afford.

As I look out over the garden, I feel a weight lifting. This was the last piece of unfinished business, the final thread connecting me to the old ways. With Leo gone, with the betrayal resolved, I can step fully into whatever comes next.

"The flights to Bali are confirmed for tomorrow," Emilio says, breaking the silence. "Security has been arranged at both ends."

"And the families?"

"They've all received notice that you'll be unreachable for two weeks. Any matters requiring attention will go through myself while you're away."

I nod, satisfied. "And Danica's plans for the corporation?"

"The preliminary paperwork is being drawn up. It will be ready for review when you return." He hesitates. "The Vincis are already asking questions."

"Let them ask. By the time we're back, they'll be desperate enough to accept her terms."

Emilio's rare smile flashes. "*Donna* Fera has changed everything, hasn't she?"

"For the better," I agree, feeling the truth of it in my bones.

***

I find Danica in our bedroom, already packing for tomorrow's departure. The sight of her—barefoot, hair loose around her shoulders, humming softly as she folds clothes—settles something in me that's been restless for years.

"It's done," I say simply, leaning against the doorframe.

She turns, pausing with a silk blouse in her hands. "You found who betrayed us?"

I nod, crossing the threshold into our shared sanctuary. "Leo Vitale. Been selling us out for months."

Her eyes widen slightly, then narrow. "Leo? The same Leo who carried me to safety when I twisted my ankle at the airport last year?"

"The very same." My voice is tight. "Dimitri confirmed it. Then Leo confessed everything."

She processes this, her clever mind connecting the dots I can almost see forming behind her eyes. "That why he conveniently missed the ambush?"

"Exactly. He won't be a problem anymore."

Danica sets down the blouse, crossing to me. "Good." A single word containing multitudes. Not judgment, not horror—just acceptance. Understanding of what needed to be done.

"The last loose end," I tell her, pulling her into my arms. "Nothing hanging over us now."

She leans against my chest, her hands sliding up to rest on my shoulders. "Perfect timing for our honeymoon."

"Two weeks of nothing but you, me, and Alessio waiting for us in paradise." I press my lips to her neck, breathing in her scent. "No ports, no families, no betrayals."

"Just us," she agrees, tilting her face up to mine. Her eyes search my expression, finding whatever she's looking for. "No more looking over our shoulders?"

"Not for this. Leo was working alone. Greedy, not ideological." I stroke her cheek. "The threat is eliminated."

She nods, returning to her packing with renewed purpose. "Then Bali awaits."

Some chapters must close before others can begin.

And now, finally, we can turn the page.

CHAPTER THIRTY-FOUR

HONEYMOON

(DANICA)

Paradise tastes like fresh mango and expensive rum, served in a coconut shell adorned with flowers I can't name.

As the sun melts into the horizon, decorating the sky in watercolor strokes of purple and amber, I stretch languidly on my pool lounger, feeling more peaceful than I have in months.

The private villa sprawls behind us, all glass and teak and luxury, but it's the infinity pool that steals the show—the way it seems to pour straight into the Indian Ocean, blues merging until you can't tell where pool ends and ocean begins. Frangipani blossoms float on the surface, their sweet scent mingling with the salty air.

This is our reward. For finally solving the puzzle.

Well, there is a lot to do but that all can wait. Paperwork takes time. And we deserve a break. Dealing with the ports is clearly more of a marathon than a sprint. But none of that matters, not here.

What matters is that I finally get to experience Bali!

And not cheap, backpacker holiday-style Bali, but lux AF Bali—the kind that comes with private chefs and towels folded like swans.

Beside me, Dante sleeps deeply for the first time in ages. His face is softer in slumber, years younger, the constant weight of being Don Fera temporarily lifted from his shoulders. A light snore escapes him, and my heart swells with tenderness.

This morning, I woke to sunlight streaming through the sheer curtains and the soothing sound of waves breaking outside. For a moment, I thought I was dreaming—surely this level of luxury only existed in travel magazines and influencer posts. But no—the marble floors cool under my feet, the private chef preparing breakfast on our terrace, the infinity pool stretching toward forever—it's all ours.

The villa itself is a masterpiece of modern design merged with Balinese tradition. Carved wooden doors tall as giants, floor-to-ceiling windows that disappear into walls, letting the outside in.

Every room opens to either ocean or garden views, though "garden" seems an inadequate word for the lush paradise of orchids and palm trees and flowers I've only seen in pictures.

We have our own stretch of private beach, accessed by stone steps that wind through tropical forest. The local staff appear like magic to attend to our needs, then vanish just as quietly, leaving us in our bubble of perfect solitude.

This is more than a honeymoon. It's a reset. A chance to breathe after months of violence and tension. A moment to just be Danica and Dante, not Donna Fera and her Don. Although...

My eyes drift to the marks on Dante's neck, just visible above his collar—reminders of last night's pleasure. Even in paradise, some dynamics don't change. Some needs don't fade. It was only the appetizer...

But for now, I let him sleep. Let him dream. Let the peace of this place work its magic on us both.

Who would have thought that I would end up here one day? That a damaged suburban nobody would become not just a Queen, but a truly happy one?

The only thing missing was Biscotti, but at least I know he's in good hands. I saw how attached he's gotten to his *babysitter*, aka Dario. Secretly, I think the guard enjoys protecting the dog more than he does protecting the family—it sure is less dangerous.

Dante stirs, and I switch my attention from the departing sun to my husband, taking his hand and kissing each finger individually.

He opens one eye, a sleepy smile on his face. "Hey, you."

"Hey..." I trail my fingers over his swim shorts, tracing the outline of his resting cock teasingly.

He groans, stretching out. "Are you trying to wake me?"

"Sonja will be up soon, don't you worry." I grin as the live animal beneath my fingers slowly squirms itself to life as predicted.

"No doubt. You know Sonja is a slut for you." He's fully awake now. Sleepy is not a state Dante can maintain for long, unlike me. Some days, I stay sleepy all day. But I'm just gonna keep blaming my stupid hormones for that.

"Sonja is a slut for everyone," I reply with a wink as I pull his waistband down to expose his cock in the fading dusk for nobody to see.

The staff have already left and Alessio is only arriving in a few days. For the time being, Dante is all mine.

"Yes, Ma'am." He shivers as I palm his erection to full hardness in the warm evening air, cocktail in one hand, cock in the other.

There is air-conditioning throughout the entire villa, in every room, but outside here, the humid air is free to stick to my skin.

Since our arrival last night, I've been unable to keep actual clothes on my body because of the heat, resolving to live in this yellow bikini for the remainder of our stay.

"You know," I grin as I put my cocktail down to give my husband my full attention, "I've always wanted to give you a blowjob outside."

Dante swallows loudly, muttering a dramatic *"Dio mio,"* much to my amusement.

"I take that as a yes?"

Climbing onto his lounger, I part Dante's thighs to make space for me between them. His whole body stiffens in anticipation.

"Please," he moans as my lips close over his cock. "Oh god." His eyes fall shut as I take all of him, swallowing him whole.

"Are you sensitive, my love?" I tease, licking him from tip to base like he's one of those big red-and-white spiral lollipops.

"So sensitive..." Dante clutches the edge of his seat firmly, trying to steady himself as I wrap my fingers around his erection to add more friction.

"I wonder why, hmm..." I remark as if I am not the one who has edged him senseless for the past few days, denying him any release. He hasn't been allowed to come since last Tuesday.

"You're driving me mad. Please let me finish, please." His voice ventures on whining as my desperate husband shakes and shudders between my lips, dangerously close to the edge within minutes.

"No, baby. Not yet. I want you nice and feral for our guest."

Before Dante can reach his climax, I pull away, giving his cock a little smack before lying down on top of him, resting my head against his broad chest while his desperate erection squirms between our bodies like an unearthed worm.

Dante lets out an exasperated huff, looking down at his painfully hard cock. "But Alessio is only arriving in four days!"

Reaching down, I trace a long, red nail up his shaft, flicking my forefinger at this tip when I reach the top. Dante gasps. Flinches.

"Oh, I know." I laugh, knowing it only fuels his need, his despair.

"Such a cruel Mistress. Please!" Dante begs as I lick my lips, smacking them together loudly.

"Wife," I correct him as my lips find his, kissing him messily, leaving his taste all over his face.

"Such a cruel *wife*."

"You don't want to see cruel." I grab his balls and tug, only lightly but enough for Dante's breath to catch in his throat.

"Danica..." he whines like a child denied a turn on the swing. "I beg you." Anguish clouds Dante's face as he arches his hips, trying to find some sort of friction for his needy cock, but there is none to be found; there is no space to move.

"You whine like a boy who thinks I change my mind easily."

Dante sighs heavily. "I get you this whole honeymoon, and you still won't let me come."

"Careful darling, you're close to pouting." I place a finger on his scowling lips.

"I don't pout."

"You also don't come. Not today. What do you always tell me about being patient?"

"You're the least patient person I know," his voice is accusatory as I get up, leaving him a puddle of need on the lounger, his orgasm successfully ruined.

I take a large sip of my water bottle before turning to the pool, diving in, purposefully ignoring Dante's flushed cheeks, his frustrated huffing and puffing. Let him stew. Torment is a good look on that handsome Italian face.

"Care to join me?" I ask when I surface again.

Dante crosses his arms, but his eyes sparkle. "You know swimming is not my thing."

"Not yet." I slip back into the embrace of the water, letting it wash away old hurts. Here, in this infinity pool at the edge of the world, with a man who loves every inch of me, my blemishes no longer bother me; I no longer want to hide them.

I surface to find Dante watching me with that look that still makes my heart skip—like I'm something rare, valuable, like every curve and scar is exactly as it should be.

"You're beautiful," he says simply, and for the first time in my life, I believe it completely.

CHAPTER THIRTY-FIVE

DADDIES

(DANTE)

T he Bali night wraps around us like silk, warm and heavy with salt air. Through the villa's open window, I can hear waves outside, a gentle counterpoint to Danica's soft breathing from the bedroom behind us.

She's having a nap, exhausted from our active afternoon.

We've been here for six days, but it's already hard to imagine a world beyond this oasis in the ocean.

Six more days of waking up married, of watching Danica smile at her ring, of feeling something close to peace.

Alessio pulls my attention back to him. "Are you going to say that to my face?" My voice is thick with mock-aggression as I push the half-naked Don against the wall in the large open-plan lounge area.

"You. Are. Such. A. Pussy," my first love taunts me with a playful grin, his hands dropping to my ass as he pulls me into

371

him. He is as hard as I am, his unmistakable erection trapped between us.

"Don't." I yank him by his open shirt, slamming his back into the wall again.

It was like he's been here all along. Yet Alessio had arrived mere hours ago, dressed in white linen that somehow stayed crisp despite the Bali heat, looking like he'd stepped out of a luxury travel magazine. His smile lit up the entire villa when Danica ran to greet him, jumping into his arms like an excited child.

I'd hung back, watching them, my heart full at seeing my two loves together again.

There's something about Alessio that makes everything brighter—as if he carried Vegas's neon glow with him wherever he went.

He'd kissed Danica first, deep and passionate, then turned to me with that knowing look that still makes my pulse race after all these years.

"Miss me, amore mio?" he'd asked before pulling me into a kiss that tasted of airplane coffee and unquenchable desire.

The day dissolved into a blur of laughter and touches and shared memories. We had lunch on the terrace, Alessio entertaining us with stories of Vegas drama while Danica curled between us on the oversized lounger. Perfect, peaceful moments that seemed impossible just months ago.

Backdropped by the setting sun, Madame Fera had finally let me come, spilling my seed all over her bikini top while Alessio watched us with a tall glass of crisp white wine in hand.

It was but the beginning...

My body ached pleasantly from our recent...*activities*. Alessio's playful wrestling turned to kisses, turned to more, until Danica took control of us both. My Queen and my Vegas Joker—they knew exactly how to take me apart and put me back together.

Danica had given me her permission to come as much as I wanted before passing out on the large fluffy bed, mumbling something about snacks before closing her eyes and not opening them again. It was an opportunity I intended to take full advantage of.

Alessio's rapid breathing anchors me in the present, in the warm evening breeze, our hard cocks pressed against one another with nothing but swimming trunks between them.

The Vegas Joker grins, running his fingers over my bared chest before gripping a nipple playfully, twisting it. "You know I love it when you play rough."

His face is mere inches from mine, his body pressed against mine. Neither of us shows any sign of backing off.

"I'm a rough guy, or have you forgotten, Don Santoro?" I kiss him before he can answer, forcing his lips open with my tongue.

Alessio's body softens against mine as he relaxes into the passionate kiss, our hands wandering all over each other, groping, tweaking, twisting, pinching.

Grinding my hips against his, I dry hump my teenage crush, rubbing our cocks together.

Free to give into my desires, I bite his neck, pulling the skin between my teeth as I mark him, pushing his hands up above his head and pinning them against the wall. He lets me.

Alessio licks my earlobe seductively as he whispers, "Fuck me, Dante," and a shiver runs down my spine, straight to my dick.

"Hmm..." I drop his wrists and reach for his cock, pulling it free from the useless material concealing it. "That tight little hole of yours stretches so beautifully..."

It was the truth.

With Alessio, we've always taken turns bottoming; the power dynamic was more evenly split than with Danica.

We expressed our desires openly, as hard as it was for me initially to find the words, to say them to him, to another man, another Don. But Alessio wasn't just any other Don, he was mine, ours.

"There is nothing I want more, darling," Alessio tells me, sliding down against the wall until he's kneeling before me, ready to take my cock down his throat.

I'm too big for Danica to fit all of me, but Alessio's gag reflex is non-existent, and he swallows me whole as I stand frozen, heart thumping in my chest.

A loud moan leaves my lips as he works his lips over my hardness, slobbering his spit all over my cock. *How is he so damn good at that?*

Grunting loudly, I grab him by the hair and pull him up before I come down his throat, dragging him to his feet so I can lick my pre-cum off his lips.

"Where's the lube?" I whisper, biting his bottom lip roughly as I pull away.

"In the kitchen." Alessio wrangles free from my grip and darts inside. I follow him, but he doesn't notice, not at first. Not until I grab him from behind and bend him over the marble island counter.

I pry the lube from his hands, keeping him bent before me. "I'll take this, thank you."

"In the kitchen? Ooh, kinky." Alessio wiggles his bum at me, and I fight the urge to laugh.

"Take off your clothes," I instruct, smacking his ass with my flat hand.

Without hesitating, Alessio turns around and strips down naked, hoisting himself onto the cold counter with those strong, muscular arms of his.

"Now you," he tells me, slowly stroking his cock as I slip off my shorts as well. "Hmm," he blows me a kiss, "Hey *Sonja*."

A scowl twists my face as I grumble, "Don't. Only Danica gets to call him that."

Alessio laughs, reaching for my cock and pressing the two heads together, rubbing them simultaneously to draw a hungry growl from my lips.

I am beyond ready, leaking in lust.

Fucking hell—again?

My hand finds his windpipe, closing around his throat as I push Alessio down on the large counter, his body shivering visibly as it makes contact with the cool marble.

Don Santoro doesn't resist, just lets me guide him where I need him, hips buckling and back arching, responding to every touch like I'm the master and he the puppet.

With rough movements, I part his thighs, sinking down between them to close my lips around that beautiful cock I'll never get enough of.

Before, I could never imagine enjoying giving blowjobs as much as receiving them. But so much has changed since Alessio came back into my life. Since Danica helped me discover my sexual freedom.

A freedom I plan to utilize fully as I smear the lube around Alessio's hole, enjoying the little gasps the cold liquid draws from his lips in reaction. Almost as much as I enjoy the hissed Italian curse he spits out when I push my forefinger into his ass moments later.

He clenches around me, humming like a little bird as I finger him.

"Stop teasing me and fuck me already," Alessio groans as I push another finger inside, stretching him.

"I don't want to hurt you. Patience," I growl, a third lubed finger joining the others.

Alessio doesn't stop complaining until I press the tip of my cock against his entrance...and then he's quiet, very quiet, holding his breath.

"You ready?" I ask.

Alessio nods. "Please."

"Can you take it all?"

"Fill me, Daddy!" Alessio begs as I carefully push inside, adding more lube for good measure. Nobody has called me *"Daddy"* in a long time, but I don't mind Alessio doing so. He can call me whatever he wants.

My first love growls loudly as I push all the way in, stretching to take all of me.

"Such a good boy," I tell him, enjoying the shift in the dynamic.

"For you, Don Fera, any day," Alessio rasps between rapid breaths, holding onto the edge of the counter as I slowly bury myself to the hilt inside him.

"Unclench, baby." I speak to him like Danica speaks to me, trying it out, drinking up every reaction, every sound, as Alessio comes undone around my cock.

No more words leave his lips, not when I wrap my hand around his cock, milking him in unison with my thrusts. Just a pretty mess, legs in the air, mine to use as I see fit.

I fuck him until my balls start contracting, warning me that I'm dangerously close to spilling my load.

Alessio whimpers. I can tell by the shaking in his knees that he must be close too.

"Words. Use your words," I demand, fucking him harder.

"C-close..." Alessio stutters like forming the simple word was incredibly hard work.

"Ask permission," I insist as I speed up my movements. He never has to ask usually, but I want to hear it this time.

He doesn't hesitate. Not for a second. "Please, Daddy. Please, may I come?" Alessio moans obediently, and I know there's not much time left for either of us.

"Come for me, *amore*. You have permission."

Alessio's only response is a loud groan. I hold onto his cock as it spasms in my hand, spilling thick cum over my knuckles.

Moments later, I release inside him, an uncontainable primal roar ripping from my diaphragm.

Leaving a sticky mess on the counter, I pull out, collapsing on the large couch behind me in the open-plan space.

When he can find his legs again, Alessio hops off the counter and joins me, snuggling his tall figure in my arms, his head on my heart, the pounding beat in his ear.

Kissing his head, I stroke his hair until both our breaths calm down. Until I'm sure our bodies have formed a singular mass of spent lust on the couch.

"You've never called me Daddy before," I remark with amusement.

Alessio chuckles softly, intertwining his fingers with mine. "What can I say? You were giving some serious Dzaddy energy today."

"I don't know what that means, but I'll take that as a compliment."

"You should." Alessio reaches up for a kiss, and I'm happy to oblige.

"I'm glad you're here, darling." The words come out softer than intended, vulnerable in the afterglow.

Alessio's fingers trace lazy patterns on my chest. "Of course. I wouldn't miss this for the world." He pauses, his tone shifting slightly. "Besides, sounds like y'all needed a holiday. Everything okay with the business?"

My body tenses instantly, the peace of the moment fracturing. "It's getting there. Thank you for your help."

"Anything for our Queen." Alessio kisses my fingers. "For you."

"It's still complicated." I stare at the ceiling, watching shadows from the garden dance across it. "But we're figuring it out."

"Your father would be proud."

A bitter laugh escapes me. "I one hundred percent doubt that."

"Well, that's not on you. You always did your best." His hand finds mine, squeezing gently.

"Not good enough, according to him." The old pain rises like bile. "I can't even count the fucked-up things I did trying to impress him. And for what? He still didn't give a shit. Even after he died, I didn't stop, I just got worse. I hated being that person."

Alessio's voice softens. "We're not all cut out for this life."

"You love it though." I glance down at him, still amazed by how naturally he wears power.

"I do, but my situation is very different. I am very different." His amber eyes hold centuries of Vegas wisdom.

"Suppose you're right." I let out a long breath. "Doesn't matter anymore anyway. What's done is done. Not like any of us ever stood a chance of going to heaven anyway."

Our shared laughter breaks the heaviness. Alessio lifts his head from my chest, those intense eyes searching mine. "Things are different now, *amore mio*. You're not that man anymore."

"My body can't take being that man anymore." We both know it's more than that.

"Excuses. Excuses." His fingers find my chest hair, tugging playfully. "Your body is fine. It's just done enough work for one lifetime, if you ask me. I think Don Fera deserves more *fun*."

My traitorous dick responds instantly to his touch. "You're insatiable, Alessio." Just like Danica—maybe that's why they get along so well.

His hand drifts lower, touch teasing and familiar, as he grabs my cock, lazily toying with the tip. "Perhaps. Want to try and find out if that's true?"

I bite back a moan, pushing myself into his hand. "Let's..."

Chapter Thirty-Six

COMPLETE

(Danica)

"What is it about you Italian thugs that make you look so pretty on your knees before me?" I tug their leashes taut, forcing Dante and Alessio to look up at me as I tower above them, naked except for my pegging harness and heels.

They don't answer, just obediently regard the Madame of the house with their hard cocks poking up from their laps like antennae, their bodies bare except for the exquisite matching collars fastened around their necks. Two adoring puppies.

I found them fucking in the pool when I woke up from my nap.

Imagine that?

Dante in the pool?

Only Alessio could convince him to do that.

After I joined them, things quickly escalated to this point where the Dons waited for my next command on their knees.

"Look how beautiful you are when you submit." I stroke each of their cheeks as they remain docile by my feet, hip to naked hip, hands on their thighs like good boys.

The lines that are supposed to box our desires have long since blurred when the three of us play together, supported by the key pillars of consent, trust, and communication. On those rest the safe space we've created, a safe space to explore even our wildest fantasies—with my husband and my boyfriend. *Oh god, I'm so lucky.*

I love all our games, but few give me as much pleasure as having them both submit to me.

"Get up, Alessio," I command, forcing him to follow the tug of his leash off the ground while Dante remains by our feet.

"Whatever you desire, *Madame.*" Oh, how I love the sound of that word.

Pulling him down to my level, I kiss Alessio deeply, enjoying the choking sounds as I pull on his leash, tightening the slip ring of his collar.

"Dante, darling husband o'mine. Don't you want to show me how good you are with your mouth?" I tug his leash toward us, and he happily takes Alessio's cock between his lips. Just enough to make Alessio fully hard, hard enough to complain bitterly when I pull Dante's head off his cock.

I push Alessio onto the bed with enough force to send him toppling onto the luxurious satin sheets with a bounce.

"You too, baby. Beside him."

Dante joins Alessio on the bed, and the boys exchange a beautiful kiss, weaving their fingers together.

My heart melts, and my insides burn with desire as I watch them, beyond aroused at the scene.

Unrolling their leashes around my fists, I give them space, letting them cuddle and play fight.

"Enough!"

They gasp, choking, as I yank the leashes, forcing their attention back to me. "Now, who's first?"

"Please, Madame. I'm ready." Alessio cries, his cock hard, desperate to be touched, but completely unstimulated.

"Very well then. Dante, you may continue touching him, but slowly. Nobody comes without permission. This party can turn from pleasure to pain very quickly if you don't respect my rules."

"Yes, Ma'am," they both echo, Alessio grunting as Dante's fingers tease the underside of his cock head—his most sensitive spot.

"Now relax. Focus on Dante's hand, on your breathing." They know the instructions by now, but I go through the motions every time, reminding them to unclench, to let me in as my lubed cock penetrates their tight asses.

I slip a condom over the dildo, positioning Alessio's ass near the edge of the bed, his knees pushed to his chest.

Dante still finds easy access, caressing Alessio's dick with such tender touches.

Carefully, I prep the Joker's ass with my finger, making sure he's ready for me.

"Now, let's see if we can make a nice little mess of you. I bet you'll take me like a good boy, won't you?"

Alessio nods furiously. "Please, fill me, Miss."

Tightening the grip on his leash, I push inside, slowly at first, until he relaxes around my cock, letting me fill him to the brim, groaning loudly as I fuck him into the bed, hitting his prostate again and again while Dante jerks him off.

I catch my husband's eye, and we exchange a smile before returning our attention to making Alessio come—a great team effort.

He doesn't last long; within minutes Alessio is screaming my name, tears streaking down his cheek, begging to come. But I don't let him, no, I leave him on the edge, crying, furious, unsatisfied.

I throw the condom on the floor and replace it with a fresh one before switching sides, pushing Dante's knees to his chest while Alessio, still hard, still needy, closes his fist around Dante's shaft, pumping him in tune with my thrusts.

I feel so powerful, on top of the world, as I frivolously toy with the Dons' pleasure, tormenting them with the one thing they need but I won't give them—permission to come.

"Please, Danica! Please!" Dante is near delirious with his need to ejaculate, but we all know the chances of me allowing that are slim.

"Leave him," I tell Alessio, and Dante crumbles in despair, his cock aching for release, on the brink, so damn close, but oh, so far.

"Please, have a heart!" Foolish boy, he knows how this conversation ends. My black heart knows no mercy for crying little boys with swollen balls and dripping cocks.

I drag myself up onto the bed, smearing the wetness between my thighs on Dante's leg as I do, straddling him with my legs spread wide.

"Don't you know good boys finish last?" I laugh cruelly, fully in character now, as I pull his leash so taut that it nearly cuts off his air supply.

Dante doesn't have a chance to reply because I shift upwards to settle on his chest, my pussy in his face.

"Eat up, puppy," I instruct as his warm breath tickles my skin. "Madame is sopping down there."

He doesn't hesitate for a second. Dante's tongue over my clit brings a gasp to my lips. So does Alessio's large hands spreading over my breasts from behind as he joins us.

Nobody told him he could move but it feels too good for me to object. I lean back against Alessio as he caresses my breasts, tweaking my nipples between his fingers, his face buried in my neck, kissing me, licking me, biting me.

Dante may or may not be able to breathe, but he doesn't ease up on his rhythm for one second, eating my pussy like a fucking boss. I know he'd signal his safe word if he really were at risk of suffocating, but his hands remain hooked over my thighs, holding my ass in place in front of his face.

My moans grow louder and louder as the climax tugs at the edges of my skin, starting warm in my belly and then growing wider and wider as it ripples outward in waves of passion, until I'm screaming—no words in particular, just a high-pitched wail of ecstasy, coming so hard!

"No more," I pant finally, when I can take no more, and Dante lets up, gasping for air between my thighs.

Alessio topples us both off of Dante, the three of us sweaty messes under the lazy ceiling fan.

Maybe it's 7 PM, maybe 11 PM. Who gives a fuck? The staff had long been sent home with the message that we would call them if we needed them.

The men sandwich me between them, wrapping me in their bodies as we all share kisses, snuggling, skin-to-skin—the most amazing feeling. Well, the second most amazing.

"I want you inside me," I smile.

"Which one of us?" Alessio asks, pinching my cheek.

"Both of you," I grin, licking his lips.

Alessio playfully smacks my ass. "Shotgun, I want the back!"

"Hey! I'm not an object."

"Not for this game, no," he concedes.

"I'm happy with that arrangement," Dante says simply as he reaches his forefinger between my legs, dragging it through the slick wetness he himself caused. I moan at the intimate touch, my skin instantly covered in goosebumps again.

And then it's my turn to get filled to the brim.

Dante sits up, supporting himself against the headboard as I climb onto his lap. Keeping my eyes on his, I slowly lower myself onto his cock, guiding it in with my free hand, the other on his shoulder to steady my movements. My orgasm is still fresh, and he slides right in, lubricated by my own cum.

"Missus Fera." Dante smiles, hugging me close to his body when his cock is buried fully inside me.

With a wide smile, I kiss his forehead and then his lips, slowly bucking my hips, riding him.

"Don Fera." He feels good inside, so perfect. The exact shape I need inside me: *him.*

Alessio gives us a moment before pushing me down on Dante's chest, spreading my ass cheeks before him.

I gasp loudly as he fingers my hole, lubing me up for his thick erection.

Oh god, to have both of them at the same time...There is nothing else like it.

My ass stretches painfully over Alessio's cock. His dick may be smaller than Dante's, but it's thick as fuck.

I'm convinced I can't take all of him, even though I have before.

Alessio strokes my breast from behind. "Relax, *cara mia.*"

The tables are turned and I have to listen to my own advice, breathing, unclenching, taking him like a good girl. For him, I do all those things, easily.

And then he's in, fully, both cocks just resting inside me for a moment as Alessio hugs me from behind, pushing me down on Dante so he can reach for a kiss too.

Dante takes a breast in each hand, firmly gripping my nipples, pinching them. Meanwhile, Alessio slowly pulls out, partially, only to thrust back in.

Oh god! So many sensations!

It forces my mind to empty, to hold onto nothing but feeling and sound and taste.

Especially when Alessio snakes his hand around to my clit, rubbing me while they both thrust inside me in some weird, synchronized movement that I cannot comprehend.

I'm on the brink of overwhelm as the intense stimulation surges through my veins. Nothing matters beyond this room. Beyond this island. It's just the three of us now. Complete.

I find Dante's eyes. They center me—emerald and pure; they are my home. Tears roll down my face, and he wipes them away.

"Are you okay, *Tesoro*?" my husband asks, concerned.

Sniffling, I smile. "I'm so happy," I cry, and I am. I have everything I've always wanted.

This time, everyone gets permission to come.

Everyone gets a turn until we collapse a sticky mess on expensive sheets, a little bit closer to a cure for the curse of the insatiable.

CHAPTER THIRTY-SEVEN

TRUTH

(ALESSIO)

I t's 3 AM. The world feels suspended between moments. Through the bedroom's open window, the waves kiss the shore, a gentle counterpoint to Danica's soft breathing behind us. Such a sleepy Queen.

Dante stands at the dresser, methodically removing his rings—a ritual I've watched him perform countless times since reuniting. Each one carries its own weight, its own story. He pauses at a gold band set with a beautiful emerald stone, turning it in the moonlight before setting it down.

"She loved this ring," he says softly, almost to himself. "Never took it off, even after everything he did."

I know which 'she' he means. Know the weight this particular ring carries. "Your mother's?" I ask carefully.

Dante nods, still focused on the band. "Wore it to church that Sunday." His fingers tremble slightly as he sets it down. "Last thing she ever wore."

The words hang between us, delicate as smoke. I've loved this man through decades of separation, but there are still doors in his heart marked 'keep out.'

"What happened that day?" I keep my voice gentle. "During the original port wars?"

Dante's jaw tightens, a muscle jumping beneath the skin. He picks up the half-empty whisky bottle from the dresser, takes a big swig. "She shouldn't have died." His voice catches. "She had nothing to do with any of it."

A long silence follows. I step closer, letting my shoulder brush his, needing to be near him. He doesn't move away.

"Do you miss her?"

"Sometimes." Moonlight catches in his eyes like broken glass. "She would've loved Danica..." He trails off, reaching for the champagne bottle.

The pain in his voice makes my chest ache. I start to speak, but he continues, words spilling out like blood from an old wound as darkness wraps us in her protective cocoon.

"Sunday Mass." Dante's voice sounds young suddenly. Small. "Luca was seven. I was ten. She always..." He takes a shaking breath. "She always held our hands. Even though I said I was too old."

The whisky bottle trembles in his fingers. I resist the urge to take it, to hold him.

"One moment, she was there, smiling down at us. Next..." His laugh holds no humor. "Bullet was meant for him. But the asshole used his own wife like a human shield...Fucking coward."

Dante stops, lost in memory. I watch his face, see the moment replay behind his eyes.

Twenty-five years of loving this man, and I never knew he carried this particular horror. Never knew he was there that day.

My heart splinters watching pain reshape his features—my proud, fierce Don reduced to that ten-year-old boy again. I want to pull him close, to shelter him from memories that can't be undone. But I know some wounds need space to bleed.

Dante speaks slowly, eyes glued to the ring like I'm not there.

"She didn't make a sound. Just..." Dante's voice trembles. "A tiny breath. Like she was trying to say goodbye. Then nothing. Nothing ever again."

His shoulders begin to shake beside me, and I finally reach for him, pressing my chest against his back to try and ground him in the present, in the warmth of my body. Anything but that memory.

Part of me regrets asking what happened. Regrets causing him this pain. But there is no putting the cork back into the bottle now. Everything is spilling out, one way or another.

"Her eyes were still open." Dante's words come out strangled. "So green. Like the forest after rain. But they weren't...she wasn't..." his voice splinters. "She was gone. Just...gone."

The first sob tears free like it's being ripped from his chest. I squeeze him as tightly as I can, feeling decades of grief shudder through his body. The fierce Don, the proud warrior, reduced to that helpless child again.

"They left us there." Each word is a battle but Dante is forcing himself through it. "In some car. All night. They just left us there. Luca wouldn't stop crying. I tried to be brave, tried to..." His breath hitches. "Emilio found us the next morning. But *him*? Our father? He never came for us. Too busy plotting revenge. Making it about him. Always about fucking him."

His fingers find the gold band again, trembling as they trace its worn surface. "Sometimes I think...if I'd been bigger, stronger...if I'd seen the car coming..."

"You were a child, *amore*." My voice breaks.

"A child who grew up to be just like him." The bitterness drips from his voice.

"No." I turn him to face me, needing him to see the truth in my eyes. "Nothing like him. Your father was an animal."

"I wish he died that day." The words finally break free, decades of silence shattering like glass. "Why couldn't he have just fucking died instead?" His voice raises slightly, and behind us, Danica stirs but doesn't wake.

"Oh, my love." I hold him tighter as fresh tears fall.

"I've never said that out loud before." His voice is barely a whisper. "Always felt so guilty, but...God, I wished it was him."

"Who could blame you? The man was a cunt. Unfit to raise children." I think of Don Fera Senior's legacy, how my father would spit at the mere mention of his name, how the old guard still speaks of his cruelty in hushed tones.

"You can say that again." Dante lowers his head. "He only had a few more years to live. But he made damn sure to leave us enough trauma to last lifetimes."

I stay quiet, giving him space to continue. Just holding him, stroking his hair lovingly.

"The first week after the funeral, he locked us in our rooms. Said he couldn't stand to look at us—we reminded him too much of her. Luca was just a little boy, crying for his mother, and that bastard..." Dante's hands clench into fists. "He said crying was for women. Said our mother made us soft."

He stares out the window into the night. "When he finally let us out, everything had changed. No more school. No more friends. Just training. Combat. Weapons. Business. If we failed..." He stops, swallows hard. "The basement had a post. For discipline."

My stomach turns, remembering the scars I'd traced on his back earlier. I'd always assumed they were from rival families, from battles won and lost. *Oh, Dante.*

"Luca was so small. Too small for the training, but *he* didn't care. Said pain builds character. Said our mother's death was a sign—we needed to be harder, stronger. No mercy." A bitter laugh escapes him. "You know what he did on the anniversary of her death? Made us practice shooting. Said we needed to learn that bullets don't care about sentiments."

I hold him tighter, feeling tremors run through his body.

"The worst part?" His voice drops to a whisper. "Some nights, he'd drink and cry over her photos. Call her name. But in the morning...in the morning, he'd beat us for leaving water rings on her picture frames. Like we didn't have the right to miss her too."

I don't want to ask more, not with each memory like shrapnel working its way to the surface. But some wounds need to be reopened to heal properly. Some burdens need to be shared to become lighter. "And after his death?"

"You know how that went." Dante laughs, but it sounds harsh. "Nineteen years old, trying to run an empire I never wanted. The other Dons circling like hyenas, waiting for the boy-king to fail." His fingers trace the heavy ring that was once his father's. "And fail I did. Everything I touched turned to blood. Every decision I made was wrong. I couldn't even protect Luca, not really. Just became a different kind of monster."

"Don't." I catch his face between my hands, forcing him to meet my eyes. In the moonlight, I can almost see that nineteen-year-old boy drowning in expectations too heavy to bear. "You were a teenager. A teenager trying to hold together a kingdom built on bones and bullets. No one should carry that weight so young."

"I had no choice." His voice cracks. "The other families would have torn us apart. Would have killed Luca just to prove a point. So I became what they feared—worse than my father ever was."

The confession hangs in the air between us, heavy with decades of guilt. I remember those years, the stories that reached Vegas about the young Don Fera. How he colored the streets red. How he made examples of anyone who questioned his authority. I never connected those tales to this man in my arms, this beautiful, broken soul I loved from the moment we met as young boys.

It's not fair. He didn't choose this life.

The contrast between our paths hits me like an unexpected brick wall on a highway. While Dante was drowning in blood and obligation, I was free—dancing in clubs, falling in love, creating art. My biggest concern was which party to attend. I was spare parts, the second-born; they never tried to mold me into a weapon.

Even now, Vegas plays by different rules. I stepped into power prepared, supported. Dante? He was thrown into fire before his voice had settled, before he knew who he was beyond his father's son.

"You did what you had to, *amore mio*," I whisper against his temple and feel him crumble.

I hold him tighter and let him cry for the boy he was, for the mother he lost, for the childhood that was stolen by a bullet meant for someone else.

Hold him like I couldn't when we were younger, when family obligations and feuds kept us apart. Hold him as the moon tracks across the sky and our skin grows cold with dew. Until the past settles back into its usual place between his shoulders.

Finally, the broken Knight's breathing steadies. He pulls back just enough to meet my eyes, and I see both the boy he was and the man he's become. Don Dante Fera, feared and respected throughout the criminal world. My first love. Danica's husband.

A man still carrying the weight of a ten-year-old boy who couldn't save his mother.

When he finally speaks again, his voice is steadier, a ghost of a smile on his lips. "She would have loved you too, you know. Would have accepted us..."

There are no words for moments like this. Instead, I press a kiss to his shoulder and feel him lean back, trusting me with his weight. With his truth.

We stay there, wrapped in moonlight and memory, until the sky begins to lighten with dawn's first blush.

Behind us, our sleepy Queen stirs in her sleep, murmuring something soft and content.

Tomorrow, we'll return to being what the world needs us to be—Dons, lovers, leaders. But for now, in this suspended moment between night and day, we're just two boys who grew up too fast, holding each other against the dark.

And maybe that's enough.

Maybe that's everything.

Chapter Thirty-Eight

Morning Light

(Danica)

Morning sun paints our villa in sunshine, streaming through the open walls to cast dappled patterns across the polished floors. Outside, the ocean sparkles like scattered diamonds—postcard perfect, almost too beautiful to be real.

I sit perched on a barstool at the kitchen counter, watching Alessio move between the stove and refrigerator with the grace of a dancer. His dark hair is still damp from an early morning swim, curling slightly at the tips. He's wearing nothing but loose swim shorts riding low on his hips, his tanned, tattooed skin gleaming in the sunshine.

"Are you going to play or just stare at Alessio?" Dante's voice pulls me back to our game.

"I'm multitasking." I wink, laying down my next card. "Gin."

"*Cazzo*!" Dante curses, dropping his cards in mock frustration. "That's the third time."

"Don't be a sore loser." I gather the cards to shuffle again, enjoying the familiar feel of them between my fingers. "Maybe you're letting me win."

"Never." Dante leans back on his stool, stretching his arms above his head.

Something is different about him this morning. The change is subtle—something in the way he holds himself, the softness around his eyes, the slightly looser set of his shoulders. After four years together, I've learned to read every micro-expression, every twitch of muscle. My Don has shed some invisible weight overnight.

I want to ask what happened, what transformation took place during the hushed conversation I glimpsed through half-closed eyes last night. But some spaces deserve their privacy, even between us.

"Pancakes or french toast?" Alessio calls over his shoulder, whisking eggs in a large bowl.

"Both," I say immediately, and Dante laughs.

"Always hungry," he remarks, but his eyes linger on my face with that adoration that still makes my chest tighten after all this time.

"For the good things in life?" I brush my fingers through his hair, longer now than he usually keeps it. "Absolutely."

"Let's start with the french toast," Alessio suggests, slicing thick pieces of bread with steady hands. "With that coconut syrup we picked up yesterday."

Barefoot and relaxed, with his usual sharp edges softened by morning light, Alessio is a revelation. The Vegas Joker—the man whose empire rivals Dante's in both scope and infamy—standing in our kitchen making breakfast in swimming shorts like it's the most natural thing in the world.

"I'm starving." I hop off my stool and pad over to the fruit bowl, selecting a ripe mango. "Anyone want some of this while we wait?"

"*Sì*," Dante follows me, reaching for a knife. "Let me."

I watch his hands as he slices the fruit with unexpected care—those hands that have ended lives now meticulously removing the stone, cutting perfect cubes. He arranges them on a plate like small jewels, his movements precise.

"You know what this reminds me of?" Alessio says, dipping bread into the egg mixture. "That morning in Santorini, after the club opening."

"God, that was, what...two years ago?" I laugh, accepting a piece of mango from Dante's fingers.

"You were so drunk," Dante says, his eyes crinkling at the corners.

"I was celebrating! And if I recall correctly, you weren't exactly sober either, Don Fera."

Alessio tosses his head back, laughing. "He even danced on the stage!"

"I did no such thing," Dante protests, but there's no heat in it. Just fond remembrance of a night when the fearsome Don let himself be just a man among friends.

"You did," I confirm, leaning against the counter. "You and Alessio both. I have photographic evidence."

"Blackmail material," Dante corrects, but his eyes sparkle with amusement.

I watch him pop a piece of mango into his mouth, juice glistening on his bottom lip. He catches me looking and winks, a gesture so uncharacteristically playful that I almost do a double-take. Something has shifted; some door has opened. I don't think I've ever seen my husband wink.

"Pass me those plates," Alessio instructs, flipping the first piece of toast with a flourish.

Dante reaches past me to grab three plates from the cupboard, his chest brushing against my back. He lingers there for a moment, arms encircling me to set the plates on the counter. It's so casual, so easy—this physical intimacy that flows between us all like water.

The smell of cinnamon and vanilla fills the kitchen as Alessio slides the first batch of french toast onto a plate. "Food's ready, lovebirds."

We move to the outside terrace with our plates, settling around the table with the ocean spread before us. Slivers of sunlight dance across the infinity pool, the water still and perfect in the morning calm.

"God, this is good," I mumble around a mouthful of syrup-soaked bread.

"Don't sound so surprised." Alessio pretends to be offended, but his eyes are warm. "I'm a man of many talents."

"Indeed you are," Dante agrees, his foot finding mine under the table, a small point of contact that feels as intimate as a kiss.

We eat in comfortable silence for a few minutes, just the sounds of waves breaking on the shore and distant birdsong. It's a perfect moment—suspended in time, the three of us together without expectations or obligations.

The morning stretches before us, unhurried and golden. We polish off the french toast and fresh fruit, trading stories and observations, our conversation flowing like a gentle current. Occasionally, Dante's hand finds mine, or Alessio leans over to brush a strand of hair from my face.

These small touches—this casual intimacy—it fills something in me I didn't know was empty. This is what love looks like when it's given room to breathe, to evolve, to find its own shape.

After breakfast, Alessio refills our coffee cups and Dante deals another round of cards. I lean back in my chair, watching them both—my husband and our lover, the two men who've reshaped my world in ways I never imagined possible.

Dante catches me watching and raises an eyebrow in question.

"Just happy," I say simply.

"You deserve to be," he replies, and there's something different in his voice—a certainty, an acceptance that perhaps extends to himself as well.

I think about the man I met all those years ago, locked in his fortress of silence and duty. The man who couldn't imagine pleasure without pain, love without loss. Who couldn't fathom the kind of unconventional happiness we've built together.

"We all do," I say, reaching for my cards.

Dante hesitates, then nods, a smile tugging at the corner of his mouth. "Maybe you're right."

"Of course she is," Alessio chimes in, shuffling his own cards. "Our Queen is always right."

"Now you're just sucking up," I tease.

"Is it working?" Alessio grins.

"Always."

The three of us laugh, the sound mingling with the rhythm of the waves. In this moment, in this unlikely found family we've created, I feel something close to perfect peace.

Later, we'll go swimming or walking along the beach. Maybe we'll nap in the afternoon heat, bodies tangled together in the massive bed. We might make love, or simply lie together, talking about everything and nothing. The day stretches before us with infinite possibilities.

But for now, there are cards to play, coffee to drink, and this quiet, profound joy to savor—the kind that comes from loving and being loved exactly as you are.

I catch Dante's eye over my cards and see a reflection of my own contentment there. Whatever burden he shared with Alessio in the darkness, its release has left room for something new to grow. Something hopeful. Something free.

And in this moment, with the sun warming my skin and the two men I love beside me, I realize that this—this unconventional, unexpected love—may be the most beautiful thing I've ever known.

CHAPTER THIRTY-NINE

'INKED

(DANTE)

It's been three days since I broke open for Alessio, spilled decades of pain into the Bali night.

The second time I told the story, the words came easier, crying into Danica's chest as she stroked my hair, wetting my cheek with her own tears.

With bleeding hands, I handed her the sharpest shard lodged in my heart, and she just folded her hands over it, wrapping it in her warmth.

Afterward, she didn't look at me like I was broken, like I feared she would. No, she looked at me like she always did, like I carved every stone of the pyramids single-handedly, like I mattered.

The vulnerability still sits raw beneath my skin—shame and relief tangled together like the roses inked over my scars.

For years, I thought sharing those memories would break me. Instead, something shifted. Loosened. Like a bone finally set right after years of healing wrong.

Alessio jetted off back to his Vegas empire yesterday, unable to stay—as always. But we made good use of our time.

Our last days together were different. Softer. The weight of secrets no longer standing between us.

Alessio knew how to hold the silence, knew when to press closer and when to give space. And Danica—my Queen who always sees through my armor—she wrapped us both in her strength, let us heal in our own way.

Now, with Alessio gone and these memories finally aired, I feel stripped bare. Exposed. But also...free. Like I've finally put down a burden I'd carried so long I forgot it wasn't part of me. My father's voice is quieter in my head. And my mother's memory hurts differently—clean pain instead of festering guilt.

Maybe that's why I'm here now. Ready for a different kind of pain, a different kind of transformation. Not hiding scars this time but choosing something new. Something that belongs entirely to me and the family I've chosen.

"You ready, baby?" Danica asks again, and I nod curtly, my jaw locked in tension. I'm glad she's here to hold my hand. This may or may not be a terrible idea, I'm about to find out.

The artist positions his clamps around the tip of my cock, and I know I will hurt. I try to brace myself. My father thought pain would make me stronger. He wasn't entirely wrong—he just never imagined I'd learn to wear it so well.

That needle looks so thick. *Jesus*. Does it have to be that thick?

I don't say anything, just grit my teeth as the most excruciating pain imaginable stabs through my flesh.

"*Puttana*!" I curse loudly as I focus all my attention on keeping still despite the blinding pain.

It hurts more than anything has ever hurt in my life.

In the shaded hut no bigger than a night shop, Danica holds my hand firmly, but I worry I might crush it as I squeeze with all my might, trying to bear the unbearable pain.

"Almost there," the piercing artist tells me in flawless English as I huff and puff through my teeth, trying to keep my consciousness through the blinding pain.

It's too late to turn around now, the needle is already sticking through my dick like some ancient torture device.

"You're going to look so beautiful, my love. Almost there. So brave," Danica coos, stroking my sweaty hair from my face. The air conditioning is working overtime but doing little to relieve the heat from the small room. Even in the most luxurious piercing studio, the heat follows us, sticking to my body like another layer.

"Jesus," I pant, trying to steady my breath as the blinding pain radiates from my dick into my body.

This seemed like a great idea before, when Danica and I lay in bed post-orgasm, discussing how we wanted to spend the rest of our remaining days on the island.

She wanted to finally get a tattoo to decorate the scar on her back—a great idea. Casually, I mentioned my lifelong

413

fascination with dick piercings, how I always wondered what it would feel like.

I didn't expect to lie here on the little black table of a stranger we've met only once before, during the consultation yesterday, my dick out with a needle through it. He hasn't even put the piercing bar through yet. *Fuck!*

"Deep breath. Exhale on my command," the little man with the thick-framed glasses informs me, getting ready to finish the job. I can't look; I'm seconds from passing out. That little drop of blood on my dick head is enough to thicken the bile in my throat, threatening to force itself up.

I scream louder than I've ever wanted to scream in public when he pushes the shiny metal bar through my glans, impaling my cock horizontally. The piercing has some fancy name that Danica has written on a piece of paper to try and remember its name, an Ampallang. But all I know is that it hurts like a motherfucker!

"So beautiful," Danica moves her phone closer to get a close-up for the recording she insists on making. We'll watch it together later, but right now I can't watch anything. My dick is on fire, and not in a good way. *This was a terrible idea!*

"All done," the little man tells us, cleaning the jewelry ever so lightly, but every movement sends blinding pain through my entire body. It's impossible to imagine ever feeling okay again. "Be sure to look after it well. All the info is in here." He hands Danica a brochure and then pushes his glasses back on his nose, eyeing her seriously. "No hanky-panky for a couple of at least two months." He shakes his right index finger to punctuate his point.

Dio mio, what have I done? Two months without coming? I struggle to survive two days.

There is something addictive about the pain as well, though, the rush of dopamine that floods my brain as my body tries to soothe the throbbing in my cock.

Danica smiles. "Don't worry, I'll make sure he heels up nicely. And when he's done..." She licks her lips at the mere thought.

Last night, we stayed up late reading first-hand experiences on Reddit of what it feels like—both for the wearer and their partner. It sounded arousing.

But it isn't just about giving pleasure or even the pain in this moment, this self-torment that feels as bad as it feels good...no, it was so much more. It was beautifully taboo, but nobody was going to tell me what to do with my body, nobody but Danica, and she wanted my body to experience all the sensations it craved.

My father would have lost his shit if he knew I got a piercing, regardless of where on my body. Tattoos were fine in his eyes, they showed you're strong, but piercings were for girls. He always had such dated ideas about gender roles, about everything really; so conservative.

This is my rebellion, my defiance of all things traditional, the final mark of ownership for my Queen, the pain I deserve for all the bad things I've done, my absolution. All of the above.

I don't know how we make it back to our villa. The boat ride isn't far, but every damn bump in the water feels like the end of the world, my cock swollen in my pants.

We really should've waited until we got back home to the city. How will I survive the trip back? Including layover, it was more than a day of flying. But what's done is done.

"I will look after you so well," Danica says when we finally reach our destination, seating me on the patio and bringing us some drinks. Probably not a good idea with the new piercing, but I need something to take the edge off.

I'm glad she went first with the tattoo, and I didn't have to sit around with my burning cock while watching them stick a little needle into her for four hours. The end result is breathtaking, though.

Danica takes off her shirt, and I can't help but stare at the beautiful lotus flowers elegantly snaking around her lower back, soft pink and greens weaving in between the tough scar tissue, creating art instead of painful memories. She deserves healing too.

Though physically, I know my own healing is still a long road ahead.

"You sure I can't give you some painkillers?" Danica asks for the third time, and I force myself not to stare at her exposed breasts, petrified of getting an ill-timed erection.

I shake my head. "I'm not putting those things in my body. I'll be fine." I've never been one for painkillers. Pain is there for a reason. It needs to be endured, not watered down.

She tilts her head sideways. "Doesn't it hurt?"

"More than a gunshot wound." It sure feels that way.

Danica bites her bottom lip, staring at me. "God, that makes me so horny. I wish I could touch it."

I protectively hover my hands over my crotch. "Don't you dare!" The mere thought of a hard-on is painful.

"In that case, I'll just have to find something else, or *someone* else, to entertain me during our last few days."

I exhale loudly. "Please. Enjoy yourself."

"The chef is quite fit." Danica winks at me mischievously. "I like her eyes."

"Normally, I'd love to watch, but this time, please keep far away from me." I groan, downing the whiskey in one gulp, the warmth burning its way to my stomach in a familiar glow that takes the edge off without doing anything to the pulsating pain.

"We'll see." Danica blows me a kiss and disappears to refill our glasses, just in time for yet another glorious sunset over the ocean.

It was nice not having to worry about my dick anymore, at least not in a sexual way. Now it's all about healing and cleaning a wound, the member reduced to a mere object. There was something peaceful about that thought. I didn't have to perform or live up to any expectations.

If only life could stay like this—so simply, undemanding.

Just thinking about of having to go back home and pick up the reigns again is beyond exhausting.

I want to be Danica's 24/7 sub, like here.

To just paint, maybe do some baking, to just be tied up at home like a good house husband, cooking and cleaning and serving my Queen.

When I told Danica that, she smiled sweetly, promising to make my dreams come true one day.

For now, my biggest concern is Danica seductively spreading her legs before me, playing with her clit.

"Stop that. You'll make me hard!" I protest, petrified of sending blood to an open wound, especially one in such a delicate area.

"Then don't look." Famous last words. *How can I look away?*

I should've tried harder.

My erection isn't even complete, but it's enough to disturb my new jewelry.

Oh god, the pain!

Some lessons you learn the hard way, and some lessons you never learn.

It is going to be a long two months, there is no doubt about it.

But I have a feeling my dick will be the least of my worries.

Bali has been fun, a welcome distraction from the reality that awaits when we return home.

Two days—that's all we have left in paradise.

I wish we could remain wrapped in this bubble of peace where my only decisions involve what to order for breakfast and which beach to visit.

But we have a business to set up, a war to keep at bay. Convincing the families *and* the authorities will be one hell of a job.

This is not going to be easy.

But there is nobody I have more confidence in than Danica—my wife, my Queen, my Madame.

If anyone can do this, she can.

CHAPTER FORTY

POWER EXCHANGE

(DANICA)

Dante insists on starting the shareholder meeting, not because he thinks I can't handle it but because he knows the other Dons are as old school in their beliefs as his father was—they need a *man* in charge to introduce change of this magnitude.

But today's the day that changes for good.

The men are sat around the freshly-painted boardroom with its stunning 180-degree view of the ocean stretching out beneath us, eight stories down. This new corporate office space—neutral territory I selected specifically for this purpose—feels worlds away from the dark backrooms where family business was previously conducted.

But nobody is looking at the ocean, nobody but me.

They're all looking at either Dante or the proposal he's about to present on screen.

I don't need to look; I've spent the four weeks we've been back from Bali fine-tuning this plan and working on the numbers with Luigi. We stayed up till 3 AM last night to review it all again to ensure every detail was solid.

To say the port business the Volkovs once controlled is a mess would be an understatement.

Things have run wild for too long, systems and processes had been mere suggestions rather than the rule. It would take time to detangle the mess, but our preliminary audit already shows the potential.

I am determined to make this work, to transform this operation into something legitimate and profitable. Something built to last. Something better than what came before.

Being apart from Dante during our audit these past days has been difficult.

But I had to figure out the ports, and he had to figure out how to hand over the other businesses. There wasn't exactly a blueprint for what we were doing.

I didn't think I would miss my darling boy this much. It took me all these years to realize just how much I can't live without him.

Those smutty books I love so much had me believe love was the instant part, the attraction, that desperate need for someone's skin against your own—that fire.

But it's so much more.

It's the after part, the work, the shared trauma, the comfort, the feeling of coming home as soon you envelop yourself in their familiar scent after a long day.

I can't wait until the initial restructuring is over, so I can spend more days working from home and see more of my Dante.

He's been a completely different person. Even in the short time since we formulated this plan, I've seen him relax more than he has in years.

The fact that he's switched to wearing actual sweatpants at home is a huge step; he used to be so anal about those perfectly ironed black pants of his.

Focus, Danica.

The meeting carries on as Dante outlines our proposal, explaining how a legitimate port management company with proper corporate structure would benefit everyone. He walks them through the transition plan, emphasizing that they'd all retain ownership stakes while gaining the protections of legitimacy.

"Gentlemen," Dante says, his voice commanding the room, "what we're proposing is not abandoning our interests, but evolving them. Every family represented here would hold shares proportionate to their current territorial claims, with the Fera family maintaining majority control."

There's muttering around the table. Don Antonio leans forward. "And who exactly would run this...corporation?"

Dante meets my eyes briefly before answering. "That brings me to the most important part of our proposal."

I take a deep breath. This is the moment we've prepared for.

"To head this enterprise," Dante continues, "we need someone with a clean record. Someone who can move freely in legitimate business circles. Someone with the intelligence and determination to make this succeed." He pauses. "And that person is...my wife, Danica Fera."

The men eye him suspiciously, some with outright disbelief on their faces.

I get up, shoulders straight, as Dante formally introduces me. "Gentlemen, I present to you the proposed Managing Director of Fera Incorporated."

The dumbfounded men just stare at me for a second, the silence deafening.

It's Don Greco who starts clapping first. "Excellent idea, Don Fera. A clean criminal record would be great for the business." He gets it.

Relief washes over me as the men start clapping, reluctantly at first.

"Thank you." I keep my voice stern, formal, as I address the room. "As Don Fera has outlined, our proposal offers a path to stability and growth without the constant risks we've all faced. The ports are a goldmine of legitimate opportunity that we've barely begun to tap."

I'm halfway through explaining our new corporate structure when Don Vinci clears his throat pointedly, his wizened face twisted in thinly veiled contempt.

"With all due respect, Don Fera," he says, not looking at me but at my husband, "this is a peculiar choice. Running the ports requires...experience. Authority." His gaze finally slides to me, dismissive. "Not someone who might be more suited to...simpler tasks."

The room falls silent. I can feel Dante tensing beside me, ready to step in. But this is exactly what I've been preparing for. If I let him fight this battle, I'll never truly command these men's respect.

I smile, the kind of smile that doesn't reach my eyes. "You're right about one thing, Don Vinci. Experience matters." I hold his gaze, refusing to be the first to look away. "And I've spent the last several weeks experiencing firsthand how inefficiently these ports have been run for decades."

A surprised murmur ripples through the room. Don Vinci's face darkens.

"You misunderstand me, Mrs. Fera—"

"Perhaps we both misunderstand each other," I interrupt smoothly, my voice calm but firm.

I slide a folder across the table to him. "This contains a preliminary report on your shipments over the last six months. You'll notice your containers have been delayed an average of fourteen days longer than any other family's. I've already identified the exact bottlenecks and have a plan to correct them immediately upon taking control."

Don Vinci stares at the folder, clearly not expecting this level of detail. I knew the asshole was going to come for me. Men like him were so predictable.

"I may not have decades in this business, Don Vinci, but what I bring is fresh perspective and determination. And unlike many"—I meet his gaze steadily—"I have no old grudges or territorial disputes clouding my judgment. Just a clear vision for how these ports should operate and the drive to make it happen."

I let that sink in before continuing. "However, if my methods don't yield the results you expect, you're welcome to challenge my position in six months. I believe in accountability, even if I'm still learning the business."

The old Don's expression shifts, not quite to respect, but to something closer to wary assessment. He nods once, sharply.

"We shall see," is all he says, but it's enough.

I catch Dante's eye and detect the barely concealed pride there. This is why we work—he knows when to stand back and let me fight my own battles.

"Now, shall we discuss the specifics of the transition?" I ask, seamlessly returning to business.

The rest of the meeting proceeds with pointed questions but gradually decreasing resistance. It's clear that some, especially Don Vinci, still have their reservations about this move, but the dynamic has shifted. They're listening now, not just tolerating.

And then it's done.

The vote is taken, the proposal approved.

Just like that.

The Dons seem finally pacified, perhaps seeing the wisdom in our plan, perhaps simply eager to write this matter off as resolved. Everyone has better things to do than sit in the Fera Inc. Boardroom discussing corporate structure.

I make sure to keep my handshake firm as I offer my hand to the men upon exit, boldly making eye contact with each one individually. When I reach Don Vinci, he hesitates a fraction of a second before taking my hand.

"An...interesting approach, Mrs. Fera," he says, the formality in his tone slightly less dismissive than before. "We'll be watching your progress closely."

"I would expect nothing less," I reply, my grip just as firm as his. Not backing down, not challenging—just equal.

It's a small victory, but in this world of old men and older rules, small victories are just the beginning.

Dante stands by my side, just a bit behind me, accepting congratulations from the Dons like he's achieved something amazing.

"Donna Fera," Don Greco nods on his way out, the final guest. It's good to see him again, but not as good as hearing him call me Donna Fera. It makes me feel important, established, powerful.

If only they knew just how powerful.

How their fearless Don Fera crawls on his knees before me.

But they will never know.

Our secrets are not for these men.

Nobody else knows about the cuts across his flesh, hidden by his fancy I'm-the-Don outfit of black pants and open-collared shirts.

I am dying to slip a collar around that neck when we get home; it looks so bare without it.

My mind drifts as we see our important guests out, standing beside Dante as so much more than just his loyal wife this time.

This is *my* legacy now.

I am eons from the person I used to be, the person Dante met that fateful night at the restaurant when the universe brought us together—if you were one of those cosmic people who believed in such things.

I'm no longer that helpless child that nobody wanted, the one who almost died in the shed as her brothers just laughed.

Fuck all of them.

When the door finally closes behind the Dons, I let out a huge sigh of relief.

I've been stressing about this meeting for weeks, even during our honeymoon when I should have been completely focused on Dante and Alessio.

I know it's only temporary, that I'm technically on probation, but there is no doubt in my mind that I'll have the results I need in six months. The foundations are there—I just need to build on them.

As Dante packs away the laptop, I lock the door behind us, plonking down on the large wooden boardroom table carved from solid oak. I picked it myself, like everything in the office. Literally picked my dream office from an online store and had it delivered and installed like I was playing The Sims. My husband paid, of course.

"What a boss bitch, as you like to say." Dante comes to me, clearly relieved to have the meeting done with too.

I kiss him deeply, messing up his perfectly styled hair with my fingers as I take his lips in mine.

"*Your* boss bitch."

Dante kisses my fingers, each one individually, then kisses my ring. "I'm so proud of who you've become. Thanks for letting me be by your side."

"My darling Dante. I am this me because of you. You make me better."

"My Queen." Dante bows before me like we're in some fancy movie, a King turned humble Knight—just for me.

I smile.

No, they will never know.

Those Dons will keep thinking Dante is in charge, that I'm just the front, the face of the company, useful only for my clean record.

But I know.

Know that I'm the boss.

I don't need anyone to protect me or to speak for me, no, I'm officially in charge now—and tomorrow, the golden nameplate will be installed on my office door to confirm it.

Danica Fera, Managing Director.

I like the sound of that.

If only my family could see me now. With my own office. My own parking spot. Hell, my own fucking empire.

But they can go to hell.

They don't deserve to share in my successes.

"You did well, baby," I tell Dante as I drop my hands over his crotch, tracing the outline of his sleeping cock. It instantly perks up, and my husband lets out a pained groan.

"You're going to drive me mad, woman," he rasps with feigned annoyance as I unbuckle his pants.

My only reply is the huge grin spreading on my face and the order to bring Sonja to the party.

"Yes, Ma'am," Dante replies as he pulls his dick free, casting a glance at the door despite knowing it's locked.

"Now..." Kicking off my heels, I reposition myself on the table so I can reach over to his erection, slowly stroking the underside with my stockinged feet.

The great Don Fera lets out a primal roar, reaching for the edge of the table to stabilize himself. "*Dio mio,*" he gasps as I gently touch his piercing with my toes.

"What is it you want, baby boy?" I whisper, trailing my foot over his balls.

Dante lets out a pained moan. "For you to stop torturing me."

"Hmm, perhaps," I reply with mock contemplation as I remove my foot again.

"P-please," my darling husband pants through quickening breaths. He's so sensitive these days with four weeks of no release—any contact has him instantly leaking.

"Well, pleasure yourself. But no touching. And no coming without permission," I lay down the rules, watching as Dante squirms uncomfortably, pre-cum glistening on his tip. I know that technically it's too soon after getting pierced, but the internet said it should *mostly* be fine after four weeks. And he clearly wants to.

"Thank you, Miss," he replies gratefully, crossing his wrists behind his back like a good boy.

"Eyes on me, *Tesoro*," I command in a stern voice as Dante rubs his cock on my foot, hands behind his back, desperate.

Mere minutes after he commanded the room with his strong voice, Don Fera whines like a little boy beneath my feet, begging me to let him finish.

This time, I am tempted to let Dante come all over my stockinged arches.

But I change my mind last minute, pushing him away with my foot on his hip.

Dante moans loudly, exasperated, so close but oh so far from sweet release.

Poor boy, I've edged him silly for nearly a month. He must be so pent-up. What beautiful devotion. What trust. To let me deny him for so long.

Just the thought of it makes me wet. Not that it takes that much.

It's not just Dante that's been denied.

Sure, I've had many releases, but I haven't had him inside me for a month. It's been a slow torture waiting for that thing to heal. I crave him so much.

But not now.

Not like this.

I want to take my time.

"Come here, darling." I pull him closer. "Don't worry, you'll come. You deserve it."

Dante lets out an audible groan, his body visibly stiffening.

Slowly, I stroke his rock-hard cock, using his pre-cum as lube, careful to avoid the piercing area. His dick head is no longer swollen, but the little holes where the long bar pierced his gland are still a bit red, not fully healed.

It doesn't take much to bring him right back to the edge; Dante is ready to come for me in less than a minute.

But I don't let him come on my hand, or my feet, or anywhere on my neatly pressed suit, no, I grab my half-drunk cup of cold coffee still on the table and milk my husband into the porcelain vessel, making sure to capture every last drop of his massive orgasm.

Dante doesn't ask questions, he doesn't say anything—he's too relieved to finally climax fully for the first time since we pierced his cock a month ago.

When there's no liquid left in his body, he collapses, panting on the floor, curled up in a fetal position. I'm sure his release hurt like a bitch with that piercing in.

I give him a minute or two before calling him to his knees again.

Lovingly, I stroke my darling Don's hair as I feed him the cold coffee streaked with his own cum. I stir it slightly with my finger and then tip the cup back, making him drink every last sip, watching his Adam's apple bob as he swallows.

Dante doesn't protest, just swallows it all down like an obedient pet. God, the things it does to the desire coiling at my core when he submits to me like that. When he gives into my kinky games.

When I put the cup down, he looks up at me with such adoration that I swear my cold heart melts. "Thank you, *Donna* Fera," he whispers, smiling contently.

I kiss the top of his forehead sweetly as I whisper the two words that will be this great Don Fera's entire undoing— *"Bravo, ragazzo."* Good boy.

433

CHAPTER FORTY-ONE

THE BOSS

(DANICA)

The familiar scent of vanilla and butter greets me before I even open the kitchen door. Two months since we returned from Bali, and the feared Don Fera has become a master baker. Imagine that.

"What smells so amazing?" I call out, dropping my briefcase by the door. The meeting with the Port Authority had run late, but coming home to this almost made up for it.

Biscotti races to greet me, tail wagging furiously. Behind him, Dante stands at the counter, flour dusting his black t-shirt, those curls he's letting grow falling into his eyes.

"Cinnamon rolls," he says, then notices my expression. "What is it? Did the meeting go badly?"

Instead of answering, I pull the papers from my bag, holding them up like a trophy. The official seals gleam under the kitchen lights.

"Are those...?" Dante wipes his hands on a dish towel, moving closer.

"The terminal operating contracts. All of them." My grin threatens to split my face. "Plus exclusive rights to stevedoring services across the entire port district. We control every ship that comes in and out of the city now."

His eyes scan the documents, lingering on the signatures of the Port Authority board members. "I can't believe you got these."

"You know I can be very *persuasive*." I hop onto the counter.

Dante kneels to help with my shoes, carefully unclasping the gold buckles of my heels. His fingers linger on my ankles before getting up. "That sounds kinky."

"I wish. Nah, it was just another board meeting. Boring as shit. They were happy to sign everything over to our new port management corporation. Anything to get rid of the 'pesky Russians.' Turns out they weren't just causing shit for us, but for everyone. Even the Port Authority was at their wit's end with those fuckers. Nothing was coming in or out on time, if at all. And so much shit just went 'missing,' never to be seen again. It was making the customs officials nervous."

"So they give us control of all the port operations in exchange for what exactly?" Dante is still skeptical, waiting for the other shoe to drop. But there is no other shoe, not this time.

"Stability. A guarantee that things will start flowing properly again. Plus..." I pause for effect, "I got us the contract to handle all customs processing and security operations. We'll have our people checking every container that moves through this city."

He arches a brow. "And...?"

A grin spreads over my face. "And...digging up dirt on three board members and the head of customs definitely helped the situation along."

"Danica! You're devious!"

"I've learned from the best." I pull him closer for a kiss, wrapping my legs around his waist.

Dante suddenly pauses. "Did you take some guards with you?"

"To a board meeting? No, silly."

"You went alone?" That worried crease appears between his brows. "Danica..."

"We're safer than we've ever been, darling." I run my fingers through his curls, smoothing away his concern. "I wish you wouldn't fret so much."

He doesn't say anything, just holds me. We both know I am right, though. Everything has changed now. Our business runs on spreadsheets and contracts now, not violence. With control of port operations, customs processing, and security services, we've got more power than any amount of muscle could give us.

This was the final missing piece to make us legitimate. The families were on board, for the most part, but we needed the government agencies to play ball too.

I feel like a fucking rock star, standing here in our kitchen, holding the key to the city's shipping empire in my manicured hands.

If my high school guidance counselor could see me now—little Danica Matthews from the suburbs, the underachiever, the failure.

Instead, I'm *La Donna* Fera, and I just outmaneuvered a boardroom full of men who've been running these ports since before I was born.

They never saw me coming. That's always been my advantage—they look at me and see a trophy wife, arm candy for a Don. They don't know who I've become, who I'm working to become.

The Port Authority suits practically tripped over themselves trying to hand me those contracts once I laid out exactly what would happen if they didn't.

It wasn't even about the blackmail material in the end—though, that certainly helped. It was about showing them a future where their precious port district could actually function the way it's supposed to. No more "lost" shipments, no more delays, no more dealing with six different families all trying to carve out their piece. Just one streamlined operation, legitimate on paper, with enough muscle behind it to keep everyone in line.

Dante squeezes my hand, bringing me back to the present, to the kitchen filled with delicious-smelling treats that would upset my trainer's perfectly designed eating plan. "Are you sure

I can't help you at work?" Dante asks, staring intently into my eyes. "I feel bad just sitting at home all day."

I stroke his cheek. "Are you bored, baby?"

"Not at all." Dante's face perks up, and I smile. "I must show you my new painting."

Ever since I bought him some paint supplies, he's thrown himself into the arts with vigor, spending hours upon hours in his new studio in the West Wing while I was out dealing with business things.

"Then stay here, enjoy your early retirement, and let me play boss bitch at the office. I'm enjoying the setting up of it all. Besides, you know I've got a legit team. You hired them yourself."

"*We* hired them." Dante smiles, pushing my skirt higher up over my thighs. "And this?" He raises an eyebrow, distracted from the conversation.

I wink at him. "You finally noticed."

"Please tell me you didn't go to work without panties?"

I blow him a kiss. "Oh yeah, I did. It makes me feel more bad-ass."

"Crazy woman." Dante shakes his head, eyes still firmly locked on my bush.

"On your knees again, darling," I command as I drop my stockinged feet onto Dante's lap, tracing the hardness forming under his loose-fitting grey sweatpants. Just lightly, oh so lightly. His cock is virtually fully heal now.

"You're the Devil," Dante gasps, bucking his hips into me, slowly rubbing himself against my dirty stockings, sweaty from my day of hustling and business-ing.

"You're not wrong. Now take that cock out."

"Danica, the staff are around. What if someone comes in?"

"Do I need to repeat myself?" I thicken my voice, tapping my fingers on the counter to accent my impatience.

"No, Madame." Dante looks around nervously before slipping his hard cock from his pants.

"Good." I trail my feet over his cock, enjoying the lust flickering over his face, the hiss as he sharply draws in breath. "I'm just teasing, baby. You know I'm not going to let you come."

"Please." Dante's voice is soft, needy.

I shake my head from side to side. "Nah-uh."

Dante sighs dejected, sitting back on his heels and looking at his sad cock, half erect but with no hope of release. Not yet.

"You could earn some *credits* in the meantime, though?" I wink at him, and he nods eagerly.

I don't pull him into my cunt, no, not today. Instead, I hop off the counter, turning around, skirt hiked all the way up to my waist.

Dante immediately gets the memo and pulls a nearby chair toward him. One foot on the floor, the other in the air, I lean forward on the kitchen counter, pushing my ass out to my husband.

My stockings are knee-high only, so there is no need to take them off.

Dante doesn't hesitate, just hooks his arms around my legs and parts my cheeks with his face, driving his tongue into the depths of my back hole.

I moan loudly, warding off people rather than attracting them—I hope.

"Just like that, oh god," I purr, wriggling under Dante's tongue as he flicks it over my asshole, devouring me like a hungry boy desperate for his dessert.

I could get used to this homecoming after a long day at work. Perhaps a nice bath afterward, a foot massage...my thoughts trail off as my circuits flood with sensation, Dante's mouth exciting more nerve endings than I remember being back there.

Gasping, I clutch the counter as he eats my ass, doing a fucking good job at that. Top marks for stress relief.

"Dante..." I moan as he fans his fingers over my clit, finding even more buttons to push.

The thought of possible discovery fuels my explosive orgasm that follows minutes later.

I come over my husband's face with little warning, my whole body jerking and squirming in pleasure that radiates from my skin through my insides. *Oh god!*

Nobody walks in, luckily. As much as the idea is hot, I don't want to traumatize the staff. They're usually quite good at keeping their distance if Dante and I are in a room, unless we explicitly call them.

Still, the perceived exposure is exhilarating! Especially for poor Dante, who wants nothing but to come all over my dirty stockings...Poor boy, not today.

And they said marriage would be boring.

Gasping, clutching the counter as the last shivers of the orgasm flash through my body. I'm desperate for more. "Let's take this to the bedroom, baby."

Just because Dante can't have any fun doesn't mean I can't.

The cinnamon rolls can wait.

La Donna Fera has some *personal* business to take care of.

CHAPTER FORTY-TWO

BROTHERLY LOVE

(DANTE)

The brush strokes flow like meditation, each one bringing the brown horse on my canvas closer to life. Classical music swells around me—a new addition to my studio, another step away from the man I used to be. Who would have thought Don Fera would find peace in Beethoven and watercolors?

I'm so lost in the details of the horse's mane that I don't hear the doorbell. Don't hear anything but strings and piano and the quiet voice in my head guiding each stroke. For three days, I've worked on this piece, finding healing in the patience it demands.

A soft knock breaks my concentration. "Enter!" I call, gesturing to dim the music.

Danica appears in the doorway, powerful and beautiful in her navy suit. My Queen turned Managing Director—the transformation still takes my breath away.

"I thought you went to work?" I move to kiss her, careful to keep my paint-stained hands away from her clothes.

"I popped out for a second." Something in her voice makes my spine stiffen. Her fingers twist together—a tell she never shows unless genuinely nervous. "I have a surprise for you, but you have to promise not to be mad."

A cold weight settles in my stomach. We both know I hate surprises. "What did you do, Danica?"

"He kept messaging me, and I felt bad, I..." The words tumble out. "Just hear him out. He seems better now. Four years is a long time. People can change, you know..."

For a moment, I don't understand. Then, the realization hits like a bullet to the chest. The paintbrush trembles in my hand. "Danica...I've told you before, don't interfere—" My tone climbs despite my efforts at control, years of buried rage threatening to surface.

"Don't be mad at your wife."

That voice. My blood turns to ice.

Luca steps into my studio, into this peaceful space I've carved for myself. My brother. My betrayer. The last person I ever wanted to see again.

"What are you doing here?" The words come out like broken glass. The zen of painting evaporates, replaced by a tidal wave of emotions I've spent four years burying.

My fists clench, the muscle memory of violence rising.

"Please don't hurt him, darling." Danica's kiss lands soft against my rigid jaw.

I don't respond, can't respond.

She touches Luca's shoulder as she leaves—the casual gesture feels like another betrayal. "Good luck," she tells him, and then we're alone with the years of unspoken pain between us.

I turn back to my easel, unable to look at him. The paintbrush snaps in my grip, brown paint splattering like old blood, fucking up the horse (and the carpet).

"Look at me, *fra*." He stays by the door, smart enough to keep his distance. We both know what these hands are capable of.

I stare at my ruined painting, the horse whose peaceful expression now seems to mock me. "Leave, Luca. I have nothing to say to you."

"Dante. You're my only family. Please."

"You are dead to me." My voice sounds foreign, harsh. "You should've been dead, full stop, but you have Danica to thank for that."

"I know," Luca answers softly. "I'm grateful."

"Don't say you're sorry," I snap before he can try.

"Dante..."

"I could've died, Luca. What the fuck?" I whirl to face him, and the sight hits harder than expected. He's older, his hair longer, something different in his eyes. But he's still Luca. Still my baby brother. Still the one who had me tied to a metal chair, waiting to die, all because of his goddamn gambling debts.

The rage I've kept locked away rises like a tide, threatening to drown all the peace I've found. All the progress I've made. Years of healing threatening to unravel in a single moment.

Luca's shoulders cave inward, making him look smaller. Younger. "Never in a million years could I have predicted shit would turn out like that." His eyes find mine, holding steady. "I was an idiot. That's the short version."

"You betrayed me." The words taste like trash. My hands itch for something more substantial than paintbrushes, though these fingers have killed with less.

"I got caught up trying to fill the unfillable void." Something different in his voice now. Steadier. "Rehab has been good for me," he adds.

"Lovely. Now leave." I turn back to my messed-up canvas, pretending to focus on the ruined horse while every nerve in my body remains attuned to my brother's presence.

"I want to make it right, Dante."

"You can't." The words snap like bones.

"Let me at least try. You don't have to forgive me."

"Good, because I have no intention of forgiving you."

"You sound just like our father now."

The comparison hits like a gut punch. "Don't you dare! I'm nothing like him!" The painting crashes to the floor, brown paint bleeding onto the expensive carpet like spilled red wine.

"You sure are acting like him. Always so violent, so unforgiving, so unavailable." Luca's accusations are soft-spoken but bitter.

"Our father was an asshole," I spit out, voice like thunder.

"Our father was a *cunt*, Dante."

"On that, we can agree." My laugh holds no humor. "But you can't keep blaming him for your lifetime of fuck ups."

"Can't I?" Something breaks in Luca's voice. "I was only a child when *Ma* died, Dante. You were all I had, and now I don't even have you."

The words pierce deeper than they should. "I can't always keep bailing you out, Luca. I have my own life now, a wife..."

"I don't need you to bail me out. I just need you to be my brother again." His voice cracks. "Jesus, Dante. We used to be thick as thieves. You were the first person I told when I kissed a boy, remember? You took a fucking black eye for me to keep Father from ending my life right there and then."

The memory hits unexpectedly—Luca trembling behind me, our father's rage like a living thing, my body the only shield between them. "He was such a bigot."

It happened a few months before Don Fera Snr. died. While I was wrestling with my feelings for Alessio, hiding who I was, Luca's beating that day made the choice for me. Made it clear what happened to sons who loved wrong.

"I'm not a bad person, Dante. Two years in therapy has finally made me realize that."

There's something different about him—a steadiness where chaos used to reign. The desperate edge is gone from his eyes.

Leopards don't change their spots.

But even as I think it, I know it's a lie. Look at me—Don Fera, the monster who painted in red, now finding peace in watercolors and cake batter. Look at Danica, the scared girl who

449

became Queen. Alessio's transformation from reckless Playboy to Don...

My mind feels like a battlefield, old loyalty warring with fresh betrayal.

"I think you should leave."

"Please, Dante. I missed you, *fratello mio*."

Part of me wants to say it back—wants to admit how many times I've picked up the phone, almost called. But the memory of rope burns and metal chairs holds my tongue. Some deceptions cut too deep.

"Just go, Luca."

"Can I come back?" Hope makes him sound youthful again.

I press my fingers to my temples, trying to hold back the tide of confusion. "I don't know; I need time to think."

"That's not a no. I'll take it. Thank you, brother."

I return to my ruined painting, dismissal clear in every line of my body.

The conversation is done.

Luca leaves quietly, knowing my limits as well as I know his. Emotions were never my strong suit—too messy, too complicated.

I pick up the canvas that is now just a brown smear, like the line between love and betrayal, between family and enemy. I stand frozen, staring at the ruin, unsure which hurts more—seeing Luca again or realizing part of me is glad he came.

"You okay, baby?" Danica's voice is soft at the door.

"Fine," I growl, but we both know it's a lie.

She moves to hold me, but I step away, shaking her off.

Danica's voice is gentle, kind...cautious. "He's your brother, darling. He wants to make amends."

"It wasn't for you to interfere." My voice comes out harder than intended, edged with the kind of darkness I've been trying to leave behind.

"It was bothering you. I know Luca was an asshole, but I believe him when he says he's changed."

"What? Like *your* brothers have changed?" The words escape like bullets, and I regret them instantly when I see her flinch. But rage makes me reckless, makes me cruel.

Danica goes still, hurt flooding those wild eyes I love. "Don't bring them into this. It's different."

"How? They almost got you killed, same as Luca did to me. Except you were a helpless child."

"Dante—"

"But it's fine; they got what they had coming." The satisfaction in my voice betrays me. *Fucking idiot, Dante.*

Danica goes perfectly still, the way she does before unleashing her Domme voice. "What do you mean?"

I stay silent, watching her Managing Director mask slide into place. The transformation is subtle but complete—spine straightening, shoulders squaring, chin lifting slightly.

"Dante...what have you done?" She moves into my space with that quiet authority that still weakens my knees, even now.

Her hands catch my face, forcing me to meet her gaze.

Those fiery eyes search mine, looking for the evil she knows still lives there.

"Nothing. Just taught them a bit of a lesson." But we both hear the old Don in my voice, the one who solved problems with blood and pain.

My wife takes a step back, arms crossing over her chest—defensive, protective. "You promised you wouldn't harm them."

"I didn't—at least not physically. But they deserved to be *humbled*." The truth tastes like victory and shame mixed together.

"An eye for an eye leaves the whole world blind." Danica's voice wavers slightly—the only indication that we're talking about her flesh and blood, not some business transaction.

"Those fuckers can be glad it was just their careers I ruined." Something dark unfurls in my chest, that old satisfaction of revenge. "You won't believe the dirt I found."

Her hands clench at her sides, knuckles white against navy silk. The muscle in her jaw jumps—fighting back words, fighting back tears, maybe. "I don't want to know."

"Let's just say they didn't magically turn into better people."

Danica turns away, staring out the window. I watch her reflection swallow hard, compose herself. When she faces me again, she's fully *Donna* Fera. "I don't need you to fight my battles for me, Dante. I'm a big girl now."

"Right back at you. Except for the big girl part."

Finally, a smile breaks through her storm clouds. "You silly man." She sighs, and some of the tension bleeds away. "I have to get back to the office, but this conversation isn't over."

"Yes, Ma'am." Making us even doesn't make us right, but it's something.

"Don't you *Ma'am* me, I'll smack that cock of yours so hard, you'll need a month to recover," she threatens, and said cock instantly jumps in my pants.

I let her pull me down, let her kiss anchor me back to who I'm trying to be. Her embrace feels like forgiveness I'm not sure I deserve.

"I love you so much, Madame Fera," I whisper into her hair that smells of soap and safety and home.

"More and more each day." Her lips brush my nose before she leaves me with my ruined art, churning thoughts, and a semi-erection. "I'll see you tonight. Be good."

My cock hurts with need. But at least it's not painful anymore to get an erection. That inevitable pain. I hated it, but I also loved it. Loved how aware I was of it at all times. But mostly, I liked how Danica licked and teased it, cared for it.

The endless edging is enough to drive anyone mad, though, but the mere thought of one day finally being able to scrape her insides with the piercing, giving her maximum pleasure if the internet is to be believed—that's enough to keep me going. I just wish she wasn't so insistent about sticking to the piercing artist's three-month 'no-hanky-panky' rule.

One more month...

I throw the painting away, its broken horse beyond saving.

Setting up a fresh canvas, I turn the music up until it drowns out the voices in my head—my father's rage, Luca's pain, my own darkness still lurking beneath this peaceful surface I've built.

The blank canvas stares back like a challenge, like redemption, like a chance to create something new from the ashes of what was destroyed.

Maybe it's time to paint something other than horses...

CHAPTER FORTY-THREE

HEALED

(DANTE)

The afternoon light streams through my studio windows, painting Danica in gold.

She perches on the highchair like a Renaissance masterpiece—all curves and shadows, naked except for her heels.

Every time I try to capture her beauty on canvas, my hands fail me.

"You have to sit still, *Tesoro*." I aim for stern, but how can anyone be serious when their Queen is deliberately testing their control?

"I'm not good at sitting still, you know that." She pouts, deliberately uncrossing and recrossing her legs like we're shooting an adult movie. "I'm bored!"

"We just got started!" Paint drips from my brush, forgotten. "What happened to you being such a new, patient person?"

"I am! But this is torture. How long still?" Danica's dramatic sigh would put theater actresses to shame.

I set my palette down, knowing I've lost this battle. Like so many before. "You're being impossible, Danica."

"Come here...maybe some kisses will make me sit still." The invitation in her voice makes my skin warm.

We both know kisses only lead to more distraction, but I'm powerless to resist. When did the feared Don Fera become so easily swayed by a seductive smile?

"You're being very naughty," I murmur against her lips. She tastes of coffee and mint and mischief—a familiar combination that makes my heart race and my dick stir.

"Darling, you know I can't be any other way." Her fingers find my tattoos, tracing the stories inked on my skin. Without a shirt, in just my sweatpants, I am fully relaxed. "I have something for you, by the way," she adds.

I press my forehead to hers, arms locked around her like anchors. "You spoil me."

"I wanted to wait until after the painting, but clearly, that will take a while." Danica rolls her eyes, a habit she still hasn't kicked despite being Missus Boss Lady at work now.

The black velvet box appears from her bag on the floor next to her.

"It's not my birthday, what's this now?" The box feels warm in my hands, heavy with intention.

She watches, silent for once, as I lift the lid.

My breath catches at what lies inside.

With a light touch I run my finger over the gold plate, tracing the letters.

"And? Do you like it?" Her hands clasp together, impatience warring with hope.

"It's so...perfect." My voice catches in my throat as I read the word again. Four letters that mean everything: *MINE*.

"Let me." Danica takes the delicate gold chain from the box and helps me fasten it around my neck.

It fits perfectly, hanging loosely around my collar to rest on my bare chest.

"How does it look?" I ask, touching the cool metal.

"So beautiful, just like you." She leads me to the mirror, and for once, I don't flinch at my reflection. The man looking back seems softer somehow. Whole.

"You are mine, forever and always, Don Dante Fera. Don't you forget it." Her words ghost across my ear, her eyes meeting mine in the glass. "Now you will always be reminded who owns you, even when you can't wear your full collar outside."

"Forever and always." I turn to face her, throat tight with emotion. "Thank you, really." *For the necklace. For loving me. For making me better.*

Words still come hard, even after months of peace in this new life. But I'm working on that.

Never in a million years did I think I'd spend my late forties at home doing domestic chores while waiting for my Domme to come home and torture me with pleasure. Well, *"chores"* is a strong word, but I do like helping around the house—often much to Missus Nell's annoyance, who insists that I'm more of a hindrance than a help, warm smile letting me know she's only teasing (for the most part).

My paintings are still shit, but I enjoy doing them.

Sometimes, I like to paint naked, dramatic music blaring from above as I completely shut off from the world, lost in the colors. It's so freeing.

Danica touches my neck as we stare at our reflections. "You know I love buying you gifts. But don't worry, I know you're all about touch…" She brushes her fingers against my straining sweatpants, stirring my semi-erect cock to life.

"Oh god," I mumble, inching closer toward her.

"Are you fully healed enough now, darling?" She drags my waistband down slowly, freeing my cock from the loose material.

"Yes…" My voice dissolves into a gasp as Danica gently traces the piercing decorating my cock with her fingertip. I want to tell her that I've been healed for weeks, but none of that matters now.

"Hmm, let's see." She leads me to the table, cock in hand, and I follow like a little obedient puppy—I would follow her anywhere.

As always, my wife seems to be oblivious to the suitable seats in the room, choosing instead to push herself onto the table, toppling various art supplies onto the floor.

I don't even try and reach for anything, just let it fall; my complete focus is on the blood rushing to my dick, the fire burning through my veins, the *need*.

Danica opens her legs and pulls me closer until the tip of my cock is touching her pussy lips.

I hold my breath as she guides me where she needs me, rubbing her clit with my pierced head.

"I've been wanting to do that for three months," she confesses, using my cock like an object as she masturbates herself.

I don't do anything, just stand as still as I can, my cock fully hard, as I watch the beautiful twists of her expression evolve into delirious lust.

"It feels so good," I rasp as the sensation builds. I've missed the feeling of her, of my dick smearing through her wetness.

If she continues like this, I'll be bursting in no time.

But Danica knows; she pulls away before both our toes start curling.

My wife winks mischievously. "I've thought about other things too…"

"Like?" Forming the word steals what little breath I had in my lungs.

"Like…one day, when you're healed proper, putting a ring through them holes so I can clip a leash onto your dick and parade you around the house."

I swallow loudly. "*Dio mio.*" The mere thought of it is exhilarating.

Danica grins widely as she continues to rub me against her wetness. "But mostly, I've thought about what it would feel like inside me."

"Me too," I confess, biting down a groan. "So much."

Danica licks her fingers before reaching down again, rubbing saliva all over my head as she massages my rock-hard cock. "Is it time?"

"Please..." There is nothing I want more; I'm feral with lust.

Danica's hand ceases. "Please *who*?"

"Please...*Donna* Fera...Madame Danica...please fuck me." I know how much she likes that title. I like it too. She deserves it.

She raises a single brow. "Here?"

"Anywhere you like. *Please*." I need her more than I need anything I can list right now; my brain can't think straight with all the blood drained to my dick.

Danica jumps off the table and leads me to the couch in the corner, pushing me down into a seated position like I'm made of clay instead of flesh.

As she turns around, I admire the beautiful tattoo on her back—it's so her, so perfect. That artist was incredibly talented; the piece healed without any issues. I often ran my hands over it at night when she was asleep in my arms, tracing the shapes of the flowers, petal for petal.

When she kneels before me, I one hundred percent forget how to breathe.

A guttural groan leaves my throat as she takes me between her lips, tongue flicking over the piercing to give me my first proper blowjob since our honeymoon.

"That good, hey?" Danica seems chuffed with herself, but I can't be amused right now. The need for release is too urgent.

I will her to stay there, to let me spill my cum down her throat, drink me dry, but my Queen has other plans.

Before I can release my load too soon, Danica climbs onto the couch, kneeling over me as she lines my cock up with her pussy. "You ready for this?"

"Yes, Ma'am," I pant, resisting every urge to grab her and force her down on top of me. We both know I'm not the one in the driving seat right now.

But this time, my patience is rewarded.

"Slowly," Danica whispers, more to herself than to me, as she lowers herself onto my dick.

At first, it stings a bit, but then I feel nothing but pleasure.

It has been far too long since I have been inside her, inside *anyone*.

My body comes undone instantly as Danica clenches around my hardness, taking all of me inside.

God, I've missed how she feels. How tight she is. How wet she gets.

"What does it feel like?" I ask her.

Danica pushes herself up on her knees and impales herself on my cock again before answering. "It feels..." she pauses, searching for words. "Incredible. Unexpected...A little dangerous." Her fingers trace my jaw as she meets my eyes. "You still okay, baby?"

"So good..." I can't give her a longer sentence because my mind isn't capable of them anymore.

The feeling of being inside her again overwhelms everything.

It feels so familiar but also a bit different, the piercing adding another level of contact.

I know most of the pleasure is for me, but I'm hoping she can feel something at least.

"We're going to have a lot of fun with this one." Danica kisses me passionately as she speeds up the rhythm of her hips, riding my dick like it's an inanimate dildo stuck to the wall rather than attached to a real person.

It's a position I'm honored to accept because I'm ready.

Ready for whatever kinky and crazy ideas my Queen comes up with.

My body belongs to her.

And only to her.

A loud groan rips from my chest as I wrap my arms tightly around Danica's body, holding her close so my ragged breathing mixes with hers, breathing the same air, trying to hold on as long as I can.

Oh, Dio mio.

If this is what retirement feels like, my only regret is not doing it sooner.

As I stumble toward the edge of the cliff, moments from toppling over, release imminent, I know, without a doubt—I was born to serve, not to lead

CHAPTER FORTY-FOUR

CONFRONTATION

(DANICA)

T he view from my executive office never gets old. Eight stories up, the entire harbor stretches before me, a playground of ships and containers that now dance to my tune. I lean back in my leather chair—not the flimsy kind, but the substantial sort that costs more than my first car—and allow myself a moment of satisfaction.

Danica Fera, Managing Director.

The gold nameplate on my desk catches the afternoon light, winking at me like we share a secret. In a way, we do. None of these port executives, city officials, or family Dons who've been parading through my office have any idea that the woman they're reluctantly respecting is the same one who ties up their fearsome Don when he begs for it.

Back home, I'm a different kind of MD, not Managing Director but Madame Danica.

467

My phone buzzes, the sound jarring me from my moment of smugness.

"Yes, Monica?" I answer, expecting another update about the German shipping contract that's been giving our logistics team headaches all week.

"Mrs. Fera, I have...visitors for you." Something in my PA's voice makes my skin tighten. "A Mr. and Mrs. Matthews. They say they're your parents."

My blood freezes in my veins. For a moment, I wonder if I misheard.

"They're insisting on seeing you," Monica continues, her voice dropping lower. "I told them you're in meetings all afternoon, but they won't leave. The woman is becoming quite...vocal."

Of course she is. That's my mother's specialty.

"Send them in." My voice comes out steadier than I feel.

"Are you sure? I can have security—"

"Send them in." I stand, straightening my navy pencil skirt and adjusting my silk blouse. Appearance is everything in this new world I've built. "Thank you, Monica."

The thirty seconds between hanging up and the door opening stretch like taffy. My heart drums against my ribs, but I force my face to remain neutral, my posture perfect. This isn't their house with its whispered insults and muffled cries. This is *my* domain.

The door swings open, and suddenly, there they are—ghosts from a life I've tried so hard to bury.

My mother enters first, all fake pearls and indignation. She's aged in the few months since I last saw her, more lines around her mouth that's already twisted in disapproval. Behind her, my father follows like a shadow—quiet, unassuming, invisible until he's needed to reinforce her particular brand of cruelty.

"Danica!" My mother's voice pierces the air like a dentist's drill. "What have you done?"

I don't move from behind my desk. Don't rush to embrace them. Don't offer coffee like the dutiful daughter they tried to mold. I simply watch them, letting the silence stretch uncomfortably.

"Hello, Mother. Father." The words taste foreign on my tongue.

"Don't you 'hello' me!" She's already in full swing, her knock-off designer handbag clutched like a weapon. "What have you done to your brothers? Is this your idea of revenge?"

My father stands silently beside her, his eyes roaming the office, taking in the expensive furniture, the harbor view, the trappings of power. Something flickers across his face—surprise, maybe. As if he never expected his disappointing daughter to amount to anything more than an embarrassment.

"I don't know what you're talking about." I sit back down, gesturing to the chairs across from my desk. "Please, take a seat."

"We will not sit! Marko has lost everything—his firm, his clients! They're investigating him for—" She stops herself, seemingly realizing she's saying too much. "And Filip! His company suddenly canceled his contract. They're saying he falsified signatures, compromised safety standards!"

Interesting. So that's what Dante found. I'll admit, I'm impressed. My husband has always had a talent for finding people's darkest secrets. I know I should be mad, that I told him to leave them alone, but actually, I just love him more. *Fuck them. Fuck them all.*

"And you think I had something to do with this?" I keep my voice level, professional. A voice that commands boardrooms now.

"We know you did! That...that *criminal* you married—"

"That would be Dante Fera," I correct her, enjoying the way her face pales at his name. "My husband."

"Filip is being audited by the IRS," my mother continues, face reddening. "Marko's wife left him! Took the children! Said she couldn't be married to someone under investigation for embezzlement and misconduct!"

I steeple my fingers, watching her unravel. "Sounds like they're finally facing consequences for their actions."

"This is your doing! Your revenge!"

"Revenge?" I raise an eyebrow, leaning forward slightly. "Is that what you call justice?"

My father finally speaks, his voice as bland as unseasoned food. "Danica, whatever grievance you think you have—"

"*Think* I have?" The words escape like steam from a pressure cooker. "Did you just say 'think,' Father?"

He blinks, startled by my tone. In their world, I never talked back. Never raised my voice. Never existed except as an inconvenience.

"You stood by and watched while your sons tortured your own flesh and blood." My voice is deadly calm now. "You watched while they locked me in a burning shed and pretended it was my own fault. While they hid my pain medication. While they broke me, piece by piece, and what did you do? *Nothing*."

"Not this again. That was an accident," my mother dismisses with a wave of her hand. "Boys being boys. You always were so dramatic."

"An accident?" I stand so abruptly my chair rolls back and hits the window. "Kingsly *died* in that fire! I still have the scars! And you—" I turn to my father, who seems to be trying to blend into the wallpaper. "You were supposed to protect me. You were my father! But you were too much of a coward to stand up to your wife or your precious sons."

All semblance of composure dissipates. So much anger. So much pain. Years of holding it all in. But no more. I'm done.

My mother's face twists with rage. "How dare you speak to us like this? After everything we did for you—"

"What exactly did you do for me?" I laugh, but it's a bitter sound. "Feed me? Clothe me? The bare minimum required by law? Or was it the part where you blamed me for my own abuse? Where you made me feel worthless? Where you taught me that I deserved to be hurt?"

"We gave you everything!" she spits.

"You gave me *nothing*!" My palm slams against the desk. "You made me believe I was unworthy of love! That I was defective! That I deserved pain!"

My father takes half a step forward. "Now, Danica—"

"No!" I point at him, and he actually flinches. "You don't get to 'now, Danica' me! Not anymore! You lost that right when you chose to protect your criminal sons instead of your innocent daughter. When you let them turn me into a punching bag because it was easier than being a parent."

"This is ridiculous," my mother huffs. "We're not here to rehash childhood squabbles. We're here because you've destroyed your brothers' lives!"

"Childhood squabbles?" The words come out so softly, so dangerously, that both my parents take an instinctive step back. "Is that what you call it when your sons tied up their sister and left her to burn alive?"

My father looks away, and for once, I see something that might be shame cross his face.

"My husband didn't touch your precious sons." I settle back into my chair, suddenly exhausted but refusing to show weakness. "He didn't need to. Their own corruption, their own cruelty—that's what destroyed them. All he did was shine a light on who they really are."

"You've ruined our family," my mother accuses, tears gathering in her eyes. Crocodile tears, the kind she's always used to manipulate.

"No, Mother. You did that long ago." I smooth my skirt, finding calm in the familiar gesture. "You ruined us when you decided that two of your children mattered and one didn't. When you taught Marko and Filip that they could do anything—hurt anyone—and face no consequences."

"We never—"

"You did. Every time you looked the other way. Every time you made excuses. Every time you chose them over me."

My mother's face hardens. "They were good boys until you turned them against us! Until you married that monster and decided to destroy everything we've built!"

"That *monster* is the only person who's ever truly seen me." My voice cracks slightly, but I push on. "The only person who looked at the broken pieces you left me in and thought I was worth saving."

"He's a criminal, Danica!"

"And what does that make you?" I ask quietly.

My father finally cracks, his voice so soft I almost miss it. "We didn't know how bad it was."

"Bullshit." The curse tastes like freedom on my tongue. "You knew. You just didn't care."

My mother grabs her purse, clutching it like a lifeline. "We're done here. Clearly, you've lost your mind. When you're ready to apologize—"

"Apologize?" I laugh, a real laugh this time. "I'm not the one who needs to apologize. "Get out.""

I press the intercom, ignoring my mother's dramatic huff. "Monica, could you have security escort Mr. and Mrs. Matthews out, please?"

"Right away, Mrs. Fera."

My mother's face turns an ugly shade of purple. "You can't do this! We're your parents!"

"No," I say, standing tall, feeling every inch *La Donna* Fera. "You're not my parents. You're just the people who failed at the job. I have a real family now—people who love me, who protect me, who would burn down the world rather than let anyone hurt me."

The door opens, and two security guards step in, looking expectantly at me.

"Please show them out," I instruct calmly.

As they're led toward the door, my father pauses, turning back. For a moment, something like regret passes across his face. "Danica—"

"It's Mrs. Fera," I correct him, my voice like ice. "And this is the last time you'll ever see me. Don't call. Don't write. Don't think for a second that you have any claim on my life or my heart. You lost that right a long time ago."

He opens his mouth, then closes it, seemingly at a loss for words.

"Goodbye, Mrs. Matthews. Give my regards to your sons. I hope they enjoy the consequences of their actions as much as I'm enjoying mine."

The door closes behind them with a satisfying click, and suddenly, I'm alone again. My legs wobble, and I sink into my chair, the adrenaline leaving my body in a rush that makes me dizzy.

I did it. After all these years, I finally stood up to them. Finally spoke the truth that has been burning inside me since I was nine years old.

For a moment, I just breathe, letting the silence of my office wash over me. Then I reach for my phone.

"Monica, I'm taking the rest of the day off. Please reschedule my appointments."

"Of course, Mrs. Fera. Is everything alright?"

I look out at the harbor, at the empire I've built from the ashes of who I used to be. "Yes," I say, meaning it for perhaps the first time in my life. "Everything is perfect."

It's time to go home.

To my real family.

To Dante, who saw me when no one else did.

Who believed in me when I couldn't believe in myself.

Who helped me become the Queen I was always meant to be.

The Queen the world never saw coming.

CHAPTER FORTY-FIVE

EPILOGUE

(DANICA)

*D*ante is up to something strange.

And I have no idea what it is.

"Keep them closed, birthday girl," my husband instructs, his hands covering my eyes. His chest is warm against my back as he guides me through familiar hallways made strange by darkness.

"What's got you so excited? You're worse than Biscotti on treat day," I tease, but my heart flutters with anticipation. Dante, usually so controlled, practically vibrates with excitement. He wouldn't even let me finish my coffee this morning, hovering and fidgeting until I gave up and followed him downstairs in only my silk robe.

The curiosity is driving me mad!

Usually, my husband was the one getting led around with his eyes closed, not me. *What's he planning?*

There is still loads of time until our dinner reservations at the super fancy restaurant he booked for us.

I had every intention of sleeping late, but my darling sub had other plans, snuggling me awake until I playfully spanked his ass and threatened him with a real punishment.

But Dante was in such a good mood, giddy almost, and wouldn't take no for an answer, dragging me from bed despite my resistance.

My first present of the day was a mind-blowing orgasm, courtesy of Don Fera's well-trained lips as he licked my pussy awake before my mind even caught up. Not a bad birthday tradition at all.

But that was but the start, he told me before covering my eyes.

As we walk, his hands tremble slightly against my face—my fierce Don, nervous about a birthday surprise. He's not the only one. Twenty-eight today, and somehow, he still finds ways to make my pulse race like a teenager's.

We stop, and I hear a door open.

"Okay," Dante's voice is soft in my ear. "Open them."

Finally.

Light floods my vision and..."Oh, my god."

We're by the library. But this is not the dusty old library that used to be down here. *Not at all!*

The transformation steals my breath.

Warm wood paneling has replaced the cold walls, but it's the books—oh, the *books*. Hundreds of them, their spines gleaming like jewels in the morning sun. I step forward.

"Is that...?" I pull out a volume with shaking hands. The complete collection of my favorite romantasy series, special editions with foiled covers I didn't even know existed. "How did you...?"

"Adira helped," Dante admits, watching me with those intense emerald eyes. "I wanted you to have a real sanctuary. Somewhere to write, to work, to just...be."

I notice the desk then, solid oak positioned to catch perfect reading light from the window. The chair behind it isn't just furniture—it's a throne. My throne.

Beyond that, plush leather couches nestle in a corner that begs for rainy-day reading sessions.

"It's like the *Beauty and the Beast* library," I whisper, hugging a book to my chest.

Dante's brow furrows adorably. "Is that good?"

A laugh bubbles up from somewhere deep inside me—pure joy breaking free.

I launch myself into his arms, peppering his face with kisses. "It's perfect. It's beyond perfect. It's..."

I stop, seeing something in his eyes. "What aren't you telling me?"

"Watch this..." Dante snaps his fingers, and the music comes on, floating in from speakers hidden behind shelves. "I had the room soundproofed. So you can listen to all those shitty pop songs of yours as loud as you want."

"They're not shitty, but also, oh my god!" I twirl around like I'm in a movie, trying to figure out how one accepts the most incredible gift in the world.

"Yeah, you can control everything from an app on your phone—the music, the lighting, the temperature, oh, and this..." He presses a button on his phone, and an electric fireplace springs to action beside the couches, instantly warming the room. It looks like real logs almost, cozy, perfect.

"This is like a...a Queen cave!" I plonk down on the couch, testing its *bounciness* or whatever the correct fancy word is.

Dante laughs. "For you, only the best. The staff has been instructed only to come when you press the button to call for them."

"You know you'll never see me. I'll just be hiding out here."

"I'm not worried." He grins. "You'll get horny eventually."

We both laugh. "That's true."

"Speaking of, I think it's time for your next *service*. It is your birthday, after all." Dante kneels before me on the plush carpet, a genuine *shag rag*, as Sasha would call it.

Without hesitation, I drop my bathrobe, enjoying the warm glow of the fireplace on my skin. "I won't say no to that."

Dante crawls toward me as I open my thighs...

***

We get so distracted rolling around on all the upgraded surfaces that we're almost late for our own reservation.

I lose count of the number of orgasms Dante gifts me.

Oh god, how lucky am I?

I'm not too phased about the dinner reservation. We can just stay home, I tell him, but Dante insists on ushering me through the shower.

"We'll be late," my husband says again, hovering as I finish my makeup. His reflection in the mirror shows barely contained excitement. *Why is he so nervous?*

I smooth down the blood-red satin gown he had made for me, admiring how it catches light like liquid garnets. Such a far cry from the baggy clothes I used to hide in.

"Since when do you care about restaurant reservations?" I tease, but he's already reaching for my hand, pulling me toward the foyer with unusual urgency.

"Dante, what—" I don't get to finish my question.

"SURPRISE!"

The word slams into me like a wrecking ball, stopping me dead in the doorway.

For a moment, I can't process what I'm seeing—faces I love, all here, all smiling, champagne glasses raised in greeting.

The foyer has been transformed with twinkling lights and flowers, making our home feel like something from a fairy tale.

"Happy birthday, *cara mia!*" Alessio breaks from the crowd first, resplendent in a charcoal suit that's perfectly tailored to his body.

He sweeps me into one of his theatrical kisses, dipping me back until I laugh against his lips. The familiar scent of his

481

cologne—sandalwood and Vegas nights—wraps around me like a hug.

"You said you were in Vegas!" I accuse when he sets me right, gripping his crisp shirt as he twirls me. "That you couldn't miss your board meeting!"

"Blame your husband." His eyes dance with mischief. "I'm just a humble accomplice."

"Humble?" Dante snorts, his hand finding the small of my back, grounding me.

Adira appears like a vision in lilac, champagne in hand. She pulls me into an embrace that smells of peaches and sin, her curves soft against my new dress. Rani's elegant frame completes our sandwich, her whispered "Happy birthday, love," tickling my ear.

The *Sinful Moon* girls descend in a wave of glitter and laughter—Sasha leading the charge in a gold dress that catches every light. Even Mary, the British dancer we saved, is here—safe, whole, thriving. No more disappearing dancers. No more broken promises.

"Missus Fera." Emilio's formal nod carries decades of protection and care. He looks distinguished as ever in his dark suit, those shoes he shines until they reflect the sun.

Then—a surprise that steals my breath. Luca, looking healthier than I've ever seen him, steps forward. "Hey, sis." His kiss on my cheek is respectful, careful—so different from the chaotic vibe he used to give.

Dante's arms slide around my waist from behind, and I lean back into his solid warmth. "Best birthday ever," I whisper, emotion making my voice thick.

For so long, birthdays meant empty rooms and echoing silence. Meant my brothers' cruel laughter and my parents' indifference. Meant being reminded I wasn't worth celebrating.

Now...Now, I'm surrounded by love that chose me.

"This is just the beginning, *Tesoro*," Dante murmurs against my hair as I try to take it all in.

"More surprises? It's been a whole day of them!"

"A Queen deserves everything."

I turn in his arms, finding his lips with mine. Around us, our chosen family chatters and laughs, filling our home with the kind of joy I never thought I'd have. The kind that makes you believe in second chances. In healing. In love that rewrites all the rules.

My birthday wish has already come true.

What we've built here—this family of misfits and criminals and dancers—is better than any gift in the entire world.

Dante holds me closer, and in his arms, in this room full of people who chose to love me, I know one thing for sure: I'll never feel alone again.

This is what having a real home feels like.

And there is nowhere I'd rather be.

Happy birthday to me.

Chapter Forty-Six

THE END

(Alessio)

From the garden, the party spills through the open French doors in waves of laughter and music. I pause by the fountain, letting the night air cool my champagne-warmed skin, and find myself captivated by the tableau inside.

Danica stands in the center of it all, radiant in that red dress that makes her look like a scarlet Queen. The confidence she wears now suits her better than any designer label could. Her head is thrown back in laughter at something Adira just said, her hand automatically reaching for Dante beside her. He catches it without looking, an unconscious dance they've perfected.

My heart swells watching them. Dante—my first love, my oldest wound, my dearest friend—has shed the weight of solitude that used to bend his shoulders. The feared Don Fera still commands respect, but the ice in his eyes has melted into something warmer. Something real. Right now, he's looking at Danica like she hung the moon, that rare, unguarded smile lighting up his face.

Who could have predicted this? That they would find not just each other, but *this*? This beautiful, unconventional family we've built.

The party guests move around them like stars orbiting twin suns. No judgment, no whispers, just acceptance. Love in all its forms, celebrated openly.

I take another sip of champagne, letting the bubbles dance on my tongue. Seven months ago, I was planning their wedding in Vegas, hoping it would stick this time. Now look at us—Dante and Danica, married and thriving. Me, still free to be exactly who I am, but with a home to return to. A place where I belong, without having to belong to anyone.

Inside, the music changes to something slower. Dante pulls Danica close, pressing a kiss to her temple. She melts into him, then reaches out a hand in my direction. Even from here, I can see the love in her eyes.

I smile, pushing off from the fountain. This is what happiness looks like—not perfect, not traditional, but real. Sometimes messy. Sometimes beautiful. Right.

As I walk back toward the warmth of the party, toward the people I love, I think about how stories don't always end the way you expect.

Sometimes, they end better.

Sometimes, the happily ever after looks like a Don and his Queen, and the man who loves them both, building something beautiful out of broken pieces.

And really, what could be more perfect than that?

Dante may have found his happy ending, but not all the Dons are so lucky. Domenico Ricci is a mean, bratty mafia heir about to get his ass handed to him. Enemies-to-lovers mafia but femdom. (Read chapter one on the next page or visit mkaynoir.com/covertdesires)

COVERT DESIRES

CHAPTER ONE

N obody knocks at 2 AM.

Not during the off-season.

And definitely not during a tropical storm.

Yet there it is again—urgent pounding that cuts through the howl of wind and rain, forcing my paintbrush to halt mid-stroke.

Every instinct, honed from yearsI'd rather forget, screams danger. The smart play would be to keep painting my black flowers, to let the storm swallow whoever's out there.

But something about that frantic rhythm stirs a dormant part of me. An itch I thought I'd buried along with my past life. When was the last time my heart raced with anything but morning cardio?

The hammering grows more insistent. A voice carries between thunderclaps—male, desperate, demanding.

Fuck-it.

I set down my brush, dark paint dripping like blood onto the newspaper-covered floor.

"Hold on!" I call out, flicking on lights as I move through my sanctuary to the inn's adjoining door.The storm throws shadows that dance like enemy combatants across my walls.

When I unlatch the door, the wind nearly tears it from my grip. And there he stands—six-foot-something of trouble, drenched to his bones.

In the dim yellow glow of the porch light, the unannounced guest looks like an unsettling mix of serial killer. He's handsome by any standard, but I'm way past the age of letting dangerous men with haunted looks upset my entire world. *Fuck that.*

His raven hair is plastered to a face that belongs in a fashion magazine, all sharp angles and dangerous beauty. But it's his eyes that give me pause—arctic blue and feral, like a wolf's in winter. They lock onto mine with an intensity that sends electricity down my spine.

"About fucking time," the man snarls, trying to shoulder past me. His expensive suit, now ruined, clings to a frame that speaks of carefully honed strength. One arm clutches a duffel bag like it contains his soul.

I plant myself firmly in the doorway. "What do you want?" Years of training keep my voice steady, even as adrenaline floods my system. You don't survive 44 years on this earth by letting strange men into your home at night, no matter how pretty their packaging.

Know your enemy; know your target.This drenched man could be either. Except I have no idea who he is.

He doesn't fit the profile of the island-adventure guests who usually stay at my inn. Even if he did, this is not the time for island adventuring.

"Room for one. This is an inn, isn't it?" His accent carries old money and fresh blood. Up close, I catch the metallic scent that rain can't quite wash away.

That's when I see it—a nasty gash on his temple, still weeping crimson. His white shirt is torn at the shoulder, revealing more than just storm damage.

This man isn't running from the weather...

Get your copy (via mkaynoir.come/covertdesires)

APPRECIATIONS

THANK Y'ALL!

This book, this series, was not written in a vacuum. I couldn't have done this on my own.

A huge thank you to my incredible team of beta readers who made sure that my characters behaved properly. Your input into this series has been undeniable. Thank you for always being willing to read my stories with minimal context.

To the ARC readers and street team, y'all are amazing! Thank you for every comment, every review, every post, shoutout, tag, and recommendation. I see you. And I feel the love. Thank you for treating my books like they are real.

To my incredible designers, Lerusha and Erika, who designed the covers for this series: Thank you for your patience and for making it all look so pretty. Your creativity knows no end, and I'm so proud of how this came together.

To my husband, thank you for indulging all my plot brainstormings and easing my freak-outs and imposter syndrome moments. Your support is incredible and I'm lucky to have a partner like you. Thank you for always believing in me—even when I don't believe in myself. And thank you for the endless brainstorming sessions and digging me out of so many plot holes.

To my friends and everyone who's listened to me go on and on about Danica and Dante (and Alessio) for literal years, you are valued. Thank you for putting up with me treating these fictional characters like people.

To my author friends, thank you for your support, your advice, and for sharing my work. Such an incredible community. Thank you for letting me be a part of the crew, even if I totally have a habit of saying the wrong thing at the wrong time.

Last but definitely not least, thank you to every reader who has picked up the *Queens & Knights* series and left a review or reached out to me. I appreciate it so much. Nothing beats that feeling of when the right reader finds your book.

Little teenage me would be so proud to know I finally did the things, finally published my stories, finally put myself out there.

Thank you all for letting me live my author fantasy.

-Kay

ABOUT THE AUTHOR

M Kay Noir is a queer romance author and journalist obsessed with moments of desire. Most of her stories are kinky, queer-friendly, polyamorous undertakings with neurotic characters who are often their own worst enemy. If you expect any regard for traditional gender roles or power dynamics, you will be disappointed.

Kay has been penning steamy moments for more than 15 years now, from fanfics to ghostwriting and now finally her own stories. Her day job also involves a lot of writing, albeit a different kind—mostly sustainability things. When she's not writing (or reading), she enjoys making her husband look at yet another sunset and watching live music concerts.

**See mkaynoir.com for the long version.

DEAR READER...

*T*hank you for reading my book.

   If you enjoyed it, wouldn't you please take a moment to leave me a **review** at your favorite retailer? It helps more like-minded people to find this very niche content.

   To get bonus content and fresh releases, join my **newsletter** or follow me on **BookBub**.

   Kay